BLACK OUT

MARC ELSBERG

TRANSLATED BY MARSHALL YARBROUGH

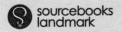
sourcebooks
landmark

Published by Sourcebooks Landmark, an imprint of Sourcebooks, Inc.
P.O. Box 4410, Naperville, Illinois 60567-4410
(630) 961-3900
Fax: (630) 961-2168
sourcebooks.com

Originally published in 2012 in Germany by Blanvalet, an imprint of
Random House Germany. The hardcover edition was issued based on
the paperback edition published in 2017 in the United Kingdom by
Black Swan, an imprint of Penguin Random House. This edition issued based on the hardcover edition published in 2017 in the United
States of America by Sourcebooks Landmark, an imprint of Sourcebooks, Inc.

Library of Congress Cataloging-in-Publication data for the hardcover
edition is on file with the publisher.

Printed and bound in the United States of America.
OPM 10 9 8 7 6 5 4 3 2 1

DAY 0—FRIDAY

MILAN, ITALY

Piero Manzano hit the brakes as hard as he could and braced himself against the steering wheel with both arms as his Alfa hurtled toward the light-green car ahead. His eyes frantically searched for an opening, some way to steer himself out of danger, but there was no time. In his mind he could already hear the awful sound of the two vehicles colliding. Brakes screeching, tires skidding, the lights of the cars behind him in the rearview mirror. Then the moment of impact.

And all the while, Manzano thought absurdly of chocolate, of the hot shower he'd been looking forward to, of the glass of wine on the sofa afterward. Of falling into bed with Giulia or Paola over the coming weekend.

The Alfa jolted to a stop, millimeters away from the other car's bumper. Manzano was thrown back into his seat. The street was pitch-black. The traffic signals, green a moment ago, had gone out, leaving only the trace of an afterglow on Manzano's retinas. An ear-shattering din of honking and scraping metal enveloped him. From the left, the headlights of a delivery truck came rushing his way. A massive jolt slammed Manzano's head against the side window, and his car was spun around like a carousel before a second impact stopped it.

Dazed, he looked up and tried to get his bearings. One of his headlights illuminated dancing snowflakes above the black, wet asphalt. A chunk was missing from the hood. The truck's taillights flashed a few meters up ahead.

Manzano didn't have long to think. His fingers flew

to his seat belt to release it; he felt for his cell phone and leaped out of the car.

He found the first aid kit and triangular reflector in the trunk and inspected his car. The truck had crushed most of the front left side and grille, the front left tire mashed deep into the mangled metal. The driver's door of the truck was hanging open. Manzano went around the front of the cab and froze.

The lights of the cars in the oncoming lane shimmered in the icy night air, creating an eerie glow. There had been a few scattered collisions, and now all traffic was at a standstill. The light-green compact was completely caved in on the driver's side, jammed crookedly beneath the bumper of the truck. Steam rose from under the hood, or what was left of it. A short, sturdy man in a sleeveless T-shirt was tugging at the twisted driver's door. The truck driver, guessed Manzano. Manzano stumbled over to the car. What he saw made him stagger.

The impact had torn the driver's seat from its housing and literally set it in the passenger's lap. The driver hung lifeless in his seat belt, his head strangely twisted, the airbag limp in front of him. All that could be seen of the passenger was her head and one arm. Her face was covered in blood, her closed eyelids fluttering. Her lips moved almost imperceptibly.

"*Ambulanza!*" he shouted at the truck driver. "Call an ambulance!"

"No signal!" yelled the truck driver.

The passenger's lips stopped moving. The small bloody bubbles that formed in the corner of her mouth were the only evidence that she was still alive.

A huge crowd of onlookers had now gathered. They stood in the falling snow and gaped.

"Back off!" Manzano shouted, but no one moved. And then he realized something. The streetlights were off. In every respect the night was blacker than usual.

"My God, what happened to you?" a man in a parka asked him. He pointed to Manzano's left temple. "You need a doctor."

Only then did Manzano feel the pounding in his head. A warm trickle flowed down and pooled at his neck.

He tried to walk, but his legs wouldn't obey. He stumbled to his knees, willing himself not to pass out. From the wreck came the sound of a car horn, ringing out into the night like a final, drawn-out cry for help.

ROME, ITALY

"What the hell's going on here?" Valentina Condotto, still punching frantically at her keyboard, glanced up at her colleague in alarm. A system alert was bleeping incessantly, while a whole battery of lights blinked on the monitors. "The frequency suddenly skyrocketed and then the automatic shutdown kicked in. The whole of Northern Italy is gone! Just like that. No warning!"

Condotto had joined the team at the Terna control center on the outskirts of Rome as a system operator three years ago. Since then she'd spent eight hours a day monitoring the flow of electricity through Italy's transmission grids, as well as the exchange of power with grids in neighboring countries.

The large projection screen in front of her displayed the Italian power grid as a myriad of colored lines and little squares against a black background. Monitors to the left and right showed current data from the networks. On Condotto's desk were four smaller screens with still more rows of numbers, curves, and diagrams.

"The rest of the country has gone yellow!" Grid operator Giuseppe Santrelli called across the room. "I have Milan on the phone; they're trying to come back online, but they can't get a stable frequency from Enel. They're asking if there's anything we can do."

"Sicily's red now too!"

The control center operated a traffic light system: green meant everything was in order. Yellow meant the grid was in difficulties. Red signaled a blackout. Every system operator in the center could tell by a single glance whether there was even a hint of a problem in the power grid. Given the complete international integration of the grid, this was an absolute necessity.

For the most part, computers handled all necessary adjustments, responding in a millisecond to increase or reduce the flow of electricity. In the event of a large fluctuation, the system was set up to automatically shut down affected parts of the grid.

The illuminated red area on Condotto's screen told her that the computer had taken almost all regions north of Latium and Abruzzo off the grid. Sicily was off as well. According to the map in front of her, only the bottom half of the boot was still being supplied with electricity. More than thirty million people were in the dark.

Condotto watched helplessly as more power surged into the rest of the grid, triggering further automatic shutdowns.

"Fffp! And there they go." Santrelli shook his head in dismay. "Calabria, Basilicata, parts of Apulia and Campania, red. Remaining service areas turning yellow. And look!" There was panic in his voice as he pointed at the screen. "The French and Austrians are in trouble now too!"

YBBS-PERSENBEUG, AUSTRIA

Herwig Oberstätter looked up from the switch box, straining to hear a repeat of the sound that had triggered his sense of unease.

Like the vaulted ceiling of a gothic cathedral, the steel-and-concrete roof of the power plant turned the interior into a vast echo chamber, amplifying the drone of the generators. Hearing nothing untoward, he leaned over the railing of the high metal walkway that wound around the southern power plant's interior and peered at the three red generators below. Their casings stood in a row like gigantic barrels, each one housing magnets that weighed several tons. Kilometers of wound wire cable spun at several hundred revolutions per minute, propelled by steel shafts as thick as tree trunks that connected them to the truck-size Kaplan turbines through which flowed the waters of the Danube, newly released from the massive dam with its thirty-four-kilometer reservoir, at a rate of over a thousand cubic meters per second.

The power plant, built in the 1950s and situated between Ybbs and Persenbeug in lower Austria, was one of the largest on the Danube. After nine years in the job and extensive training in mechanical engineering, Oberstätter understood the process by which the rotating magnetic field induced voltage in the stator's conductors, thus converting kinetic energy into electrical energy. Even so, he never ceased to marvel at the power of the three sleeping red giants under his care, miraculously generating the power that drove modern life, even in the remotest hut in the country. Aware that the instant this power dried up the world would come to a standstill, he tended his machines like a father watching over his children, constantly monitoring their progress. And tonight his senses had picked up on some irregularity that as yet he couldn't quite place.

It was Friday evening. Workers were returning home, looking forward to opening the front door and being warmed by central heating, a hot shower, cooked food, relaxing in front of the television. Even with Austria's power plants running at full capacity, at this time of day it was necessary to import power to meet demand. Oberstätter moved a little further along the walkway to listen again. And as he did, the noise level in the power plant began to increase.

Instantly grasping the implications of what he was

hearing, he reached for his radio to alert the switch room to the problem.

Through the static hiss and popping of the receiver, it was all he could do to make out his colleague's response: "We see it too. We've got a sudden drop in frequency across the grid!"

The droning in the room was now punctuated by an irregular pounding. Oberstätter cast a nervous eye over the cylinders; what he was seeing was the exact reverse of a drop in frequency. The generators were clearly overburdened, not under. Who could be using so much power all of a sudden?

He shouted into the microphone, "The frequency's too high—the generators are cracking up. Activate shutdown immediately."

If the frequency in the power grid was so unstable that it was reaching his generators, this was a much scarier problem than a surge in demand caused by a small part of the grid dropping off. Had the power gone out over large areas? If so, tens of thousands of Austrians were now in the dark.

Oberstätter looked on, horrified, as the red giants began first to vibrate, then to jump. If the number of revolutions became too great, their own centrifugal force would destroy the machines. The system should automatically have shut down by this point, but the safeguards had obviously failed.

"Cut it!" he bellowed into the radio. "Shut it down now, or this whole place'll be blown apart!"

He froze, transfixed in the face of this power. The three supermachines rose and fell unevenly. His heart pounded in his chest, anticipating the moment one of them would explode through the roof like the lid blowing off a pressure cooker.

And then the vibrations began to decrease; the giants stopped their jumping and settled down once more. The shaking could only have lasted seconds. To Oberstätter, it had seemed like an eternity.

The silence that followed was eerie. It took a while for it to sink in that the striplights had all gone out. The power plant was illuminated only by the red glow of the emergency lights.

BRAUWEILER, GERMANY

"Sweden, Norway, and Finland to the north, Italy and Switzerland to the south—all gone," said the operator whose shoulder Jochen Pewalski was looking over. "Same with parts of Denmark, France, Austria. Also some regions of Slovenia, Croatia, and Serbia. E.ON is reporting a few outages; Vatenfall and EnBW have gone completely yellow. Same story from suppliers in Poland, Czech Republic, Hungary, and Britain."

Jochen Pewalski looked up at the vast display board for confirmation. Sixteen meters wide and four meters high, it delivered up-to-the-minute information on energy transmission throughout Germany, Belgium, Bulgaria, the Netherlands, Austria, Poland, Romania, Slovakia, the Czech Republic, and Hungary. Around him, systems operators manned workstations loaded with state-of-the-art technology. It was a far cry from the office he'd occupied when he first joined Amprion GmbH thirty years ago. The Brauweiler building on the outskirts of Cologne had been transformed in the intervening years, thanks to the ever-increasing demand for energy. Transmission grids were no longer confined by regional or international borders; nowadays, energy flowed right across Europe, from the place where it was generated to wherever there was demand. And as head of Grid System Management, it was Pewalski's job to oversee and coordinate this constant give-and-take of energy, not just for Amprion's own transmission grid and those of the other German operators, but for the entire northern sector of Europe.

Usually the board that loomed above him reflected a

state of energy equilibrium that could be maintained by relatively minor adjustments to generate precisely the amount of energy needed. Tonight the display showed a network in chaos.

"This is worse than 2006," groaned one of the operators.

Pewalski recalled the night in question: Saturday, November 4, 2006. A cruise ship from the Papenburg shipyard was being towed along the canals to the coast, and to allow it to pass under overhead cables, E.ON had shut off the power. Unfortunately, they had failed to give neighboring networks prior warning. As a result, lines became immediately overburdened, triggering automatic shutdowns. Despite the efforts of Pewalski and his colleagues to balance the system, the cascading effect proved unstoppable. Fifteen million people across Europe found themselves plunged into blackout. It took an hour and a half to reestablish operations. They had come within a hairsbreadth of the complete collapse of the entire European grid.

The current situation was looking far more catastrophic.

"The Czech Republic is totally red now too," the young man reported.

Twenty minutes earlier the Italians had been first to experience problems. Then, as things were falling apart to the south, the Swedes had started having massive difficulties, followed by the rest of Scandinavia. And already reports were coming in that the cold winter weather was claiming victims all over Europe.

"We have to secure the German grid at all costs to ensure the east-west connection isn't interrupted," Pewalski urged his team.

He commanded the operators to redirect power to lines that were still clear, shut down power plants, bring others online, and send any surplus energy to pumped storage plants for as long as they still had the capacity to receive it. Where necessary, they began load-shedding—which left some factories on a mandatory break and thousands of people in the dark.

But just when their efforts seemed to be working, a number of lines on the board suddenly began flashing red.

Pewalski tried to remain calm, but his mind was racing. Provided a substantial part of the grid continued to function, they could use the power generated to reactivate downed networks relatively quickly. But if the blackout were to spread until the entire grid was taken out, it would be a very different story. Nuclear reactors and coal-fired power stations could not be brought back online within minutes.

"Spain's gone yellow."

"OK, that's enough," Pewalski declared, reaching a decision. "We're sealing Germany off." And then, more quietly, "If it's still possible."

A FEW KILOMETERS FROM LINDAU, GERMANY

"I hope we've got enough gas left," said Chloé Terbanten anxiously.

Her friends, Sophia Angström and Lara Bondoni, who'd been sitting in the backseat admiring the snow-covered landscape, both leaned forward to peer at the dashboard. Fleur van Kaalden, in the front passenger seat, broke off tapping her thigh in time to the music on the radio and suggested, "Maybe we should fill up again before we cross the border, just to make sure."

The Austrian border couldn't be far now. And then they'd be only an hour away from the ski cabin they had booked for the coming week. The foothills of the Alps were already visible in the moonlight, which now and again peeped out from behind the clouds. Sophia could make out the shapes of individual farmhouses, all in darkness; people in this part of the world must go to bed really, really early.

They were traveling in Chloé's Citroën, the trunk

crammed with oversize suitcases, skis, and snowboards. They had already stopped for gas once en route, spending longer than they'd intended in the service station café, drinking coffee and flirting with a couple of young Swedish guys who were on their way to Switzerland to go snowboarding.

"Services in one kilometer," said Fleur, pointing to the sign as they whizzed past.

Sophia scanned the roadside for the lights of the service station, but all she could see was the moonlit landscape.

Chloé took the exit, a long, drawn-out curve.

"It's probably on the other side of the autobahn," said Lara, as a wide expanse opened up in front of them with lights dotted at intervals along the off-ramp.

Chloé slowed. "What on earth…?"

The gas station was in darkness. The lights they'd seen turned out to belong to the cars queuing for the pumps, their headlights casting bright spots on the front of the building. Here and there, beams of light darted back and forth in the night—flashlights, probably.

Leaving the headlights on, they got out.

Immediately Sophia felt the cold penetrate her jeans and sweater. The car ahead of them had a German license plate. She spoke the language better than the others, so she went forward and asked what was happening.

"Power's out," explained the driver through the half-open window.

She then approached a man in overalls standing by one of the pumps. He gave the same answer.

"So we can't get gas here?" she asked, beginning to panic a little.

"The pumps are powered by electricity from the grid. Until it comes back on, we can't get the fuel up from the underground tanks."

"Don't you have backup power?"

"Nope." He shrugged in apology. "It should be back on any moment, though."

"How long is it going to be?" asked Sophia, glancing back at the long line of waiting cars and the restaurant's packed parking lot, also in darkness. A traveling Friday before a week of winter holidays.

"Maybe fifteen minutes."

Not a hope, thought Sophia as she made her way back to the others. Chloé, having reached the same conclusion, pounded her hand on the roof of the car and yelled, "Get in, guys. Let's go find the next service station!"

BERLIN, GERMANY

"What do you mean, you don't know?"

The interior minister, a tall man with a red face, thinning hair, and a thunderous expression, stood before the screen. He had probably been pulled out of a gala dinner, judging by his tuxedo. Frauke Michelsen couldn't remember ever having seen him in the Interior Ministry's incident room. Probably because she herself rarely attended.

Tonight the room was full: civil servants, information technology specialists, federal police, public security, as well as crisis management and civil protection. Michelsen knew more or less all of them.

Helge Brockhorst from the Joint Federal and State Information and Command Center in Bonn could be seen on the screen. "It's not that simple."

Wrong answer, thought Michelsen.

"With your permission, Minister," Secretary of State Holger Rhess spoke up. "Perhaps Mr. Bädersdorf here can shed some light on matters for you."

Michelsen groaned inwardly. Bädersdorf had worked for the German Association of Energy and Water Industries for years, until eventually the lobbyists had succeeded in installing him within the ministry itself.

"Imagine the power grid as a human circulatory system," Bädersdorf explained. "Perhaps with the difference that instead of one heart, there are several. These are the power plants. From the power plants, electricity is distributed to the rest of the country, like blood being carried around the body, only instead of blood vessels, the grid relies on power lines. High-voltage power line wires are the main arteries, transporting large quantities across broad stretches; then there are cables with average voltage, which transport the energy farther, to the regional networks, which then distribute to the individual end receivers—these are the capillaries that bring blood to every cell."

As he spoke, he tapped on the relevant parts of his body. This wasn't the first time he had delivered this particular lecture, and Michelsen had to acknowledge, without envy, that it wasn't a bad analogy.

"Pivotal here are two aspects. First, in order to keep the grid stable, a consistent frequency must be maintained. We can compare that to blood pressure in a human. If it gets too high or too low, we keel over. That's unfortunately what has happened with the power grid.

"Second, you can't really store power. Like blood, it must flow continuously. That means it must be generated if it is to be used. The quantity needed varies dramatically throughout the course of the day; so in the same way that the heart has to beat faster if a person suddenly breaks into a run, power plants must deliver more energy at times of peak demand—either that or additional power plants must be brought online. Make sense so far?"

He looked around the room and received several nods. The interior minister, however, was frowning.

"Yes, yes, but how does that explain what's happening across Europe? I thought the German power grid was secure?"

"It is—in principle," answered the lobbyist, as Michelsen secretly dubbed him. "That can be demonstrated by the fact that Germany was one of the last countries to lose its power supply and one of the first to start bringing individual regions back online. But the German grid is not an island within Europe."

He tapped away at the keyboard on his computer and the large projection screen came to life, displaying a map of Europe that was covered with a thick network of colored lines.

"This is a map of European power grids. As you can see, they are tightly interconnected."

The image on the wall changed into a blue graphic on which symbols for power plants, transformer stations, factories, and houses were connected by a network of lines.

"In days gone by, national energy providers both generated power and distributed it. They also managed each aspect of the supply chain. Through the liberalization of the energy market, however, this structure has fundamentally changed. Today there are, on the one hand, those who generate power…"

The power plant in the graphic changed from blue to red.

"And on the other, there are those who operate the grid."

The connection lines in the graphic turned green.

"Completing the circuit between them, so to speak, there are now additionally"—in the loop appeared another building symbol with a euro sign—"energy exchanges. Here, power generators and power traders negotiate prices. The power supply today therefore consists of many different actors, who, in a case such as the one we have before us, must first coordinate with one another."

Michelsen felt obliged to expand on his remarks. "And their foremost concern is not optimally supplying energy to the population and to industry, but rather securing a profit. That means bringing many different interests together under one roof. And, in the event of a crisis, doing so within minutes.

"As yet, we don't know the cause of the outage. But you can be sure that everyone is working toward the same goal."

"Why don't you know the cause of the outage?" asked a staffer from the Public Security division.

"The systems these days are far too complex for that to be determined immediately."

"How much time will it take to reestablish the supply?" asked the secretary of state.

"According to our information, most regions should be getting power back by tomorrow morning."

"I hate to be the voice of doom," Michelsen spoke up. "But we're talking about most of Europe here. The corporations have no experience whatsoever with a crisis of this magnitude." She took care to maintain a controlled tone. "I'm accountable for crisis management and civil protection. If tomorrow morning public transportation isn't running, train stations and airports are at a standstill, offices and schools can't be heated, telecommunications are down, and the water supply for large parts of the population cannot be guaranteed, we're going to have a huge problem. The best thing we can do now is start preparing."

"How exactly will the supply be reestablished?" asked the interior minister.

Bädersdorf got in before Michelsen could speak. "In general, you go little by little, build up small grids around the power plants, make sure that they maintain a stable frequency, and then successively enlarge them. Then you start to join these partial grids together and to synchronize them."

"How long does each of these steps take?"

"For building back up, it depends—anything from a few seconds to a few hours. At that point, the synchronization should go relatively quickly."

"You say regions throughout Europe have been affected," said the minister. "Are we in contact with the other countries?"

"Happening as we speak," confirmed Rhess.

"Good, put a crisis team together and keep me up to date as things develop." The minister turned to go. "Good evening, ladies and gentleman."

Speak for yourself, thought Michelsen. For some of us, it's going to be a very long night.

SCHIPHOL, NETHERLANDS

Delayed.

Delayed.

Delayed.

In the past hour, the departures and arrivals boards had shown one flight after another as delayed.

"Will it be much longer?" asked Bernadette, her favorite doll clutched to her chest.

"Read it yourself," ordered her older brother pompously. "It says right up there that our flight is delayed."

"But I can't read."

"Baby," mocked Georges.

"Am not!"

"Baby! Baby!"

Bernadette started to whine. "*Maman!*"

"That's enough now," François Bollard told his children. "Georges, stop annoying your sister."

"So now it'll be midnight before we get to Paris," groaned Bollard's wife, Marie. Dark shadows had appeared under her eyes.

"Friday night," said Bollard. "It's not like this is the first time."

They stood among a cluster of people craning their necks in front of the announcement boards. The new departure time was ten p.m.

The long rows of seats in the waiting areas were over-flowing. Those without seats were squatting on their suitcases. In the fast-food restaurants, massive queues had formed. Bollard looked around to see if he could find a quiet spot for them somewhere, but everywhere he turned there were hordes of people.

"What's up there now?" asked Bernadette as the boards above them suddenly came to life.

"Oh, great," Bollard heard his wife say. He looked up at the display.

Canceled.

Canceled.

Canceled.

PARIS, FRANCE

Lauren Shannon kept her camera trained on James Turner, CNN's correspondent in France, as he thrust the microphone under the nose of his interviewee.

"I'm standing here in front of the headquarters of the Paris fire department on Place Jules Renard," said Turner. "With me now is François Liscasse, *général de division*, head of the Brigade de sapeurs-pompiers de Paris, as the fire department is called here in the French capital."

In the glare of the headlights, the snowflakes shone like fireflies.

Turner turned toward Liscasse.

"Général Liscasse, Paris has been without power for more than five hours now. Has there been any information on how long the situation is going to continue?"

Despite the weather, Liscasse wore only a blue uniform. His cap made Shannon think of Charles de Gaulle, which in turn triggered a recollection that the Paris fire department was a military unit that reported to the Interior Ministry.

"I cannot provide any information on that subject at the present time. Throughout Paris and the surrounding areas, all available men have been mobilized—several thousand in all—the largest firefighting organization in the world, after New York. The population of Paris can therefore feel secure. At the moment, we are busy freeing people caught in the Metro and in elevators. In addition, there have been many traffic accidents and a few scattered fires."

"Does that mean that some will have to wait until tomorrow morning to be rescued?"

"We're assuming that power will be back on soon. But we will free every single individual; that I guarantee."

"Général—"

"Thank you. Now if you'll excuse me, please, I must get back to work."

Brushing off the dismissal, Turner faced the camera and intoned, "James Turner, Paris, on the 'Night without Power.'"

As soon as he'd given Shannon the signal to cut, he pulled up the fur collar of his coat and set off in the direction of the car, calling over his shoulder, "It's about time I asked these guys at the Interior Ministry a few questions. Come on, let's drive there now."

As Turner's camerawoman and chauffeur, Shannon had mastered the art of weaving her way through the streets of Paris—or so she'd thought, until the traffic chaos of a few hours earlier. The situation on the roads had calmed since then, but even so it took them more than twenty minutes to cover a distance they could have walked in ten.

The Rue de Miromesnil was blocked off to prevent access. Without giving it a second thought, Shannon parked in a driveway.

She had lived in Paris for two years. The plan had been to travel the world after college, but she'd ended up here. Her intention to continue studying journalism had also fallen by the wayside when she landed the job as camerawoman for Turner. The job took up way too much of her time, and Turner was an arrogant scumbag who thought he was Bob Woodward—despite the fact that she was a better researcher, found better stories, and had a better grasp of how to tell them, he refused to let her in front of the camera—but on the plus side, she'd been around a lot and had learned loads. In her meager free time, she made her own features and put them up on the web.

They hurried to the blockade on foot.

"Press," Turner informed the police guard, flashing his credentials.

"Step aside, please" was the policeman's only response.

Shannon saw the headlights of several cars coming toward them.

Without slowing down, the cars drove past them through the small gap that had been cleared by the police officers. Shannon kept the camera on them and turned when they did but couldn't make out a thing behind the darkened windows.

"Well?" asked Turner.

"I got the shot," Shannon answered. "Looking was your job. So who was it?"

"No idea—too dark to see."

SAINT-LAURENT-NOUAN, FRANCE

"For God's sake!" huffed Isabelle Marpeaux as her husband, Yves, pulled a thick jacket on over his warm sweater. "You work in a power plant, and here we sit, fifteen kilometers away, without electricity."

Covered in layers of sweaters and jackets, she looked even more unshapely than usual, sitting there in the candlelight.

"And what am I supposed to do, huh?" he demanded.

"It's the same thing with the kids," she repeated for the umpteenth time.

She had managed to track down their son on his cell phone an hour and a half after the power had gone out, their daughter a few minutes after that. Their son lived with his family near Orléans, their daughter in Paris. "I've been trying forever to get through," she had explained, "but the cell phone network…"

Marpeaux hadn't been able to tell the children anything, except that they too were without power.

"You can imagine how your mother is complaining."

He closed the door behind him and left his wife there in the cold, dark house. After all the hours of nagging he'd endured, it was a relief to be getting away. Outside, his breath was a white cloud rising into a sky that was free of stars.

The Renault started without a problem. On the way, Marpeaux surfed the radio for the latest news. Many stations were silent; one or two were playing music. In the end he gave up.

Looking out at the dark winter landscape of bare fields and leafless trees, it was hard to believe that he was driving through one of France's most popular holiday destinations. When spring came, millions of tourists would flood into the region, shopping for wine and souvenirs and hoping to catch a whiff of savoir vivre as they ventured into the heart of France on the trail of bygone generations of aristocrats who'd inhabited the castles in the hills along the Loire. Marpeaux had come to the region twenty-five years ago, not for its beauty, but for a well-paid job as an engineer at the Saint-Laurent nuclear power plant.

After twenty minutes, the village of Saint-Laurent-Nouan, uncommonly dark that night with the streetlights off and no lights on in the windows, appeared silhouetted against the sky. Behind it, lit up as if in mockery, rose the cooling towers of the reactor. As always, it reminded him of a giant steam engine house, the kind they'd built in the early nineteenth century. The fundamental concept underlying the technology remained pretty much the same, as did the riverside location to allow for drawing water from the Loire. The main difference was that instead of burning wood to power the generators they relied on fissionable uranium or plutonium.

Marpeaux passed the security checkpoint at the entrance and parked the car in his usual spot. France received eighty percent of its energy from nuclear power plants. If the news reports of the past few hours were correct and the grid had almost completely collapsed, then most of the reactors would have been shut down, thought Marpeaux. The automated mechanisms would sink the controlling rods between the fuel rods in order to bring the nuclear chain reaction to a halt—or, at least, as much of a halt as possible. The reactor would continue to produce heat and would therefore need to be cooled to prevent a meltdown. Normally the cooling systems drew their energy from the grid; in the event of an outage, the emergency systems sprang into action. The facility in Saint-Laurent possessed three of these per block, each independent from the others, all fed by diesel engines, with sufficient fuel for seven days.

As he opened the door to the control booth he was greeted by a cacophony of alarms. A twenty-year veteran in the job, Marpeaux didn't bat an eyelid. Inside, a dozen of his colleagues were calmly going about their work, monitoring screens and gauges, making adjustments. Even the less experienced members of the team had been well drilled in dealing with emergencies; during their training they'd have been through simulations of every conceivable emergency scenario.

The duty shift leader came across to greet him. "One of the diesels in Block 2 broke down, right at the outset."

"The others are running?"

"Without any problems."

"Do you suppose it had anything to do with the test?" Marpeaux asked. Three days ago they had checked over the emergency power systems, and their readings had shown that one of the diesels was defective. When the engineers had gone down to examine it, they could find no problem; it appeared to be working perfectly. At the time, they'd put it down to a malfunction of the instruments used to perform the test.

The shift leader shrugged. "You know how it is. We

might know in two months when we've investigated and reconstructed everything."

Marpeaux groaned at the thought of the paperwork that investigation would entail, then donned his shift supervisor badge and nodded for his colleague to begin the handover briefing.

MILAN, ITALY

"Deep breaths, in and out," instructed the doctor.

The cold stethoscope pressed into Manzano's back.

"I'm telling you, I'm absolutely fine."

The doctor, a young woman with TV star looks, came around to face him and shone a small flashlight into Manzano's eyes.

"Headache? Dizziness? Nausea?"

"No, nothing."

Manzano sat bare-chested on a gurney in a tiny room in the emergency ward of the Ospedale Maggiore di Milano. Although he had regained consciousness after briefly losing it at the scene of the accident, the paramedics had insisted on taking him with them. There was nothing left of his car but scrap anyway—the fire department would deal with it before he could.

"Mouth open."

Manzano complied, and the doctor inspected his throat. How this was supposed to help with a small laceration on his forehead was a mystery.

"Sew this thing up and let me go home," he told her.

"Is there someone there who can look after you?"

"Was that an offer?"

"It was not."

"That's a shame."

"Are you sure you don't want to stay here?"

"If we can share a bottle of good wine, I'm perfectly happy to stay."

"Tempting," she replied with a cool smile, "but here we only use alcohol for disinfecting."

"Well, in that case, I suggest a decent Barolo back at my place. Hopefully we can do without the X-ray."

"That we can," she said and pulled out a syringe.

Manzano felt sick when he saw the needle.

"I'm giving you a local anesthetic, close to the wound, and then you can go. Watch out; this is going to hurt a little."

"Is this really necessary?" he asked.

"Would you like me to sew up the wound without the anesthetic?"

Manzano began to sweat. Keeping a tight grip on the gurney, he turned his gaze to the floor so as not to have to look at the doctor. "The power's out here too?" he asked, hoping to distract himself.

"All over the city, it looks like. For the past hour I've been getting nothing but guys like you in here. There's more waiting outside. Car accidents, because all of a sudden the lights aren't working. People who fell over when the Metro came to a halt. So, there you go. There'll probably be a small scar, nothing too bad. Makes a man more interesting."

Manzano relaxed again. "As interesting as Frankenstein's monster."

This time a real smile skittered across her face. Manzano put his shirt back on, with its blood-stained collar, then his coat, which had red stains on its sleeves. He thanked the doctor and found his way out.

Outside he looked in vain for a taxi. He asked the man at the information desk, who shrugged apologetically.

"Assuming I can get through, I'd be happy to book a cab for you, but right now the wait time runs to at least an hour. With public transportation out of action, the taxis are in demand. It's like the big blackout of 2003."

A date every Italian remembered: the whole country

had been without power for twenty-four hours. Hopefully this one wouldn't last that long.

He thanked the man, turned up his coat collar, and trudged off.

In the streets, the lights of the cars blurred together into a single stream that sluggishly pushed its way through the dark canyons between buildings. The icy wind sliced through his coat.

He weaved slowly through the alleys toward the cathedral, accompanied by a never-ending concert of car horns in the background. Once past the church, he turned down Via Dante in the direction of Parco Sempione. The honking grew louder as drivers grew increasingly frustrated at finding their progress blocked by abandoned trams. He continued walking through the dark, congested streets, at times having to squeeze between shop fronts and cars that had mounted the pavement in an effort to continue their journey. Most of the shops were closed, even if the signs showing their opening hours said differently.

Fascinated, he realized he was discovering things that he'd never noticed by daylight or streetlight. Clever bits of signwriting above shops, for example, or buildings he would have passed by, where now he paused to look at the facades. In a tiny *alimentari* a stooped figure was rummaging around by candlelight. In the glass door hung a sign that read *Chiuso—Closed*. Manzano knocked all the same. The figure inside stopped rummaging and came to the door; it was an older man in a white smock. He eyed Manzano suspiciously for a moment before opening up. A bell chimed above the entrance.

"What do you want?"

"Can I buy something?"

"Only if you've got cash. Electronic payments won't work."

The smell of sausages and cheese, antipasti and bread met Manzano's nose. He fished out his wallet and counted.

"I've got forty left."

"That should do. You don't look like much of an eater. What happened to your head?"

He left the door open and went off behind the counter. "Small accident on account of the power outage."

Manzano chose bresaola, salami finocchietta, taleggio, goat cheese, marinated mushrooms and artichokes, and half a loaf of white bread. All for sixteen euros. He said good-bye and left with his spoils.

For three years Manzano had lived on the fourth floor of a crumbling building on Via Piero della Francesca. With no light on in the entrance, he could barely see a hand in front of his face as he climbed the stairs. But once inside his own apartment, he was struck by how he'd managed to get there as if on autopilot: lifting his hand to exactly the right height to find the keyhole, locating the coat hook by touch, setting down the laptop bag and groceries, making his way to the bathroom—all without seeing a thing.

There was a rattle after the flush, and that was it for the water. Manzano missed the soft hiss the water normally made as it filled the tank. He turned the old-fashioned tap at the washbasin, which coughed out a few drops before going quiet.

This blackout was beginning to get on his nerves. He could get by for a while without power, but now he was supposed to get by without water too? It wasn't a prospect he relished, considering how dirty he was.

The knock on the door made him jump.

"Boo! It's a ghost!" The face of neighbor Carlo Bondoni appeared in the doorway. He looked like something straight out of a Caravaggio painting, the candle in his hand giving off just enough of a glow to reveal his wrinkled face and the unkempt white hair that circled his bald spot. He held up the candle so he could see Manzano, then cried out in shock, "Dear God, what happened to you?"

"An accident."

"There's not a light on in the whole city," Bondoni reported. "Said so on the radio."

"I know," replied Manzano. "The traffic lights went out. My Alfa's a total write-off."

"It was before."

"You always did know how to make me feel better."

"Here, light a candle for it," said Bondoni, producing a candle from his pocket. "Now you won't have to sit in the dark."

Manzano lit it from Bondoni's flame.

"Thanks. I've got a box of candles stashed away somewhere; this'll make it easier to find them."

"Hey, you know all about engineering and IT—can't you do anything to fix this mess? No TV, no internet—I don't even know where I am anymore. I blame these new-fangled electric meters..."

Manzano was hungry. He had known Bondoni long enough to guess where this conversation was headed. Without television, the older man was bored and desperate for entertainment. Well, what the hell. It wasn't as if he had any plans.

"Come on in," he said. "It's too cold to hang around out there. Have you eaten?"

NEAR BREGENZ, AUSTRIA

"Nothing's working here either!" cried Chloé. "It's unbelievable!"

Sophia leaned forward from the backseat and peered through the patch of windshield cleared by the wipers. It was snowing heavily, and the gas station they'd just pulled into was a repeat of the previous three: cars abandoned on the forecourt, others parked on the off-ramp, drivers trying to weave their way out of the chaos. She peered at the Citroën's fuel gauge. A yellow light indicated that they were now running on reserves.

"We won't make it to the cabin on what we've got left," she reasoned. "That leaves us with two options: wait here till the pumps start working again—"

"Which could take all night," remarked Chloé.

"—or leave the highway and look for a place to stay," Fleur suggested.

"But we can't look for long," Chloé pitched in. "Because we won't get very far. And I don't want to end up stranded on some Austrian country road in this weather. At least here we'll freeze close to a fresh supply."

Sophia took out her smartphone to search for accommodations nearby, then swore under her breath. "No internet connection," she moaned, putting the phone back in her bag.

The clock showed 10:47.

"What I really wanted was to be sitting in front of a cozy fire with a mug of hot punch by now," she sighed. "OK, who's for finding a hotel, who's for waiting here? And… Go!"

A chorus of four voices. "Wait here."

"I'm hungry," Lara Bondoni added.

"The shop and restaurant look closed," observed Chloé.

"Well, I need to go to the bathroom, so I'm heading over there anyway. Who's coming with?" said Lara.

"Me," answered Fleur.

Sophia and Chloé looked at each other and nodded, then the four of them set off.

The gas station was indeed closed, most of the cars empty. They circled the building and found the bathrooms at the back. A horrific stench wafted out when they opened the door. It was too dark to see.

"Oh my God, I am *not* going in there," Sophia declared.

They turned and made their way to the restaurant building. Weak light could be seen through the fluted glass of the large double doors. As they stepped inside, Sophia felt a thrill of adventure—a childish sort of adventure, like when she was at summer camp and they'd sheltered from a thunderstorm in an abandoned hut. Every table in the restaurant was occupied, and there were candles flickering on a couple of them. Some customers made conversation; others sat in silence or slept. There was a musty smell, but at least it was warmer here than outside.

A man got up and came toward them. He was wearing a down jacket. A bow tie hung loose around his neck.

"We're full," he said. "Light, water, bathroom, stove, refrigerator, heating, booking and payment systems—none of it's working. I was supposed to be off three hours ago. But we can't lock people out. If you can find a little spot for yourselves, you're welcome to stay."

YBBS-PERSENBEUG, AUSTRIA

The nine men stood motionless, staring at the monitors in the control booth.

"And… Go!"

Oberstätter pressed the button.

For three hours they had argued, run simulations, and phoned colleagues in other stations, trying to establish what had gone wrong. So far, all they could say for certain was that most of Europe was without power. The power plants that supplied the grid had gone down like dominoes as automatic safety measures triggered by the sudden spike in frequency kicked in to deactivate the system.

Ybbs-Persenbeug should have shut down automatically too. Oberstätter still couldn't understand why it hadn't, and why the displays in the control booth had registered a drop in frequency even as the generators were shuddering and jumping before his eyes. He only hoped that the facility hadn't been damaged. Run-of-river hydro plants like this one had a vital role to play in reestablishing the supply, since they could start up again without assistance. Not that it was a simple process of pressing a button. They had to let the water through the turbines, switch on the generators, and then activate the various pressure valves and other components step-by-step. Only then could they start feeding power into the grid.

"And stop," sighed one of Oberstätter's coworkers.

He turned, frowning, to see what the problem was.

The man leaned toward his screen and read aloud: "Short circuit risk on XCL 1362."

Oberstätter shook his head in dismay, then waved a hand in the direction of the door. "Armin, Emil, get down there; check it out."

"That means at least another hour's delay," groaned one of the men.

"We have no choice," replied Oberstätter. "If everything's not in order, we can't come back online."

Frowning, he reached for the telephone and dialed the number for Crisis Management.

BERLIN, GERMANY

Michelsen hurried past the open door to the conference room, where the interior minister was in urgent discussion with his European counterparts via video link. As she entered the hallway, seven staff members from various divisions were lying in wait for her; they fell in behind her as she strode to the press room, the spokesperson for the interior minister leading the pack.

Questions were flying back and forth between them.

"Do we know what caused it yet?"

"No. No clue whatsoever. For the media, that translates as: our number one priority at the moment is reestablishing the power supply. Investigation into causes will be carried out as soon as people can put the heat back on, go shopping again, and get back to work."

"Foreseeable end to the outage?"

"Hard to say. The providers have been optimistic. But

they've been trying to get the grid back online for six hours now, with no result. For the media: the providers are hard at work and striving to reestablish the power supply."

"How can this happen throughout the whole of Europe? That can't be normal."

"Unfortunately, it can, given modern interconnected power grids. For the media: the minister has for some time now devoted his utmost attention to modernizing power grids and power systems, especially at the European level."

"First responders?"

"Are working around the clock. In the past few hours, the fire department has freed thousands of people from elevators and subways. The Red Cross and others are caring for the sick, the elderly, and travelers who have been stranded on the roads."

"Why's that?"

"You can't pump fuel without power."

"You're not serious!"

"Unfortunately, I am."

"And this on the first day of winter holidays."

"The Federal Agency for Technical Relief has been alerted and is fully mobilized."

"The military?"

"Is standing by, prepared to support relief workers wherever necessary."

"And what are we going to tell people who still don't have power tomorrow?"

MILAN, ITALY

Manzano had the feeling that time had slowed down since the power had gone out. He listened, conscious of the stillness, acutely aware of what was missing. The soft buzzing of the refrigerator. The bubbling of water in the pipes. The muffled chatter of a neighbor's television. Now, only Bondoni's heavy breathing, gulping down his wine, the scratching of his shirt against his sweater when he set the glass down on the table. The clock above the kitchen door showed half past one.

"Time for bed," announced the older man, getting to his feet with a groan.

As Manzano was seeing him out, an odd feeling came over him. He shrugged it off and was about to clap Bondoni on the shoulder and bid him good night when he realized what was different. Through the door to his study, which was standing open, there came a weak beam of light.

"Hold on a second," he told Bondoni and went into the study, a small cluttered room with two windows looking onto the street.

"The streetlights are back on!"

Bondoni was already standing next to him. Manzano hit the light switch. On, off. On, off. It remained dark inside the study.

"Weird. Why are the lights on out there but not in here?"

Manzano walked back out into the hallway and opened the circuit breaker. All the individual switches were in the right position, the main switch as well. The meter's display read *KL 956739*.

"The power's back here," he murmured to himself and then to Bondoni, "Will you try the light switch by the door?"

Click, clack. Nothing.

"Hmm, let's take a closer look here…"

"What?"

Manzano disappeared into his study and returned with a laptop.

"What are you up to?" asked Bondoni.

"Back when they installed the modern electric meters, being the curious type, I couldn't resist taking a closer look at that little box there."

He started to type.

"These electric meters are basically tiny computers. That's why they call them smart meters. They allow the power companies not only to collect data on your electricity use, but also to control the meter remotely."

"I know. They can shut my power off too," said Bondoni.

"In order to do this, the electric company uses various codes…"

"Like the one that's on there now?"

"Exactly. And we can set up a link with this box, if we put a little effort into it."

Bondoni grinned. "I take it this isn't entirely legal."

Manzano shrugged.

"And how do you set up this link?" asked Bondoni.

"With a very basic infrared interface. These days, almost any computer can do it. Or even your cell phone. That's what I did back when they installed them. I wanted to see for myself just what this hardware can do—and how it does it."

"Don't you need passwords for that? Isn't that data encrypted?"

"Of course it is. But this kind of encryption is, for the most part, easy to crack. And as far as the passwords go, you'd be amazed what you can find on the internet when you know where to look."

"That is most definitely not legal."

Now it was Manzano who grinned.

"A man likes to know who he's dependent on, don't you agree?"

By now the files he had been looking for were up on his screen.

"I managed to pick out the operating codes—here's the list I saved. You see this one—that's the electricity supplier giving the order to share the current usage. That one there allows the supplier to cut usage by two hundred watts, and so forth."

Bondoni studied the list. Looked back up at the meter.

"The one on the display is on your list too. But in red."

"And right there is where it starts to get interesting.

The meters are manufactured by an American firm—for domestic use as well as international. Some of the codes they use are different. They also have functions that aren't utilized in Italy at all. For example, a command for total cutoff from the grid—the disconnect command. This one right here, you see it?"

Bondoni slowly read off the sequence of letters and numerals. "KL 956739. I'll be damned!" As he turned to Manzano, the laptop screen cast a blue glow on his face, giving it a ghostlike quality. "Does that mean the Americans took you off the grid?"

"No. The disconnect command isn't recorded anywhere in the Italian instruction manual, but clearly it works all the same. I tried it out back then. And guess what: there's a sting in the tail. Because the function isn't intended for use in Italy, the meter doesn't send any information to the power supplier if the disconnect command is activated."

"Hold on, hold on—does that mean this cutoff order gets activated and the people at the power company don't know a thing about it?"

"For an old man with a bottle of wine under your belt, you catch on fast."

"But how does this command get activated?"

"That's the question. A system error, maybe. But you've given me an idea. Come on." He pushed Bondoni toward the door. "Let's go have a look at what your meter's up to."

Manzano waited impatiently for Bondoni's fingers, clumsy with age and too much wine, to fit the key into the lock.

As they passed through the hallway to get to the circuit breaker, Manzano looked at the pictures on the wall. Photos of Bondoni, his late wife, and his daughter, Lara, a petite, lively woman with a mane of brown hair.

"How's your daughter these days?" He knew she worked for the European Commission in Brussels, though he could never remember in which department.

"Fantastic! She just got promoted again. You won't believe how much she's making now. And all of it from my taxes!"

"So the money stays in the family then."

"Most of it goes to rent—the cost of living in Brussels is unbelievable! Today she's off to Austria on a ski trip. As if you can't go skiing in Italy!"

Bondoni opened the circuit breaker box to reveal the smart meter.

The device showed the same jumble of digits as Manzano's.

COMMAND HEADQUARTERS

He wished he could see the view from the International Space Station at that moment—swaths of darkness across Europe, where usually the delicate veins and shining nodes of the electric grid radiated across the land. According to the first reports and their own assessments, at least two-thirds of the continent were without power. Still more regions would follow. He imagined those in charge, frantically trying to identify the cause, apportioning blame—the winter weather, a technical fault, or human error. They had no inkling what it was they were actually dealing with.

Accustomed to being in control, they'd assume it was a passing occurrence and tell themselves that in a few hours everything would be back to normal. No doubt they were even now collecting amusing anecdotes to entertain their friends. Oh, they'd have stories to tell all right, but not the frivolous ones that were going through their minds now. Unlike previous blackouts, where the legacy was a jump in the birthrate nine months later, this one would lay waste to the so-called civilization of the West. Only then could history be written anew.

SERVICE STATION NEAR BREGENZ, AUSTRIA

After a night on the restaurant floor, Sophia was awoken by a murmur. Still dazed from sleep, it took her a while to realize that people were getting up and making quietly for the exit. Fleur's head was resting on her shoulder, obscuring her view of the exit, but as she watched, more people seemed to be waking, looking around sleepily, then joining the exodus.

Gently extricating herself from Fleur, she stood up, stretched her legs, and crossed the room, an obstacle course of resting bodies. She smelled damp clothing, sweat, melted snow, cold soup. She hadn't yet reached the entrance to the parking lot when someone shouted, "Hey! The pumps are back on."

By the time Sophia reached the door, people were crowding in behind her, jabbing her in the back, and shoving her out into the open.

It was biting cold outside, and the night was still starless. The gas station shop shone out like a beacon in the gloom, and she could see people cramming themselves inside, gesticulating at the man behind the counter.

She clumsily brushed her thick hair away from her eyes and stepped into the store. Already most of the shelves and coolers were half-empty. The people around her were agitated, speaking so quickly it was hard for her to translate, but she understood enough to grasp that the pumps weren't working after all. She grabbed what she could: bread, sandwiches, cookies, as well as a few bottles of soft drinks still rolling about the emptying shelves, and got in line at the register.

"Cash only," said the man behind the counter in a dialect she barely understood. Sophia took out her wallet, fished out one of the few bills, collected her change, and left.

There were masses of people streaming out of the restaurant. She badly needed to go to the bathroom, and she was ravenously hungry, but the first priority was finding her friends.

It turned out they were waiting for her in the Citroën.

"Breakfast," she announced and held up her shopping.

Then she walked quickly to the hedge that separated the parking area from the neighboring fields. The moment she reached the bushes, she was met with a terrible stench. In the first light of dawn, she saw that the area had turned into one big communal toilet. Treading carefully in her graying sneakers, she skirted the hedge in the hope that it wouldn't be as bad farther away from the parking lot. Only when she came to the end of the hedge did she finally risk entering the bushes. The ground was littered with white, wet scraps. Sophia decided not to look too closely. Two meters away, she caught sight of a squatting figure. Murmuring something unintelligible that was meant to be an apology, she hurried onward to another spot. To her right, another girl huddled. In front, a woman held on to a little boy who was peeing merrily. At last, she found a spot where she thought no one could see her. She still had tissues and wet wipes from the night before.

In the car, Lara and Chloé were nibbling on the bread as they listened to the news on the radio. As Sophia climbed into the backseat, she could see her breath in the cold air.

"They're saying the power went out in half of Europe last night," said Lara.

"What are we going to do?" asked Chloé. "We can't sit here and freeze our tits off. And I don't much like that makeshift refugee camp over there."

Fleur climbed in and joined them with a shiver. "This place is vile," she said, rubbing her hands to warm them. "I'm not staying here for another second."

In the distance, someone began sounding their horn. Others joined in, as though that would help matters.

"No power, no phone, no gas—what's next?" Chloé had

to yell for the others to hear her over the noise. Everyone, it seemed, was releasing their pent-up frustration.

The four friends could only look at one another, at a loss as to what to do next. They sat in the car, unspeaking, listening to the swelling din.

DAY 1—SATURDAY

PARIS, FRANCE

"We've got tons of material," Turner announced as he pulled open the door to the editing room. Then he fell silent when he saw candles flickering in the darkness.

"What the hell's going on here?"

Shannon turned to him in disbelief. "Seriously? We've just spent the entire night running around in pitch-black and—"

"OK, OK, oo power's out. But there ought to be a backup power system here."

"No shit," said Eric Laplante. "The only computers still working are the ones whose batteries had enough charge. I've been trying to come up with some alternatives."

"You've got to be kidding," said Turner. "We've shot hours of material and we can't do anything with it?"

"We can edit on the laptops," Shannon offered.

"What is it you've got?" asked Laplante.

"Scenes at Gare du Nord after all the signs went off, the ticket windows were closed, the power went out in the shops, and most of the trains were canceled…a few car accidents…interview with the chief of the fire department, firefighters rescuing people stuck in elevators…chaos in and outside supermarkets and malls."

As he spoke, Turner played some of the raw footage on the screen.

"We need this one," he said, indicating a scene shot in the subway.

Only because you're in the frame the whole time, thought Shannon. She fast-forwarded to the footage at the

Interior Ministry. When the car drove by, she hit Pause. It was possible to make out the outline of a face behind the tinted windows. She put on a few filters; the edges got sharper, the contrast deeper.

"I know that face," murmured Turner.

Yeah, but you don't know the name that goes with it, thought Shannon.

"That's Louis Oiseau, head of Électricité de France," she explained.

"I know that," Turner snapped.

"It's an awesome opening scene," Shannon remarked. "Energy boss heads to Interior Ministry on secret mission."

In the foreground of the shot, Turner vanished behind a flurry of snowflakes.

"Nah," he said. "Nobody cares about that."

"I wouldn't say that," Laplante said. "After all, half the country's in the dark. And other countries are affected too. There's no word yet as to the cause or how soon it will be fixed."

"Exactly!" cried Shannon. "So we should sign off with the scene at the ministry. First the human drama and at the end the question: Are things going to get even worse?"

"Lauren, please," groaned Turner. "You're the camerawoman. These are decisions for journalists and editors."

Without me you'd be nowhere, thought Shannon. She clenched her teeth and said nothing.

MILAN, ITALY

The taxi stopped in front of the glass palace that housed Enel, one of the largest power suppliers in Europe. As he dropped the fare in the driver's palm, Manzano realized that he was spending the last of his cash.

The doors to the lobby were closed; a row of security guards formed a cordon across them, holding back journalists, curious onlookers, and disgruntled customers.

Manzano pushed his way through the crowd and told one of the black-clad security men that he had to get inside.

"Nobody gets in today."

"I know what started this whole mess. And I have to let the good gentlemen inside know. How about you let me through and spare yourself the embarrassment of having to explain to your employers that you got in my way? Believe me, you will have to explain."

The security man exchanged a wavering glance with another guard. Then, without taking his eyes off Manzano, he said something into his mouthpiece. Manzano stared stony-faced at the guard as he listened to the response. Finally, he beckoned him forward. "Come with me."

Manzano followed the man to the long, curved reception desk, behind which were three dazed-looking employees. One of the women greeted them with a pinched expression.

"Please wait here. Someone will be down in a moment."

Twenty minutes later, he was on the verge of walking out when a junior manager appeared. He could have come straight out of central casting: young, tall, dapper, every hair in place, in suit and tie—quite an achievement in the current conditions. Only the bags under his eyes betrayed that he'd had less sleep than usual the night before. He introduced himself as Mario Curazzo. Straightaway he demanded, "How do I know you're not a journalist?"

"Because I don't have a camera or a voice recorder with me. And I haven't come here to ask you anything. Instead, I want to tell you something."

"You sound like a journalist to me. If you waste my time, I'll throw you out of here myself."

And he could do it too. Manzano didn't doubt that for a moment. Curazzo was a head taller than he was and looked to be in very good shape.

"Does KL 956739 mean anything to you?" asked Manzano.

Curazzo stared back at him with a blank expression.

Then he answered, "A code for the electric meters; we don't use it."

Now it was Manzano's turn to be surprised. Either the subject was Curazzo's area of expertise, or the man was really good. Or they already knew.

"Then why was it showing on my meter last night?"

Again that same look, penetrating, giving nothing away.

"Come with me."

He led him along deserted glass hallways.

They arrived at an enormous room with gigantic screens decking one of the walls. Under them, in desks arranged in circles, dozens of people sat in front of computer monitors. The air smelled rancid. A curtain of sound woven of multiple discussions filled the room.

"The control center," Curazzo said.

He led him to a group that stood leaning over a table. When Manzano was introduced, he looked into drawn faces. Curazzo explained why he had brought him here. The group didn't seem particularly impressed. Again Manzano repeated his story.

An older man with his shirt collar open and his tie loosened asked, "Are you sure you didn't just dream all of this up?"

A name tag on his chest identified him as L. Troppano.

Manzano could feel his face turning red.

"One hundred percent sure. Have you not had any reports about this yet?"

The man shook his head.

"Could the code have been activated by mistake?"

"No."

"I heard on the news that the outages began in Italy and Sweden. Is that true?"

"They were among the first, yes."

"The two countries where practically every home is fitted with a smart meter. A strange coincidence, don't you think?"

"You think the meters were tampered with?" asked a man with a mustache and blow-dried hair.

"I was able to do it. Why shouldn't somebody else be able to?"

"Tens of millions, throughout Italy?"

"The problem isn't the meters," said Troppano. As he spoke he turned to the others, as if to remind them of something that had already been discussed. "We have instabilities in the grid that we've simply got to get a handle on." To Manzano he said, "Thank you for making the effort to come to us. Mr. Curazzo will see you out."

Manzano was about to answer when Curazzo discreetly took hold of his elbow.

On the way to the exit, Manzano urged Curazzo to look at the meters and to share what they found out with other companies. Had he sown a seed of doubt that would take root in the next few hours? He didn't have much hope.

FARM NEAR DORNBIRN, AUSTRIA

Sophia knocked a second time on the old wooden door. Their car was parked ten meters away, at the end of the drive that led to the farm. Lara, who could still remember German from her school days, stood patiently next to her. The mooing of cows floated in the air.

Still no one came to the door. It was clear that someone was there—the animals couldn't look after themselves. So they went around the back to the cowshed. The door swung slightly ajar. The cows' cries were so loud now that Sophia only made a show of knocking before pushing it open with force. The smell inside the cowshed filled her with a warm, contented feeling. Inside stretched a long aisle of cows standing in stalls on either side. But no human in sight.

"Hello?" Sophia called out.

"Hello!" Lara called louder.

They spotted a farmhand sitting on a stool, half-hidden by a cow's flank.

"Hello! Excuse me!" Sophia called out again.

Years of working outdoors showed in the man's face. He looked suspiciously at her. Then without standing up or taking his hands from under the cow, he said something.

As much as her German allowed, Sophia introduced herself and explained what she was after.

The man's face didn't get any friendlier, but he stood up and wiped his hands on his apron. He wore rubber boots and a patchy, oft-mended sweater. Behind him she could see a bucket of milk under the cow's udder.

Sophia still couldn't understand what he was saying. With a smile she held out her road map. The farmer gave her a look, then ran his finger over the map. As he did so, he explained, now in more intelligible language, how they could get to the nearest train station.

Sophia and Lara were about to leave when one of them asked, "Why are the cows mooing so loudly?"

"Their udders are killing them," he said grimly. "Without power, the milking machines don't work. So we have to do everything by hand—and with more than a hundred cows, it's going to take ages. Their udders are already past full." He stood up. "So excuse me, but I need to get back to work."

Sophia caught the look Lara was giving her. The same thought had popped into both their heads.

"Is it difficult?"

"What?"

"Milking. Is it difficult to learn?"

MILAN, ITALY

Completely frozen through, Manzano reached Via Piero della Francesca. It had taken him three hours, walking from one side of the city to the other in old shoes that he hadn't gotten around to replacing. He fantasized about a hot shower. Instead, he stepped through the door to find it was about ten degrees Celsius in his apartment. At least my food will keep even without the refrigerator, he thought. He kept his coat on. He was just bemoaning the fact that he couldn't even make himself an espresso when there was a knock at his door. Old Man Bondoni.

"And you're completely sure?"

Manzano told him where he had been.

"I'm sure somebody is tampering with the power grid. I know I'm not exactly an expert, but to me it looks as though somebody deactivated all the meters at once, causing an abrupt spike in the power grid. That resulted in a chain reaction, till finally nothing was working. Who am I supposed to go to now?"

"Well, if nobody in Italy will listen to you, you have to try somewhere else."

"Fantastic idea," scoffed Manzano. "And who was it you had in mind? The U.S. president?"

"The European Union."

"Wonderful! Sounds really promising."

"Why don't you try listening to me for a second instead of poking fun? Think about it! Who do we know on the payroll up there?"

Slowly it dawned on Manzano what Bondoni was getting at.

"Your daughter. So what are we waiting for?"

Bondoni put on a pained face.

"Lara is off skiing in Austria. Tyrol. Ischgl. She gave me the address. Just in case."

"I've been there." Manzano thought for a moment. "Do you still have a few of those jerricans that you're always filling up when the prices are low?" he asked.

A wrinkle formed between Bondoni's eyebrows. "Why?"

"Yes or no?"

"Yes."

"And your Fiat's tank is pretty full?"

"I think so. But…" Bondoni caught on. He started wagging a finger excitedly, as if he were warning a naughty child off of playing a mean trick. "No. No. Absolutely not. You're nuts!"

"Have you got a better idea?" He grinned at Bondoni. "Or anything better to do? It'll take us four, five hours. Best of all." He flicked the collar of Bondoni's coat. "The car's got a heater."

FARM NEAR DORNBIRN, AUSTRIA

"Ah, that is magnificent!" Chloé leaned against the tile stove in the farmhouse. Sophia sat with the others at a long wooden table, enjoying the food that the farmer's wife had set out so generously. Rye bread, butter, cheese, cold cuts, and a glass of fresh milk to wash it all down. Everyone dug in eagerly, though Sophia noticed Fleur leaving her milk, still warm from the cow, untouched. It was pungent stuff, and she was having a hard time lifting the glass herself.

With their fractured German, they made conversation with those who lived in the house and others who had come to help out, joining in with the laughter at their clumsy milking. The farmer imitated their inexpert technique with his knobby fingers, clutching his belly with mirth. Then they discussed how they should get on their way.

"How much further is it?" the farmer asked.

"Maybe an hour, about sixty kilometers," said Sophia.

"Ten liters ought to be enough for your car. I've got a full tank and can give you some from mine."

"That would be great! We'll pay you for it, of course."

"That's what I was thinking," said the man, the same plain look on his face. "Four euros per liter."

Sophia swallowed. That was more than double the normal price. She shared a look with Lara. They were thinking the same thing: don't get upset now. Supply and demand have nothing to do with what is just or fair. They would have fuel to continue their journey; that was the main thing.

YBBS-PERSENBEUG, AUSTRIA

Calm and unrelenting, the Danube wound its way through the landscape. It had finally stopped snowing, and the fields on either side of the river were covered in a blanket of white, dotted with the occasional farmhouse and the leafless skeletons of trees.

Oberstätter's gaze followed the swirling water as he took another drag on his cigarette and pondered the events of the last twenty-four hours. He and his team had been at the plant the whole time, staying on even after the night shift came in to relieve them and making do with a couple of hours' sleep on makeshift cots. They had tried again and again to get the power plant started up, and every time their efforts had been brought to a halt by a system alert warning of some malfunctioning component—a different one each time. As if it wasn't bad enough that they had to abort the restart while a team went to inspect the relevant component, they had yet to find a single problem with the machinery. Oberstätter stamped out his cigarette, deposited it into the ashtray, and went into the control booth.

"It's got to be the software," he told the shift leader.

"I've been thinking the same thing," he said. "Problem is, where do we begin?"

All manner of programs were put to use in a power plant. The most complicated were the so-called Supervisory Control and Data Acquisition systems. SCADA systems had a wide range of applications, from industrial manufacturing processes to the management of airports, corporate headquarters, shopping centers, and space stations. They made it possible for a handful of people to pilot a gigantic oil tanker across the ocean, for a few dozen workers to operate an automobile factory, and for millions of travelers to take off and land at airports all over the world.

"No idea. The SCADA systems were exhaustively tested before they were installed. Anyway, as far as I know, we can't access the system directly. I guess we should start with the PCs."

The shift leader stared through the giant glass windows into the machine room. Oberstätter knew what was playing out in his head. If he decided to suspend the attempts to restart until they had looked over the software, days could go by before the power plant was producing electricity again. In the end, it was down to the operator to make the decision.

"Hopefully, nobody's planted anything like Stuxnet on us," said Oberstätter.

"You don't joke about things like that."

"Wasn't a joke."

The malicious virus had caused an uproar in autumn 2010 when an Iranian nuclear facility was targeted.

"Well, it's pointless to continue when we keep having to abort," Oberstätter's superior said finally. "We're stopping the resuscitation attempts. I'll notify headquarters."

RATINGEN, GERMANY

There were only a few vehicles scattered across the wide expanse of the parking lot, but still more than usual for a Saturday in February. Gusts of wind swept over the whisper-thin covering of snow, churning up puffs of white and leaving behind gray asphalt. In this bare winter landscape, the ten-story glass-and-concrete cube seemed almost forlorn. Atop the building the large blue letters of the logo jutted into the gray sky: *Talaefer* AG. Lights shone in a few windows.

James Wickley parked the SLS Roadster and made his way to the basement. The building was equipped with diesel-powered backup generators, which meant he'd still be able to use the elevator and his office on the top floor would be heated.

As soon as he reached the office, he threw his coat over a chair and started up his computer. The son of a diplomat, Wickley considered himself a citizen of the world: born in Bath, raised in London, Singapore, and Washington, educated at Cambridge and Harvard. And as chief executive officer of Talaefer AG, he saw himself as the vanguard of a brave new world, thanks to his company's innovations in the field of smart grids.

For the last four years he'd been predicting the end of the old order, whereby large, centralized energy producers generated electricity and distributed it across interlinked international grids. The system had functioned by predicting demand for power and meeting that demand with hydroelectric, coal, and nuclear plants that delivered power constantly, with peak-time assistance from more flexible thermal (primarily natural gas–fired) plants.

In Wickley's vision of the future, power would be supplied by a multitude of small entities harvesting electricity from unreliable sources, like the sun or wind, or even capturing energy generated by individuals walking, thanks to micro–power plants in the soles of shoes.

Classic grids were incapable of managing countless small, independent, and unpredictable electricity providers. Already, the growing number of wind and solar power facilities presented a threat to grid stability. Circumstances would become completely uncontrollable if in the future every household, every individual even, were to become a mini power plant, generating electricity and sending its excess output into the grid.

Smart grids would get around this problem by linking together all the microgenerators to form virtual power plants, with countless high-speed sensors at every possible point in the grid to measure power quality and voltage in real time. Users would receive smart meters; in accordance with European Union guidelines, large parts of Europe would be retrofitted by 2020.

In the meantime, it appeared the collapse of the existing grid was keeping him from getting on the internet, so Wickley abandoned his office for the large conference room where his senior management team had gathered. The night before, he had ordered that they be here in case the power outage continued, which indeed it had.

"So far we haven't received any feedback from operators, facility contractors, or even from individual power plants," announced the head of sales. "I've set up a call center on-site in case customers require support."

"Good," said Wickley. "Are there enough technicians to handle it?"

"For the time being, yes," replied the head of human resources.

"Communication?"

The question was directed to the chief of communications, a sharp-featured man with prematurely graying hair.

"So far, no questions from the media," he replied. "I am, however, planning to have off-the-record conversations with select journalists as soon as possible. Naturally, I'll forefront the reliability of our products as well as the high degree of competence among our software developers and engineers, particularly in regard to our projects in development."

"Excellent! The man uses his brains. And with that I come to the most important point in our discussion."

Wickley leaned forward, letting his gaze sweep over the twenty men assembled around the conference table.

"This blackout is a huge opportunity! In a few hours it will be gone—but not forgotten. I'll make sure of it." He jumped up from his seat. "Right now, we need to drive home the message that the competition's ideas are shortsighted, well past their sell-by date. If we're to avoid a repeat of this situation, radical innovations are essential."

And it was his hope that those radical innovations would, over the coming decade, deliver double-digit annual growth rates for Talaefer AG.

He turned to the head of sales. "First thing Monday morning, I want you to start setting up meetings with key policy and decision makers."

No longer would they have to rely on luxurious "educational" trips to foreign countries to woo clients and investors. Instead they would rely on presentations that highlighted the failure of the existing system and the virtues of Talaefer products. He placed both hands on the long table, leaned forward, and fixed his colleagues with a penetrating look.

"By Monday evening I want to see a presentation from every single department, with the blackout as the point of entry and as a key thread running throughout."

He could see in their faces that this wasn't something they had counted on. Most of them had families who were sitting at home without heat, water, or means of communication, hoping their spouses and parents would be home soon. Well, they would just have to get by without them.

"Get to it! Let's show the world what energy is."

PARIS, FRANCE

The music woke Shannon, and she cursed her roommates. She got up and padded along the hallway to the bathroom in just her T-shirt and shorts. Eyes barely open, she turned on the taps—it was an old-fashioned washbasin with one hot, the other cold—splashed water on her face, and washed the bad taste out of her mouth. She looked sleepily into the mirror, her wild brown hair hanging over her face.

The water was running. She heard music. She'd used the toilet. It flushed.

She put on her bathrobe and went into the kitchen. Marielle and Karl were having a late breakfast, French hip-hop playing on the radio. "Morning," she greeted them. "Power's back on?"

"Thankfully," said Karl.

As she poured coffee and milk into a demitasse, Shannon recalled her fleeting glimpse of the head of Électricité de France as his limo roared into the Interior Ministry. So that meeting was all for nothing, she thought. Or perhaps he'd been summoned there for a reprimand that had had exactly the desired effect, namely getting the power back on as quickly as possible.

After luxuriating in a hot shower, Shannon sat down at her laptop and uploaded material from the night before. She worked for Turner as a freelancer, which meant she could take her unused footage and use it herself. While she waited, she surfed a few news sites and checked her various social media accounts. Finally, she put some footage together and added a voice-over, then posted the resulting report on YouTube.

When she was done, she put on warm clothes and went shopping in the small supermarket two blocks away. From what she could see, Paris had already returned to normal.

She arrived back at the apartment building at the same time as her neighbor, Annette Doreuil. The elegant sixty-something had also gone out to pick up a few groceries.

"Annette!" she called. "That was some night last night, wasn't it?"

"It was terrible! Our daughter and her family were supposed to be flying in from Amsterdam, but all the flights were canceled."

"What a shame. I know how much you've been looking forward to seeing your grandkids."

The elevator shuddered to a halt between two floors; a knot formed in Shannon's stomach, but then the elevator started moving again.

"That'd be all we need right now," Annette laughed nervously. They stood in silence, watching the floors go by through the glass panes of the door until they stopped at the fifth floor. Shannon was happy to step out onto firm ground.

Maybe now she'd take the stairs more.

"Say hello to your husband for me. Hopefully your grandkids will come soon."

"I hope so too."

NEAR BELLINZONA, SWITZERLAND

There seemed to be less traffic on the roads than usual. Bondoni had let Manzano take the wheel, and once they were out of Milan, he'd put his foot down on the accelerator and pushed the 1970 Autobianchi 112 to its limits at 140 kilometers per hour. Stowed away in the tiny trunk were four jerricans holding twenty liters each. Bondoni had turned on the radio; together, they followed the news and special reports that most of the stations were carrying. They weren't saying anything good. Europe was still largely without power.

They were already in Switzerland; they had left Lugano behind them and were headed toward Bellinzona when the fuel gauge drifted into the red.

"We have to fill up," said Manzano when he saw the sign for a rest area.

Four tractor trailers parked one after the other occupied the entire left half; to the right were three cars. Next to one of the cars, a man paced back and forth, smoking. Manzano and Bondoni got out and stretched their legs. Manzano opened the trunk, lifted a canister out, and began to fill the tank.

He listened to the quiet glugging of the fuel while every now and then in the background a car rushed past on the highway.

"Hey! You're like a mini tanker truck," a voice called out next to him and let out a hoarse laugh at its own joke.

The smoker, now without his cigarette, eyed the trunk of the Autobianchi with interest.

"And we've got a long way ahead of us too."

"Where's your load taking you then?"

"To Hamburg," Manzano lied.

"Wow! That's a long way for a purse on wheels like this."

Manzano had emptied the canister, closed it, and put it back. As he did so, he looked over the roof of the car and took note that two more men were coming toward them from the smoker's car. Manzano liked them as little as he did their buddy. He closed the trunk.

"You'll never get to Hamburg in this thing," said the man. "Wouldn't you rather sell us a canister or two instead?"

Manzano had the driver door handle in his hand, was ready to get in.

"Sorry. But like I told you, we've got a long way to go. We need every drop for ourselves."

By now the smoker's companions had reached them. One planted himself in front of the vehicle; the other headed toward Bondoni, who was about to get in on the passenger's side.

At that moment, the smoker grabbed Manzano's arm.

"We need gas," the man said flatly. "Until now, I've asked you nicely."

No mistaking that. Manzano didn't hesitate. In one hard motion, he kicked the man between the legs. The guy hadn't counted on that. He doubled over. Manzano pushed him away; the man stumbled backward and fell onto the asphalt. Manzano jumped into the car. Bondoni took advantage of the moment of surprise and all but threw himself onto the passenger seat.

Manzano slammed his door shut and locked it while turning the ignition key with his other hand. Outside, his attacker pulled himself to his feet. The guy in front leaned on the hood, as if he could stop the car that way. Manzano put the car in gear, stepped on the accelerator, then let the clutch out. The Autobianchi leaped forward; the man was flung over the hood into the windshield. He rolled off to the side and took the smoker with him. Manzano upshifted and shot out of the exit.

"Those bastards," yelled Bondoni. "My beautiful car. That guy had better not have put a dent in the front!"

BERLIN, GERMANY

Michelsen had suggested a change of venue, and the minister had given his approval. Instead of a conference room in the ministry, they had rented a room for the short term in the building next door. The law practice that occupied the premises had closed on account of the power outage, hardly surprising, given that the temperature in the building had fallen to twelve degrees. Michelsen wore thin thermal leggings under the jacket of her pantsuit.

Even from the fourth-floor window, she could make out the confusion of the companies' executives as they got out of the car and looked for the address. They were received below by an official who would open the door for them and show them the way to the fourth floor. Without the elevator, unfortunately. Handshakes in the conference room. The new arrivals took their coats off. Some of them still had beads of sweat on their brows from the climb. After a few minutes, everyone was seated.

One of the company bosses who looked to be in better shape—Michelsen recognized him as the CEO of E.ON—began to rub his hands as if he were trying to warm them. The climb hadn't made him sweat, so he was the first to feel the cold.

When the interior minister stepped inside, everyone stood up.

"Everyone," he greeted the guests, "please, sit."

"We chose a somewhat unusual venue for our meeting today. Unfortunately, due to the lack of power, I can't offer you any coffee or tea. And I must ask you to save using the toilet for another time and for a place where you can find running water and wastewater disposal."

Now the minister took his seat as well.

"I'd like for us to be continually reminded during this meeting of what close to sixty million German citizens have been going through for the past twenty-four hours."

Surreptitiously Michelsen observed the dignitaries' reactions. Most maintained detached expressions of interest. Only one man's mouth twitched for a moment into a fleeting, derisive grin.

"Emergency personnel are working at the limits of their capacities. We can't ask for any help from abroad, because they're going through the same thing. You are responsible for this. And I'm damned tired of the excuses."

He subjected each of his guests to a piercing look. "It's time for you to tell me what's going on. Do we need to declare a countrywide state of emergency?"

Michelsen studied the faces. Had the CEOs made some arrangement among themselves? Probably. That meant they had a strategy too. Or had they been divided? If that was the case, everyone was now waiting for someone to be the first to come out of hiding. There were furtive glances up and down the table. She saw a resolute-looking man in his midfifties, with gray hair parted on the left, stiffen almost imperceptibly. Curd Heffgen was head of one of the largest transmission grid operators.

"I admit," began Heffgen, "that we haven't yet managed to resynchronize sizable areas of the grid…"

Bravo, thought Michelsen. He doesn't just hold his helmet up on a pole; he sticks his whole head out. We'll see where the shells land.

"Which, among other things," he continued, "is due to the fact that sizable areas of the grid are currently offline. And it hasn't been possible for us on the regional level either. The frequency in the few areas that are online is too unstable."

What do I mean, bravo? Michelsen reconsidered. The man was merely giving his "It's not our fault," an elegant lead-in to take the edge off.

"Perhaps one of my colleagues from the electricity producers can explain things." Heffgen leaned back and crossed his arms over his chest to signal that he had said enough.

And now he was passing the buck. Who would take it next?

"Herr Bädersdorf, perhaps?" the minister prompted.

The man addressed, somewhat overweight and with skin showing the open pores of a smoker, nervously ran his tongue over his lips.

"Um. There are more problems with the power plants than expected, even in such a case as this," he explained. "None of us has ever been confronted with a situation of this kind. The test scenarios had assumed outage rates of up to thirty percent. In reality it's more than twice that. We're still looking into—"

"Are you trying to tell us," the interior minister cut him off, his voice dangerously quiet, "that you still cannot guarantee the reestablishment of base-level supply in the coming hours?"

Bädersdorf gave the minister a pained look. "We've got every employee available hard at work. But for our part, we cannot make a guarantee." He bit his lip.

"And the rest of you?" the minister asked the group.

An embarrassed shaking of heads.

A feeling began to take hold of Michelsen, a feeling she had last felt a few years earlier, when two police officers had knocked on her door to break the news that her parents had been killed in a car crash. In the others' faces she could see that they too had slowly begun to catch on. Despite the temperature in the room she broke into a sweat, and her heart began to beat in her throat.

ISCHGL, AUSTRIA

Relieved and impatient, Sophia took in the snow-covered mountains that rose up all around them. So close to their destination, the girls were in high spirits and spoke longingly of baths; proper toilets; hot water; clean, warm beds; and an evening in front of the fire. As they wound slowly up the mountain, they fell silent, eagerly scanning the foothills for a sign of their destination. Ten minutes later, they spotted a cluster of cozy little wooden houses huddled together on a steep slope, smoke rising from the chimneys. They parked in the small parking lot and headed to the closest cabin, which had a "Reception" sign over the door.

Inside, a young woman in uniform greeted them and led them between the cabins over narrow paths strewn with salt to one at the lower edge of the group. The view across the valley and the mountains was stupendous.

"Unfortunately, we too have been hit by the power outage," said the woman. "There's no electric light or running water in the cabins, and the heat isn't working." Sophia, Fleur, Lara, and Chloé exchanged looks of profound disappointment.

"However," the woman quickly added, "we will be doing everything we can to make your stay as pleasant as possible."

She unlocked the door and let them step inside. A narrow hallway opened into a simple but comfy den with a rustic seating area and a tile oven.

She led them into a tiny kitchen. "The stove in the kitchen can also be lit with wood—and we've plenty of it. I don't know if you want to do any cooking yourselves, but in any case, for the time being, you can also melt snow here and heat water for a bath." She laughed. "And there's certainly enough of it outside. It's just like the old times! Authentic, right?"

She grew serious again and showed them the two small bedrooms, which they reached by means of a narrow, steep wooden staircase to the second floor. "Here is the bathroom.

Have a look. We've already set pails out so you can fill the bathtub with snow and top it off with hot water." When she saw the skeptical looks on her guests' faces, she added, "You will of course be receiving an adjustment for these inconveniences. Despite all the unpleasantness, you can even use the sauna cabin, which I'll show you in a moment, and the restaurant cabin, as both can be operated with wood fires." They were standing in the den again. The woman gave them a big smile. "And I hope that tomorrow you will again be able to enjoy the full comfort of your lodgings as normal. Incidentally, there is a working telephone at reception, in case you can't get any service on your mobile devices."

She showed them the sauna and restaurant. Afterward, they got their bags and got settled in.

"Who gets to take the first bath?"

They flipped a coin. Fleur got lucky. She jumped up and down like a child.

"First milking cows, then hauling buckets of snow," grumbled Chloé.

"Let's just look at it as an adventure," Sophia said pertly and set about carrying pails of snow inside.

———

It was already dark by the time Manzano and Bondoni arrived. After they had explained to the friendly woman at reception who it was they were looking for, she led them to the cabin.

"Dad! What are you doing here? And you, Piero?"

Manzano had met Lara, albeit briefly, during her visits to her father. He got along well with her.

"Come in! What did you do to your forehead?" she asked, leaning in to inspect Manzano's stitches.

"A little accident," he said, as a flash of memory overtook him—the image of the girl in the passenger seat, her mouth bubbling with blood.

A second woman appeared in the hallway. She too appeared to be in her mid- to late thirties. She was taller than Lara, thin, with long, straight dark hair that contrasted strikingly with her blue eyes. Lara introduced her as Chloé Terbanten.

The cabin seemed small, but snug. In the den a cozy fire crackled in an open hearth. On the bench that ran along two of the walls a third woman was sitting with her feet propped up. When Manzano and Bondoni entered, she stood up politely. Like Chloé, she was tall, but her curves were visible even beneath the thick Nordic print ski sweater she wore. She had a cute, upturned nose with a sprinkling of freckles, and her blond hair was cut in a chin-length bob. Her blue eyes seemed to shine. They peered briefly at his forehead, but their owner didn't ask. I could get to liking it here, thought Manzano, the three women crowding around him.

"Sophia Angström," said Lara Bondoni. "The Swedish member of our quartet. The fourth, our Dutchwoman, is still upstairs in the bathtub."

"You have hot water?" cried Bondoni. "And a bathtub?"

His daughter let out a laugh. "Only if we work hard for it. Don't tell me you two came here from Milan for a hot bath."

BRUSSELS, BELGIUM

Terry Bilback hadn't felt this happy to be at work in a long while. His office was warm, the toilet flushed, and there was hot water. The lights, the computers, the internet, and even the coffee machine—they all worked. Not like in his overpriced two-room apartment in the suburbs, which he couldn't get to in any case because there was no public transportation.

His happy mood didn't last long. Like his colleagues in the European Union's Monitoring and Information Center, MIC for short, he had counted on the power outage being over soon. Instead it had dragged on, and with each passing hour the situation seemed to be getting worse. What had started as a trickle of reports and requests for help from member countries was turning into a flood.

The MIC was staffed around the clock by thirty officials from various nations and had three areas of responsibility. First, it served as a continent-wide communications center. In the event of a catastrophe, requests for help and offers of assistance from all member nations were channeled via the MIC. Second, it kept member states and the general public informed about current activities and interventions. Third, the MIC was tasked with coordinating assistance measures, which included sending experts to affected areas.

His phone rang. Something it had been doing all day. He didn't recognize the number. An Austrian country code.

"Hello, Terry! It's Sophia."

"Sophia, did you make it all right?"

Sophia laughed. "With a few difficulties, but that's not why I'm calling. Listen, I've just heard a strange story. We're not the right people to deal with it—I'm guessing that would be Europol. But I don't have the number with me."

"What's it about?"

"The best person to tell you that is the friend of a friend I'm here on vacation with. His name is Piero Manzano; he's an Italian programmer, and he's turned up something rather disturbing…"

THE HAGUE, NETHERLANDS

François Bollard stood at his living room window and looked out at the falling rain. It was slowly getting dark. The lawn was hidden beneath an array of buckets, bowls, pots, glasses, mugs, plastic containers, soup dishes—every last container they could lay their hands on. He watched the raindrops splashing off the hard surfaces. Behind him, the kids were playing happily together for once. His wife sat reading by candlelight on the couch. A fire was burning in the open hearth. It was the only room in the house that was comfortably warm.

The prospect of a two-year stint abroad, living and working in a city that seemed to symbolize Europe and its administration, had always appealed to him, and the reality had more than lived up to expectations. Bollard and his wife and their two children lived fifteen minutes from the ocean, in a charming nineteenth-century house with steep staircases and a wood-paneled interior. The children attended the international school, and his wife worked as a translator. They'd been living the good life—until now, at least.

Bollard went out into the hallway and put on his rubber boots and rain jacket. He took a large bucket and emptied seven almost-full containers into it, then set them back out. He took the bucket into the bathroom on the second floor and emptied it into the quarter-full bathtub. Then he put it back in the yard and went to join his wife inside.

"Can't you find a backup generator for us somewhere?" asked Marie.

"Europol doesn't have any; at least, not for employees' private use."

His wife sighed. "This isn't right. The power should've come back by now."

"One would think," said Bollard.

The phone rang and Bollard hurried to the hall to pick it up. The caller turned out to be a Dane working the weekend shift, who wanted to put him through to a British colleague who had received a call from an Italian in Austria. Bollard was still processing this information when there was a click and a British voice came down the line.

He introduced himself as Terry Bilback from MIC and then launched into a bizarre account about rogue codes in Italian electric meters. Bollard listened attentively, then asked for a name and phone number so he could speak to this Italian in person.

ISCHGL, AUSTRIA

Manzano hung up.

"And?" Sophia asked him as he joined them all in front of the reception cabin's log stove.

"That was someone from Europol," he explained. "He says he'll inform the Italian and Swedish authorities."

"I hope he doesn't go through official channels," Fleur spoke up. "If he does, we'll be huddling around fires like cavemen for weeks."

Manzano's brief discussion with the French officer from Europol about the possible consequences of his discovery had left him more troubled than ever. Pushing the thought aside, he forced a smile and asked, "Do I get something to drink too?"

Lara handed him a mug of something steaming and sweet. "We've managed to get you two accommodations in one of the empty cabins. It's got to be cozier than your freezing-cold apartments." She laughed, clinking her mug against his.

Manzano drank and hoped that the alcohol would drive away his dark forebodings.

"Now tell me again exactly where it is you work," he said to Sophia. "You seem to have some very useful connections."

THE HAGUE, NETHERLANDS

As soon as he ended the phone call, Bollard put his rain jacket back on, then stuck his head around the living room door.

"I have to go into the office for a bit."

"On a Saturday night?" Marie looked up anxiously, trying to read his face in the dim light. If he was needed urgently, she knew it must mean trouble. "Should I be worried?"

"No," he lied.

The journey through the darkened streets to Europol HQ in the Statenkwartier took him ten minutes. He strode through the corridors to one of the few offices with a light on, where he found Dag Arnsby, the Dane who had put the call through to him.

"I need everything you have on an Italian named Piero Manzano."

Arnsby typed in the name.

"Is this him?" asked Arnsby.

An image filled the monitor: a middle-aged man with sharp features, prominent chin, thin nose, short brown hair, brown eyes, pale complexion.

Bollard nodded for him to scroll down, then skimmed the profile, reading aloud: "Piero Manzano. One hundred eighty-seven centimeters, sixty-eight kilo, forty-three years old, programmer. Former member of a group of Italian hackers that infiltrated the computer systems of companies and state institutions in order to expose security deficiencies. One conviction in the late nineties, though most of the charges were dropped. Popped up at a number of demonstrations in connection with the 'Mani Pulite' investigation. Briefly detained in 2001 at the G8 protests in Genoa."

The massive riots that took place during the meeting of the world's eight most influential government leaders had been met with extreme brutality by some members of the Italian police force. One demonstrator had been shot dead; hundreds more were injured, some seriously. A number of officers were subsequently convicted by the courts, though many more escaped censure thanks to the lapsed statute of limitations.

"So he comes from that world," said Bollard, who looked upon activists, particularly those on the left of the spectrum, with skepticism.

"Officially, he works as a freelance IT consultant. Unofficially, the Italian authorities suspect he's still up to his old tricks, but they haven't been able to pin anything on him. Looks like he knows what he's talking about when it comes to malicious codes," said Arnsby.

"It would seem so. He's given me some tips to pass on to the Italian power companies. Apparently, they should start by checking the logs for their routers—whatever that means."

"If he's telling the truth, does that mean what I think it means?"

"I wouldn't want to spread panic unnecessarily," said Bollard, who had spent the short drive to the office running through every possible scenario. "But so far it doesn't sound good. Not good at all."

"You mean if someone in Italy can infiltrate the power grid, manipulate and shut it down, then he can pull the same stunt elsewhere."

"At this stage, we can't rule it out."

MILAN, ITALY

The two men didn't look like police officers. One introduced himself as Dottore Ugo Livasco, the other as Ingegnere Emilio Dani.

"What can I do for you?" asked Curazzo. He had slept for precisely one of the past thirty-six hours.

"We have orders from Europol to conduct an investigation," said the *ingegnere*. "They've received information indicating that Italian electric meters were tampered with and that this could be the cause for the power outage."

Blood rushed to Curazzo's head as he remembered the guy from that morning.

———

The staff at Enel headquarters had been sallow-faced with lack of sleep when the police IT specialists showed up, demanding to examine the logs of the company's routers.

"Why those, exactly?" they grumbled.

"We received a tip-off."

Within minutes, the search had uncovered something that turned their faces as white as sheets.

The smart meters in Italian homes were connected to one another through routers, much like any other computer network. The log data from these routers documented all the signals sent to the meters.

"It's actually in here—the command to interrupt the connection to the power grid!"

Four dozen people had gathered in front of the large screen on which the head of Crisis Management, Solarenti, pointed out the relevant data sets and graphics.

"These commands aren't coming from us, though," Solarenti continued. "Someone smuggled them into a meter, and once in the system they spread to every meter in the country."

"How? Was it a virus?" someone asked.

"They didn't need a virus—the command was probably forwarded by radio."

He let his words sink in. Curazzo couldn't hear a single person breathing, only the soft hum of the machines.

"But how could that happen?" someone cried. "What about our security systems?"

"That's what we're trying to find out."

"So whoever did this literally turned the lights out on us," another commented. "On the whole country."

"It's not just the lights they turned out," said Solarenti. "When they took all those homes and businesses off the power grid, it caused the grids to fall apart. And then, when we eventually managed to patch together a few relatively stable grids in a couple of regions, another outside command turned the meters back on so that there was a flood of homes and businesses coming back on the grid in an instant. This led to further frequency fluctuations, which overloaded the grid and brought it crashing down again."

"So somebody's playing cat and mouse with us!"

"That's the bad news. We have good news as well,

though. Now that we know the cause, we can block this command. The IT guys are already working on it—they figure they'll have it fixed in two hours."

In the movies, cheers and applause would erupt at this point, but the crisis center remained subdued. Colleagues formed huddles, whispering among themselves. Slowly their minds began to grasp the implications. The Italian power grid had fallen victim to an attack.

"This is a disaster," groaned Tedesci, the head of technology. "Gentlemen." He turned to the two policemen who stood next to him. "Let's not do anything rash here."

The two looked at him, puzzled.

"Under no circumstances can the public find out about this," Tedesci continued. "And I see no real need to report the matter to Europol either. You heard it yourselves: in two hours it'll all be over!"

Ingegnere Emilio Dani shook his head in disbelief. Dottore Ugo Livasco looked at the executive, stony-faced.

It was Dottore Livasco who spoke. "I understand your concerns. But could it not be the case that whoever has carried out these manipulations has done the same in other countries? It's our duty to warn—"

"But these paper pushers in Brussels—"

"Europol sits in The Hague," Livasco corrected him.

"Whatever! They have nothing better to do than tell the world about all this to make themselves look good!" Tedesci talked himself into a rage. "I'm going to call my friend the president right now. Let him decide what needs to be done. This is a matter of national security!"

Livasco's features hardened. A thin smile formed on his lips. "I'm afraid this lies outside of the president's jurisdiction. But go ahead and call your friend. Meanwhile, I'll be contacting Europol."

"Don't you answer to the interior minister?" asked Tedesci.

"Indeed. And he will be duly informed. I'm sure he will then report our findings to your friend the president."

"I don't think you understand," hissed Tedesci. "Do you want to continue your career as a policeman?"

Livasco's smile tilted sarcastically. He fixed the executive with a look. "Oh, we'll see soon enough whose career continues."

Curazzo looked on as a colleague hurried into the room and whispered something to Solarenti, who then approached Tedesci.

"I have news," Solarenti announced, with a look toward the investigators. He gestured toward a computer graphic of the power grid. "As we now know, the codes entered the system through a handful of meters and then spread throughout the entire country."

The graphic changed to show red lines spreading across the grid until every single line had changed color.

"Based on the time stamps recorded in the logs, we were able to trace this spread and follow it back to identify the three meters that started it."

The red lines on the screen receded until only three red points remained.

"Are you saying," asked Dottore Livasco, "that we know the exact locations where the attackers planted these signals?"

Solarenti nodded. "All three of them. My colleague will give you the addresses."

DAY 2—SUNDAY

TURIN, ITALY

"This is it," said Valerio Binardi, taking up position in front of an apartment door with oak veneer. Next to it was a doorbell with no nameplate. Behind him, six men from the Nucleo Operativo Centrale di Sicurezza, the antiterrorism unit of the Polizia di Stato, moved into place. Like Binardi, they wore bulletproof vests and carried machine pistols; one had a battering ram at the ready.

Six more members of the squad were waiting at the open windows of the apartment directly above, waiting for the order to abseil down and force their way in through the front windows. On the roof of the building across the street were snipers, their infrared scopes trained on the apartment windows. Troops had been stationed at every entrance to the building and the entire block was cordoned off. So far, they were all keeping out of sight; the tech van and troop transporters were parked around the corner where they could not be seen by anyone inside the apartment.

Over the radio came the signal to move in.

The battering ram smashed the door off its hinges. Seconds later a flash bang exploded in the entryway. They stormed inside. It was dark in the apartment. Binardi ran to the first door and pulled it open. Toilet: empty. Second door. Shower: empty. The door to the living room stood open. The rappellers came crashing in through a shower of broken glass. No one there. Nothing but an old couch and a few bookcases. Two closed doors remaining. The second team took the one across the way, Binardi and his team the other. A room with bunk beds. On the top bunk a child stared at Binardi, eyes wide open in panic. Before he could stop himself, Binardi raised his gun. The kid started screaming. Then a second one in the bottom bunk. Binardi stood to one side and covered his men while they checked underneath the beds and tore off the covers. No one else in the room. They held their guns raised. The children cowered in the furthest corner of their beds, shrieking.

Twenty seconds later, the speaker in Binardi's helmet relayed the other team's situation report. "One man, one woman, in bed. Apparently, we woke them up. Other than that, nobody."

"Secure," Binardi confirmed. He felt the wave of adrenaline subside. It appeared they could have just rung the doorbell.

THE HAGUE, NETHERLANDS

Bollard switched off the projector. Judging by last night's revelations, they would need to save every last precious drop of diesel in their backup generators.

After briefing his colleagues in Italy and Sweden, he had driven home and gone to bed in his freezing-cold room, hoping he would wake up to the news that those responsible had been apprehended. At four in the morning the ringing of the telephone woke him from a dreamless sleep. The Swedes had reported in first, the Italians twenty minutes later. Manipulation of signals via the electric meters had been confirmed in both countries.

Within half an hour, Bollard was sitting at his desk, sounding the alarm to everyone he could reach and assessing the initial findings from Italy and Sweden. By seven a.m., the majority of the team had gathered in the meeting room; in fact, the only one missing was Europol director Carlos Ruiz. The Spaniard was attending an Interpol conference in Washington, so they'd had to arrange for him to take part in the meeting via a secure audio-visual link.

Bollard summarized the results of his early morning fact-finding on the subject. Critics of modern electric grids had highlighted the dangers from the outset, but most experts had been of the opinion that the systems were too complex and too secure to be taken out for long, or over a large area. European power grids adhered to the n-1 criterion, which allowed for a system component—be it a transformer, a power line, or a power plant—to go offline without the system becoming overburdened as a result. The safeguards had been proven to work—in the event of an isolated incident. But when malfunctions or inclement weather led to several such incidents occurring simultaneously, or when human error led to breaches in safety protocol, power outages were inevitable. Until now, there had been very few targeted attacks on the power supply; the worst of these had been the so called Night of Fire back in 1961, when nationalist extremists in south Tyrol blew up a number of pylons.

"We have to assume what we're dealing with now is a coordinated action," Bollard stated. "Our colleagues in Italy and Sweden have each identified three infiltration points. The special units on-site were able to inspect the apartments in question within hours of our initial call. Investigations into the residents or former residents are in progress."

On the video screen, Director Ruiz nodded his approval before announcing, "Effective immediately, all leave is canceled. All personnel are to report back to their posts as quickly as possible."

"Is it true," he asked, "that the tip-off came from an Italian programmer?"

"Piero Manzano. He's in our files," Bollard answered.

"In what connection?"

"A hacker—and a rather good one."

"White hat or black hat?" asked Ruiz.

"Hard to say," Bollard answered. So far as he was concerned, all hackers were criminals. The white hats might claim they only broke into networks in order to expose security gaps, but they were still intruders. Black hats stole and vandalized into the bargain.

"Could he have something to do with this?"

"Can't be ruled out."

"If he's clean and as good as you say, it's possible he can help us. He's done it once already. We need every good person we can get right now—independent contractors included. And if it does turn out he's involved in the sabotage, we'll have him close by and can monitor his every move."

"But we might be inviting the devil into our midst," Bollard countered.

"True. Which is why I'm leaving him in your capable hands," said Ruiz.

COMMAND HEADQUARTERS

The Europol director's response had taken Bollard by surprise. Who'd have thought it: Europol, that bastion of bureaucracy, opening their doors to a hacker!

He scanned back through the video, savoring the expressions on the faces around the conference table when the director ordered them to enlist the Italian's help. The Frenchman wasn't the only one who seemed appalled at the prospect. Quite right too—it was nothing more than clutching at straws, a sign of their desperation in the face of forces they could not understand.

Well, let them bring in the Italian. He might have managed to disrupt their schedule with his irritating intrusion, but he wouldn't be able to help Europol. Not when the next phase of the operation got under way.

ISCHGL, AUSTRIA

Sophia closed her eyes and let the rays of sunshine play upon her face. She clutched the warm cup between her hands.

"I'm never drinking glühwein again," said a voice from somewhere above her.

She opened her eyes. Before her stood Manzano, careful not to block her light. She laughed. "I swore the same thing when I woke up."

He took a deep breath and turned, gesturing toward the mountains. "Isn't it magnificent? Hard to believe all is not right with the world when you look at that view."

"Too true," she said. "Would you like a drink?"

"I don't want to use up your supplies."

"I'm sure we can order more."

"In that case, I'd love a coffee."

Sophia grabbed a cup and the thermos from the kitchen. Someone upstairs was stirring; the cabin was slowly coming to life. She filled the cup and went back outside. Manzano sat down on the bench next to her and wrapped both hands around the steaming mug. Leaning his head against the cabin wall, he closed his eyes.

"Last night was nice," he said. "Despite it all."

"Yes," she agreed, and did the same.

Everyone had lingered around the fire in the reception cabin, drinking glühwein and chatting until three in the morning. Manzano had shown an interest in her work at EUMIC, then as the evening wore on their conversation flowed, taking in heaven and earth and everything in between. Sophia suspected that Fleur fancied the Italian; she had certainly laughed the loudest at his jokes, but then again she had been knocking back the glühwein. Sophia did not want to be inside her head this morning.

"Hey there, you two turtledoves." Chloé stood in the door holding a cup. "Is there room for me?"

Sophia found Chloé's appearance at that moment irksome. She had been feeling so contented when it was just the two of them out here on the bench.

"Here," said Manzano, without opening his eyes, and patted the space beside him on the bench.

The moment of calm was past. Chloé started chattering away; every now and then Manzano would respond. Sophia was about to get up when she heard footsteps crunching in the snow.

One of the young women from reception was coming up the path between the cabins.

"Mr. Manzano, a Mr. Bollard called for you. He'll call back again in ten minutes. He said it was urgent."

———

Sophia had followed Manzano's phone call with mounting anxiety, drawing her conclusions from his answers. Afterward he confirmed her fears.

As they wound their way back to the cabin, Sophia asked, "How come you don't want to go?"

Manzano shrugged. "Where the police are concerned, my experiences haven't been good. Besides, I don't see how I can help."

"You already helped once. So why not again?"

"I'm not an expert in this area. These are highly specialized systems."

"But it's IT."

"That's like saying you should switch from coordinating disaster relief to organizing a world ski jump championship. With one day's notice."

"Well, it would be a nice change of pace. But I see your point."

In the cabin, the others had already set the table for breakfast. Even Old Man Bondoni had crawled out from under the covers. Manzano told everyone of the latest development.

"Of course you're going!" Bondoni spoke up, outraged. "Or do you want to leave it up to those dopes to save us? No, my boy, you can't duck your responsibility so easily. Have you forgotten what made you go storming the police barricades back in the day? Because you wanted to save the world. Now you've got the chance to do it."

"Oh, let him be," Lara said to her father. "It's Piero's decision."

"If I've understood correctly what it is you do there in Brussels," Manzano said to Sophia, "your colleagues are going to be very busy over the next few days."

Sophia gave a rueful nod. "I've been thinking about that. If you do end up deciding to go to The Hague, ask Bollard whether he can arrange two seats on the plane."

Manzano looked at her, puzzled.

"From The Hague it's only two hours to Brussels by car," she said. "One way or another, I have to get back. They'll need everyone there now."

BERLIN, GERMANY

To those who knew its history, the Bundeskriminalamt complex at Treptower Park called to mind a litany of conflict: it was from here that the Kaiser's battalions had once marched off to war; the Wehrmacht designed munitions for the coming war of extermination; and from 1949 it had been home to the cynically named *Volkspolizei*—the people's police. In the aftermath of 9/11, the building had become the epicenter of Germany's fight against international terrorism, housing not only the Berlin branch of the federal criminal police force, but the Joint Counter-Terrorism Center (GTAZ) as well.

Jürgen Hartlandt, a detective in Division ST35, was one of a number of officers making their way to the emergency briefing that had been called that Sunday morning. As they took their seats, it became apparent that no one could do more than hazard a guess as to why they were there. After fifteen minutes, by which time the room was completely packed, the head of GTAZ stepped up to address the gathering.

"This morning we received confirmation from the Italian and Swedish authorities that the outages were caused by deliberate manipulations of their electric grids."

He paused a moment to allow the agitated murmuring that greeted this announcement to subside, then continued, "The extent and nature of the crisis leads us to fear that we must expect more reports of this kind."

As the briefing continued and more details were provided, Hartlandt realized that the situation was far worse than news reports on the radio had led him and millions of others to believe. With the grids likely to remain out of action for several days, governments were considering emergency measures on an unprecedented scale—including mass evacuation.

The identity of the culprits remained unknown, as did their motive. "At present we cannot rule out a politically or religiously motivated act of terrorism, or even an act of warfare."

The last comment sent a new round of murmurs through the room.

"In two hours, I want to see a preliminary report reassessing all the facts at our disposal. I want to know why we were not forewarned. Hartlandt, you'll coordinate the investigation."

THE HAGUE, NETHERLANDS

Marie carried the suitcase out to the car. The children each carried a small backpack with their favorite toys.

"We're going on vacation!" Bernadette skipped out of the door with excitement.

"But I don't want to go," whined Georges.

"Please, Georges, stop. You were happy enough when we went to the airport to visit Grandma and Grandpa on Friday."

"But we didn't go anywhere."

"Well, we're going somewhere now—come on, in the car."

Marie was afraid. Last night, when he finally made it home from the office, her husband was more agitated than she'd ever seen him. He could not and would not tell her what had made him so worried. All he would say was that he had made arrangements for her to take the children away for a few days. Paris wasn't an option; they didn't have enough fuel left to make it to her parents' place. So he'd found them somewhere local that could offer guaranteed power and hot water.

"Is Papa coming too?"

"Papa has to work. He's coming tonight."

Marie locked the front door. In the narrow street with its old townhouses, everything seemed as it always had.

Traffic was heavier than usual. No surprise—everyone had switched to driving. She turned on the radio. The only stations still operating were broadcasting nothing but news reports on the outage. Marie wondered where the radio stations got the power to broadcast.

Past Zoetermeer, the GPS led her off the expressway. She followed the instructions until they reached a stately farmhouse, the exterior made almost entirely of timber, crowned with a steep sloping thatched roof. In the graveled courtyard stood a four-wheel-drive vehicle, two sedans, and a tractor.

"Time to get out, kids!"

She rang the brass doorbell, and a woman with blond hair and a kind face opened the door. Marie estimated her to be about her own age, and she was dressed like a typical farmer's wife in corduroy trousers, a plaid shirt, and a wool sweater.

Bollard introduced herself and the children. "I believe my husband spoke with you," she said.

"Maren Haarleven," said the mistress of the house, a smile lighting her face. "Welcome. Would you like a little something to drink, or do you want to see your room first?"

"The room first, please."

It was warm in the house. There seemed to be few straight walls or edges, but it was charming and well maintained, and the furnishings had been tastefully selected in keeping with the style of a country estate. Their room turned out to be spacious and comfortable, with soft sofas and armchairs covered in a floral fabric, rural antiques, plenty of white.

"This is one of our suites," said Maren. "Here we have the living room. Next door you'll find a kitchen with a dining table, leading off to a bathroom, and two bedrooms."

"A bathroom!"

Marie tried one of the taps. Running water! She let out a happy sigh, imagining the shower that she would be taking as soon as possible.

"Oh, this is marvelous."

"Yes," laughed Maren. "The power outage is nothing to us—it would be disastrous if we suffered a blackout. Come with me, and I'll show you. Don't worry about your things—I'll have them brought up for you."

Maren led the way downstairs and out the back of the house. To the left and right stood two large outbuildings, one of which had a large wooden gate. Inside, Marie could see the floor was teeming with chicks. Lamps hung from the ceiling, giving off a warming light.

"This is where we raise chickens."

Georges and Bernadette squealed with delight.

"Imagine what would happen if we didn't have heat. After a few hours they would all freeze to death."

She shut the gate and set off in the direction of a modern extension with a metal door. The room beyond was dimly lit, and all Marie could see was a large green box with pipes and wires leading off of it.

"Our heat and power system," Maren explained. "It can be fueled with logs and wood pellets. Thanks to this, we don't have to rely on the public power grid. We've got our own well too so the blackout hasn't had much of an impact here so far." She closed the door. "Except that all of a sudden we have guests in winter. In fact, since this morning, we're all booked up. Within a half hour. Some of your husband's colleagues, I gather. Haven't a clue what's going on."

We'll all find that out soon enough, thought Marie, and she felt her eyes prick with tears.

PARIS, FRANCE

"Ladies and gentlemen," Guy Blanchard greeted the horde of journalists crowding into the press room. Ordinarily he would have been beaming with satisfaction at the size of the turnout, but he was conscious of the TV cameras and photographers recording his every move and knew it wouldn't do to be captured looking smug. "Today is a good opportunity to point out that it's time Frenchwomen, Frenchmen, Europeans, and the rest of the world recognize the initials CNES belong not only to the Centre National d'Études Spatiales, our illustrious space exploration agency, but also to the control center for France's electric grids, Le Centre National d'Exploitation du Système—among whose directors I, in all humility, count myself. If it weren't for the Centre Système, the space agency wouldn't even have power to make coffee."

This witty aside prompted a journalist from one of the regional papers to point out that, for the past weekend, no one south of Lyon had had power to make coffee.

"Granted, the current pan-European outage has not spared the French power grids. We regret this inconvenience and would like to apologize to the French people, who have had to go without light and heat. However, thanks to the heroic efforts of our employees, we have managed over the course of one night to reestablish the power supply in many regions, at least partially—unlike many of our European neighbors. An outage on this scale places great demands on everyone involved. For example, France derives the majority of its energy from nuclear power. To shut down and then restart the reactors is no simple task, but thanks to our highly trained technicians the procedure was handled in textbook fashion."

"Monsieur Blanchard." The insistent voice of his assistant sounded in his earpiece. Taking no notice, he continued his lecture.

"We are one of the very few countries in Europe to have managed this."

"Monsieur Blanchard, it's really very important." The voice in his ear was beginning to annoy him.

"Our stable French grids will provide a base that will allow us to rebuild those in the rest of Europe."

"Stop the press conference."

What was that the button in his ear said?

"Stop the press conference. It's an emergency."

Wondering what kind of emergency could possibly warrant interrupting his carefully rehearsed speech, he reluctantly informed his audience, "I'm afraid that's as much as we have time for. My thanks to all of you for coming."

Ignoring the journalists hurling questions at him, Blanchard hurried off the podium and strode out of the side door to find his assistant.

She was waiting for him, her eyes wide as if in fright.

"This had better be important, or you can start looking for another job right now!"

"You're needed in the central control room, immediately."

"Why? Come on, woman, spit it out!"

"They don't know. That's the problem."

Cursing her incompetence, Blanchard took the elevator. When the doors opened to the control room he froze, taking in the scene. Some of the operators were gesticulating frantically, arguing with colleagues or engaged in urgent telephone conversations. Others were simply staring at their screens with dazed expressions, as if unable to comprehend what they were seeing. The large display on the wall showed the graphic of the network, apparently unchanged from the last time he'd seen it, just before the press conference got under way: some green regions, some red ones.

The screens at the workstations, however, were all blue.

His stomach dropped to his knees.

Turner stared blankly at the empty podium. Around him, irate journalists were yelling at the CNES press officer, demanding that Blanchard return to take their questions. But the podium remained empty. After a while, they began to pack their things and leave. Eventually, Turner gave up too; grumbling about the lack of professionalism and shoddy media relations, he made for the exit with Shannon following in his wake.

Shannon tuned out his whining, preoccupied with trying to fathom why someone who craved media attention as much as Blanchard would call a sudden halt to his moment of glory. As they drew near the exit, her suspicions grew. She heard cars honking in the street. Through the glass doors she saw people running, people waving their hands in agitation as they spoke, people typing nervously on their cell phones...

The sky was gray. An unpleasantly cold wind was blowing as they stepped outside. And then Shannon registered the cause of the commotion: not a single window display along the street was lit, the traffic lights at the intersections were dark, traffic was gridlocked.

"Not again," groaned Turner. "Didn't the guy just announce that this was all over with?"

"OK, so we go back in," Shannon suggested. "They owe us an explanation."

She turned on her heels, ready to stride back into the building, but the security guards had already locked the doors.

ISCHGL, AUSTRIA

After breakfast, they all sat out on the bench in front of the cabin. Those who couldn't find a seat set up deck chairs. This is surreal, thought Sophia. But how else were they supposed to deal with the situation? Wailing and gnashing their teeth wouldn't help anyone. After swearing off alcohol that morning, they had quickly thrown their oaths overboard and ordered a bottle of prosecco. She and Manzano were the only ones not drinking. Fleur and Chloé had made a plan to spend the afternoon cross-country skiing. But as they uncorked a third bottle of prosecco, Sophia doubted it would happen.

In the distance, they spotted two men in uniform walking toward them between the cabins. "Piero Manzano and Sophia Angström?" the shorter of the two asked.

Sophia sat up, suddenly alarmed.

"We're from the police. We've come to pick you up. There's a helicopter standing by in the valley."

There was an immediate hush among the friends. Piero and Sophia exchanged nervous glances. When Bollard had said that he would arrange to fly them both to The Hague, they'd assumed that, with civilian flights grounded, he would arrange transportation from the nearest military base and phone back with details of where they needed to get to and what time their flight was due to leave. It had never occurred to them that he would send a helicopter—it suggested that the level of urgency had increased in the few hours since they'd last spoken to him.

One of the police officers tapped his watch and signaled for them to get a move on, so they hurried into the cabin to retrieve their bags. When they emerged, the others were standing, silently waiting for them. In their faces, Sophia read the worry and fear that up till then they had been pushing away with alcohol. She hugged her friends and watched as Manzano embraced old Bondoni. The warmth between them surprised her. Or maybe it was that the older man had an inkling of the dangers that might await them.

"Dare I leave you here alone?" Manzano asked Lara's father in a playful tone.

"What do you mean, alone? Look at me, surrounded by beauty," replied the older man, as if they were just engaging in their usual banter.

Lara wasn't fooled. She put an arm around her father's shoulders and said, "Don't worry about us. Just take care of yourselves."

SAINT-LAURENT-NOUAN, FRANCE

The director of the power plant, accompanied by a PR officer, had arrived at the control room in search of good news. They wanted to be able to tell the head office that finally, after all the aborted attempts and delays, the restart was going ahead in textbook fashion and the reactor would soon be up and running. Instead, they found the control room in chaos.

There were manuals aplenty in evidence. Plant operators were frantically scanning the pages, trying to find explanations for the various alarm signals and codes and warnings the system was churning out. The shift leader was tearing back and forth between them, discussing a possible course of action here, shouting an instruction there. Then he got on the phone. When he was finished, he came over to the director.

"The pressure in the reactor and the temperature in the primary cooling system are climbing again," he reported, wiping a thin film of sweat from his forehead.

Marpeaux came over to join them as they ran through

the countless possible reasons for the anomaly, from the vents opening or closing by mistake to electronic malfunctions in the system controls or defects that no one knew about.

"What about the diesel engines?" asked Marpeaux.

"According to the computer, two of them didn't come on, but the one that was showing as defective last time did. Three teams are down there, inspecting the machines as we speak."

Marpeaux and the shift leader both knew that if they couldn't trace the cause of the problem and fix it, the temperature in the primary coolant loop would continue to rise, along with the pressure in the reactor vessel. Before long, they would reach a point at which the only way to avoid a meltdown would be to employ drastic measures, such as letting off radioactive steam into the atmosphere. And with no television or radio, how would they be able to transmit a warning to the population?

"Paris won't be happy about this," remarked the director.

At that moment, Paris's happiness was the least of Marpeaux's concerns. He was far more troubled by the fact that no one seemed to have a clue what was going on in the reactor. For the last hour, they had been as good as flying blind.

THE HAGUE, NETHERLANDS

The helicopter had delivered Manzano and Sophia to a military airport near Innsbruck. From there, a small jet had flown them to The Hague. On board with them was an Austrian liaison officer for Europol.

Cold winds and a light drizzle greeted them as they stepped off the plane. At the foot of the stairs was a man with short, reddish-brown hair that was starting to thin. He introduced himself as François Bollard.

"What happened to your head?"

Manzano wondered whether he should have a witty answer ready for when people asked about his stitches, but right now he wasn't in the mood to crack jokes.

"A traffic light went out," he replied.

"And not just the one. We'll take you to your hotel now, Mr. Manzano. It's located within walking distance of my office. There's a preliminary meeting scheduled in two hours—and we'd like you to take part. Ms. Angström, we've arranged a car so you can continue your trip to Brussels. It will be waiting for you in front of the hotel when we arrive."

Manzano felt a twinge of regret that he would be losing Sophia's company. She was a good listener, with a great sense of humor, and he had come to appreciate her direct manner.

"By the way, when you're working with us, you'll prob ably want to use your own computer," said Bollard. "First, of course, we'll need to give yours a quick check for mal ware. OK with you?"

Manzano hesitated. "So long as I'm present for it," he finally agreed.

Bollard drove them through the streets of The Hague in silence. It was Manzano's first time in the Netherlands, and he was taken with the pretty historic homes that reflected the merchant city's former wealth.

"Wait, I have a somewhat shameless request," Sophia said suddenly as the hotel came in sight. "Would it be all right if I came up to your room to take a shower? In my apartment in Brussels it'll probably be a while before I can have one."

"Of course." Manzano was happy for the delayed farewell.

Bollard placed a small map of the city in Manzano's hand and showed him the route he should take to Europol headquarters.

While Manzano opened and closed the drawers in his

room before unpacking, Sophia tiptoed off to the bathroom. Manzano sat on the single chair in the room and took off his shoes. He studied the hotel brochure and listened to the rushing of the shower. He let his imagination run wild for a brief moment, then he turned on the television, channel-hopping till he found a news broadcast in English.

A female reporter in a woolen coat stood outside a large warehouse. Behind her, men in white overalls were at work.

"…beginning to spoil. I'm feeling very cold here outside; it is only nine degrees. But, it's not much colder inside this cold storage facility behind me…"

The camera zoomed past her to a large, open sliding door that led into the warehouse. Palettes of packaged goods were stacked on high shelves.

"…Inside, nearly two thousand tons of food worth several million euros has been stored, but after over twenty-four hours without power, it is no longer fit for consumption. And this is only one of many across Europe. So the citizens of countries further to the north and in Central Europe might complain how much colder it is for them than it is for us in the United Kingdom, but at least their food stays properly refrigerated and edible even without power. I'm Mary Jameson in Dover."

Sophia stood outside the bathroom in her jeans and a wool sweater.

"Ah, that was wonderful. So what's the latest?"

"Nothing we don't know already."

She took hold of her travel bag and swung it by her side.

"I'm ready."

Together they went down to the lobby.

She gave him an earnest look. "Good luck," she said, then hugged him.

"You too," he said, hugging her back—for perhaps a

while longer than would have been usual for people who had just met.

"When all this is over, let's get a drink together, yeah?" she suggested when they finally let go of one another. He noticed that she had to force herself to smile.

She slipped her business card into his pocket.

She stepped into the car and was gone. Manzano felt a lump in his throat as her blond head receded into the distance. Then the street was empty.

PARIS, FRANCE

"All right, what have we got?"

Blanchard wiped the sweat from his forehead. He had gathered the software specialists together in the computer center of CNES. Nearly a dozen men clustered around their laptops.

"We have a virus in the system," explained Albert Proctet, the acting head of IT, a young man with a three-day beard and a loud shirt.

"A virus?" Blanchard roared. "What do you mean, a virus?" He realized he was shouting and lowered his voice. "We have one of the best security systems in France, and you're telling me someone has breached it?"

Proctet shrugged. "There's no other explanation for the crashes. Right now we're scanning the system with antivirus software. So far without any success. And it's going to take a long while yet."

"No, it will not!" Blanchard was shouting again. "An hour ago I stood out there and praised the reliability of the French power grids! We're making fools of ourselves in front of the entire world! Why are we paying millions for this technology if anybody can just waltz right in and shut it down? What about the backups?"

Like most grid operators, CNES cloned its systems as a backup, so that in the event of files becoming corrupted or infected by a virus, they could simply load the cloned version.

"Same thing," said Proctet. "Somebody did a thorough job here."

"Somebody has caused a shit storm!" Blanchard roared. "People are going to lose their heads for this; you can bet your life on it."

"At the moment we need all the heads we've got," Proctet reminded him, unfazed.

The young man's refusal to be cowed by his rage only infuriated Blanchard all the more, but he made an effort to rein in his anger before he spoke again. "What sort of timetable are we looking at here?"

"Right now we're restarting the system, per the standard installation protocols," Proctet explained. "We'll let it run for a while and then we'll test it. That's going to take a few hours. The problem is that many of the software packages that we'll need for our investigation are only available on the internet. And thanks to the power outage, some sites are out of action and the internet itself is overburdened."

Blanchard groaned. "This cannot be happening—any of it! How come we don't have these things here on DVDs or servers?"

Proctet grinned at him.

"Unfortunately, we don't have DVDs, and the servers are infected."

"For God's sake, what kind of security—" Once again Blanchard bit down on his anger and struggled to compose himself before continuing. "OK. Now what?"

"Once we've got the software we need, we'll check over the systems. We've also called in a few specialists. They're on their way."

THE HAGUE, NETHERLANDS

With help from Bollard's map, Manzano reached Europol

headquarters in ten minutes flat. He saw no signs of the power outage in the building complex. Silhouetted against a murky gray sky, light shone out from some of the windows. Busy people strode across the courtyards and through the halls. Manzano announced himself at the reception desk. Bollard himself showed up to collect him.

At a small conference table sat a small, heavyset man, a laptop in front of him. Bollard muttered a French-sounding name and explained, "He'll scan your computer."

Manzano reluctantly handed over his laptop. While the man started it up, Bollard handed Manzano a document.

"A confidentiality agreement."

Manzano scanned the text but kept an eye on his laptop screen as he did so.

Standard boilerplate. He'd signed identical contracts for the many private firms that used his services. He wasn't counting on learning or having to keep quiet about any grand secrets. He scrawled his name on the form and gave it back to Bollard. Then he turned back to the IT technician.

The phone rang. Bollard answered. Manzano could hear the voice of the person on the other end but couldn't make out what he was saying.

"I see," said Bollard. Then, "OK. I understand. Not good."

He hung up, went to his desk, and checked something on the computer.

"Not good," he repeated. He jabbed hard on a button. The printer next to the desk came rattling to life. Bollard pulled out the papers and waved them in the air.

"There's been a development." He looked at the clock. "Damn! You'll have to excuse me—our meeting's about to start but I've got two phone calls to make."

"You're still able to use the telephone?"

"We've got backup power systems that also feed the telephone equipment. With long distance you can still get through from time to time. Locally, it's as good as ever."

Bollard dialed, waited, then started speaking in French.

Manzano had taken four years of French in school so he had no trouble understanding "*maman*" and could pick up enough of the words that followed to get the gist of Bollard's conversation.

He was warning his mother.

"No, I can't say any more right now. Tomorrow, or at the latest the day after that. Now, listen to me very carefully: take the old radio out of the garage and keep it on. Be careful with the food you have stored up. Make sure the well stays in good order. I'm going to try to send the Doreuils to you from Paris. Please be nice to them. Put Papa on."

He went silent, holding the receiver to his ear.

Sitting at the table, the little fat man snapped his laptop shut and said, "Everything checks out. Thanks."

"So the internet's still working?" Manzano asked him.

"For the general public, barely. Here, we've got a direct connection to the backbone." Meaning to the good, thick cables whose substations could be provided with sufficient backup power. "It's remained stable so far."

He gave Bollard, still on the telephone, a thumbs-up and left the room.

Manzano put away his computer while Bollard continued his conversation.

"Papa, I'm trying to arrange for the Doreuils to come and stay with you. Please treat what I'm about to tell you with the strictest confidence. Tomorrow morning, as soon as the bank opens, take out as much cash as you can get. I don't want to cry wolf here, but make sure that your rifles are cleaned and loaded and that you have enough ammunition. But say nothing to *Maman* and the Doreuils. Let's hope I'm worrying for no reason. I love you both. *Salut.*"

Manzano tried not to show his astonishment. He wondered what kind of news was on those printouts Bollard was clutching. Meanwhile, Bollard dialed a new number. Again he spoke in French. Manzano realized he was speaking with his father-in-law. After he had ended the call, his face seemed paler and more haggard than before. He turned to Manzano.

"Time for our meeting. Let's go."

———

The conference room was dominated by a large oval table. Six large screens hung on one wall. Most of those present were men. Manzano spotted only three women. Bollard showed him to his seat and then took his place at the table, directly under the monitors.

"Good day, ladies and gentlemen," Bollard addressed the meeting in English. "If one can call a day like this a good one."

He held a remote in his hand. A map of Europe appeared on the screen above him. The majority of the continent was in red. Norway, France, Italy, Hungary, Romania, Greece, and numerous small regions in other countries were crosshatched red and green.

"Until further notice, this room is our base of operations. By the end of this briefing, you will understand why. As you are aware, for almost forty-eight hours now, large areas of Europe have been without power, although intermittently some areas have managed to secure a basic supply. These latter are shown as crosshatched on the map. This morning we learned that this outage was brought about deliberately, by persons unknown.

"It started when a code was fed into the smart meters of half a dozen private homes in Italy and Sweden.

"It has now been reported that a significant number of power plants are experiencing difficulties with their computers that are preventing them coming back online."

"Stuxnet?" someone asked. "Or something like it?"

"They're looking into it now. Of course, it could take some time until they find anything. Since ten o'clock this morning, computer crashes have taken out the headquarters of grid operators in Norway, Germany, Great Britain, France, Poland, Romania, Italy, Spain, Serbia, Hungary, Slovenia, and Greece."

Countries that were previously crosshatched on the map began to turn red. From the audience came gasps of shock and dismay.

"As a result, many of the grids that were in the process of being restored have broken down a second time. Initially, each of the companies affected assumed they were the victim of an unfortunate malfunction, but as one after another was hit it became clear that this was no accident. Ladies and gentlemen, someone is attacking Europe."

A stunned silence.

"Do we have any idea who?" a man at the other end of the table asked.

"No," answered Bollard. "And so far we have little to go on. The operators identified six meters that were used to feed in the malicious codes: three in Italy, three in Sweden."

The screen filled with images supplied by the Swedish and Italian authorities.

"The residents at each address stated that they had been visited by service technicians from the local power company days before the outage. Despite initial doubts, their statements have checked out. With their help, facial composites of these supposed technicians are being prepared.

"I don't need to tell you that the outage is hampering our investigations more with every day the power stays off. Despite those difficulties, I must stress the need for close cooperation with liaison officers in each country. Independent national initiatives will be futile in the face of this pan-European threat."

"If the public finds out about this…" murmured a man on Manzano's left.

"They won't—not for the time being," Bollard said firmly.

———

Manzano waited for Bollard outside the conference room.

"Do you really mean that?" he asked him.

"What?"

"That the public won't be getting any information."

"The public will be informed that the outage could go on for another few hours, or in some areas a few days. If they were told about the attack, it would only trigger panic."

"But it's not going to be just a few days in a couple of areas!" protested Manzano, appalled.

Bollard gave him a penetrating look, then set off in the direction of his office.

Manzano followed. He wasn't done asking questions.

"The software for the operation and control of power grids and power plants is very complex and highly specialized. Worldwide, there are only a few companies that are capable of developing these kinds of systems. Stuxnet was just mentioned. Would it be possible to put together a list of all power plants, grid operators, and other energy companies that are having problems, together with a list of their software providers?"

"I'll see what I can do."

PARIS, FRANCE

The elevator in Shannon's building was, of course, not working. Exhausted, she climbed the stairs to her apartment. At least it warmed her up after the long, cold walk home.

When she got upstairs, she saw suitcases and bags in front of her neighbors' door. Bertrand Doreuil was in the process of balancing another piece of luggage on the pile. Before his retirement, the tall, gaunt man with the scant gray hair had been a leading official in one of the ministries. She knew him as a witty conversationalist and a helpful neighbor.

"Good evening, Monsieur Doreuil. Making a run for it?" she asked, laughing. "I can understand why."

Doreuil gave her a confused look.

"Huh? Oh, no. We're going to stay with my son-in-law's parents for a few days."

Shannon eyed the luggage. It didn't look like a few days to her, more like a trip around the globe.

"You're taking a whole lot of gifts for your hosts, I see," she said, nodding at the suitcases. "Hopefully there's power where you're headed."

His wife appeared behind him. "Psh, the Bollards burn wood for heat when they have to. And when we want something to eat, they take a hen out of the coop and slaughter it," she joked.

Her husband smiled sourly.

"I've just come from a press conference where a director of CNES declared that everything will be running again soon."

"Oh, I'm sure it will," Madam Doreuil singsonged.

"Moments after the press conference ended, the power went out again." Shannon watched as they each took a suitcase from the pile. "I thought your daughter and her family were supposed to be coming for a visit?"

"Oh, they had to postpone the trip on account of the power outages. And my son-in-law can't leave The Hague at the moment."

Her husband gave her a sharp look. Annette smiled at him sheepishly and then turned back to Shannon. "Um, could you be a dear and keep an eye on our mail while we're away?"

Too many ohs and ums. This awkwardness didn't suit the Doreuils. They were normally so poised.

"But of course," Shannon replied as casually as possible, while thoughts raced through her head. She had met the Doreuils' son-in-law a couple of times. He was a high-ranking officer in Europol—responsible for counterterrorism, if she remembered correctly. Why would a power outage force him to cancel his vacation? And why had Doreuil given his wife such a scolding look when she mentioned it? Shannon's journalistic instincts were stirring.

"Is your daughter doing well?" she asked.

"Well, there's no electricity where they are either, but, yes, she's doing fine. We just spoke with our son-in-law—"

"Annette," her husband cut in, "we need to get going, or else it will be dark when we arrive."

———

Shannon sent up a silent prayer of thanks that neither her landlady nor her roommates had ever invested in a fancy new telephone. After a few tries with the old-fashioned landline she reached the production studio. "There's something behind it," she told Laplante. Turner couldn't be reached. "Notify the correspondent in Brussels."

"I can't get through to her."

"Then I'll go to The Hague myself. If I take the car, I can be there in five hours."

"You don't have a car."

"Well, here's the thing. I thought maybe you could lend…"

"And how am I supposed to get between the office and home when there's no public transportation?"

"The network could spring for a rental car…"

"Because you've got a vague hunch that something's not right? No way."

"So you're not interested?"

"I'll keep trying to reach our correspondents for the Benelux countries—"

"By the time you do, there won't be a story anymore."

She hung up.

She packed a rucksack full of warm clothes, her two digital cameras, all the spare batteries she could find, and her laptop. She put on her woolen jacket and heavy boots, shouldered the rucksack, took one last look around, stepped out, and slammed the door.

THE HAGUE, NETHERLANDS

"So what's he up to?"

Bollard had given a cursory knock and walked straight into the hotel room. It was different from other guests' accommodations by virtue of the towers of electronic equipment stacked up on top of and next to the desk. Three small screens showed black-and-white scenes from another hotel room. On the middle screen, Bollard recognized Manzano, who was sitting on his bed, the laptop on his lap. He seemed to be reading intently, but every now and then his finger briefly touched the keys.

"Not much," answered Manzano's tail, a surly thirty-something in a jean jacket. "Made three phone calls. The first was to MIC in Brussels—asked for Sophia Angström. Then Angström's personal number. Couldn't reach her on either one, though. The third number was in Austria. A resort near Ischgl. But that one was dead. Since then he's been sitting on the bed, reading on his computer."

"Nothing but reading?"

"As far as I can tell, yes."

"OK then. I'm out of here. Let me know if he does anything suspicious."

———

A dozen cars were parked in front of the farm. Bollard parked his among them, rang the doorbell, and was let in by the proprietor, a blond woman who introduced herself as Maren Haarleven.

"Come in," she said. "Your family is sitting down to dinner."

Bollard followed her into a dining room with a few large tables that were all occupied. He recognized a number of faces. After he had secured a place for his family, he had passed the address along to his colleagues.

His children greeted him with excited patter about the farm and its animals. During the meal, they didn't mention the power outage. Only when the children were asleep did Marie finally ask him quietly, "Are you going to tell me what's going on?"

"You three will have to stay here for a couple of days. The kids certainly seem to like it."

"On the news they said that the power is out again back home."

By home she meant France, Bollard realized. He nodded.

"I called my parents on the phone. And yours."

"How are they?"

"Good," he lied. "I asked your parents to go and stay with mine."

She frowned. "What for?"

"In case the outage lasts for a long time."

"Why should it?"

"You never know."

"And why go to your parents? Because the countryside is so nice? To visit the Loire castles again?"

"Because they have their own well, a stove they can heat with wood, and a couple of hens."

BERLIN, GERMANY

Until now, Michelsen had only been in the chancellery on public occasions. With her were members of the crisis team from every area. After that morning's news, they had stepped into a new phase of heightened security— and heightened anxiety. The guards at the entrance were more thorough than usual when carrying out their checks.

Instead of allowing them to make their own way to the third-floor conference room, a young man escorted them to the door, then a couple of technicians ran checks on their laptops before hooking them up to the system.

They waited in silence, everyone avoiding looking at anyone else. Nobody wants to reveal the fear in their eyes, thought Michelsen. On one wall of the room were ten video screens, linked via satellite to delegates unable to attend in person. Among them, Michelsen recognized two of the energy bosses from yesterday afternoon's meeting: Heffgen and Bädersdorf. They fiddled with their jackets or shuffled documents in front of the computer's camera eye.

The minutes ticked slowly by. The Berlin sky was as dark as her thoughts. Approaching footsteps tore her away from her reverie.

The chancellor was the first to enter. Prompt, resolute, serious. He shook hands with everyone present, exuding an air of resolve and vitality. Behind him came the full cabinet and the heads of government for all the member states.

"I'd like to thank you all for coming and also extend my greetings to the ladies and gentlemen who are with us via satellite," the chancellor began his address.

A face was now looking out from each of the ten screens on the opposite wall.

"As a result of developments over the last few hours, this meeting has taken on a new significance. Security agencies have confirmed that the blackout is the result of a concerted attack on Europe's power systems." He paused and took a sip of water before continuing. "This will have dire and far-reaching consequences for all member states. You are, I am sure, familiar with the report *Endangerment and Vulnerability of Modern Societies—as Seen in the Example of a Wide-Reaching and Long-Lasting Failure of the Power Supply* that the Committee on Education, Research, and Technology Assessment presented in spring 2011."

Not a chance anyone here's read it, thought Michelsen.

On the wall opposite where the ten satellite delegates looked out, a vast screen came to life, showing edited television reports from the past few days, followed by a montage of photos featuring a dark, deserted supermarket. This was Michelsen's cue. As the minister announced that he would now hand the meeting over to the acting head of Civil Protection and Disaster Management, she rose to her feet. Behind her, the screen filled with images of shipping containers being unloaded from cargo ships by huge cranes, freight trains hauling wagons, automated warehouses, and cold storage facilities.

"As a result of the blackout, the entire manufacturing and delivery chain is at a standstill," Michelsen began.

Large sheds with cows lined up in narrow metal stalls.

"Take one of our staple foods: milk. The majority of our supplies come from industrial operations, which rely on automated machines, not only for milking the thousands of cows they hold, but also for heating and ventilation of the cowsheds where the herds are kept and for supplying feed. The larger firms have backup power systems that will hold up as long as they have diesel—a few days, in most cases. Some have their own autonomous power supply, not that it will be much use to them. Because milk tankers cannot collect when they have no diesel."

Images of cars lined up outside a gas station.

"Refueling is impossible when there is no electricity to pump fuel from the underground tanks. And even if the tankers could pick up the milk and transport it to the dairies, the machines there are idle."

Images of idle processing plants—shining metal pipes, stalled conveyor belts.

"Products that had been processed before the outages are stockpiled in cold storage facilities. These—you guessed it—cannot refrigerate goods without power. Again, many have backup systems, but they need fuel to keep them running. Again, there's the problem of transportation.

Without fuel, goods cannot be transported from the warehouses to the stores. And speaking of warehouses…"

She pulled up the relevant images.

"Modern manufacturing relies on stopover facilities, where goods are stored for twenty-four hours; most of these are already empty. Supermarkets are completely reliant on electronics; the entire ordering and storage system is run by computer. Doors are designed to open and close automatically—provided there is electricity. Cash registers and checkout conveyor belts cannot function. Most of the staff can't get to work because there's no public transportation and their cars have no fuel."

She sensed that some of the delegates were about to raise objections and hurried to forestall them. "Yes, doors can still be opened manually. Money can still be exchanged for goods on a piece of paper. But the volume of demand will be such that there is a danger of rioting and looting breaking out. Most supermarkets dare not open under these circumstances."

She called up images of dairy cows penned in milking machines.

"To return to the problems facing milk producers: farmers can deal with only a fraction of the herd by hand. The vast majority of cows have therefore gone unmilked for two days. Even if we were able to supply backup generators within the next couple of hours, for many it would already be too late. Millions will suffer agonizing deaths as their swollen udders lead to glands becoming infected—that's if they haven't already starved, suffocated, or died of thirst. And we can't even slaughter them to put them out of their misery because we lack both the means and the manpower.

"It's the same story across Europe, in every form of industrialized agriculture. Millions of chicks and hens will either freeze or starve to death. In industrialized vegetable and fruit cultivation, the failure of watering, heating, and lighting systems will cause crops to fail, and firms will be forced into bankruptcy as a result. That means a critical situation for food supply in the medium term as well—even if we manage to resolve the outage within the next few days. The disruption the industry has already suffered will lead to many businesses failing."

She stopped to give her listeners the opportunity to digest the implications. If they thought they'd heard the worst, they were mistaken.

"As you have just seen, effects in one area spill over into the next. This is especially true where the water supply is concerned. In many regions, the pumping stations have shut down, so there is no running water. Even if we can find a way to supply drinking water, without which millions will die, water is needed for a number of other purposes, including—to name one of the most, literally, burning needs—putting out fires. So long as the power remains out, the risk of fires caused by short circuits in homes and industries does go down, but there will be an exponential increase in blazes caused by people lighting fires to cook or keep warm. In the industrial sector—especially where chemicals are involved—the failure of emergency and safety systems will lead to an increase in fires.

"And then there's the hygiene problem. Imagine a high-rise apartment building in which no one can use the toilet, but has to go anyway. In no time at all, our cities will be ravaged by epidemics such as cholera that will kill thousands. We have only one hope of preventing this: we must begin large-scale evacuations into emergency shelters immediately. In the initial phase alone, we are talking about more than twenty million people."

Shocked silence filled the room. Everyone stared at the screen, where Michelsen showed images from emergency shelters housing victims of the 2005 flooding in New Orleans and the Japanese earthquake of 2011: gymnasiums, meeting halls, convention centers, indoor stadiums, with thousands of makeshift beds and long lines of people queuing for food and water. Germany was no stranger to such images, on such a scale, but only in black and white—people in dated clothes in television documentaries of a war that most of those present hadn't been alive to experience, it was so long ago. And none of them had thought they would ever live to see such images in their own time.

"I will now hand you over to my colleague from the Ministry of Health, Mr. Torhüsen."

Michelsen sat down with a sigh as Torhüsen began to address the assembly. "Generally speaking, European health systems are among the best in the world. We are well prepared, even for crises—but not for a crisis on this scale. Allow me to describe what is happening out there as we speak, right here in Germany. First, we've got the hospitals…"

Images of patients lying on gurneys in corridors, sitting on floors in emergency departments, wards with no spare capacity.

"The sudden onset of the outages resulted in a high number of road accidents and injuries, causing a surge in demand for beds and medical care."

Images of intensive care units, beds surrounded by tubes and monitors and machines. Operating rooms crammed with technology.

"Our hospitals have backup generators, but as Ms. Michelsen has pointed out, these depend on fuel, which will have to be conserved. Resources for intensive care units will have to be cut back, likewise neonatal divisions."

At the sight of the red, wrinkled babies in glass incubators, skin so transparent you could see every little vein, Michelsen's throat constricted.

"Rescue workers and paramedics are hopelessly overburdened as it is. Doctors can't get to their surgeries or their patients without transportation. Patients struggle to obtain the medication they need because pharmacies are facing the same problems as supermarkets. Those with chronic conditions—diabetics, patients with heart disease—are particularly hard hit. Access to dialysis machines has become impossible for many patients whose kidneys cannot function without assistance. We are threatened here with hundreds if not thousands of human casualties."

Michelsen realized that she was biting her lower lip. A year before, she had witnessed a friend's slow death from an incurable nerve disease. How horrible this helplessness must be for patients—and for their loved ones—especially knowing there was a treatment that could save them, if only it were available.

"Nursing homes and assisted living facilities will turn into death traps—I'm sorry, but there's no other way to describe it. Aside from medical machinery ceasing to function, there will be no heating, no cooking facilities, no running water, no laundry facilities. Many of the staff won't be able to get to work. Those that do will be completely overwhelmed."

"My God," whispered a voice.

Out of the corner of her eye, Michelsen tried to see who had let out this exclamation. To judge from their pale expressions, it could have been anyone in the room. Many of them probably had parents in care homes and took for granted that their care would be guaranteed for the remainder of their lives.

"We need to ensure at least a rudimentary provision for public health and the most severely ill. And we need it immediately. This includes, among other things, setting up medical centers equipped to deal with dire cases and epidemics, emergency directives for dispensing medication, and every means of support that we can get from the army's medical units. To this end, we are currently finalizing a plan of action. Rolf?"

Torhüsen sat down, and Rolf Viehinger, leader of the Interior Ministry's Public Security division, got to his feet.

"Crises," he began, "often bring out the best in people. In the past forty-eight hours, many in need have found Good

Samaritans coming to their aid. The Red Cross, the fire department, and other agencies have been inundated with volunteers offering their services. But let's not kid ourselves: the longer these circumstances last, the weaker these structures will become. To borrow a phrase from Britain's: 'We're four meals away from anarchy.' As people see the lives of their families and loved ones threatened by deprivation, they will turn from rallying to the aid of others and begin fighting to protect their own. We must be prepared for civil unrest and to safeguard our citizens from criminal activity.

"Security personnel have been informed that all leave is canceled immediately. Even so, we will need support from the state police and the army."

"In a civilian capacity, or militarily as well?" asked the environmental minister.

"Whatever circumstances demand," the interior minister answered curtly, taking his seat.

"I thought most districts were energy autonomous," said the foreign minister.

"In practically every case, energy autonomous means independence not in actual but in accounting terms," Secretary of State Rhess jumped in. "Under normal operating conditions, these municipalities might indeed produce more electricity than they themselves use, saving them from having to buy power from elsewhere. But without the grid, their energy production is of no use to them—they simply don't have the capacity to establish a stable grid in miniature."

"So you're saying they can still produce power, but they can't deliver it to users?" the minister asked in disbelief.

"Precisely. The same applies to the larger power plants," affirmed Rhess.

The chancellor took the floor before any other questions could be put. "I suggest we take a short break. Let's stretch our legs, and in ten minutes we'll resume."

Everyone stood up, the smokers racing to the elevators

to get outside. Michelsen noticed that no one reached for their cell phones, as the multitaskers would ordinarily have done at such a moment. By now everyone had received the message that the cellular network was out of action.

PARIS, FRANCE

Shannon had walked clear across the city, over the Île de la Cité, and finally to the Gare du Nord. Streetlamps, traffic signals, and the lights in most of the buildings were out; the only light came from the headlights of cars. It was shortly after ten p.m. by the time she reached the train station, and here too it was almost completely dark, except for the odd flickering emergency light. Clusters of people crowded around the entrance to the station's main hall. In the dim half light, the stranded travelers had converted the hall into an emergency shelter. Everywhere she looked people were sitting or lying on the floor, children fretting and wailing. Despite the cold, a musty smell hung in the air that carried a hint of feces.

The arrivals and departures boards were blank. Shannon picked her way through the bodies to the far side of the hall until she found a placard on which she could faintly make out the sign for buses. She followed the arrow out of the building to a terminal where buses were lined up one after the other. There were lines of people clutching their bags, searching, waiting. It took her ten minutes to find the bus to The Hague.

"*Oui, La Haye*," the driver responded to her question.

"Where do I get a ticket?"

"Today, from me. The ticket windows are closed. Fifty-six euros. Cash only."

Shannon paid and made her way to the back row, where there were two remaining seats. She stowed away her rucksack in the rack and took the seat by the window. What an idiotic idea this had been, she told herself. But there was no going back now. At least inside the bus it was warm.

The driver turned on the engine, and moments later, the bus lurched into motion.

Shannon folded her down jacket and stuck it between the window and her head to use as a pillow.

Outside, the shadows of the city glided past her. At some point the silhouettes grew fainter, and the landscape vanished into almost complete darkness under a starless, moonless sky. Shannon stared into the gloom and thought of nothing at all.

BERLIN, GERMANY

"Money rules the world, as the saying goes," Secretary of State Rhess opened his presentation.

Nice, thought Michelsen, throwing these words at people in government. She wouldn't have thought he had the guts.

"The question is, who rules when there is no money?"

Tense, they waited to find out where he was going with this.

"So long as the backup generators are working, customers can withdraw cash. And the supply of cash will continue for as long as the security vans transporting money can get fuel. After three or four days, however, every bank in the country will be closed. Look in your own wallets. How much cash do you have on you? Once the supply of cash dries up, companies won't be able to pay salaries, no one will be able to pay for goods.

"The European Central Bank and the clearing houses that process financial transactions will open tomorrow— but the markets will close early. As soon as news gets out that the pan-European blackout was caused by a deliberate attack that breached our defenses, markets all over the world will experience a bloodbath. The value of European companies will plummet; many will fall victim in the coming months to hostile takeovers by foreign firms. To say nothing of the collapse of all those small and midsize businesses that lack the resources to survive such losses."

Michelsen saw people shaking their heads in disbelief.

"And there is one more pressing matter we have yet to touch upon: communication. The public phone network and the cellular network have collapsed. The emergency networks are struggling to cope. The satellites are overburdened, as is the internet. We have already had to introduce bandwidth-rationing, giving priority to state and emergency services.

"It will take two days for the army to set up a provisional network. In the meantime, we are launching an initiative to enlist the aid of amateur radio operators. Their equipment is relatively robust, but even so their usefulness will be short-lived since most will have no means of recharging their batteries.

"It is therefore imperative that we do not delay in getting information to the general public while we still can. The various emergency services—paramedics, fire departments, police, and federal relief agencies—still have functional communications networks. We must secure these networks and use them to inform the public as to what measures need to be taken. The employees of these agencies, in addition to their traditional duties, must now assume the role of an information service."

"What is the prognosis for reestablishing a nationwide power supply?" asked the chancellor.

"We are not in a position to make any predictions at this stage," Rhess answered. "Much will depend on the cooperation of our fellow member states and global allies. I ask, therefore, that we continue to support Europe-wide cooperation as much as it is in our power to do so. The Foreign Office is also seeking international aid—"

"International aid?" the minister-president of Brandenburg cut in. "Where's it supposed to come from?"

"From the United States, Russia, and Turkey, for the most part."

"And you say we still have no idea who launched this attack?" asked the minister-president from Hessen.

"No," said the interior minister. "Investigations are proceeding at full speed."

"Why Europe?" asked the defense minister. "It makes no sense. From an economic standpoint, no one will benefit from doing this much harm to one of the world's largest and strongest markets. We have half a billion consumers who boost the economies of Russia, China, Japan, India, Australasia, and the United States by buying their goods. If things aren't going well for Europe, those economies will suffer too."

"Could it be a military attack?" asked Rhess.

The defense minister shook his head. "It's true there have been tensions recently with Russia and China, and naturally we're in constant contact with NATO headquarters, monitoring developments on that score. But at this time we have no indication of hostile activities by any nation."

"Organized crime, to extract a ransom?" suggested the minister of health.

"Surely we would have been given their demands by now, if that were the case. Besides, anyone who tried something like this would be pursued throughout the entire world. There'd be no safe haven for them."

"And with that we come to the most likely scenario: an act of terrorism," said the interior minister.

"On this scale?" asked the defense minister, incredulous.

"Maybe it wasn't planned to be this big. Let's remember 9/11. The terrorists wanted to hit the towers of the World Trade Center, but they may not have been expecting them to collapse."

"Ladies and gentlemen," the chancellor interrupted the discussion, "in light of the situation, I'm recommending we declare a state of emergency. As of now, the government in Berlin will take over leadership and coordination."

DAY 3—MONDAY

THE HAGUE, NETHERLANDS

Shannon woke to a stabbing pain in her neck. Then it hit her that something was different. The noise of the bus's engine had stopped; she didn't feel it vibrating anymore. She opened her eyes. Her eyelids felt swollen. Outside, the darkness was total. She could hear passengers standing up to get their luggage down from the racks and cursing as they jostled for the exit. Slowly, she stretched her stiff limbs and looked out the window for some indication of where she was.

In the darkness she spotted a sign: *The Hague.*

Shannon rubbed her eyes and checked the time. A little before seven. The bus was late. More than ever she longed for a hot bath and a steaming cup of coffee, but judging by what she could make out through the window, she wouldn't be getting either in the foreseeable future. As in Paris, there were no streetlights, darkened buildings, few people. She waited till everyone else had disembarked before leaving the bus. A biting cold wind assailed her cheeks, nose, and ears. She pulled up the hood of her jacket and took out her gloves while trying to get her bearings.

It seemed they had arrived at a train station. She found her way into the central hall, where a few travelers stood around helplessly. She approached a man who looked more aware than the rest. "Are you from here?"

"Yes."

She held the sheet of paper up to him on which she had written François Bollard's address in capital letters.

"Any idea where this is and how long it'll take me from here?"

The man studied the paper. "About half an hour on foot," he said, pointing down the long straight road that led from the station. "Just head that way and keep walking."

He was right. Twenty-eight minutes later, she stopped in front of the house and double-checked the address on her piece of paper. So, this was where her neighbors' son-in-law lived. There was no sign that anyone was home, but with everywhere in darkness it was hard to tell. She knocked hard on the elegant wooden door, then waited a moment before knocking a second time. Since there was no electricity, there was no point in her trying the doorbell. She put an ear to the door. Not a sound. Knocked again. Waited, listened.

After ten minutes she gave up. François Bollard wasn't home. All at once she could feel the accumulated weariness of the last few days—indeed, of the last few years: the cold, the hunger and thirst, her longing for a shower. She began to shiver, and her eyes welled with tears. She suddenly felt alone. Her lips quivered; she gasped for air and took deeper and deeper breaths to calm herself down. She had to find someone who could tell her the way to Europol.

————

Bollard had barely slept. He'd slipped out of bed at five in the morning and stealthily left the small apartment in the farmhouse. A half hour later he was sitting at his desk in the Statenkwartier. He wasn't the only one. Half his team had spent the night in the office.

One of the technicians, Christopoulos, waved a stack of printouts at him.

"We've finally got the facial composites from Italy and Sweden. Six of them in all."

Bollard took them and went to the incident board to post them: three images for the Swedish group, three for the Italian. All the suspects were male. As usual, the e-fit computer renditions seemed ageless and soulless. It must have something to do with the eyes, thought Bollard.

He stepped back to look at the board. Five with dark hair, two with stubble, one mustache, two full beards. One had Asian-looking eyes.

"According to witnesses, they were between twenty and forty. Four of the six were described as southern, possibly Arabic—though one witness had them down as Latin American or Asian." Christopoulos shrugged. "About what you'd expect from witness reports... In Sweden, though, there was also a blond guy with them. At the moment, the images are being circulated among the power companies, but they'll probably draw a blank. None of the utilities' service schedules show any appointments for the days and addresses in question, so it's unlikely these are bona fide employees."

"It's a start though. Anything in our database?"

"We're running them through now. Interpol and the FBI are working on it as well."

"That's everything?"

"On these investigations, yes, unfortunately. A few reports have come in from the International Atomic Energy Agency in Vienna. Temelín in the Czech Republic is reporting ongoing problems with its cooling systems, but the authorities say it's only level 0 on the International Nuclear Event Scale—the same in Olkiluoto in Finland and Tricastin in France."

"Let's hope it stays at level 0," said Bollard.

"There is one plant experiencing more serious problems with its emergency cooling systems," Christopoulos continued. "The Saint-Laurent reactor in France." Bollard felt as though someone had tightened a thick belt around his throat, cutting off his air supply. The facility at Saint-Laurent-Nouan was twenty kilometers away from his parents' house.

"What's the INES level?"

"Hasn't come in yet. The situation is still unclear.

All I know is there's talk of increased pressure and rising temperatures."

"Excuse me," said Bollard.

He hurried into his office and turned on the computer, scanning in vain for reports on the incident. Surely if it had been made public, there would be something? He checked the time. A little before eight. He dialed his parents' number.

The line was dead. Bollard nervously pressed the hook, tried it again. Nothing.

———

Manzano was lounging on the sofa in his hotel room and working on his laptop when there was a knock at the door.

Bollard stepped inside.

"Did you sleep well?" he asked.

"And had a decent breakfast too," replied Manzano.

Yet he didn't seem at all comfortable in his surroundings. He'd been much more relaxed last night, less jittery.

"Grab your coat—we're going shopping," said Bollard.

"Are the shops open again?"

"For us they are."

They drove through the empty streets, Bollard making small talk along the way, pointing out a few landmarks.

They drove past a large department store. Bollard parked the car on a side street.

"We'll take the side entrance," he said, taking a bag out of the trunk.

At the delivery entrance, a middle-aged woman let them in after Bollard had exchanged a few words with her and shown her an ID.

It was so dark inside Manzano could barely see. From his bag, Bollard took out two large flashlights. He handed one to Manzano. He pointed the other across the expanse of floor, throwing light on shelves, tables, and racks crammed with clothes.

"Pick some things out for yourself."

"I feel like a burglar," Manzano remarked.

"You should be used to that by now," Bollard replied.

Manzano didn't understand the remark, and he didn't care for the tone.

"As a hacker, I mean," Bollard added.

Manzano said nothing, determined not to engage. But Bollard wouldn't let up.

"You're breaking in and trespassing on other people's property there too."

"I never broke in; I used security gaps. And I didn't steal or damage anything." Manzano felt compelled to defend himself now. To end the conversation, he went over to another table and shone his flashlight on the shirts.

"If you forgot to lock your door," Bollard stubbornly kept at it, "would you think it was all right for complete strangers to walk into your apartment?"

"Do you want to argue with me or work with me?" asked Manzano. He picked up a sweater, held it up to his chest. "This might do."

———

The Dutch police officer had watched the screen as Bollard and the Italian left the hotel room.

"And that's my cue," he said to his partner. "Back in a second."

He left the surveillance room and took the stairs, two flights down to the Italian's room. Using the duplicate key, he let himself into the suite. Manzano's laptop was on the desk. They had already seen the password on the surveillance cameras. Next he inserted a USB stick. He entered a few commands until the download bar came up on the screen. Two minutes later the program was installed on the computer. Three minutes after that he had covered his tracks and hidden it well enough that the Italian wouldn't be able to find it. He shut down the computer and left it exactly as he had found it. He went to the door, took one last look, turned off the light, and left the room as quickly and inconspicuously as he had come.

———

Shannon had walked forty-five more minutes in the cold to Europol headquarters. In the new building's lobby, she had been informed that François Bollard wasn't in the office but was expected back soon.

She plopped down in one of the clusters of chairs. It was warm here, and she could use the bathroom, of which she had already taken advantage, washing herself as best she could.

Shortly after ten, Bollard walked in, accompanied by a lanky man with a freshly stitched-up scar on his forehead, his hands weighed down with shopping bags.

"Hello, Mr. Bollard," she introduced herself. "Lauren Shannon, I'm a neighbor of your mother- and father-in-law in Paris."

Bollard looked at her, alert.

"What are you doing here? Is there something going on with the Doreuils?"

"That's what I'd like you to tell me," answered Shannon.

"You go on ahead," Bollard said in English to the other man. Once he was out of earshot, he continued, "I remember you. The last time we saw each other, you were working for some TV network."

"Still am. Yesterday afternoon your wife's parents left Paris in a big hurry—the in-laws of the man heading up counterterrorism at Europol. They were off to stay with your parents, Mr. Bollard, if I understand correctly. As they were leaving, your mother-in-law let a comment slip that piqued my curiosity."

"It must have, if it brought you here from Paris in the middle of the night. All the same, I can't help you. Members of the media must deal with our press office."

Shannon hadn't expected him to tell her anything willingly. "So we don't have to consider the power outage as in any way related to a terrorist attack? Or that the blackout might go on for quite some time?"

"When the power comes back on, you'll have to ask the electric companies, not me."

He made a show of stepping past her.

"So terrorists aren't behind the outages?"

"How familiar are you with the European power system?"

"I see and hear that it's not working. That's enough."

He was right. She didn't have a clue.

"Not entirely," he answered with a pitying smile. "Because if you understood how the system works you would know how complex it is. You can't simply turn the whole continent off like the lights in your living room. Now, if you would excuse me, please. Our press office will be happy to answer any further questions."

"So why were your wife's parents in such a hurry to get out of Paris?" she called after him. "To stay with farmers who have their own well, can burn wood in the fireplace for heat, and—how did Madam Doreuil put it?—simply slaughter a chicken from the coop whenever they need something to eat."

He turned and walked back to her.

She continued, "Sounds to me like the actions of a couple who know this situation is going to go on for some time. And who else could they have found this out from?"

Again Bollard considered her with a forbearing look, as if dealing with a child who was acting up.

"With all due respect to your imagination and your efforts, Ms...."

"Shannon. Lauren Shannon."

"I have work to do. Even if it's not what you're thinking. I suggest you go back to Paris."

———

It was slightly warmer outside. A few raindrops fell from the sky. Manzano hurried to reach the hotel before the rain got heavier. On the way, he stayed alert, keeping an eye on his fellow pedestrians and the occasional driver passing by. He envied them their ignorance of what lay in store for them.

He'd no sooner stepped into the entrance of the hotel than he heard a woman's voice behind him, speaking in English. "Excuse me, didn't I see you earlier with François Bollard?"

Behind him stood an attractive brunette carrying a small rucksack. Aside from the receptionist, there was no one in the lobby. Her face seemed familiar.

"You're the woman from the lobby at Europol," he said, responding in English.

"I'm a neighbor of Bollard's wife's parents in Paris," she replied. To Manzano's ears she sounded American.

"What are you doing here?"

"This is a hotel. I'm looking for a room."

"I'm afraid the place is full—it's one of the few places with a functioning backup power supply and running water. But what I meant was, what are you doing in The Hague?"

"I'm a journalist. I saw Bollard's in-laws leave Paris in a hurry yesterday afternoon. I don't believe it's a coincidence that the in-laws of the man in charge of counterterrorism at Europol would take such a trip during the biggest blackout in the history of Europe. Bollard wouldn't tell me anything."

"You followed me here from Europol."

"I have to know what's going on. I spent the whole night in a bus for this."

"You look like it too."

"How charming, thank you."

Her eyes shone, and she jutted her chin at him defiantly.

"The whole night in a bus? And nowhere to stay? Have you eaten since you arrived?"

"A couple of candy bars."

Manzano went up to the receptionist. "Is there a room available?"

"No," the man answered.

Manzano turned back to the young woman and shrugged apologetically. "As I thought. And I bet you're desperate for a shower right now."

"And how!" she sighed.

"Then come on. I'll treat you to one."

She eyed him warily.

Manzano had to laugh. "Not what you're thinking! I prefer to eat lunch with people who wash. You've got to be hungry, I'm sure."

She still looked hesitant.

"As you like. I'll wish you the best of luck then."

He started to walk up the stairs.

"Wait!"

———

While his new acquaintance was busy in the bathroom, Manzano hung up his new clothes in the wardrobe. Then he read the latest news on the internet. The first rumors had surfaced of police raids in Italy and Sweden that were supposedly connected to the power outages. There was no comment on this from official sources. Manzano didn't think this was the best strategy. The governments knew by now that they were dealing with an attack. It had to be clear to them that large parts of the population would have to manage without power for days to come.

Shannon came out of the bathroom in a bathrobe, drying her hair with a towel.

"That was fantastic. Thanks!"

"Don't mention it."

"Is there anything new?"

"Not really."

"Well, you were right about one thing," she said. "I am so hungry…"

———

Ten minutes later Shannon was sitting with Manzano in the hotel dining room. Half the tables were occupied. He ordered a club sandwich. Shannon asked for a hamburger.

"What'd you run into?" she asked, gesturing toward the stitches on his forehead.

"Crashed my car when the traffic lights went out."

"Do you work at Europol?"

"I work for Europol. Bollard brought me in."

"What for?"

"What network do you work for?"

"CNN." She showed him her ID.

"Do they not have people here?" Manzano asked.

"I'm here, aren't I?"

"And how do you report? Without power? How do you get your material to the network? How do you get it on television? Apart from the fact that hardly anybody can still watch television."

"They can outside of Europe," she countered. "I put the stories up online. So long as parts of the internet are still working."

"Which won't be the case for long," said Manzano. He looked around as if he was worried about being watched. None of the other guests showed any interest in them. He lowered his voice. "I only got here yesterday myself. I'm not permitted to speak about what I'm doing here. I had to sign a confidentiality agreement." He flashed her a grin.

"But nobody can forbid me to talk about what I discovered before I got here."

After he finished, Shannon could barely stay in her seat.

"Why haven't people been informed about this?" she whispered.

"The authorities are afraid that it would cause mass panic."

"But people have a right to know!"

"Journalists always say that to justify their actions."

"We can discuss journalistic ethics some other time. Besides, you didn't tell me this so I could keep my mouth shut."

"No."

"You've got an internet connection in your room. May I use it?"

"That won't be necessary. The whole hotel has Wi Fi. The hotel has a direct connection to the internet's backbone because it's often used by Europol's guests and diplomats. You just have to ask the receptionist for a code."

"And he'll ask if I'm a guest with a room number."

"Give him mine."

"Aren't you afraid they'll throw you out?"

"They want something from me, not the other way around."

"After this, maybe not."

"Let me worry about that."

"Do you agree with them—about mass panic?"

"Interesting concept," he replied. "To cause a panic across an entire continent... Do you believe it?"

Shannon hesitated. A journalist got a chance at a story like this exactly once in a lifetime, if at all.

"I think we underestimate the public," she answered finally. "This isn't some trashy disaster movie. There's been barely any unrest or looting so far. People are helping one another; they're being peaceful."

"They've still got food in the pantry."

"You know what? I think the news of a hostile sabotage of the power grid will cause people to pull even closer together. After all, against a common enemy, you have to stick together."

"You would make a great propaganda minister."

———

"We couldn't hear what they were saying," the policeman told Bollard. "There was too much background noise."

Lost in thought, Bollard gazed at the laptop screen that showed the images from the camera in Manzano's room. The Italian was sitting on his bed, his laptop in front of him. He appeared to be working.

"Where is she now?"

"Downstairs in the restaurant, with her laptop. Writing."

Bollard's thoughts wandered. He still hadn't managed to reach his parents. Neither the IAEA nor the French authorities had issued any updates on the situation at the Saint-Laurent nuclear reactor. He forced himself to concentrate.

"And naturally we don't know what she's writing, either."

"Luc is working on finding out right now. He's tapping into the Wi-Fi."

Bollard stood up.

"Keep me updated."

———

Shannon reached the Paris bureau via its satellite connection.

Her fingers flew over the keyboard.

> I'm sitting on the mother lode here. For me to be able to keep going, the network's got to take over the costs for accommodation and supply a rental car. Assuming I can get one.

OK, came the answer. And Laplante added details of the company credit card.

Good work, Lauren.

Shannon pumped her fist in triumph. She strode over to the front desk.

It took the receptionist a few minutes before he was able to make a short phone call. He laid a hand on the mouthpiece and asked her, "This is the only company I could get through to, and they've got one car left. It's not cheap, though."

"How much?"

"A hundred and fifty euros. Per day."

"What is it, a Ferrari?"

"A Porsche."

Shannon shrugged her shoulders. Laplante would flip.

"All right."

"And you have to pay cash."

Shannon stiffened. Laplante wouldn't flip quite yet. If she wanted to get the car, she'd have to dip into her own cash reserves to pay for it.

And so what if she did! What did it matter now!

———

An hour later, she was putting the key into the ignition of a silver sports car with bright stripes down the sides, like a racing car. Gingerly she tried out the clutch and the gearshift. The engine roared. The employee at the rental car company watched her with alarm. Before he could change his mind, she gave him a wave and rolled out of the garage.

On the way back to the hotel, she kept the hot rod in check as she negotiated the traffic.

She knocked on Manzano's door. When he answered,

she confessed, "I have a problem. I need to stay in The Hague overnight, but there's not a room to be had in the entire city. And so I thought, since you've already helped me out, maybe…"

"What? That you could hide out with me?"

"I don't know anybody else."

"What about your neighbors' son-in-law, Monsieur Bollard?"

"He won't speak to me."

"You must have a lot of faith in strangers." Manzano snorted, shaking his head. "Asking to share a bed with a man you don't even know."

"To share the room!"

"Which has one double bed. The sofa is too small to sleep on."

"I'll stay on my side," promised Shannon.

"You'd better hope you don't snore," said Manzano.

BERLIN, GERMANY

Hartlandt and his colleagues at Treptower Park had worked nonstop, sifting data from previous years while at the same time collecting, analyzing, and categorizing new information as it came in.

Hartlandt himself was focusing on the industries that generated and distributed energy. Assisted by three colleagues, he was analyzing reports from engineers on the power outage.

"Far too many power plants are having problems starting up again," said one of the group. "As a result, not enough power is being generated, and they can't get the grids synchronized."

"So far we've had two instances of damage reported," Hartlandt noted. "Fires have destroyed multiple transformers in the Osterrönfeld and Lübeck-Bargerbrück substations."

The man opposite Hartlandt groaned. "That means they'll be out of commission for the next few months."

But Hartlandt was no longer listening. A new message had come in. The sender, one of the large grid operators, had attached pictures.

"Look at this." Hartlandt showed his colleagues.

The images showed the spindly frame of a transmission tower lying on its side in a brown field, its arms sticking up awkwardly into the gray winter sky, broken wires dangling like strings torn off a gigantic marionette.

Hartlandt was convinced. "This tower was taken out with explosives."

THE HAGUE, NETHERLANDS

"Someone out there is taking advantage of the chaos of the power outage to go after not just the software but also the hardware of the electric grid," Bollard announced to those gathered in the operations center. He pointed to Spain on the map. "A report's come in of another bombed transmission tower. And there may be other acts of sabotage occurring even as we speak. The grid operators and power producers don't have enough service teams to check all facilities and line routes. So far, only a small number of them have been investigated."

"Could it be copycats?" someone suggested.

"It's possible. But it could be that someone is hell-bent on causing the most damage possible," Bollard said. "The attacks on the software might have been only the beginning. A rudimentary supply should have been up and running within a few days of the outage. But it's a completely different prognosis when strategic infrastructure like switchgears and transmission lines are destroyed. It takes time to repair that sort of damage, which makes reestablishing the power supply more difficult."

RATINGEN, GERMANY

At Talaefer headquarters, the heads of sales and technology, the chief of development, the director of corporate communication, and four members of the media agency handling the Talaefer account had fought their way through the blackout to attend a marketing presentation. Thus far, Wickley was unimpressed with the agency's efforts.

"What we're asking of people is nothing less than a paradigm shift. If we can't win over consumers, the energy revolution will fail—and with it our chances of making a profit. We need to come up with compelling arguments to make people understand why they can no longer take energy for granted, why they're going to have to pay more. You need to convince consumers that they stand to gain something—and this 'freedom of choice' and 'self-management' pitch you people keep pushing is not going to cut it." He waved dismissively at the bullet points projected on the wall. "I mean, seriously, 'Earn money with your car battery,' is that the best you can—"

The text vanished. The room was suddenly plunged into darkness.

"What now…?"

One of his coworkers wrestled with the projector's remote control. Another jumped up and hurried to the light switches beside the door. Their button pushing had no effect. Wickley reached for the telephone on the table and dialed his personal assistant's number. No ringtone. He tried again. The line was dead.

Wickley stormed out of the room. It was even darker in the hallway. He threw open the door of his office and saw his PA silhouetted against the window. She was trying to use what daylight was left to see the buttons on her telephone.

"Nothing's working," she said.

"Light some candles then!"

"We don't have any," she protested.

Wickley stifled a curse. The entire continent had managed to adapt to the blackout, but apparently it was beyond her capabilities.

"Then go get some!" he snapped, then turned and roared into the darkness, "Lueck—where are you, man!"

"He's gone down to the basement," a voice shouted back.

Wickley set off downstairs. After jogging down several flights of stairs, he found he had lost track of which floor he was on. A door opened and someone entered the stairwell.

"Have you seen Lueck?" he asked.

"For several minutes now I haven't seen a thing," a woman's voice answered.

Wickley was irritated at the woman's nerve, until he realized that not everyone would recognize him by voice alone. And he was forced to admit to himself that he had no idea where the backup generators were located. He just kept jogging down the stairs until he could go no further. He felt for a door and opened it. The room was black as night.

"Lueck?" he shouted.

No answer. Wickley called out again.

At the far end of the hallway a flashlight beam came into view.

"Here," Wickley heard. He strode to where the sound had come from.

He found Lueck, divisional head of disaster management, in a large room with claustrophobically low ceilings. It was packed full of machines, cables, and pipes that seemed to vibrate in the glow of the flashlight. With him were two men in gray overalls with the Talaefer logo on the back.

"What the hell is going on here?" Wickley hissed, making an effort to control himself.

Lueck's large glasses reflected the flashlight as he squinted up at Wickley. His thinning hair was damp with perspiration.

"The backup power generator is broken," he explained, aiming his flashlight at a large tank toward the back of the room.

Wickley felt a pounding at his temples. "We are one of the most important suppliers for the energy industry and we don't have power! Do you understand how embarrassing that is?" His voice rebounded off the various metal parts.

"The backup power supply is—was—designed to run for three days. It was probably overloaded, but even if it hadn't been, we're almost out of diesel," said Lueck. "The installation of a long-term autonomous power system was vetoed three years ago. Cost considerations, if I remember correctly."

The bastard had a nerve, bringing that up! Unfortunately, Wickley remembered all too well the directors' meeting in question. Spending five million euros on a system they would probably never use had seemed like throwing money down the drain. The only executive to vote in favor was no longer working for the company. If he had been, Wickley would have fired him for not pushing the project through, regardless of the board's resistance.

"We need replacement parts and diesel," Lueck explained. "At the moment, we've no chance of securing either."

"Then go get portable generators!"

"They're all in use—"

"Money talks, Lueck. Go wave some cash under the right noses and—"

"They've been commandeered by the Technical Relief Agency for use with hospitals, emergency shelters, rescue work…" Lueck answered with aggravating calm.

Wickley hated Lueck for letting him run up against a wall of argument that he had nothing to counter with. Together they climbed back up the stairs.

When they opened the door and found employees milling about in the darkened lobby, he told them, "We're done for today. We'll pick up where we left off tomorrow.

Let's say two o'clock. And you." He turned to Lueck. "See to it that tomorrow morning everything is up and running. Or else you won't be seeing to anything at all at Talaefer."

BERLIN, GERMANY

Michelsen was drinking her fifteenth coffee of the day. The previous night, and the one before, she had barely slept. Since the chancellor had declared the state of emergency yesterday evening, she'd hardly eaten. People were packed into the operations center. They had expanded the team significantly, recruiting every kind of expert they could find.

Michelsen spent most of her time on the phone with higher-ups from the various emergency services. In the clamor of voices, it was all she could do to hear herself speak. The Federal Agency for Technical Relief and the army had begun setting up shelters. In every major city in Germany, they were fitting gymnasiums, stadiums, and other suitable locations with mattresses, cots, blankets, portable sanitary facilities, basic medical supplies, and foodstuffs. In the affected areas, the police were out in cars with loudspeakers calling to people to make use of the shelters. Families with children, the sick, and the elderly were given priority. Many elderly people who lived alone couldn't hear the loudspeakers or were too weak to leave their homes—especially after two days of cold, often without food or water—and had no way of leaving their buildings with the elevators out of order. Those who didn't have relatives or neighbors to look after them had to rely on police officers going door to door.

Meanwhile, the Relief Agency was installing backup power generators in local administration buildings, health centers, and farming operations, but there simply weren't enough to go around. And there wasn't enough fuel to keep them running. Many hospitals were having to cancel operations because the diesel stores for their backup systems had been exhausted.

With over twenty-five million tons in strategic oil reserves, the German government had sufficient stores of crude oil and petroleum products to cover demand for around ninety days. Most of the crude oil was stored in decommissioned salt mines in Lower Saxony, but the refined products were distributed across the country in aboveground tanks. This meant they didn't require pumps to fill tankers. Their problem in the coming days wasn't so much the amount of fuel available as the means of delivering it to where it was needed as fast as possible.

Elsewhere in Europe things were no better. While temperatures in Germany hovered around zero degrees, in Stockholm it was eighteen below. South of the Alps the temperatures were positively mild in comparison—which was no help to those battling to keep the Saint-Laurent nuclear reactor from overheating now that its cooling systems had either partially failed or failed completely; no one knew exactly. Unbeknown to the public, the International Atomic Energy Agency in Vienna had in the meantime raised the event to INES 2. The word was that the plant had been forced to release radioactive steam in order to lower the pressure in the reactor. Michelsen pushed away the thought that diesel shortages could lead to reactors all over Europe being forced into similar measures.

Stranded trains had left many railway lines blocked. Where the lines were open, signals and switches could only be operated by hand. Passenger services in most areas had therefore been suspended until further notice. Even in the power islands where trains were still running, there were numerous cancellations and long delays.

The one bright spot was that, despite the grim conditions, there had been no reports of serious public order breakdowns. So far, there hadn't been a massive rise in criminal activity and no large-scale looting. But

Michelsen wasn't feeling too complacent on that score; communication networks were down in about forty percent of the country, leaving local authorities and emergency services struggling to make contact with the government's crisis center, so it was possible that incidents were occurring that had yet to be reported. And the longer the situation continued, the more inevitable the emergence of black markets, which would further erode trust in official institutions.

"Damn!"

Michelsen looked up to see the man next to her straighten up and stare intently at the row of screens tuned in to the handful of TV networks that were still broadcasting. Only then did she notice that most of the others in the room had also stopped what they were doing. It had become significantly quieter in the room. Someone turned up the volume for CNN.

The monitor showed a young woman with brown hair speaking into the camera. The caption identified her as Lauren Shannon, The Hague.

Michelsen read the news ticker at the bottom of the screen.

Europe-wide power outage—terror attack suspected. Italy and Sweden confirm manipulation of their electrical grids.

Michelsen felt something inside her break. Now the public would learn about the cause of the calamity from a television network, instead of from the authorities or the chancellor. Their failure to "come clean" meant those institutions would forfeit a large measure of the public's trust. Hopefully they wouldn't have to pay for it in the days to come.

"We're lucky hardly anyone can still watch television," whispered the man sitting next to her.

"Doesn't matter. Everyone in this country will have heard the news by midnight," Michelsen replied, without taking her eyes off the screen. "And speculation will be rife."

Now all that's missing is a story on the accident at the French nuclear power plant, she thought.

THE HAGUE, NETHERLANDS

"I should tear up your contract immediately," raged Bollard. Shannon followed the discussion from the couch in Manzano's room.

"I didn't say a word about my work here," said Manzano. "As stipulated by our agreement. Your own press office confirmed the suspicions to Shannon."

"After you told her about the codes in the Italian meters!" The Frenchman was still incensed.

"Which I found out about before we began working together."

"Most governments and several energy companies have been forced to issue confirmations after your girlfriend's"—he pointed at Shannon—"inquiries."

The images of the reporters who had picked up Shannon's story ran across the television screen. Almost every channel was running a special report.

Bollard sighed. "What am I supposed to do with you now?"

"You let me get back to work. Or send me home."

"You can be sure about one thing: all this sneaking around is over," Bollard said, and with that, he stormed out of the room.

"We kicked the anthill, all right," observed Manzano. "I don't know about you, but I'm shattered," he announced.

"Me too."

"You go ahead and take the bathroom first."

While Shannon got ready for bed, Manzano followed the TV reports, deep in thought. He still hadn't been able to reach Bondoni, and he couldn't stop wondering how the older man and the three women were faring in the mountains.

The American reappeared, now dressed in a T-shirt and shorts. "Thank you. For letting me stay here. And for giving me the story."

"Don't mention it."

He was still a little incredulous that she would spend the night in a room with a man she didn't know without a second thought. She could almost be my daughter, he thought. Not to mention she was drop-dead gorgeous.

Manzano sauntered wearily into the bathroom. He wondered how long the hotel's backup generators would continue to provide electricity and hot showers.

When he came back into the room, Shannon was lying under the covers on her side of the bed. Her breathing was deep and even. Quietly Manzano turned off the television, got into bed, and was asleep the moment his head hit the pillow.

DAY 4—TUESDAY

THE HAGUE, NETHERLANDS

Shannon woke up from a nightmare, bathed in sweat. She breathed deeply and slowly got her bearings. She was in the hotel room. The walls were flickering with blue and orange light, like in a discotheque. Next to her someone turned restlessly in the bed. Of course, the Italian. She stood up, went to the window, and pushed the curtains aside.

Down the street a building was burning. Flames were shooting out of the windows and the roof. Thick smoke rose into the night sky. Several fire engines were parked haphazardly on the street; two ladders were extended, from which streams of water sprayed into the inferno. Firefighters ran back and forth, evacuating the residents of neighboring buildings. People in pajamas, with blankets around their shoulders. Shannon felt for her camera on the bedside table and started filming.

"Probably someone trying to start a campfire in the living room to keep warm," she heard from behind her, and she gave a start. She hadn't been aware of Manzano getting out of bed.

"Easy for us to say, in our warm hotel room," she responded. "It's the start of the fourth day without heat and electricity. People are desperate."

She zoomed in on a top-floor window from which thick smoke was billowing. Then through the lens, she spotted something moving.

"Oh my God…"

A shadow waved, clutched the window frame, climbed out. A woman in soot-covered pajamas, hair whipped by the wind, blowing across her face. In the dark opening someone else appeared alongside her, someone smaller.

"There are people in the building," she stammered, not lowering the camera. "A mother and child…"

The woman had taken the child by the arm. She stood on the windowsill, her free hand clutching the frame, leaning with the child as far away from the smoke as possible.

"They can't get there with the ladder," whispered Manzano.

Flames shot out of the window. The woman let go, swayed, and fell.

NANTEUIL, FRANCE

Annette opened her eyes and stared into the darkness. Her bedroom smelled different. Then she remembered that she wasn't in her own bedroom but at the Bollards'. The uncomfortable conditions brought about by the power outage, their son-in-law's mysterious hints, the hurried flight from Paris had made for a restless first night. But after last night's news reports, sleep was impossible. Bollard Senior had tried without success to reach his son on the landline in the hope of verifying whether there was any truth in the story. The four of them had then sat up discussing what it might mean, until weariness got the better of them. Annette had lain awake for a while, listening to her husband's long, calm breaths interspersed with brief snoring sounds. Much as she was doing now.

But then another sound made its way to her ears. It sounded like a staticky voice ringing out from far away. Annette listened. The monotone singsong—she couldn't understand a word of it—grew louder, seemed to get closer. Then silence.

A few seconds later, the murmur started up again. Again growing louder but still just as unintelligible. She sat up and shook her husband by the shoulder.

"Bertrand, wake up. Do you hear that?"

"What's going on?" he grumbled, irritated at being woken.

"Listen! There's an announcement coming from outside—in the middle of the night!"

The covers rustled, and she heard her husband shuffle into a sitting position.

"What's going on? What time is it?"

"Shh. A little after four. What are they saying?"

Again her husband groaned; he ran a hand over his face, then listened intently.

"I can't understand a word they're saying," he said after a while. His wife heard his feet patter across the floor, then the window and the shutters clattered open.

"…await further messages," announced the staticky voice, louder now. After a short pause it started back up again. Though it seemed to be moving farther away.

"Please stay in your homes and keep the windows closed." The clipped voice was still hard to understand, but Annette could piece together the gist. "There is no danger and no reason to worry. Turn on the radio and await further messages."

Her husband turned to her.

"Did he just say…?"

"We're supposed to keep the windows closed."

"Why though?"

"Go on; do it!"

Her husband closed both windows.

Annette got up and put on her robe. She grabbed the flashlight that she had left sitting on the nightstand, just in case, and opened the door. Her husband followed her. In the hallway they ran into their host.

"Did you hear it too?" asked Annette.

He nodded. "Stay in the house and keep the windows closed."

"But why?"

"No idea," said Bollard.

THE HAGUE, NETHERLANDS

"Let's go through everything one more time," said Bollard. "We'll start with Italy. By this point they've checked out the residents of the apartments where false codes were fed into the meters."

He turned to the corkboard in their improvised operations center and pointed at the images of apartments and their residents.

"They focused on those from the past few months and years. Aside from the odd tax offense, which isn't considered a real crime in Italy, the occupants were thoroughly unsuspicious and respectable. There continues to be no trace of the alleged electric company employees."

Bollard pointed to an image of a modern Italian electric meter.

"Technicians from the Italian electricity provider Enel have checked the access protocols of the internet firewall and discovered a string of suspicious incidents, starting almost eighteen months ago, where internal systems and data banks were accessed. The IP addresses of the intruders lead to Ukraine, Malta, and South Africa. This was probably how the perpetrators got their hands on access data for the meters. They also reconfigured the routers so that the disrupt codes could be distributed across the entire grid."

"How did these attackers know how to break in to the Enel network and to mess with the meters in the first place?" asked one of the female detectives on the team.

"Practically every critical infrastructure has been breached at some point in recent years. Some think hackers are to blame; some claim that states are behind it— from the Chinese to the Russians on up to the Iranians or North Koreans. Whoever they are, those responsible for such attacks are pros; they have all manner of ways to dodge firewalls and get into internal IT networks, ranging from bogus websites that implant a Trojan or a worm on anyone who visits, to USB sticks 'left lying around' for an employee to find, or simply through innocent-looking emails. The vulnerable points are always people. That's why many institutions have banned the use of data storage devices and restricted employee access to websites. Unfortunately, people don't always obey the rules.

"As for manipulating the electric meters, that couldn't have been simpler. These things are in every home, and you can buy secondhand ones on eBay. Take one apart and you can soon figure out the way they work. And there's plenty of literature on the internet to help you, some of it from the manufacturers themselves, explaining how well equipped these little boxes are for a plan of this sort—the most important feature being that every meter in the system is capable of broadcasting data to all the other meters."

"But surely there's some safeguard in place to prevent meters accepting random data from unknown meters. Don't they require some kind of authentication?"

"They do, but the attackers probably snatched that up when they infiltrated the internal IT networks and data banks at Enel. They might even have found it on the internet. Once they have the authentication, the rest is child's play. Which gives us reason to assume that the authentication for the Italian data sources was weak. All the attackers had to do was imitate the requested data source and enter their desired command code."

"Aren't these the systems that all of Europe is supposed to be outfitted with in the next few years?"

"Indeed" was Bollard's only reply. He turned to another row of photos. "And with that we come to Sweden. The attackers there acted according to the same method: three residences were selected. And here too the residents have turned out to be respectable and cleared of all suspicion after intensive investigation. As in Italy, it's highly probable that the codes were fed into the meters by the men who passed themselves off as technicians from the electric company."

He placed himself in front of the map of Europe in the middle of the wall.

"In addition to the attacks on the IT systems, we also have reports of arson in substations and transmission towers downed by explosives. As yet, however, there is no distinguishable pattern behind these attacks, which is going to make it difficult to catch the saboteurs."

With that, Bollard ended the presentation and hurried back to his office. He checked his computer to see if there were any new reports out of Saint-Laurent. Since that morning, the incident had been raised to INES 3 by the French Nuclear Safety Authority. The population within a twenty-kilometer radius was being told to stay indoors. Once again Bollard tried his parents' number. The line was still dead.

———

Shannon had to pull into the opposite lane in order to drive around the mass of people outside the building. Only then did she realize that it wasn't a crowd trying to get into a supermarket. These people were mobbing a bank branch. Two minutes later she was right there among them.

"I have seventy euros left in my wallet," a portly man told her, waving his wallet at the camera in frustration. "Anything that you're still able to buy you have to pay cash for. And who knows how much longer it's going to be like this? That's why I wanted to get enough money out. And now this!" He gestured behind him. "If they're already out of money, what will it be like in a few days' time? Without question, I'll be here at dawn tomorrow."

"Wait a minute," said Shannon. "Are you saying the bank is out of money?"

"For today they're out; that's what they told us. More cash will be delivered tomorrow. We all waited here for nothing."

Shannon filmed the men and women who were still pounding furiously on the bank's windows before they gave up and gradually went their separate ways. She panned to the handwritten sign behind the door.

> Closed due to technical disruption.
> Cash can be withdrawn as of tomorrow.
> The maximum amount for withdrawal
> will be €250 per person.

So the bank had closed. No cash till tomorrow, and even then there would be a limit. In the lobby she caught sight of the tellers standing in a group and gossiping. She knocked several times until one of them turned around. He shook his head. When Shannon showed him the camera, he turned away.

PARIS, FRANCE

"I need results," Blanchard stated wearily. "The president, the interior minister, you name it—everybody is calling for our heads." He didn't care to recall that, only a few days earlier, he had threatened everyone present that their heads would roll. Now his own lay on the chopping block.

"Oh we've got results," said Proctet. "But they're not good."

Blanchard closed his eyes for a moment. He saw the blade fall on his neck. For two days the entire IT department and two dozen IT forensics specialists they'd brought in to assist had been working around the clock. And yet it seemed all they could come up with was more bad news.

"We've found parts of the malware that acted as a trigger. It's been inside the system for more than eighteen months. This attack was planned well in advance. It means our current data protections are unusable, because they too are contaminated."

"So we fall back on the older ones then."

Proctet shook his head. "Eighteen months in the digital age is like a century in the real world. Those data protections are hopelessly outdated."

"Which means?"

"We have to wipe every computer."

"There are hundreds of them!"

"A few dozen would be enough to start with," answered Proctet. "If it weren't for the other thing."

Blanchard stared, aghast, at the young man. "What other thing?" he asked under his breath.

"The few servers that were still running tried to access computers they had no business accessing."

"You're trying to tell me…"

"…that the servers are infected too. Precisely."

"This is a disaster," mumbled Blanchard. "How long do you think it's going to take?"

"A week," Proctet said quietly. Everyone in the room heard his words. Blanchard thought he saw the young man grow even paler. Then he added, "At least."

"Are you out of your fucking mind?" cried Blanchard. "Did you see the news this morning? We're looking at a nuclear meltdown in the middle of France if the people in Saint-Laurent don't get power for their cooling system soon! Who knows where else it could happen?"

THE HAGUE, NETHERLANDS

Bollard scrolled down the website's news ticker in disbelief.

**+ Plant operator confirms controlled
release of radioactivity +**

(5:26 a.m.) Électricité de France, the company that operates the crippled power plant in Saint-Laurent, confirms the controlled release of small amounts of radioactive steam into the air surrounding the facility in order to ease the pressure in the reactor container.

+ Nuclear Safety Authority:
"No damage to reactor shell" +

(6:01 a.m.) France's Nuclear Safety Authority (ASN) declares that the reactor container in Block 1 of Saint-Laurent is undamaged. The cooling systems in Block 2 are functioning without issue.

+ Block 2 will assist Block 1 +

(9:33 a.m.) According to an announcement from the power plant's operator, one of the three redundant backup cooling systems in the uncompromised Reactor Block 2 is to be repurposed for Block 1 as quickly as possible. Experts consider such a solution both unfeasible and dangerous.

+ Government: "Other nuclear facilities secure" +

Without taking his eyes off the screen, Bollard entered his parents' phone number on the number pad and put the receiver up to his ear. On the line he heard an ominous, quiet hiss.

———

"Oh my…" Shannon called out as Manzano entered the room. She was sitting on the edge of the bed, two cameras next to her on the comforter, one of them hooked up to her laptop with a cable. But it was not her computer that had her transfixed; it was the television.

"Look at this!" she exclaimed. "And this!"

On the screen, an anchorwoman in the CNN studio announced, "Asian markets were hit hard by the news from last night. The Nikkei index fell a further eleven percent, the broader Topix even more at thirteen. Shanghai lost ten percent, and the Hang Seng gave up fifteen percent."

"What did you expect?" asked Manzano. "You must have considered the risk of falling stock prices before you sent your news blast around the world yesterday."

Manzano was fairly clueless about financial markets, but it had been perfectly clear to him that Shannon's news would cause stocks all over the world to plummet. Someone who bet on those falling stocks at the right time could make a lot of money.

"I don't mean that," she said. "Read the ticker."

The text ran in a red strip at the bottom of the screen: *Accident at French nuclear power plant. Cooling system fails. Radiation escapes. Special program coming up.*

Manzano watched Shannon gnaw on her fingernails.

"   turn now to our correspondent James Turner in France. James?"

"Damn it, damn it, damn it!" hissed Shannon. "And I'm not there!"

"Be glad you aren't."

The American stood in a field. Way off in the distance behind him stood the cooling towers of a nuclear facility.

"According to an official statement, the backup cooling systems in Reactor Block 1 in the Saint-Laurent nuclear power plant have given out. No one knows how long it's been in this state. We're about five kilometers away here, on the other side of the Loire river. Regarding damages to the reactor core, there is still no precise indication..."

"This asshole kept me doing grunt work for years, and now he's got the top story again!"

"But you had it yesterday."

"There's nothing as old as yesterday's news."

"...any damage could have serious effects on the environment."

"How's he even getting on air?" Manzano asked.

"He's got the satellite truck, probably."

Behind the reporter a cloud burst forth where the cooling towers had been. Even on the television, Manzano heard the dull blast.

"Whoa, what was that?" Turner spun around, his eyes fixed on the broadening cloud.

"There's been an explosion!" he yelled into the microphone. "There's actually been an explosion at the nuclear power plant!"

"If I were you, I'd start making tracks," murmured Manzano.

"An explosion!"

"Can't he think of anything else?" groused Shannon.

"He should get out of there," noted Manzano.

But Turner turned back to the camera. Behind him the cloud climbed slowly higher and became more transparent.

"Did you see that? Did you get it? Damn it! Can we see it again? Studio?"

And in fact the producers were already running a slow-motion replay. There was nothing to be seen that hadn't been seen the first time. Where the cooling towers had stood, all that could be seen now were bursts of white cloud.

"Shit," whispered Shannon.

"So, would you still like to be there?" asked Manzano.

COMMAND HEADQUARTERS

Saint-Laurent was something they hadn't counted on. Overnight, the whole enterprise had taken on a new dimension. The intention hadn't been for Europe to become uninhabitable—on the contrary.

"We have to call it off, before something worse happens," some of them bleated. But their voices were drowned out by the committed majority, who had no time for dilettantes who were only interested in playing at revolution. Even if it turned out that Saint-Laurent was not an isolated event but the first of many such incidents, so be it. It had been obvious from the start that there would be victims. Many victims. That was the price of change.

And change was what it was all about. To call it off now would mean giving up on their goals, dishonoring the sacrifices they had made in order to come this far. Worst of all, it would concede the right to control the future to a society obsessed with money and with power, with order and productivity and efficiency, with consumption, with entertainment, and with ego, and with how to take as much of everything for themselves as possible. A society in which people didn't count, only maximizing profit. In which community was merely a cost factor, the environment a resource. Efficiency a religion, order its shrine, and the ego its God.

No, they could not stop now.

RATINGEN, GERMANY

"This is a disaster," said Wickley. "For all of us. Energy revolution, modern energy networks, the smart grid, and all the rest of it—for the next few years we can forget the whole thing."

The conference room in the executive suite was not as well staffed as the day before. Even fewer people had made it in to work. The communications agency was represented by two people instead of four: Hensbeck and his assistant. Everyone wore their coats or down jackets.

Lueck had been unable to procure either a new generator or more diesel.

"Numerous European grid operators have confirmed fatal attacks on their IT systems," said Wickley. "Unofficially, I was able to find out that some estimate repairs could take several days or even weeks."

"As bad as the news and the situation are," Hensbeck offered, "the situation does create a huge opportunity, doesn't it? It makes it clear that the current system is flawed and a change is necessary."

"I applaud your determination to think positively, Hensbeck, but it's not that simple. Right now the cause of the outage is painfully clear: the IT system—the very thing that was supposed to play a key role in our plans for the extension of the smart grid, a vital part of our core business. Every last one of our visionary development projects depends on the power grid being governed by a communications network. And now the thing that banks, credit card companies, and insurance companies have been fighting for years has landed in our sector. Only with far worse consequences. Once the dust has settled after all this, every development project related to IT will be evaluated, reviewed—and halted."

"No system can ever be absolutely secure," the head of technology spoke up. "But we go far beyond every industry standard."

"That's the argument the nuclear power industry will make right up to the next meltdown. It won't be enough. After this attack, there will be only one talking point in the energy sector: security. Or, to be more precise, energy security. Climate and environmental protection will be forgotten. Europe will be happy just to get back on its feet again. That's a complete turnaround since the start of the new millennium; no one was talking about security as an issue then."

"Excuse me? Of course they were. There was even a movie…" Hensbeck struggled to recall.

"Yes, yes, the fourth *Die Hard* movie. Complete nonsense…"

"But the topic was in the air," insisted Hensbeck.

"OK, so we've only ourselves to blame, because back then, everyone wrote off the dangers as so much craziness from doomsday prophets. Naturally, it's also a question of cost. Security costs money."

"Well, events have now shown that it costs even more to ignore it."

THE HAGUE, NETHERLANDS

Shannon had edited her report and was uploading it. The TV was on.

Manzano came back into the room, having been out for a stroll.

"Anything new?"

He threw himself onto the bed, popped open his laptop, and followed the news on the television while the machine was starting up.

"Hmm," answered Shannon distractedly, with a look toward his computer and the strange green sticker on its case.

The news out of Saint-Laurent sounded bad. Blurry images taken from afar showed the power plant with smoke rising out of it.

"That's not steam we're seeing coming out of the cooling towers," said the anchorwoman. "After the explosion at midday, the situation continues to be unclear…"

Manzano was scanning the live news feed on the internet. For most of the reports, he just stuck to the headlines.

+ European markets closed +

+ Stoppages in all European automobile factories +

+ Munich recalculates damage to date
of up to 1 billion euros +

+ Correction: Six workers at Saint-Laurent nuclear
facility injured; two exposed to radiation +

+ World Ice Hockey Championship in Sweden canceled +

+ Government estimates victim count in Germany
after power outage at up to 2,000 +

+ United States, Russia, China, Turkey prepare aid +

+ Power temporarily restored to area around Bochum +

+ Interpol releases facial composites of suspects +

+ NATO high command discusses situation +

+ Oil prices in free fall after power outage +

+ Nuclear Authority: Saint-Laurent is
not Chernobyl or Fukushima +

"They said the same thing in Japan for the first few days," murmured Manzano. "Until it got out that the reactor had been out of control from the start."

BRUSSELS, BELGIUM

"Requests for help are still within bounds," Zoltán Nagy, the Hungarian director of the MIC, summed up the meeting. "The International Atomic Energy Agency in Vienna is looking into Saint-Laurent and Temelín. They've dispatched experts and are keeping us updated."

For the last thirty minutes they had discussed the latest developments. Things were far worse than Sophia or anyone else at the EUMIC had feared. The only thing still unclear was the level of breakdowns in technology.

"One request is from Spain in connection with the explosion in the Abracel chemical plant near Toledo. Poison gas has escaped. The authorities still don't have an accurate victim count, but they assume dozens. Several thousand have been evacuated, some of them from the emergency shelters that had just been set up. The United States and Russia are sending teams of technicians to assist in sealing the leaks. Additional accidents involving escaped harmful substances and fatalities were reported to us from Sheffield in the United Kingdom, from Bergen in

Norway, from the area around Bern in Switzerland, and from Pleven in Bulgaria. None of these nations has asked for international assistance; in each instance the victim count is reportedly single-digit figures.

"Right, so much for the current state of affairs. The next status meeting will take place in three hours." Nagy was about to stand, but then something else occurred to him. "Oh, before I forget. The Brussels transit authority has informed us that they will operate a twice-daily shuttle bus service covering a radius of forty kilometers around the city, exclusively for employees of select authorities, including the police, government ministries, and essential departments of the European Commission. That includes us. You will be able to get on at special gathering points in the morning and will be brought back in the evening. Your employee identification card acts as proof that you're eligible. You'll find the routes and pickup locations on the bulletin board."

BERLIN, GERMANY

Hartlandt jumped as someone behind him clapped his hands. He looked around, embarrassed that he'd been caught napping on the job.

"I've got news that'll wake you up," his colleague announced. "The fire department thinks that the blaze at the Osterrönfeld substation was arson."

"Shit! Why are we only learning this now?"

"Because the fire department has its hands full out there. Cause-of-fire investigations aren't top priority."

Hartlandt got up to study the giant map of Germany on which they had marked all known incidents in various colors. There was hardly any land visible under the colored pins.

"Then…maybe it's not a coincidence," he murmured. "Since the power went out we've had reports of fires in eight substations."

He went back to his desk and rifled through the files.

"Here." He handed his colleague a sheet of paper. "That's a list of the substations that have been hit. Get on the radio and contact every fire station involved. They're to check what caused the fires immediately."

ZEVENHUIZEN, NETHERLANDS

François Bollard almost ran into the car that was parked at the farm's entrance. In the glow of his headlights, he saw that cars were parked all the way up to the building. He steered onto the lawn and drove on up to the house. In some of the cars he saw people stretched out, wrapped in warm clothes and blankets.

"They won't let you in," someone called as he got out of his car.

"Unless he's one of the special ones," another jeered. A few men followed him to the door. Bollard unlocked it, and immediately a hand from inside grabbed him, pulled him in, and slammed the door shut. From outside, Bollard heard angry yelling. Jacub Haarleven stood in front of him. He seemed shaken. Only then did Bollard notice the sound of raised voices in the house.

"We couldn't take in all of them," Haarleven explained, and he walked down the corridor. As they passed by the breakfast area Bollard understood what he meant. The tables had been pushed to one side, and at least forty people were lying on the floor. The smell of unwashed bodies assaulted Bollard's nose. Someone snored; someone else whimpered in their sleep.

"I've told them we won't be able to feed them," Haarleven continued. "But what was I supposed to do? There are kids, sick and old people. I can't let them freeze to death out there!"

"And the people outside?"

Haarleven looked at him helplessly. "I can only hope they'll remain rational."

"What are you going to do tomorrow morning, when these people wake up hungry?"

Haarleven shrugged it off. "I'll think about that tomorrow. All we can do now is improvise. If the power doesn't come back on soon, we're looking at a massive problem."

Bollard marveled at the man's naiveté.

"You're with the EU, aren't you…"

"Europol," Bollard corrected.

"Isn't there something you can do for these people?"

"What about the Dutch authorities? They have emergency shelters."

"Not enough, the people are saying."

"I can't do anything today," replied Bollard. "Tomorrow I'll see what I can do."

Which wasn't much more than to call the city and ask why there were no shelters for people. And if necessary the police, in order to protect Haarleven's property and the people inside. He could already imagine what the answers would be.

Bollard climbed the stairs to his family's rooms. He had barely opened the door when his wife had her hands on his shoulders.

"Have you heard anything from our parents?"

He had dreaded this moment. "Not yet. I'm sure they're fine."

"Fine?" Her voice had a hysterical undertone. "There's a nuclear meltdown happening twenty kilometers from them, and you're sure they're fine?"

"Where are the kids?"

"They're asleep. Don't change the subject."

"It's not a meltdown. The government says—"

"Oh, and what else are they supposed to say?"

"Marie, stop—you'll wake the kids."

She started to sob, pounding on his chest with her fists. "You sent them there!"

He tried to calm her down, to take her in his arms, but she pulled herself away and kept hitting him.

"You sent them there!"

Anger and helplessness flared up inside Bollard. He pressed her so tight against his chest that her arms were pinned. At first she continued to resist, but he held her until he could feel her relent and she was leaning against his shoulder, sobbing uncontrollably.

Only four days, he thought, and already our nerves are raw. He closed his eyes, and for the first time since he was a child he prayed.

THE HAGUE, NETHERLANDS

"We've got it good," said Shannon. She wound noodles around her fork with relish. "This became even clearer to me after today."

"You certainly do anyway," replied Manzano. "Getting to drive that Porsche from one disaster site to the next."

"Believe me, I'd rather have no Porsche and report on how everything is back to normal again. Haven't you got anywhere yet?"

Manzano grinned. "My dear, I know that you're looking to build on your coup, all the more so now your esteemed colleague in France is enjoying everyone's undivided attention. But don't even go there. My work, as you well know…"

"…is highly confidential. I got that."

"How about you tell me about yourself instead."

"You know the important stuff. I grew up in a hick town in Vermont. I started college in New York, then I went on a world tour that ended with me being left stranded in Paris."

"Not the worst place to get shipwrecked."

"Granted."

"That was the important stuff. And the unimportant? Most of the time it's much more interesting."

"Not in my case."

"Weak story, Madam Journalist."

"Is yours any better?"

"Haven't you done your research yet?"

Now it was Shannon who grinned.

"Of course. But there's not much on you. You don't seem to live a very exciting life."

"I'm with the Chinese on that point; they only wish an exciting life on their enemies. But the way things have been going recently, looks like somebody did so in my case."

"Was it easy for you to just leave Milan at a moment's notice? No wife, kids?"

"Neither nor."

"Why not?"

"Is that important?"

"Pure curiosity work related illness. Besides, we've got to talk about something."

"Hasn't happened yet."

"Aha! Looking for Miss Right? I thought it was only women who did that."

"You, for example?"

She laughed. He liked her laugh.

"What about your parents? Are they in Italy?"

"They're dead."

"I'm sorry."

"Car accident. It was twelve years ago now."

He remembered the day when he'd heard the news. The strange numbness he had felt.

"Do you miss them?"

"Not…really." He realized that he hadn't thought about them in a long time. "Maybe there would've been something more for us to talk about. You know, some things you're only ready to discuss later in life. But maybe, even then, you still don't talk about them. I mean, who knows. And yours?"

"Got divorced when I was nine years old. I stayed with

my mother. My father moved to Chicago, then to Seattle. I didn't see him very often."

"And since you've been in Europe?"

"I Skype with Mom. Sometimes with Dad. They always say they've got to come visit me sometime. But so far neither of them has come."

"Siblings?"

"A half sister and a half brother, the kids from Dad's second marriage. I barely know them."

"An only child then."

"As good as," she replied, twisting her face into a dark grimace and declaiming in a theatrical voice, "Stubborn. Egotistical. Inconsiderate."

"My girlfriends always say the same thing."

"The current one too?"

Manzano's expression left the question unanswered.

"What'll she say when she finds out that you're sharing a bed with me?" asked Shannon.

"She won't find out a thing from me." He stuck with the singular. He had no interest in explaining his open relationships with Paola and Giulia, or worse, in having to justify himself. Sophia Angström popped into his head. "And what about Mister Right?" he asked.

"He'll turn up one of these days," she replied, taking a sip of wine. Her eyes flashed flirtatiously at him over the lip of the glass.

YBBS-PERSENBEUG, AUSTRIA

Oberstätter walked through the deserted hallways of the power plant. Only a few technicians were present, the minimum number of staff necessary to get the plant running again—if they could get to the bottom of things, that was.

Oberstätter asked himself where things went from here. Already the damage was devastating. The farmers in the area had lost large numbers of livestock. The cattle and sheep had starved or frozen to death, the dairy cows died in pitiful agony from their swollen udders. For days the cries of pain could be heard for miles. The father of one of his friends had a stroke and died because the ambulance arrived too late.

Some had simply taken off, and who could blame them. Since the news had emerged that some parts of Austria were able to maintain a basic power supply, more and more people had been trying to reach them.

For his part, he continued to live here in his tiny paradise. Like his coworkers, he also brought his family in from time to time, so that they could warm up and experience a sliver of normalcy, at least for a few hours.

As soon as Oberstätter reached the south generator room, he radioed the control booth.

"Are you all set?" he asked.

Upstairs, five engineers were anxiously watching the displays. Once again they were going through the steps to bring the power plant back online. So far the system hadn't reported any problems. One more button to push and they'd be generating electricity again.

"Here we go!" He heard crackling through the speaker.

In front of him, the red giants sprang to life with a deep throb.

"We're rolling!" Oberstätter cried into the microphone.

"Woo-hoo! They're working!" his colleague yelled back.

Oberstätter was flooded with relief. His whole body trembled with hope. For four days they had received error signals in every single phase of activation. The team had been working around the clock, inspecting components or replacing them.

"Shit!" Oberstätter heard from the radio.

"What's up?"

"They're spinning too fast!"

"No they're not. I would hear it," shouted Oberstätter.

"But that's what we're reading up here."

"They're fine, I tell you."

"It's too risky. We're shutting down."

"Let them run!" ordered Oberstätter. "If it's critical, they'll shut themselves down."

"And if they don't?"

"Down here everything sounds normal," said Oberstätter.

"The displays are giving us the order to shut down" came crackling over the radio. "We have to. We can't risk the generators!"

The quiet drone grew weaker until it faded completely.

"Damn it," whispered Oberstätter.

He marched upstairs to the control booth.

"It's not the machines," Oberstätter said. "Those generators were purring like kittens. The problem must be with the software."

"The SCADA system?" asked the IT expert. "It's been checked from top to bottom."

"If we get an error signal, we switch out the components and the error signal goes away—only for another one to pop up. There can't possibly be as many broken parts as we've replaced. I swear to you, the machines are working perfectly. It's the software; it's been giving off false alarms the whole time."

The man shook his head. "Why should this problem pop up now, of all times? And if it were a virus, how could it possibly have gotten in? The SCADA suppliers are giant corporations with massive quality control mechanisms and security protocols."

One of his colleagues disagreed. "I think there might be something to this theory. We should report it to headquarters in Vienna, see what they've got to say."

DAY 5—WEDNESDAY

ZEVENHUIZEN, NETHERLANDS

François Bollard was woken well before dawn by noises he couldn't at first place. With an effort he got up and crept barefoot to the window. Below, about twenty people had gathered at the front door and were demanding to be let inside. He pulled on yesterday's clothes and rushed downstairs. He couldn't get past the landing. A throng of people, all talking over each other, were pressuring Jacub Haarleven to open the door. The proprietor, a rifle held level with his chest, was keeping the mob at bay.

His time as a police officer on active duty was long in the past, but it was clear to Bollard that, ultimately, Haarleven didn't stand a chance. From outside came the dull thud of someone pounding on the door; inside, people were muttering ominously. He ought to take the rifle away from Haarleven, before he was forced into doing something stupid.

"Get back," the proprietor said to the group in front of him, and he let the gun drop. "I'll open the door, but you have to understand you still won't be able to stay. The authorities will take care of you."

"They haven't so far!" someone shouted.

"Yeah!"

"They let us starve!"

"And freeze to death!"

Bollard was already thinking of where else he could put his family. The way things were looking, they would have to go back home. They had enough wood for the fireplace, but neither food nor water. He himself would still be provided for by Europol for a while yet. But for how much longer?

From another room came the ugly sound of glass shattering, followed by a thud, then more shattering. Haarleven clutched his rifle and took a step forward. The crowd backed up. Bollard hurried over and gently pressed the gun down in Haarleven's arms.

"Somebody broke a window!" a woman yelled from the breakfast room. "Stop!"

On the stairs Bollard caught sight of his wife's anxious face. He motioned for her to go back upstairs. He had made his decision.

"We're packing," he said. "Fast."

Marie didn't need an explanation.

Twenty minutes later, they were clattering down the stairs with their luggage.

"The kids are riding with me," said Bollard.

They loaded both cars, Marie's and Bollard's, and backed out of the packed parking lot.

A few minutes later, the two cars had swerved off of the property. Within moments, the low fuel warning light in Bollard's car began to flash. Bollard cursed and banged his hands on the wheel. There was no way he'd used it all. When he arrived the night before, the tank had been half-full.

They had barely reached The Hague city limits when behind him his wife began to flash her headlights. Bollard slowed down, but Marie had already stopped on the side of the road and put her hazard lights on. He reversed and parked in front of her.

"You two stay here," he said to the kids, and he got out.

"I'm out of gas," Marie said. "But I'm sure that the tank was almost full when I got to the farm the day before yesterday. I haven't driven anywhere since then."

"So I was right," he replied. "I'm driving on fumes too."

They checked the fuel cap covers. Both had been tampered with.

They moved the suitcases over, pushed Marie's car off the main road, and drove on together in his car.

"I hope we can still make it home," Georges spoke up quietly from the backseat.

"When will this end?" whispered Marie, tears in her eyes.

THE HAGUE, NETHERLANDS

François Bollard stayed home long enough to help Marie unpack the car, then drove on to Europol.

So here Marie was, home again. First she lit a fire in the living room fireplace, so that at least one room in the house was warm. After putting away the suitcases, she inspected the refrigerator. She had already used up frozen items and quick-to-spoil foods on the first days without power. There hadn't been much left after that. Since they had planned to stay on the farm, they hadn't bothered to stock up. During their absence, most of what remained had gone bad. In the pantry, she found various canned goods, enough for one or two days. There would be some odd mixes of ingredients, but now wasn't the time to be fussy. It was important to get herself up to speed. Maybe their neighbors knew where someone could get food. Maybe François knew, or perhaps he could use his connections. Next she tried the TV and the telephone, already knowing that she would get not so much as a flicker out of them. Her thoughts turned to her parents. Without television, she'd have no way of knowing what was happening with the reactor at Saint-Lauren-Nouan. She wondered whether it was better not to know.

———

+ Breaking News: France Evacuates Population +
The French Interior Ministry confirms that an evacuation has begun for the population within a five-kilometer radius of the Saint-Laurent power

plant in the *département* of Loir-et-Cher. Affected
areas include cities such as Blois, with its world
famous castle, and suburbs of Orléans, among
others. Further evacuation measures have not
been ruled out.

"My God," moaned Bollard. Nanteuil lay between Blois
and Saint-Laurent. Again he reached for the telephone.

+ Cash Withdrawals Limited to
100 Euro Per Day +

After yesterday's run on banks in most European
countries, the European Central Bank is calling
for calm. "The supply of paper money is secure,"
stresses President Jacques Tampère. However,
until further notice withdrawals will be limited to
€100 per person per day. Tampère confirmed that
the ECB made an additional €100 billion available
to prop up markets.

———

+ Radioactive Cloud Headed for Paris? +

Since early this morning, reports of a cloud bearing
radioactive particles from Saint-Laurent being driven
toward Paris by winds have been causing concern.
According to the nuclear plant operator EDF, mildly
radioactive steam was released from the plant
yesterday in order to reduce pressure in the reactor.
According to statements made by EDF, however,
the amounts were not health endangering.

There was a knock at Bollard's door.
"Come in."
Manzano stepped inside.
"Do you have a minute?"

Bollard put the receiver back down and motioned him toward the conference table.

"You look pale," Manzano remarked.

"I'm not getting enough sleep these past few days."

"Who is?" sighed Manzano. He opened the laptop in front of Bollard.

"You remember the information on software providers for power plants that I asked you for?"

"Yes."

"I think I've found something there that could shed light on the mysterious technical problems at the power plants. Now, their software is very specific and *very* complex. So complex, that mounting a far-reaching attack on this many power plants is far too complicated. I asked myself how I would go about launching such an attack, if I had the time and money to prepare. For a start, I'd need a gateway that would grant me access to as many potential targets as possible. Something that is the same for as many power plant control systems as possible. Thinking along these lines, it doesn't take long to narrow it down to SCADA, the software systems that power plants use. Of course, the developers do design specific solutions for each power plant, but certain parts of the software are replicated on most systems. So, as an attacker, all I need to do is manipulate some of these parts."

"But SCADA systems are extremely secure, by virtue of their structure," countered Bollard. He furrowed his brow. "Unless…"

"We're dealing with an inside job at the SCADA manufacturer," Manzano finished Bollard's thought. "At this point, I've reason to believe that *could* be the case. In the last couple of years, SCADAs have become increasingly less secure."

"Less secure in what way?" asked Bollard.

"Relatively speaking, only the first-generation SCADA systems were secure, those for which the manufacturers used their own software protocols and architecture. Modern SCADA systems increasingly make use of standard protocols used on every computer and on the internet. This consistency makes them easier to use, but it drastically increases the security risks," Manzano explained. "I have to stress, though, that at this stage, this is just a suspicion based on a few random statistics."

On the monitor, he brought up a map of Europe with many blue dots.

"These are the power plants that have been affected, according to the latest information. I've run a simple comparison of the software provider for each. The results are striking."

He pressed a button. Most of the points turned red. "Every one of these power plants was outfitted by one SCADA manufacturer."

He waited to let the words sink in.

"Naturally, I cross-checked to make sure. The remaining twenty-five percent were supplied by other large SCADA suppliers. But an overwhelming majority of the power plants that are unable to function are working with systems that come from the one outfitter: Talaefer."

COMMAND HEADQUARTERS

The Italian was starting to get tiresome.

Of course they had taken into account that thousands of investigators across Europe would find a lead sooner or later. But they had expected it to happen significantly later. And again the Italian was to blame. First the electrical meters in Italy and Sweden, now this. It was time they set a trap for him—after all, they had access to his computer. They'd have their fun with the bastard yet.

He typed a few commands on his keyboard. On the screen in front of him appeared a list of names, Manzano's among them. Next to it was the word "offline." As soon as the Italian turned his laptop back on and went back online, he'd find a little surprise waiting for him.

He couldn't help feeling a little sorry for the guy. Like them, Manzano had stood against the cops, had taken a beating from their batons. Like them, he had dared to enter forbidden territory, effortlessly hacking his way across the unending expanses of the internet, surmounting and dissolving barriers. But at some point, he, like so many others, had taken a wrong turn. Now, it was time to put him back on the right path.

If they couldn't, they would have to eliminate him.

THE HAGUE, NETHERLANDS

"What do you think?"

Frowning, Bollard looked into his laptop camera. In a small window in the upper right-hand corner of his screen he saw Carlos Ruiz. Europol's director was traveling again, this time in Brussels, to confer with various leading officials of other EU organizations.

"It's a lead that we should pursue," said Ruiz. "We can't afford to ignore information that might help put a stop to this. Time is getting away from us."

"How about," Bollard suggested, "we send Manzano to Talaefer as support, to help them out?"

Bollard waited with bated breath for the response. This was the opportunity he had been waiting for. Manzano's cooperation with the American journalist had confirmed his worst fears. Even if, strictly speaking, Manzano hadn't broken the confidentiality agreement, he trusted him less than ever. He wanted this criminal pseudo-revolutionary out of there. Let the Germans deal with him.

"If you don't need him..." said Ruiz.

"We need every man we've got, but if there's something to his theory, I'm sure Talaefer will be happy for the help."

"Go ahead and recommend it."

Finally, thought Bollard. *Ciao*, Piero Manzano!

RATINGEN, GERMANY

"They want what?" asked Wickley.

"To get at the software," repeated the chief technology officer. He had managed to obtain a satellite telephone and had the Bangalore office on hold. "We were just now able to reestablish contact. We're only getting through three or four times a day."

"Were there any other requests?"

Outside, a gray sky stretched over the Talaefer AG building. The winter was dismal, especially when it was ten degrees in the office and you had to wear a scarf and winter coat. They presented a ridiculous sight. Wickley dreamed of Bangalore.

"Three operators are reporting problems at several of their power plants that they can't explain. They'd like our support."

"Then we've got to make sure they get it. What is it they're struggling with?"

"We don't know yet. Normally, our service people log in to check the system. But as long as the internet isn't working, that's not possible."

A strange noise started in Wickley's ears that turned into a drone. He had already gone through two separate treatments for sudden hearing loss. He needed another incident like he needed a hole in the head. The sound grew louder and louder and developed chopping undertones.

"What's that?" asked the head of technology.

"You hear it too?" Wickley tried to hide his relief. It wasn't the moment to show any sign of weakness.

The noise now filled his head. A shadow darkened the windows of the executive suite. Wickley could see a dark-blue silhouette, then the whirring rotors of a helicopter slowly descending on the parking lot in front of the building.

"What the—"

They rushed to the window and watched as the aircraft touched down between the cars. Four figures had jumped out toting heavy bags that they tossed on the ground. Two of them ran toward the building, bent over; two stood where they were. Wickley was able to make out some lettering on the side of the helicopter.

"Police?"

"What are they doing here?" cried the head of technology.

Crates were being handed out from inside the helicopter, which were received by the two remaining men and set down on the ground next to the bags. Two more passengers jumped out. One of them gave a signal, and the helicopter lifted off and rose in a long arc, up and away. The entire operation had taken less than three minutes.

Someone rapped on the door.

———

Wickley escorted them to a small conference room off the lobby. The CEO waited while they took their seats, then cleared his throat and demanded, "What is the nature of this investigation you're conducting?"

Hartlandt was accustomed to dealing with executives from large multinational corporations. He didn't care for Wickley's superior attitude, but he was unfazed by it.

"To put it simply, our investigation concerns the activities of a terrorist organization. I'm not assuming you're wrapped up in it..." He wasn't about to let Wickley off the hook, but he didn't want to antagonize him unnecessarily. "But someone at your firm could be. If that's the case, you surely want to get it cleared up as quickly as possible, yes?"

Wickley weighed Hartlandt's words. "Our SCADA systems? Impossible!" he snapped, indignant at the suggestion.

Hartlandt had expected this reaction. He took out the statistics that Europol had sent him, laid the paper out in front of the CEO, and gave him the facts.

"It has to be a mistake," Wickley insisted.

"Mistake or not," replied Hartlandt, "we have to look into the matter. I'll need a list of every employee who has worked on these projects. Additionally, we'll need to interview those members of the management team who were responsible—preferably today. My colleagues here are IT forensics specialists. They'll support your people in finding any errors."

"It's not going to be that simple, I'm afraid," Wickley finally admitted.

Hartlandt could see that this admission wasn't easy for him. He said nothing, waiting for the man to continue.

"Our backup power system wasn't designed for an event such as this one. Without power, we cannot access our computers where all the data is stored. In addition, with no public transportation and no fuel, many employees have been unable to get to work."

Hartlandt resisted the temptation to joke about a multinational energy supplier lacking a power supply. Instead he gave a nod. "I'll take care of it."

THE HAGUE, NETHERLANDS

As he watched the convoy of military vehicles and tankers moving across the screen, Manzano couldn't help but be reminded of an action movie.

"The accident in France has caused unrest all over Europe. This closely guarded convoy of diesel tankers is required to ensure a sufficient supply for the power plants' backup systems."

Everyone in the conference room at Europol followed the report.

"With the exception of Saint-Laurent, the situation at power plants on the continent and in Britain is currently stable," declared the news anchor. "The International Atomic Energy Agency is reporting low-level incidents at twelve facilities. Only at the Czech Temelín power plant does the situation remain tense. There is, however, more bad news from the damaged French power plant…"

Since the European TV networks had all ceased broadcasting, they were now dependent on CNN for news coverage. Blurred, grainy footage showed one of the Saint-Laurent reactors swelling up like a balloon, then suddenly it vanished behind a massive cloud.

"This was the second explosion in the compromised facility. Buildings were severely damaged as a result."

Figures in hazmat suits stalked the terrain around the power plant like giant insects, rattling boxes in their hands.

"An hour later, a thirty-fold increase in radioactivity was measured."

Another insect-man, a Greenpeace logo emblazoned on his jumpsuit, held a measurement device up to the camera.

"Environmental organizations claim to have measured life-threateningly high levels of radiation twenty kilometers away from the facility."

Columns of military trucks traveling along an otherwise deserted road masked members of special units crowded in the back.

"The French government has announced that it will, in the interim, be evacuating the population within a twenty-kilometer radius."

Manzano watched as Bollard reached for a telephone and dialed. He followed the report with the receiver pressed to his ear.

Toy-like tractor trailers trundled across an airfield and into the rounded bellies of giant planes, like plankton into the maw of a whale. More footage showed soldiers as they loaded crates and directed traffic.

"The United States, Russia, Turkey, China, Japan, and India prepare to send the first wave of aid units."

Bollard put down the receiver, without, as far as Manzano could tell, having spoken to anyone.

"We have to put a stop to this madness," someone said.

The others remained silent.

RATINGEN, GERMANY

Hartlandt had set up their base of operations in one of the conference rooms off the lobby at Talaefer AG. The tables had been pushed together to form a long rectangle. At one end were laptops for Hartlandt's people. The other end was used for conferencing. The backup generator behind the building produced enough power for their computers and a few sanitary facilities on the first floor, as well as for the servers. The building technicians had disconnected the elevators and upper floors, forcing Wickley to abandon his top-floor executive suite and set up a makeshift office just down the hall, albeit with a few rooms' buffer in between. For the moment, though, he had joined them at the table with some of his staff to deliver a briefing.

"Our SCADA leadership team consists of seven people, two of whom are here today. The full staff totals about 120 people. Mr. Dienhof will give you the details."

At this, a gaunt individual with gray hair circling a bald pate and a full beard, looked up from the notebook in front of him and said, "Three of our managers are on vacation; we haven't yet been able to reach them. Two more live in Düsseldorf, but it seems they've had to move into a shelter and we haven't been able to trace them. Maybe you could help us in this?" He looked to Hartlandt.

"I'll take care of it," he affirmed.

"As for the rest of the team, we've only been able to

round up ten so far—we don't have enough people or cars with fuel to reach the others, and some of the addresses we called at were empty."

He laid the paper aside.

"Let us have a list of names and addresses," said Hartlandt. "We'll find them."

Dienhof nodded. "As to the SCADA systems—we've started our analyses. The systems are based on certain shared basic modules but are then individually tailored for each customer. Naturally, we're looking at the shared elements first. If in fact our systems are partly responsible for the problems, the cause would most likely be found there."

"Good," said Hartlandt. "Keep at it. In the meantime, we'll locate as many of your people as we can and bring them here."

———

The event hall was a modern, functional building. People huddled together around the entrance, talking and smoking. Hartlandt made his way past them and through an open door into what would have been the place where people met up with their friends and loaded up on popcorn and soft drinks before going in to see the show. Now it was full of people in winter clothes, even though it was warmer here than it was outside. Signs had been hung over the display boards for ticket, snack, and drink prices. In plain black letters against a white background, they announced, *Check-in, Red Cross, Volunteers, Supplies*. There were arrows pointing to toilets, showers, and food stations. On a long wall hung scraps of paper and photos, a kind of community bulletin board, guessed Hartlandt.

He made his way to the check-in. A heavyset woman greeted him sullenly. He showed his identification and put a list in front of her with thirty-seven names on it.

"Are any of these people staying in this shelter?"

Without a word, the woman turned toward a tall cabinet and pulled out one of the drawers. She began riffling through files. Every now and then, she glanced at Hartlandt's list and made notes on a slip of paper.

He found himself observing the people in the hall. They seemed neither agitated nor anxious. It was almost as if they were waiting for the show to start. Their conversation blended into indistinguishable chatter that filled the room.

"Eleven of them are here," the check-in woman announced to Hartlandt's back.

The main hall consisted of one giant space filled with rows of single beds. In some places, towels had been hung between them as a makeshift way of screening off individual areas. The air was stale; it smelled musty—damp clothes, sweat, and a hint of urine. People sat or lay on the beds. Others chatted, read, stared into space, slept.

Hartlandt glanced down at his map, at his list, then headed toward his first stop.

———

At Talaefer they had removed the portable wall partitions between the conference rooms on the ground floor and created a single large space. On two long rows of tables sat 120 laptops. A good two-thirds of the workstations were occupied, mostly by men, many of whom hadn't shaved in days. Hadn't showered either. Hartlandt's team had commandeered two portable showers with water tanks and were setting them up for the employees' use.

"We've got eighty-three," announced Hartlandt. "Of the rest, thirty are on vacation. Ten we haven't yet been able to locate. Among management, everyone is here except for Dragenau, Kowalski, and Wallis. According to his colleagues, Dragenau is on vacation in Bali, Kowalski is in Kenya, and Wallis is in Switzerland on a ski trip. We will continue trying to get in touch with them."

"We're pretty much set up now," said Dienhof. "Nevertheless, it's going to take a while. We'll need to sift through modifications from previous years, because if there really is a saboteur in our midst, he can't have modified the software overnight. Plus, we need at least two people going through everything."

"Why's that?" asked Wickley.

"If the saboteur is checking something he's tampered with himself, he's hardly going to tell us," said Hartlandt.

"The biggest challenge, however," Dienhof continued, "is that we don't know what we're looking for. We're searching in the proverbial haystack, but we have no idea if we're looking for a needle, a tick, or a mushroom."

"Or for nothing at all," Wickley added.

DAY 6—THURSDAY

RATINGEN, GERMANY

Hartlandt woke before dawn. Quietly he slipped out of his sleeping bag, dressed, and used the employee bathroom. He would go without a shave for the time being.

They had secured their provisional operations center with locks so only he and his people could gain entry. Inside, they had set up their computers, servers, and a TETRA radio, with which they could also transmit data.

Along with his field duties at Talaefer, Hartlandt was still responsible for leading the task force on energy producers and distributors. He fired up his laptop and looked over the most recent data to come in. Berlin had sent the reports he'd requested on fires in substations. Sure enough, four of the six cases appeared to be arson: Osterrönfeld on Saturday, Güstrow on Sunday, Cloppenburg on Tuesday, Minden last night.

Hartlandt pulled up his interactive map of Germany, on which he had marked all the incidents reported thus far. The locations were scattered across northern Germany.

His colleague Pohlen, blond and tall as a giant, padded sleepily into the room.

"Look at this," said Hartlandt. "Fires were started in four substations serving the transmission grid."

Pohlen peered at the map. "They'd need a whole army of saboteurs to cover that area."

Hartlandt cleared the points off the map. "The fires didn't all happen at once," he said. "They were spread out." One by one, he replaced the points on the map.

"First north, then east, then west," Pohlen said. "But that doesn't make any sense."

"It's as though someone was zigzagging across the country, burning down substations. But there's another report—four transmission towers that were blown up."

He entered the locations into his system.

"Unfortunately, the teams on-site couldn't establish the exact time of the explosions. But…" he trailed off. Now that all the points were showing on the map, Hartlandt connected the locations of the fires with a line from Lübeck to Güstrow in the east and from there to Cloppenburg and Minden in the west.

"Two of the blown towers lie right in the vicinity of the Güstrow-Cloppenburg transmission line. It looks as though somebody is systematically sabotaging strategic infrastructure."

"In that case the remaining infrastructure has to be protected right away!" cried Pohlen.

"Impossible. Do you have any idea how many transmission towers and substations there are? We can't possibly guard them all; the police and army are stretched to the limit as it is." He reached for the radio. "Let's see how the folks in Berlin see it."

THE HAGUE, NETHERLANDS

"We've started following up on your suggestion," Bollard told Manzano. "Even as we speak, German authorities are looking into Talaefer's SCADA systems. Ideally, I'd send one of my own people to assist, but we have no one to spare." He leaned forward and propped his elbows on his desk. "So, to get to the point, how would you like to go to Talaefer's HQ in Ratingen and put your talents to use there?"

Manzano raised his eyebrows in surprise. "I'm not a SCADA specialist."

"I believe you on a lot of things, even your theories, but not on that." Bollard flashed him a grin. "And even if it were true, you have the ability to recognize errors and anomalies in the system. Why don't you download the reports—they're already on our network. I can't guarantee that there'll be any hotels in Ratingen with hot water and working toilets…"

"You really know how to make the job sound appealing."

"But you'll have a car at your disposal. I'm sure we can come to an agreement about your fee. Just don't tell your girlfriend anything about it."

"She's not my girlfriend."

"Whatever you say. So, are you going?"

————

"As of now, the room's all yours," Manzano told her as he packed his bag. Shannon had returned moments earlier from a trip around the city, taping a few short segments.

"You're leaving? Where to?"

"Not important."

In the bathroom she heard the toilet flush, then the tap, then out stepped Bollard.

"Ah, the star reporter," he sneered. "Would you mind leaving us alone for a few moments?"

Shannon hesitated; after all, it was her room too. Well, OK, not really. She laid her camera down on the desk, left the room, closed the door from the outside, and pressed her ear up against it. She could only catch a word here and there. Then a complete sentence.

"Assuming, that is, that the Germans can connect to the internet," said Manzano. So he was going to Germany, Shannon thought feverishly.

"You can say what you want about the Germans, but they are organized," replied Bollard. "The BKA at Talaefer is sure to have the necessary equipment. Here are the car keys. The car is in the hotel garage, a black Audi A4 with Dutch plates and a full tank. It'll get you to Ratingen"—he pronounced the name with the stress on the last syllable, Rating*en*—"and back without any trouble."

Shannon heard footsteps and ran on tiptoe two doors down the hall. There she leaned against the wall and crossed her arms, as if she had been waiting for an eternity.

Bollard nodded to her as he passed.

Shannon padded back to the room. Manzano was standing with his suitcase and laptop bag in hand, ready to head out.

"Been a pleasure," he said and held his hand out to her. "I hope we see each other again when this whole mess is over. Maybe you'll do a story in Milan sometime. You've got my address."

Shannon waited till the door had clicked shut behind him. Then she began stuffing her belongings as fast as she could into her rucksack.

NEW YORK, UNITED STATES OF AMERICA

Tommy Suarez was standing in a packed car of the Brooklyn-bound A train. Fellow passengers were wiping snow from their steaming clothes, texting their friends, reading, listening on earphones, or staring into space. Then the lights went out.

The squeal of brakes fused with the cries of the passengers. Strangers' bodies slammed into Tommy's, and the handrail cut into his wrist; he felt like he was in a giant washing machine, caught up in the spin cycle, his ribs, spine, and legs getting painfully pounded. Then with an almighty jolt, everything came to a stop. The stillness in the car stretched for the span of a single breath before people started screaming. Suarez had no idea how far it was to the next station. He hoped the train would be able to continue on its journey; he didn't want to have to walk through the tunnels or spend hours stuck down here. The voices around him grew louder. He looked at his watch. Quarter of seven. Where was the announcement from the conductor?

"Great!" said an older woman somewhere behind him. "I hope it's not another blackout! I was stuck in one of these things for two hours back in 2003!"

"Two hours?" cried a young woman, barely suppressed panic in her voice.

"And I was one of the lucky ones!" the older woman went on, relishing the effect her words were having. "Some people were trapped—"

"I'm sure it'll start moving in a second." Suarez cut her off before she could frighten the young woman any more than she already had. Not everybody could keep their cool in dark, cramped spaces surrounded by a lot of people. Especially not with the prospect of having to endure it for several hours. He knew how the young woman felt. "Nothing bad can happen to us."

Next to him, he could hear someone tapping on his cell phone.

"Figures, this thing doesn't work either."

"What do we do if this keeps up?" asked a man with a Southern accent.

"If what keeps up?" asked a woman.

"The lights are off; we're not moving."

"I can tell you that," the older woman spoke up again. "Wait. Wait and freeze."

Suarez would have liked to belt her one to shut her up, but it would have been like hitting his mother.

"And what if we've been hit too?" asked a woman. "Like in Europe?"

The young woman, now in full panic mode, began to whimper, then to scream. Suarez felt his blood run cold, felt her panic spreading to him and the others. He had to stop himself from shouting at her; instead, he attempted to reassure her, patted her on the shoulder, tried to take her in his arms.

She lashed out.

"Leave me alone! I want to get out of here!"

THE HAGUE, NETHERLANDS

Bollard walked into the hotel room two floors above Manzano's and saw that the towers of surveillance equipment had been dismantled and were now being packed away.

"I'm heading off," he said. "I'll see you back at the office."

"Before you go," said the Dutch officer who'd planted the bug in Manzano's laptop, "that American journalist took off immediately after Manzano did. Where she's headed, we don't know."

"Probably chasing him," said Bollard. "He was good for one story; she's probably hoping for another."

The Dutchman pointed to his computer screen. "Shortly before he set out, he sent an email."

Bollard leaned over to read the message.

> Headed to Talaefer. Looking for a bug. Won't find a thing. Will keep you posted.

I knew it! thought Bollard triumphantly.

"Who was it sent to?"

"A Russian address: Mata@radna.ru. That's all we know so far."

Bollard reached for the telephone to call his boss. When he finished briefing him, Ruiz cursed under his breath.

"We can't take any more risks. Inform that guy at the BKA who's working the Talaefer case—what's his name again?"

"Hartlandt," answered Bollard.

"Right. They should arrest the Italian and see what they

can get out of him. I'm sure the CIA will be more than happy to help."

"Why the CIA?"

"Haven't you heard the news?"

"What news?"

BERLIN, GERMANY

"The United States?"

For an instant, the Interior Ministry's operations center was like a freeze-frame. Everyone stood, frozen in midstride, to stare at the few active screens. The clocks showed 14:07.

"The same as us?" someone asked.

Rhess nodded. He held a phone pressed up to his ear and kept on nodding. Michelsen's gaze jumped back and forth between the TVs and the secretary of state.

"If that's true," her neighbor whispered, "we're completely fucked—pardon my language."

Rhess hung up. "The foreign minister has confirmed that large parts of the U.S. power grid have collapsed."

"No coincidence," someone said. "Less than a week after Europe."

"So we won't be getting any help from there," stated Michelsen.

"The West is under attack," Rhess declared. "Minutes from now, NATO high command will gather for an emergency meeting."

"They don't think it was the Russians or Chinese, do they?"

"Every possibility has to be taken into consideration."

"Heaven help us," whispered Michelsen.

COMMAND HEADQUARTERS

The American power grids had turned out to be far easier than they had imagined. After what had happened in

Europe, they'd assumed security would be tightened, loop-holes closed, and connections to the internet guarded with new improved firewalls. Given the choice, they would rather have struck both continents simultaneously. But as it turned out, this way was good too. Even better, perhaps. For almost a week, the world had been speculating over who was behind the attacks. The outage in the United States would feed new rumors. The military would be champing at the bit. Such a far-reaching attack pointed to a nation-state as the likely culprit. A few came to mind: Iran, North Korea, China, even Russia. Naturally, they would all deny it, but so long as the true perpetrators remained undetected, who would believe them? There were no tracks that could lead back to the culprits; in the global network, it was far too easy to cover them. In the meantime, theories would pile up. Investigators with the police, military, and intelligence agencies would chase clues, leads, tangents; there would be so many leads they'd have no option but to divide their resources, leaving time for only the most cursory investigation.

The psychological effect would be even more devastat-ing than in Europe. The world's last superpower, already reeling from the economic crisis, and now unable to defend itself. Pearl Harbor and 9/11 would pale into insignificance in comparison. Soon the American public would see that this couldn't be fixed by sending in the army. Because they wouldn't know where to send it. Then they would realize how helpless they were. How helpless their government was, their so-called elite, their entire system. A system in which they had long since ceased to feel at ease, let alone content, but that they chose over the unfamiliar.

They would understand that they had been left behind. A new age was dawning, and the United States of America would be powerless to stop it.

RATINGEN, GERMANY

For the first few miles, Manzano had tinkered with the radio, trying to pick up stations, but only static emerged from the speakers. Since then, he had driven in silence. It felt good after the excitement of the last few days.

The GPS led him off the highway and through the suburbs of Ratingen to a fifteen-story glass and concrete monolith. Manzano parked the car in a visitor's spot. He took his laptop with him. The rest of his luggage he left in the trunk.

At reception he asked for Jürgen Hartlandt. Two minutes later he was greeted by a man of roughly his own age; he looked as though he spent a lot of time in the gym, but this was no muscle-bound beefcake. His light blue eyes seemed to assess Manzano in a heartbeat. He was accompanied by two younger men, also in casual attire.

"Jürgen Hartlandt," the leader introduced himself. "Piero Manzano?"

Manzano nodded, and the two others placed themselves on either side of him.

"Follow me, please," said Hartlandt in barely accented English, without introducing his colleagues. He led Manzano into a small conference room and closed the door behind them. One of his men remained standing by it.

"Please sit. I've received a message from Europol. For security reasons I need to look over your computer before we start."

Manzano frowned. "It's private property."

"Do you have something to hide, Mr. Manzano?"

Manzano started to feel uneasy. He didn't like Hartlandt's tone and wondered what he was getting at. He'd come all this way at their invitation, so why were they treating him with suspicion?

"No. But I like to protect my privacy," he replied.

"We'll do it another way then," offered Hartlandt. "Explain to me please who mata@radna.ru is."

"Who's it supposed to be?"

"I'm asking you. You sent an email to that address."

"Definitely not. And even if I had, how would you know?"

"You're not the only one who knows his IT and can look around in other people's computers. Europol had you under surveillance, of course. So who is mata@radna.ru?"

"Again, I don't know."

One of Hartlandt's men took Manzano's laptop bag from him before he could stop him. Manzano jumped up. Hartlandt's other colleague pressed him back down into the chair.

"What is this?" cried Manzano. "I thought I was supposed to be assisting you."

"That's what we thought too," said Hartlandt, turning on the laptop.

"Fine, I'll be leaving then," Manzano said.

"No, you won't," replied Hartlandt, without looking up from the screen.

Manzano tried to stand but was again held back.

"Please remain seated," ordered Hartlandt. He turned Manzano's laptop around so that it was facing him. "So you deny sending this email to mata@radna.ru."

On the screen, Manzano saw an email sent from his address.

Headed to Talaefer. Looking for a bug. Won't find a thing. Will keep you posted.

He read it again. He looked at Hartlandt, speechless. Stared at the screen again. Finally, he managed to get the words out. "I neither wrote nor sent that."

Hartlandt scratched his head. "But this is your laptop, yes?"

Manzano nodded. His thoughts were racing. He saw the time stamp on the email. Somewhere around the time he had set out from The Hague. He crossed his arms over his chest. "I didn't write this. I have no idea who did. Search the computer. Maybe it's been tampered with. I'd be happy to do it myself, but I'm guessing you won't allow that."

"You're right there. We'll be the ones searching the computer." He handed the laptop to one of his men, who left the room with it. "In the meantime, we can talk a little more about your email contacts."

"There's not much to talk about," replied Manzano. "I don't recognize that message or the address. Therefore, I can't tell you anything about them."

Hartlandt brought up a file on his own laptop and scanned the contents. "You are Piero Manzano. In the eighties and nineties, you enjoyed some notoriety as a hacker—quite a brilliant one, it seems. You were also a political activist; at the G8 summit in Genoa, you were briefly detained."

"Please don't tell me my life story; I know what I've—"

"Somebody out there is attacking Europe and the United States! And your email gives us every reason to—"

"Wait a minute, wait a minute! What do you mean, the United States?"

"—suspect that you are in contact with those responsible."

They suspected that he was one of the people behind this? That he was some political cyberactivist turned terrorist!

"This is…this is…absurd!"

"That's for us to find out," replied Hartlandt, a deep fold between his eyebrows.

"Well, you need to get on and find out fast. What's this about the United States?"

"Didn't you hear it on the radio?"

"I couldn't pick up any stations still on air."

"As of this morning, large parts of the United States are without power."

"Oh my God…you're not serious?"

"I'm in no mood for jokes. And it's better you start talking now, before the CIA takes an interest in you too."

———

Shannon reached for her wool jacket on the Porsche's cramped backseat and put it on. It was freezing inside the car. She had been waiting for an hour outside the giant office building on the outskirts of the city. The top story was emblazoned with *Talaefer* AG; under normal circumstances, she would have done some research on the company while she waited. But these weren't normal circumstances; she had no internet connection and even the radio wasn't working. The wait was turning out to be quiet and boring.

So she climbed out of the car and took a walk. Still a couple of cars here, she thought. Maybe they have backup power inside.

In the lobby a woman sitting alone in the vast space greeted Shannon with eyebrows raised.

"What can I do for you?"

Shannon looked around, nonchalant. A little stand on the desk held company brochures. German version. English. Perfect.

"Do you speak English?" she asked.

"Yes."

"I think I'm lost. I need to go to Ratingen."

The woman's expression brightened. In clumsy English she told Shannon that all she had to do was take a right from the parking lot and after about a kilometer she would be in Ratingen.

Shannon thanked her, casually flipped through one of the brochures, and tucked it away before turning to leave.

Back in her ice-cold car she nestled deep into her jacket and studied the leaflet, every now and again stealing a quick glance at the doors through which Manzano had vanished.

NANTEUIL, FRANCE

"I'm out," said Bertrand, shaking the empty medicine packet. "I'll have to get more; I can't do without my pills."

"But we're not supposed to leave the house," said his wife.

"I can leave the house and get right in the car. What's going to happen?"

He went down to the kitchen, and Annette followed. Celeste Bollard was sitting at the table plucking a chicken. She was collecting the feathers in a large basket, but more than a few were landing on the kitchen floor.

"I haven't done this in years," she sighed. "I'd completely forgotten what a tedious chore it is."

Vincent Bollard walked in through the door, huffing as he carried a basket full of firewood in each hand. With a crash he set them down.

"Where's the nearest pharmacy?" asked Bertrand.

"Blois," Vincent told him. "Assuming it's open. Is it urgent?"

"Yes, my heart medication."

Vincent nodded.

His wife exchanged a glance with Annette.

"We really aren't supposed to go outside, you know," puffed Bollard, still short of breath. "But if we must, we must." He gave his wife a kiss on the cheek. "We'll be back in a while."

RATINGEN, GERMANY

Hartlandt had grilled Manzano for a full two hours.

"What do you mean, 'won't find a thing'? Is there something to find? Did you come here to stop us finding it? Or is there nothing to find? What have you given away already?"

Endless questioning. Manzano fired back his own questions.

"Why would I be so stupid as to send a message like

that without encryption? I would just press delete as soon as I'd sent it."

The door opened and a police officer walked in with Manzano's laptop tucked under his arm. "We found more emails in which you give information to various recipients about your stay in The Hague."

"That's crazy," said Manzano. "What the hell do you mean?"

Hartlandt sat up. "Mr. Manzano, we're placing you under arrest. The Central Intelligence Agency has also expressed an interest in questioning you."

At the thought of the American intelligence agency's infamous methods, Manzano grew sick with fear.

NANTEUIL, FRANCE

At the sound of a car pulling up outside the house, Annette hurried into the hallway. Two men came through the door, breath steaming, and closed it quickly behind them.

Her husband held up a medicine packet, and she felt the relief sweep over her.

Then he crumpled it in his large fist. It had been the old, empty one.

"Nothing," he said. "No more in stock anywhere now."

DÜSSELDORF, GERMANY

After driving for half an hour, they approached signs for Düsseldorf. Hartlandt's driver steered the car into a sprawling building complex. A few spaces in the parking lot were occupied by droning generators, the exhaust fouling up the air around them. Thick bundles of cables snaked through a small flower bed on their way into the building.

Manzano felt the cold strike his cheeks as he got out. Hartlandt hadn't considered it necessary to put him in handcuffs.

"I have to go to the bathroom urgently," he said. "I can't wait till we get inside. Can I step over there really quick?"

Hartlandt gave him a look. "Before you piss your pants on us."

Manzano hurried over to the generators, Hartlandt and his man following closely behind. Manzano placed himself next to the machines, gave the two of them a glance to say, Don't look, and unzipped his pants. The two of them ignored him and stood as close as they could. Manzano could hear their breath while he surreptitiously inspected the machines and their cables. There was nothing for it. He turned around and directed his stream toward Hartlandt's colleague.

"Son of a bitch!"

The man leaped back. Manzano swung over toward Hartlandt, who also jerked backward. Both men looked down in horror at their pants. Manzano used the moment and took off running.

With long strides, he crossed the parking lot, zipping up his fly with fevered fingers. Behind him he heard the two of them calling out.

"Stop! Stay where you are!"

Not a chance. Manzano was a practiced runner. Whether he could outrun trained police officers remained to be seen. The blood pounded so violently in his ears that he barely heard the shouts. He had to get off the street. One of them was sure to try to head him off in the car. His feet seemed to barely touch the ground. He scoured the street for a place to turn off.

Another yell that he didn't catch. He dashed down a side street, knowing in an instant that this was a mistake. He had to take the next street. Behind him were the racing footfalls of his pursuers. He couldn't make out if it was one or two. By now his breath was trying to drown out his heartbeat. He felt the sweat on his forehead. A car engine roared. Up ahead was a yard, surrounded by a fence taller than a man, with a hedgerow. A few steps more, he leaped as high as he could and just cleared the fence. Behind him, squealing breaks and cursing. Manzano ran toward the building, a large mansion. The windows were dark. He ran around the side; the yard in front of him was also surrounded by a hedge and a fence. With a mighty leap he managed to grab the top of the fence. He hauled himself up, swung his legs over, and dropped neatly onto the pavement. Gasping for breath, he knew he wouldn't be able to keep this pace up much longer.

Another shout. So he hadn't shaken them off then. On the contrary, the voice sounded very close. Manzano couldn't catch the words. There was a sudden bang. He kept running along the side street. Up ahead another intersection. Another bang. He felt a dull pain in his right thigh. He stumbled, kept running. He was slowing down. Suddenly he was slammed from behind and thrown to the ground. Before Manzano could defend himself his arms were painfully twisted behind him. He felt a blunt object in his back. Metal clicking, then he felt the cold handcuffs snap closed around his wrists.

"You jerk." He heard the man panting for breath behind him. "I thought you had some sense."

Manzano felt hands traveling down his legs.

"Let's see the damage."

Only now did he become aware of the pain. His right thigh was burning, as if someone were holding a red-hot iron against it.

BERLIN, GERMANY

"There is not even the faintest sign," the NATO general conceded. Each of the conference room's ten monitors was split in four; at least one face looked out from each screen: the heads of state of most EU countries or their foreign ministers; six NATO generals, patched in from headquarters in Brussels; and the president of the United States. Behind them sat members of their various crisis teams.

"But the extent of the attacks—surely only nation-states have the necessary resources at their disposal," said the general.

"Who would be capable of such a thing?" asked the U.S. president.

"According to our assessments, around three dozen nations have built up capacities for cyberattacks in the past few years. Many of these have now been hit: France, Great Britain, other European countries, and the United States. In addition, allied nations such as Israel and Japan."

"So who is being considered?"

"Our information tells us that Russia, China, North Korea, Iran, Pakistan, India, and South Africa could be capable."

"I would consider India and South Africa allies," the British prime minister objected.

"Initial diplomatic aid—to the United States as well—has come from many nations. The offers come from almost every state mentioned, with the exception of North Korea and Iran."

"For as long as we're in the dark about what's behind this, we must concentrate on the needs of the population," said the German chancellor. "The attack on the United States demands that we rethink the coordination of international aid. Aid personnel in the United States who were mobilized for Europe will now be deployed within the United States itself."

"The question is, how do we handle the remaining offers of help?" asked the Italian president. "Do we want to accept Chinese or Russian aid when we're unsure of their culpability? Maybe we're already at war with Russia or China and we just don't know it. More saboteurs could be smuggled in alongside relief forces."

Is he paranoid, Michelsen asked herself, or am I too naive? Surely we have to take all the help we can get!

The defense minister, who also held the office of vice chancellor, pressed the button to mute the microphone so that the other participants in the video conference couldn't hear what he had to say.

"I have to agree with the Italian president," he said to the chancellor. "There is a certain risk present." He released the button. The chancellor raised an eyebrow. Michelsen could see him pondering the argument.

"According to the information I've received," said the Swedish head of state, "the first aid flights out of Russia are scheduled for the day after tomorrow, Saturday. The first truck convoys and rail transportation are also due to set out then. Planes bringing aid from the Chinese are expected as of Sunday. I recommend that, for the time being, we push ahead with the preparations. Should we gain any new intelligence by the time the transportation actually begins, we'll still be in a position to stop them."

Thank God for common sense, thought Michelsen, stealing a look at the defense minister.

DÜSSELDORF, GERMANY

Three ambulances were parked outside the hospital. Two bulkily dressed figures were pushing a wheeled stretcher out of the building. On second glance, Manzano could see that a patient was lying under the sheet. A half-full IV pouch swung from the metal arm above his head. A young man dressed in white ran along behind and gestured excitedly with his hands. The two pushing the bed shook their heads and kept pushing their load in the direction of the street. Eventually the man in white gave up, made a rude hand gesture, and hurried back into the hospital.

Hartlandt drove past the strange troupe and parked behind one of the ambulances.

"Can you walk a few steps?"

Manzano shot him a furious look. It probably wouldn't be too difficult, but why should he cooperate with someone who considered him a terrorist and shot him in the leg?

"No!"

Hartlandt disappeared through the hospital entrance without a word. His colleague watched Manzano's every move. Manzano's hands were bound behind his back, and the pounding in his leg was extremely painful.

Hartlandt came back with a wheelchair. "Sit in this."

Manzano obeyed reluctantly. Hartlandt pushed him into the building. His colleague didn't budge from Manzano's side.

They had barely passed through the entrance when the smell hit him. It was overwhelming. Even though it wasn't much warmer here than it was outside, the place stank of decay and feces laced with traces of disinfectant.

In the reception area, beds with patients in them were being moved around by men and women who didn't look like nurses. There was mass confusion, though Manzano thought he could detect a general move toward the exit.

Hartlandt pushed him down a hallway. Beds occupied by the sick and injured were lined up along the walls. Some were silent; others groaned or whimpered. There was a figure standing among them, more likely a visitor than a doctor. The temperature was still way below normal room temperature. Except for the white-clad man outside, Manzano still hadn't seen any hospital staff.

Finally, they reached the emergency ward. Every one of the chairs in the waiting area was occupied. Hartlandt took out his ID and showed it to the admitting nurse.

"Gunshot wound," he announced. Manzano's German wasn't particularly good, but he could still follow the conversation. Two semesters as a student in Berlin, a year with a German girlfriend, and years of trips—albeit not completely legal ones—inside the systems of

German companies were paying off. "We need a doctor immediately."

The nurse was unmoved.

"You can see for yourself what's going on here. I have to tell people we can't treat them. The hospital should have been evacuated a long time ago. But do you think anybody is listening to me? Are you listening to me?"

"Now you listen to me," Hartlandt insisted. "I need a doctor right now. Do I have to mention national security before you go get somebody?"

She scowled and disappeared.

There were at least fifty people waiting in the room. A woman was trying to calm her wailing little boy. An older man sitting on a chair was leaning against his wife, his face white as chalk, his eyelids fluttering. She whispered something to him over and over and stroked his cheek. Another woman was lying in her chair, her head tilted back, her skin waxen, one arm raised to chest height, the end of it a stump of once-white gauze drenched in blood under which there had to be a hand. Manzano looked away. He stared at the wall instead.

"What's going on here? Who do you think you are?"

Behind Manzano the nurse had reappeared; with her was a man in his midforties carrying the usual doctor's implements in a coat that was no longer entirely white. There were dark bags beneath his eyes, and his face hadn't seen a razor in days.

"An emergency," explained Hartlandt, "and a priority case."

"And tell me, please, why?"

Hartlandt held up his ID. "Because he might be one of the people responsible for the situation we're all sitting in."

Manzano thought he misheard. Was this crazy idiot turning him into a scapegoat in front of everybody here?

"All the more reason not to treat him!" The doctor snorted.

"Hippocrates would've been proud of you," remarked Hartlandt. "But it might be that your patient here can also help us to solve the problem. First, however, I need him with a stable pulse and no blood poisoning or infection."

The doctor grumbled under his breath, then he said to Hartlandt, "Come with me."

He led the way to a small examination room and pointed at a table.

"What is this?" asked the doctor when he saw the hand-cuffs. "Take them off. I can't treat him like this."

Hartlandt undid the cuffs.

The doctor cut away the bandage Hartlandt had applied, then Manzano's pant leg. He explored the wound and was careful in touching it; still, Manzano couldn't help but cry out in pain.

"No tragedy here," the doctor concluded. "There's only one problem. We're out of anesthetic. Do you want to—"

"Do it," Hartlandt interrupted him.

"I'll disinfect first," said the doctor, tipping a bottle of liquid onto a piece of gauze and dabbing at the wound.

Manzano let out a howl.

"This is a nightmare," said the doctor. "I feel like I'm in the Thirty Years' War, giving the wounded a bottle of schnapps before sawing off their leg."

Manzano closed his eyes and hoped that he would pass out. His body didn't oblige.

"Well?" asked the doctor.

Manzano took a deep breath and answered in English. "Get it out."

"Sure thing. Grit your teeth. Or better still"—he put a bandage in Manzano's hand—"bite down on this."

He poured disinfectant onto another piece of gauze and used it to wipe a set of forceps. "We don't have any sterile instruments left," he explained with a shrug.

Someone stabbed a burning spear through Manzano's thigh and rooted around in his flesh. Manzano heard an animal sound, pushing its way out of the depths, a drawn-out muffled howl. Only when he ran out of breath did he realize that it had come from him. His lungs gave out on him. He tried to sit up, but Hartlandt pressed down on his shoulders, his colleague leaned on his knees, and together they held him to the table.

From the corners of his teared-up eyes, Manzano saw the doctor hold the forceps up to his face. Something bloody was caught between the tips.

"Well now, we've got it."

He tossed the bullet into a waste bin.

"Now I've got to sew it up. That won't hurt as much."

What could possibly hurt now? thought Manzano, breaking into a fresh sweat. I should really take a deep breath, he remembered, then everything went dark.

PARIS, FRANCE

Laplante pointed the camera at James Turner, who had positioned himself in front of an industrial building. And all the while, Laplante cursed Shannon for clearing off and leaving him with this jerk. Behind Turner, the occasional lone figure or small group of people emerged from the darkness of a giant doorway, carrying large packages.

"I'm standing in front of the main storage facility of a large food company south of Paris. Since the moment the doors were forced open earlier tonight, people have been taking whatever they can find inside."

Turner approached a group of looters and stood in their way. They carried plastic bags brimming with something that Laplante, as cameraman, couldn't identify.

"What have you got there?" asked Turner.

"None of your goddamn business," answered one of the men, pushing Turner out of the way.

The journalist steadied himself, keeping his composure.

"As you can see, people are already on edge. On the

sixth day of the power outage, not counting the brief and only partial restoration on day two, the people of Paris have been doing without just about everything. The news that a radioactive cloud from Saint-Laurent could reach the city has made the mood much worse. Which brings us to our main topic."

Turner pulled the device, which he had been carrying with him since their brief trip down to Saint-Laurent, out of the belt of his coat.

"Now for what's become our obligatory measurement report," he announced solemnly. "With this dosimeter I can determine the current radiation level."

He raised the device into the air.

"What we have here is a small digital instrument, not the clicking things you know from the movies. They are, however, calibrated so that, upon detecting critical or dangerous dosages, they emit alarm noises…"

A loud beeping interrupted Turner's performance. Confused, he looked up at the little box above his head before it dawned on him that, in order to read it, he had to bring it back down to eye level.

Laplante zoomed in on his face, which showed first bewilderment, then disbelief, and finally horror.

He raised the device up in the air again, waved it to one side, then the other, and took a few steps forward. Laplante followed his movements. In the background more looters crept past.

Turner held the little box in front of the lens.

"Zero point two microsieverts per hour!" he proclaimed. "That's double what is classified as an acceptable dose! The cloud has reached Paris!"

DÜSSELDORF, GERMANY

"Wake up; we're done."

Manzano needed a moment to get his bearings. He lay

on his back, feeling a stabbing pain in his thigh. Three faces were peering down on him. Then he remembered.

"Not a bad way to do it," said the unshaven doctor. "This way you didn't feel me stitch up the wound."

"How…how long was I…?"

"Two minutes. Now you stay here for a few more hours for observation. Then everybody must leave the building, no matter what."

"Why?" asked Hartlandt.

The doctor took Manzano by the arm and pulled him up to sitting. "The backup power supply has been on reserve since the day before yesterday," he explained. With Hartlandt's help, he hoisted Manzano back into the wheelchair. "We won't be getting any more fuel," he continued as they left the examination room, "since there's not enough available for all the hospitals in Düsseldorf. Now we have to look at how we're going to get rid of our patients. Tonight the lights are going out here, literally."

"Shouldn't we go and find somewhere else right away?"

"He needs to rest a few hours. Besides, you won't find any room in the few hospitals that are still open. They need the beds and staff for more severe cases."

"Hey, I got shot," Manzano said, his voice weak.

"That was nothing. Believe me, you don't want to know what kinds of operations I've had to carry out without anesthesia in the past few hours. Unfortunately, I can't give you any pain medication," said the doctor. "Used it up a long time ago. You're going to feel that wound for the next couple of days." He put two packets in his hand. "Here, now at least you've got an antibiotic. In case you get an infection. Maybe it'll help. Best thing would be for you to sleep a little."

Without another word he turned and walked away.

"All right then," Hartlandt said to his colleague, "find the gentleman a bed. I could use one myself. But I'm headed back to Talaefer. I'll return later or send a car."

Then he pushed his way down the corridor and outside. Manzano watched until he was gone.

"What's your name, anyway?" Manzano asked his guard. "Seeing as how we've got to spend the next few hours together…"

"Helmut Pohlen," the man answered.

"All right then, Helmut Pohlen, let's find me a bed."

———

Shannon waited a few minutes. When Manzano and his guard didn't come back out of the room, she crept closer to the door. Then she knocked quietly and opened the door without waiting to be invited. The room was so tiny that Manzano's bed completely filled it.

The Italian seemed to be sleeping. His guard jumped when he saw Shannon peering inside. But she had already seen what she was looking for: there was neither a window nor another door in here.

"Sorry," she whispered and closed the door again.

She walked stealthily down the hall, looking for a secret spot from which to watch the exit to Manzano's sick quarters.

What the hell had the Italian done to make them shoot him?

RATINGEN, GERMANY

Dienhof stood in front of a flip chart on which diagrams had been drawn: pictograms of buildings that were connected to one another by lines. Aside from him and Hartlandt, only Wickley, Hartlandt's colleagues, another Talaefer executive under whose purview matters of security fell, the chief security officer, and the company's head of human resources were present.

"We have assumed the worst possible scenario," Dienhof

began. "Namely that our products could in fact be to blame
for the problems experienced by the power plants. These
products are based on basic modules, some of which we
have developed ourselves, but also on standard modules—
protocols, basically, which today are used regularly, for
example on the internet." Dienhof accompanied his presentation with gestures, pointing at the drawings on the
flip chart. "On this basis, however, we develop custom-
built solutions for every customer. This means, logically
speaking, that for an error or a deliberate manipulation
affecting so many power plants, we must first look in one
of the basic modules."

"Could be somewhere else, though, too," one of
Hartlandt's men interrupted.

"In theory, yes, but in practice, unlikely. So what we
must ask ourselves is, who develops them, or, who among
us has write access to the basic-module. This was the first
group that came under focus for us."

"Write access?" Hartlandt interrupted him. "Does that
mean that only these people can alter the basic module?"

"Exactly," Dienhof affirmed. "Nowadays it isn't the
case that the power plants get the system from us and
then never hear from us again. These products are hugely
complex and are constantly being improved. So companies
are always receiving updates to their software. Here too we
naturally have a particularly interesting group of employees, namely those who have direct access to the producers'
systems already in operation.

"It goes without saying that both these employees and
the update procedure itself are subject to the most rigorous security standards. A general security standard within
our company is the strict separation of staff in different
units such as development, quality inspection, and customer service.

"A software developer isn't permitted to be one of the
inspectors, or one of those who end up implementing it

on behalf of the customers. In order to get a bug through to the customers, someone would have to write it so ingeniously that the inspectors and their instruments wouldn't spot it…or we have an error in the authorization system for the source code archive."

"What does that mean?" asked Hartlandt.

"Only certain individuals are permitted to alter the source code. Each of these changes must be checked and signed off by others."

"But if you had an error in this system…"

"…then a developer could smuggle a program code past the inspectors. I consider that to be out of the question, however."

A lot of ifs and buts, thought Hartlandt. Clearly Mr. Dienhof could not entertain the thought that the responsibility for this mess could rest with his company.

"It's a good start," he said encouragingly. "But what if it wasn't just one person operating alone?"

"No, I think we're looking for an individual, one who can alter the routines that are used by all programs. After our research into the access administration of the source code archives, we were able to determine only three people who fit that bill. The first is Hermann Dragenau, our chief architect. Alongside his program design activities, he can also make adjustments within the standard libraries."

Hartlandt recalled the name from his search for absent employees. "He's on vacation in Bali," he said.

"That's the information we have too. The second is Bernd Wallis. He is skiing in Switzerland; we haven't been able to reach him either. The third is Alfred Tornau. He was on the list of people who couldn't make it to work since the outages. You didn't find him at home, however, and he couldn't be located anywhere else, if I understand correctly."

"We're still searching for him and a few others," answered Hartlandt. "Let me see if I have this straight. We have three people who are under suspicion: one is in Bali, the other's in Switzerland, and the third has disappeared. Well, that's great news."

THE HAGUE, NETHERLANDS

Bollard stuck another pin into the map of Europe. After the Germans had called that morning, he had passed the information along to all the liaison officers present to make further inquiries in their home countries. By midday, reports had come in from Spain, France, the Netherlands, Italy, and Poland. In Spain, a case of arson had been reported at a substation, along with two blown towers; in France, four towers had fallen; and two each in the Netherlands, Italy, and Poland. Still, each country stressed that the information was preliminary and possibly incomplete, as they had only skeletal teams to investigate. For every sabotaged facility, he stuck a pin in the board.

"New information just in from Germany," said Bollard. "The ruling of arson in Lübeck was rescinded, and the transmission towers in the north falling was also due to natural causes, apparently. That casts doubt on Berlin's theory that the saboteur was following an east-west route. At the same time, we have another possible arson in southern Bavaria and a downed tower in eastern Saxony-Anhalt."

"Don't we have to assume that someone is driving across Europe, disabling substations and transmission towers?"

"That would take a lot of troops," said Bollard.

The ringing of a radiophone interrupted their deliberations.

When Bollard picked up, it was Hartlandt on the other end of the line. "I've been trying to get through to you for an hour."

At first Bollard couldn't believe Hartlandt's account. The Italian had been shot while attempting to escape and was now lying in a hospital in Düsseldorf. Hartlandt related how Manzano had stubbornly insisted that he had not been responsible for the incriminating emails from his computer.

Bollard ended the call and jumped nervously to his feet. "I'll be right back," he said to his colleagues.

The IT department was two floors down. Many of the offices here were empty too, he noted.

The acting director, an affable Belgian who'd been on secondment to Europol for years, was in his office with one of his team, analyzing data on the four monitors that stood on his desk.

"Can you spare two minutes?" asked Bollard.

The Belgian nodded and motioned for him to come in.

"I'd prefer to discuss this in the hall," said Bollard, gesturing over his shoulder with his thumb.

The Belgian shot him a hostile look, but Bollard had planted himself outside the door and made it clear that he would wait there as long as it took for the other man to follow.

"What's this about?" demanded the Belgian.

Bollard closed the door behind him and ushered him along the hall where they couldn't be heard before telling him about Manzano, the emails, and the Italian's accusations.

"Bullshit!" the Belgian exclaimed.

"These saboteurs have crippled the power grids of two of the biggest economies in the world. How can you be so sure they haven't found their way in here too?"

"Because our system employs state-of-the-art security!"

"So did the others, supposedly. Listen, we both know that there's no such thing as an absolutely secure network. And I am also aware that there have been successful attempts to infiltrate our networks—"

"But only in peripheral sectors!"

"And if it turns out you're wrong and they have breached our security—would you rather be the one who discovered it or the man who buried his head in the sand while someone observed and manipulated us via our own system?" Bollard locked eyes with the Belgian, gave him enough time to consider, but not enough for an answer. "If that is what's happening," he continued, "would he notice once you start looking for signs of a breach?"

"Depends how we go about it," groused the Belgian. "But I've nowhere near the number of people for what you're suggesting. Half my team have stopped showing up. The rest are near collapse."

"As are we all. And now we've got our backs up against the wall."

DÜSSELDORF, GERMANY

Manzano woke from the burning pain in his thigh. He had no clue how long he had slept; for a long moment, he didn't even know where the hell he was. But the pain quickly brought the events flooding back into his mind.

Pohlen was still sitting at the foot of his bed.

"How are you doing?" he asked.

"How long did I sleep?"

"Over two hours. It's seven o'clock."

"The doctor never came back?"

"No."

Manzano remembered why he was in Düsseldorf in the first place. He couldn't let these police officers get the better of him.

"I have to go to the toilet."

"Can you walk?"

Manzano tried to lift his legs off the bed. His right thigh protested bitterly. He propped himself up, determined to stand. He declined Pohlen's helping hand.

The dark hallway was in chaos. Beds were still being pushed toward the exit. People were shouting in confusion; whimpers, moans, and cries of pain punctuated the din. Manzano could not spot a single hospital uniform.

"What's going on?"

"They're evacuating the hospital," said Pohlen.

By the time they made it to the toilets, he noticed that his leg was hurting less. He decided to continue limping conspicuously. It might come in handy if Pohlen thought he was incapable of walking.

When he'd finished using the toilet, Manzano suggested, "Let's go to the emergency ward and look for the doctor."

Manzano limped along. Under an abandoned bed, he found crutches that had been tossed aside.

"I could use those," he said to Pohlen.

The BKA man bent down and handed them to Manzano.

Word of the evacuation had apparently gotten around. The waiting room of the emergency ward was deserted, as was the room where he had been treated.

"You're not going to find him," said Pohlen. "But you seem to be doing better anyway."

"What next?"

"We wait for the car that Hartlandt's sending for us. Then you're going to jail."

Under no circumstances was Manzano planning on ending up in a German jail. "I think there are some painkillers under there," he pointed to the lowest shelf of a tall storage unit. "Could you grab them for me?"

Pohlen bent down. "Where?"

Manzano hooked the handles of the crutches around the two supporting poles of the metal unit and yanked hard. The whole thing came crashing down on Pohlen, burying him. Manzano pulled the crutches free, shut the door smartly behind him, and crossed the waiting room as nonchalantly as possible. Behind him, he could hear Pohlen shouting and cursing and trying to extricate himself. Even with the crutches, every step sent an excruciating jolt of pain from his thigh to his brain, interfering with his efforts to work out where he needed to go.

But when he made it to the hallway, where the people continued to push toward the exit, he had an idea.

———

From her hiding place, a recess behind a door, Shannon watched as Manzano stepped out of the emergency ward, looked nervously around, limped down the hallway against the flow of fleeing patients, and finally disappeared down a side passageway. She was about to run after him when his guard appeared, running from the emergency ward. Shannon held her breath as the policeman hesitated for a moment to scan the room, then pushed his way through the mass of people toward the exit.

Only when he was out of sight did she abandon her hiding place to follow Manzano. She knocked into people, who pushed and shoved her out of their way, until finally she reached the end of the wall where Manzano had vanished around a corner.

The Italian was gone.

———

It was dark in the room. Manzano could walk over to the window with no danger of being seen, even from outside. He gazed down at the open space in front of the hospital: people were running this way, illuminated by the flashing blue lights of the ambulances. With no elevators in operation, getting to the sixth floor had been a daunting prospect, but once he'd figured out how to climb stairs on crutches, he had managed it in a matter of minutes. It seemed his plan was working. Despite the poor lighting, he spotted the gangly policeman looking for him in the crowd. Then he saw a second man making his way through the crowd, his gait totally different from everyone else. Hartlandt.

To ease the stabbing pain in his leg, he pulled a plastic

chair over to the window and sat down. Now he could keep vigil on the street. He hoped he could still sense danger in the darkness. Soon, if the doctor had been right, the remaining lights in the building would go out. Then he would be completely alone.

Shannon searched one room after the other but gave up before she'd even finished the ground floor. The building was too big. She would never find the guy here. Maybe he'd slipped out of the hospital in all the confusion. For a while she stood and watched the mass exodus, then she gave up and stepped into the throng, letting herself be carried out of the building. Once she was clear, she looked back one last time; she hesitated. Then she ran to the side street where she had parked the Porsche in a no parking zone.

"Help!"

Manzano didn't know how long he had been sitting at the window. The area in front of the hospital was almost empty. Now the only light came from the half moon. Had he been imagining things?

"Help!" The voice was very faint, as if it came from far away. Slowly Manzano felt his way down the dark hallway, using his crutches to check that there were no obstacles in his path. He listened. Maybe his mind had been playing tricks. Then he heard another sound. At the end of the corridor, a weak shaft of light filtered through the gap below a door. Limping clumsily toward it, he passed several open doors. From one of them came the stink of decay and feces. After a pause, he hobbled into the room and in the darkness came close to falling over a bed. He bent over to peer at the face resting on the pillow. It belonged to an older person. Manzano couldn't tell whether it was male or female. Bones covered by paper-thin skin, eyes closed, open mouth. No movement.

Where is the staff? he asked himself. Maybe over where the light was coming from?

Cautiously, he left the room and made his way toward the light.

The door was ajar. He could make out voices. His German wasn't perfect, but he could pick out a few scraps of conversation.

"We can't do this," pleaded a man's voice.

"We have to," answered a woman.

Someone was sobbing.

"I didn't become a nurse to do something like this," said the man.

"Nor I a doctor," the woman responded. "But they're going to die in the next few hours or days, even with optimal care. None of them will survive being moved, let alone the cold and lack of facilities at the shelter. To leave them here means subjecting them to unnecessary suffering. They'll starve, go thirsty, and freeze to death, slowly, lying in their own excrement. Is that what you want?"

The man was crying now.

"Besides, how are we supposed to get them downstairs with no elevators working? Do you think you can carry a five-hundred-pound patient down the stairs?"

A shudder ran through Manzano's body as it dawned on him what was going on.

"Don't think for a moment that this is something I want to do," the doctor continued. Manzano heard the quiver in her voice.

The nurse's response was to sob louder.

"None of the patients is conscious," said the doctor. "They won't feel a thing."

Who was it calling for help, then, Manzano asked himself. Had the two of them not heard? He broke into a sweat.

"I'm going now," the doctor declared, her voice thick.

Manzano moved away from the wall and hurried as best he could into the room directly across the hallway from the one where the elderly patient lay. He didn't dare close the door, for fear of arousing suspicion. As he pressed himself against the wall next to the door frame, footsteps sounded in the hallway.

"Wait!" said the nurse.

"Please," whispered the doctor, "I have to—"

"You shouldn't have to go through this alone," the nurse cut her off, his voice firmer now. "And these poor people shouldn't have to either."

Manzano heard the soft squeaking of their rubber soles as they went into the room across the hall.

Cautiously he peered around the corner. They were carrying flashlights, so he could see them as they approached the bed. The doctor, a tall woman with shoulder-length hair, placed her flashlight on the bed so that the light was cast onto the wall. The nurse, a thin young man, placed himself at the side of the bed, took the patient's frail hand, and began stroking it. As he did so, the doctor took out a syringe. She removed the tube from the IV bag, stuck the needle of the syringe into it, and injected the medicine. Then she reconnected the tube to the bag. The nurse continued to stroke the patient's hand. The doctor bent over the patient and gently caressed the patient's face, over and over. As she did so, she whispered something that Manzano was too far away to hear. He stood in the doorway, transfixed, as if the blood had frozen in his veins.

The doctor stood up and thanked the nurse, who nodded wordlessly, not letting go of the dead person's hand.

She picked up her flashlight, and for a moment the beam of light passed right over Manzano's face.

Manzano jumped back, hoping they hadn't seen him. Across the hall he heard a whisper, then steps in his direction.

Harsh light blinded him. He closed his eyes.

"Who are you?" The nurse's voice was close to cracking. "What are you doing here?"

Manzano opened his eyes, held his hand in front of his face, and stammered, in English, "The light. Please."

"You speak English?" demanded the doctor. "What are you doing here? Where are you from?"

"Italy," he answered. They had guessed he understood German fairly well and had listened in on their conversation.

The doctor fixed Manzano with a look. "You saw us, didn't you?"

Manzano nodded. "I think you're doing the right thing," he whispered in English.

The doctor continued to stare at him. Manzano met her gaze.

After a few seconds, she broke the silence. "Then get out of here. Either that or help these people."

Manzano wavered. Was this really help? He wasn't competent to judge the medical condition of these patients, so he had no choice but to rely on the doctor's assessment. But what about moral responsibility? If he were suffering with a terminal illness or facing a lingering, agonizing death, Manzano would have no hesitation in choosing assisted suicide. Yet when it came to ending the life of someone else, someone who couldn't even give consent… Thoughts raced through his head in a torrent.

But what was happening here wasn't some academic debate about assisted suicide. The doctor had been clear: either get out, or help these people. Clever woman. She hadn't asked him, "Help us." No, she had emphasized the—ostensible—selflessness of what they were doing. This way Manzano wouldn't have to see himself as an accomplice but a Good Samaritan. Except he knew he couldn't do that.

He leaned against the wall for support. Only now did he

understand what the nurse must have felt, but also what the doctor was going through. He took hold of the handles of his crutches, stood up.

"What should I do?"

"Just be there," answered the doctor in a gentle voice. "Do you think you can do that?"

Manzano nodded.

She turned to the lonely figure in the bed behind them, only revealed to Manzano now in the glow of the flashlight beam. The face belonged to a woman; her cheeks were sunken, her eyes closed. Manzano could detect no signs of life.

"Hold her hand," the doctor instructed him.

"What's wrong with her?" asked Manzano as he sat down on the edge of the bed.

"Multiple organ failure," said the doctor.

Hesitantly, Manzano reached for her hand. It was a soft hand, with slender, well-cared-for fingers. It felt cold and clammy. There was no response to his touch; the hand sat unmoving in his own. Like a small, dead fish, he thought, though he didn't like the comparison.

The doctor readied another syringe.

"Her name is Edda and she's ninety-four," she whispered. "Three weeks ago she had a major stroke, her third in two years. She suffered substantial brain damage. She has no chance of ever waking up again. A week ago, pulmonary edema occurred, and as of yesterday her kidneys and other organs began to shut down. Under normal circumstances I might give her twenty-four hours. But the machines have stopped working."

She had drawn the liquid from the vial into the syringe. She repeated the procedure with the tube connected to the IV bag that Manzano had already watched in the other room.

"Her husband has been dead for years; her kids live near Berlin and Frankfurt. Before the power went out, they managed one visit."

Manzano noticed that while the doctor related this he had involuntarily begun stroking the older woman's hand.

"She was a teacher; she taught German and history," the doctor continued. "Her children told me."

Images of a younger Edda appeared in Manzano's mind's eye. Did she have grandchildren? He caught sight of a framed picture on her bedside table. He leaned over for a closer look. It showed an old couple, formally dressed, surrounded by nine adults and five children of all ages, all dressed up to have their photo taken. The doctor plugged the tube back into the IV pouch. "It takes about five minutes," she whispered. "We'll go to the others. Do you need one of the flashlights?"

Manzano said no and watched as they left the ward. In the darkness he held Edda's hand and felt the tears run down his cheeks.

He couldn't bear the silence, so he started talking to her. Italian, because it came most easily to him. He talked about his childhood and youth in a small town near Milan, about his parents, about how they had lost their lives in a car accident and he hadn't been able to say good-bye to them, even though there was still so much to say, so much to resolve. About the women he had known, and about his German girlfriend with the French name, Claire— Claire from Osnabrück, with whom he had long been out of touch.

He assured Edda that her children and grandchildren wanted to be with her right now, but circumstances made it impossible for them, that he would tell them how she had passed gently and peacefully into the next world. He talked and talked, as if his life depended on it. He must have sat there a long time, longer than the five minutes the doctor had mentioned, until he could feel that there was no more life in the hand that he held.

Gently he laid it back on the sheet and brought her other hand to rest on top of it. Edda's expression hadn't changed in all this time. He didn't know if she had heard a single word he had said, if she sensed that she wasn't alone in her last moments. In the darkness he saw only the cavity of her mouth and the shadows into which her eyelids had sunk.

His skin tightened where the tears on his face had dried. He rose, took up his crutches, and left the ward.

Across the hall the nurse was getting to his feet. It occurred to Manzano that neither he nor the doctor had introduced themselves. Maybe it was better if they stayed nameless.

In the next half hour, Manzano held the hands of three more people: the thirty-three-year-old victim of a car accident, a seventy-seven-year-old multiple heart attack patient, and a forty-five-year-old who after a thirty-year career as a drug addict had shot up for the last time.

None of them showed any awareness of Manzano or the medical staff. Only the addict let out something like a sigh before she fell silent. After Manzano had let go of her hand, he felt an emptiness inside himself.

Only slowly did his reason for being here work its way back into Manzano's consciousness. His leg hurt, but instead of wishing the pain away he was almost glad that he still felt something. That he was alive. He stood up and held himself upright without crutches.

The doctor held her hand out to him. "Thank you."

The nurse held out his hand too. In tacit agreement they preserved their mutual anonymity.

"You'll need this," said the doctor, and she handed him her flashlight.

Manzano thanked her and hobbled down the hallway toward the stairwell.

He had no idea what to do, where to go. If Hartlandt hadn't come for him by now, he wouldn't be coming at all. Maybe he should stay here overnight. Next to the elevators he found a directory that told him which departments he would find on which floor. After making his way through the list, there was only one option he would consider. He made his way to the third floor, to the maternity ward.

———

The hotel lobby had been repurposed by people desperate for shelter. There was hardly enough room for a baby to squeeze in, let alone a full-grown woman. But as Shannon had discovered over the past few hours, every other hotel had closed its doors.

Shannon turned away, wondering where to go next. All she wanted was a bed for the night. The Porsche wasn't an option; the seats were not designed for sleep, and in any case the thermometer was showing two degrees above freezing

As she slipped into the driver's seat, Shannon had an idea. She headed back to the hospital where she had last seen Manzano and drove into the underground parking lot—the gates had probably been open for days. It was pitch-black inside the hospital. She dug out a mini flashlight from the car's tool kit, shouldered her rucksack, and went upstairs to the reception area. The hospital's halls were deserted; there were sheets everywhere, rags, medical supplies. The smell was repulsive. The circle of light from her flashlight hovered over the directory beside the elevators.

Third floor, maternity ward. The only beds in which she would feel at ease. She took the stairs.

———

"Quietly," said Hartlandt. "So he isn't warned, if he's still here."

Eight police officers and four dogs followed him into the hospital. As they moved through the deserted corridors and rooms, they pointed their flashlights into every possible hiding place.

Hartlandt led the way into the emergency room where Manzano had been operated on. He rummaged around in the overflowing waste bin, fished out the scrap of Manzano's jeans that the doctor had cut away, and passed it to the dog handler. The dogs sniffed nervously at the rag. One of them headed for the door. The others followed, straining on their leashes.

———

Lying under four blankets, Manzano gazed through the window into the darkness. He could only dream of sleep. The events on the sixth floor had shaken him too deeply. What was more, the smell of feces, decay, and death that pervaded the other floors was seeping into the maternity ward as well.

For a moment he thought he heard footsteps, saw a beam of light. No, he couldn't get paranoid now!

He turned onto his other side, restless. For the second time he thought he heard something, thought he saw a weak glow moving around in the hallway outside, but it vanished immediately. He got out of bed and limped to the door. This time he heard footsteps quite clearly. And hushed voices. And another sound that he couldn't place. As if someone was tapping on a stone floor with plastic spoons.

Then a whimper. Dogs! And a hissed command. He felt himself break out in a sweat. Hastily he limped back to his bed and reached for the crutches. Then he went outside the ward and listened.

The sounds were coming from the stairwell. Manzano looked around, frantic. Was it Hartlandt after all, prowling after him?

Manzano stood by the elevators, listening to the approaching footsteps. It was too late to flee into the stairwell now.

And he didn't know where the hallway ended. Fair chance it was a dead end. In his fear, he could think of only one escape route. His eyes turned to the window.

Then, from the hallway, he heard barking.

———

"Police! Who's there? Come on out!"

Shocked and blinded by the sudden light, Shannon put her hands in front of her eyes.

"I'm a journalist!" she cried, in English. "I'm a journalist!"

"What's she saying?"

"Hands up! Get out of the bed!"

"I'm a journalist! I'm a journalist!"

"Out! Let's go!"

Dogs barking.

Shannon couldn't see a thing. She kept shouting as she tried to free her legs from the tangled sheets.

"It's a woman!"

"What's she saying?"

"She says she's a journalist."

Finally, Shannon's feet came free and she swung them over the side of the bed. She stood up, one hand shielding her eyes, the other held up as if in greeting. From somewhere behind the flashlights she could hear dogs growling.

"Who are you?" asked a tall, muscular man with short hair. He spoke English with only a hint of a German accent. "What are you doing here?"

"I couldn't find a hotel to stay the night," said Shannon, truthfully.

The man shone his flashlight on her, examining her from head to toe. Now she recognized him. He had led Manzano away, chased him, and taken him to the hospital.

"Have you seen anyone else around?"

"No."

The men searched the other beds. When they had

finished, their leader told her, "You should find yourself a better place to stay."

Shannon stood by the bed while the men stormed into the next ward. She could feel herself shivering, but she didn't know if it was on account of the shock or the cold. She crawled back under her blankets and listened to the police officers in pursuit. Their voices and footsteps faded, then returned, marched straight past her room, and died away.

———

On the fourth floor, Hartlandt and his people searched with as little result as on the fifth. It was long past midnight. Both men and dogs were dead tired after the previous day's duties. The dark building, with its forsaken, deserted wards, was even more depressing than a hospital under normal circumstances. With eyelids drooping, they worked their way down the hallway of the sixth floor. Then the dogs started to whimper louder and louder.

"Could that be him?" Hartlandt asked one of the dog handlers.

"Maybe. Although this whimpering usually signals something else…"

The animals were pulling eagerly now. The men let themselves be led until they came to one of the last wards. The beams of their flashlights wandered over the outlines of beds, eight in total, packed in tightly. Sheets covered the patients from head to toe.

Hartlandt stepped up to the first bed, threw the sheet back, and looked into the pale, emaciated face of an older woman. He had seen enough dead people over the course of his career to recognize one when it was lying in front of him. He hurried to the next bed. Awaiting him there was the corpse of a gaunt woman—a junkie, thought Hartlandt, judging by the bad skin and rotten teeth.

By then two of his colleagues had checked the beds on the other side.

"It looks like they stowed the dead patients in here," one of them surmised.

The dogs waited in the doorway, whimpering, tails tucked between their legs.

"With no elevators working, the staff probably couldn't manage to get them down to the morgue," said another.

Hartlandt swept his flashlight beam over the remaining beds. Two of the corpses appeared to have been truly obese. "Nobody could carry these two down the stairs." He turned away. "And what would be the point? The morgue's freezers aren't working."

He gave the men a signal and they left the room.

"Let's keep going."

———

As the footsteps died away, the corpse began to weigh even more heavily on Manzano. The dead man's head lay next to his, the torso covering his own. Manzano hardly dared breathe. Weight, fear, pure horror robbed him of breath.

The stench was unbearable. The sheets beneath the dead man had been covered in dried blood and feces—but this Manzano discovered only when he was already lying halfway under him. More than once Manzano had been forced to stifle his retching as he felt his clothes grow damp from liquids secreted by the corpse. Still he waited until the silence had gone undisturbed for several minutes before throwing the limp limbs aside and swinging his own stiff limbs off the bed.

As he bent to retrieve his crutches from under the bed, he stumbled forward until he fell against the wall, his gaze focusing in horror on the shadowy shapes on the beds around him. His breathing was shallow, and tears ran down his cheeks. At some point, he took a couple more steps toward the door.

He listened again, for a long time. The hallway was totally silent. He opened the door a crack. Nothing. Then he felt his way down the corridor in pitch-darkness. The doctor and the nurse were gone; presumably they'd left before Hartlandt and the dogs had shown up. His entire body was shaking uncontrollably. His pants were wet from his hiding place and smelled of something truly repellent. He pulled them off. Now he was in his boxers. If only he could have a shower—a long, hot one, with plenty of lather.

A small eternity later he had cautiously made his way down to the third floor, having seen no sign whatsoever of the men with the dogs. He made his way back to the ward, to the bed he had left a few hours earlier. He crawled under his four blankets, his entire body trembling. He did not expect to sleep a wink for the rest of the night.

DAY 7—FRIDAY

THE HAGUE, NETHERLANDS

"I think I have a fever," groaned Marie, standing in the doorway with shoulders slumped, her arms hugging her torso. Despite the cold in the house, a thin sheen of sweat covered her pallid face. Her eyes were red. "I can't make it to the food line today."

Bollard put a hand on her forehead, his mind elsewhere, thinking about the calls he needed to make as soon as he got to the office. "You should go back to bed," he told her. "Do we have any flu medicine?"

"Yes. I'll take some. You need to go—if you don't get there early, there'll be nothing left."

"Go where?" he said, confused.

———

Bollard chained the bicycle to a signpost. He wouldn't get any farther on it. Hundreds of people were packed into the small square. He could make out a number of horse-drawn carts, surrounded by sturdy young men armed with clubs and pitchforks. From a distance came the low rumble of a truck as it slowly drew closer. There was a ripple of movement through the crowd. From a street on the opposite side of the square, a weak beam of light filtered through. It grew brighter, then the truck pushed its way into the sea of people. Immediately some of the waiting crowd began to climb up on the running boards and bumpers. Bollard pushed into the middle of the square. He wasn't the only one. Soon he was completely boxed in by people. There was cursing and shouting. This is what it must feel like to be caught in a riptide that you can't swim against, he thought. He tried to hold his ground but he was pushed off to the side instead of toward the delivery truck. People were hanging off like bees on a hive.

The rations truck came to a halt in the middle of the square, and for the next minute, it sat there. Then the crew finally managed to open the doors that the crowds had been blocking. It took them a few more minutes, escorted by two police officers, to make it to the back of the truck. They opened two big swinging doors and climbed onto the bumper. On either side of them, police officers used their batons to keep the crowd at bay.

Bollard saw two small children bobbing above the crowd, hoisted on their parents' shoulders to signal that here was a family in need of provision. Behind him, the first scuffles broke out.

Stoically the men handed out packages to anyone who managed to get to the edge of the loading deck. Inside the truck, identical bundles were stacked right up to the ceiling. Bollard was too far away to stand a chance of claiming a food parcel.

In the tangled mass of people, fighting broke out in earnest now. Some took advantage of the situation and forced their way past the brawlers. Bollard, at a loss, wondered how Marie had managed to come home with food the day before.

The police officers defending the cargo were losing their battle to maintain order. Beating off the crowd with batons was having no effect; for every rioter that fell, another would take his place. Then one of the officers pulled out his service weapon and fired a shot into the air.

For an instant the crowd froze. The drivers seized the opportunity to slam the doors. After pressing one last package into each policeman's arms, they jumped down from the truck. The officers then escorted them, guns drawn, as they shoved their way back to the cab and climbed inside.

Within seconds the cab disappeared beneath a swarm of people.

Bollard heard the deep churning of the engine and looked on helplessly as the truck slowly made its way through the disappointed crowd. Whoever got in the way could count on being run over.

Above the baying of the crowd, Bollard heard the clear and terrible crack of a cobblestone striking the windshield. The vehicle began to pick up speed. Bollard heard ugly, dull thuds; the truck reached the street and accelerated. Those who had been clinging on had either let go or fallen off. Some picked themselves up, faces twisted in pain, and dusted themselves down; others lay still on the ground.

DÜSSELDORF, GERMANY

Manzano didn't know where any of the official food distribution sites were in this city, and he wouldn't have dared to visit them anyway. Hartlandt would most likely have circulated his description, assuming he would turn up in need of food. After he had searched the empty and deserted hospital kitchen yet again, he wound his way back to the entrance. On the way he looked into the ward, hoping to find some winter clothing that would fit him. He found Band-Aids, bandages, tape, and disinfectant, which he stuffed into his jacket pockets. He also grabbed a pair of scissors and two scalpels. Finally, he came upon a room piled high with bags full of white trousers and shirts—all soiled and presumably destined for the laundry service, had it been operating. He climbed back up to the third floor and tried the gynecology and internal medicine departments. In a cabinet he stumbled upon two pairs of trousers that someone had left behind. The first was too small; the other seemed clean enough and was even his approximate size.

He sat down heavily on a bed, changed his bandage, and

slipped into the trousers. Now he could at least risk going out on the street without immediately arousing suspicion. But where would he go?

"Piero?"

Manzano jumped out of his skin. He looked around in a panic.

"Hello, Piero."

In the doorway stood Lauren Shannon.

"What…what are you doing here?" he stammered.

"I spent the night in the hospital."

"But how did you get here?"

"I followed you from The Hague. I have a fast car, as you know."

"But…"

"I followed you all the way to Talaefer. I saw them taking you into custody, you trying to escape, you getting injured. It was last night, here in the hospital, that I finally lost you, after you got the better of your guard. What exactly is going on here?"

"I'd like to know that myself."

He sat back down on the bed.

"Are you alone?" he asked carefully.

"What is it?" she asked. "You're giving me this weird look."

"Who told you where I was going when I left The Hague?"

"Nobody. I saw you packing, so I did the same and went after you."

He sat there, studying her face intently, conscious of the wound in his thigh pulsing. Then he told her the whole story.

THE HAGUE, NETHERLANDS

The jostling in the square had quieted down. Most of the crowd had moved on; those that remained gathered around the farmers on their horse-drawn carts, trying to outbid one another for a few potatoes, turnips, carrots, heads of cabbage, or withered winter apples. The guards, armed with pitchforks or shotguns, saw off any unruly customers. Bollard took out his wallet and checked its contents. Thirty euros. How much could he buy with that?

He had to try at least. He pushed his way to the front, held his cash up in the air, and shouted, "Here! Over here!"

The farmer on the cart ignored him. In other outstretched hands, Bollard saw significantly larger sums. Why the hell didn't the police stop this craziness? he wondered. As a Europol officer, this was outside his jurisdiction. And without a gun, there was nothing he could do in any case. A police badge would only encourage derision. Exhausted, he let himself be pushed aside.

They had enough canned goods for Marie and the kids' lunch, he thought as he made his way back to his bicycle. But what about tomorrow?

DÜSSELDORF, GERMANY

"So what now?" asked Shannon.

"No idea," Manzano replied.

"Hey, you're the computer genius. If it's really true that some unknown person sent the emails from your computer, can you find out how they did it, or even who it was?"

"Maybe. Depends on how professional this person is. If he's good, there won't be any clues. But I need my laptop to find out."

His injured thigh throbbed.

"Let's assume that our friends in the police force are upstanding officers who are only doing their jobs. How would the attackers have known about your trip?"

"They'd have to be spying on Europol somehow. Bollard had my laptop under surveillance. He could have opened a gateway for the attackers."

"If someone has actually infiltrated the Europol system, would it be possible to detect the intrusion?"

"If you knew where to look and looked long enough, most likely yes. Unfortunately, their software specialists have more important things to do at the moment."

"OK. You wait here. I'm going to try something."

"What am I supposed to do in the meantime?"

"Rest. Believe me, you'll have a hard time finding a better spot at the moment. I'll pick you up in a couple of hours."

THE HAGUE, NETHERLANDS

There was no need for Bollard to get off his bicycle. He could see the bank was closed. He pedaled on past. A couple of blocks farther on, he found another. Behind its door was a handwritten sign saying the bank was closed until further notice. Increasingly anxious, he pedaled on toward Europol. Oh God, he thought. Oh God, oh God. He passed three more banks. Lights off in every one. His last-chance saloon—the Hotel Gloria, where he had lodged the Italian—was on the way. Built to accommodate guests of Europol, it was better equipped than the other hotels in the city.

A few lone lamps shimmered in the lobby. Bollard thrust his ID toward the receptionist. The man nodded grimly. Bollard passed swiftly through the deserted restaurant and swung through some doors into the kitchen.

He was greeted by a cook wiping his hands on a soiled apron.

"Entry for staff only," he said.

Bollard showed him his ID. "I need a few meals. What have you got?"

"Are you a guest?"

"Do you want to keep your job?"

"Potatoes with vegetables or vegetables with potatoes—your choice," the man responded drily.

"I'll take some of each. I need it to go."

"I don't have takeout containers."

"Then I'll come back with some later. If you care about your job, make sure you pile the portions high."

DÜSSELDORF, GERMANY

Shannon uncovered a couple of rubber tubes, scalpels, funnels, and a bucket from the hospital. Abandoned cars littered the underground parking lot. Flashlight gripped between her teeth, Shannon measured the opening to the fuel tank of her Porsche, then she walked to the nearest car. The fuel cap cover was locked. She returned to her car, found a wrench in the emergency tool kit along with a second tool for leverage. Then she went back to the other car, pried off the cover, fed the tube into the tank, crouched next to the car, and started to suck. The driving force of our civilization, she thought. How much longer?

After two more rounds of siphoning, Shannon's Porsche had a full tank. She threw her fueling utensils into the trunk—she might need them again. She stowed the tools she'd used for breaking the cover off in the trunk. The scalpel she dropped into the compartment on the driver-side door. In the underground parking lot, the roar of her car's flashy exhaust was twice as loud as on the street.

RATINGEN, GERMANY

Hartlandt opened his laptop and brought up the message that had come in the previous day.

"CORRECTION" blared the subject line, just to make sure everybody would catch on right away. Granted, the news warranted the fanfare, even if it did shatter the one potential lead they had on the attackers. In the message, Berlin revised the reports from the previous day about arson in substations and the dynamited transmission towers. Suddenly, most of the cases weren't acts of sabotage after all but were attributable to other causes. The fire in Lübeck had originated from a short circuit, and two of the towers in the north had collapsed under the weight of freezing rain and snow.

He picked up the radiophone and called the people who'd sent the message at headquarters in Berlin.

"You're the third guy to call me about this" was the man's answer. "No, I didn't send that message. And I don't know anyone else who could've done it either. And on top of that, we have no information from the utilities."

"But I'm looking at the message right now," argued Hartlandt.

"I'm not disputing that you received the message," said the other. "Or that it was sent from my computer. But—"

"So some jerk is sending out information from your computer, but neither you nor your colleagues know anything about it?"

"Looks that way to me."

"Does that mean that the original information is still accurate?"

"Well, no one's told us any different," the other replied, hesitant now.

"Then get it clarified, ASAP!" Hartlandt bellowed, and he hung up.

He called Bollard.

"You're not going to believe this," he said and recounted his conversation.

"And your colleague in Berlin denies all knowledge of this message?" said Bollard.

"Yes," said Hartlandt. "Just as the Italian denied sending that email."

———

In the Talaefer parking lot, there were fewer vehicles than the day before. Shannon parked the Porsche behind a van so that it wouldn't be so noticeable from the entrance. Manzano's car was still standing right where he had left it. Shannon slung the bag with her camera and laptop over her shoulder.

The same woman was sitting at the reception desk, the same woman who had witnessed her "little girl lost" act the previous day.

"Have you lost yourself again already?" she asked in heavily accented English.

"I'd like to see Mr. Hartlandt," Shannon announced. "And I'm going to stay right here until I get to see him or until he exits the building."

From the woman's confused look, Shannon could tell that that had been beyond her poor grasp of English. She repeated it more slowly.

"If you don't leave, I will call security." So the woman had got the gist.

"Go ahead. I'm a journalist and I'll file a report on it."

The receptionist sighed and reached for the telephone.

Moments later, two men appeared behind the desk. Shannon turned as three more entered from a hallway. Shannon recognized one of them immediately.

"I've been looking for you," she called out to Hartlandt.

Hartlandt and his crew, a man and a woman, stopped. Shannon felt uneasy under his gaze. Did he recognize her as the woman from the hospital last night?

"What do you want?" he asked her in English.

Behind her, the security guards inched closer.

"I'm a journalist from CNN. I'm interested in what German investigators are looking for at one of the most important manufacturers of power plant control systems worldwide."

He fixed her with a look and said, "Excuse me, I didn't catch your name."

In that moment, Shannon was praying for three things:

that he hadn't watched too much TV in the past few days and so had missed her "fifteen minutes of fame"; that Bollard hadn't sent through anything about her connection to Manzano and her disappearance from The Hague; and that she could somehow untangle herself from this mess she had so blithely walked into.

"Sandra Brown."

"What can I do for you, Sandra Brown?"

Shannon threw a look of triumph at the two men, who by that point had grabbed her by the arms. They loosened their grip.

"You can tell me what's going on here. People are aware now that the power outages were caused deliberately. What's Talaefer's role?"

"Follow me."

With a shrug, she left the meatheads from security standing.

Hartlandt led her to an office on the ground floor. The room was flowing with crates and computers.

"Can I offer you anything? Coffee? A snack?"

Yes, yes, yes! screamed the voice in her head, but she managed to say, "Sure, thanks."

The moment he'd gone, Shannon cased the room. It looked like an improvised workspace. On a file cabinet next to the wall, there were stacks of hard drives and laptops. The one on top looked a lot like Manzano's. She took a closer look. There was the same green sticker she'd seen on Manzano's computer.

That was almost too lucky.

She returned to her seat in the nick of time; Hartlandt walked back in seconds later. When he placed the coffee, a bottle of water, and a sandwich before her, it took an act of will not to wolf all of it down at once.

"So," he said with a smile. "Ask your questions. Since you don't have any recording devices, we can go ahead and speak openly."

"Maybe I could charge my camera here?"

"Sorry, but energy is very valuable at the moment. We need the electricity for more important things," said Hartlandt.

"And what would those be, exactly?" asked Shannon.

Shannon sank her teeth into the sandwich. She couldn't remember ever eating anything so delicious. She chewed slowly and intently.

"You've already guessed," answered Hartlandt.

"You confirm then that you're here at Talaefer as part of your investigation into the blackout?"

Another bite. Then a sip of hot coffee, with milk! It didn't bother her at all that there was way too much sugar, quite the opposite.

"Every manufacturer is assisting with the investigation at the moment," said Hartlandt. "Talaefer is no exception."

"Have you found anything yet?"

"So far, no."

Shannon didn't ask any more; she ate her sandwich instead. Let Hartlandt be the one to talk. Meanwhile, she tried to figure out a way to get hold of Manzano's laptop without being noticed.

"Is it good?"

Shannon nodded.

"Would you like anything else?"

"Another coffee would be great."

He had barely left the room when she grabbed hold of Manzano's laptop and stuffed it in her bag. When Hartlandt returned a few minutes later, she took the coffee from him and poured it down her throat in one go. Then she said, "I take it there's not much more you're going to tell me, right? Thanks for your time."

"Can you still get through to your network?" Hartlandt asked as they walked toward the exit.

"It ain't easy, but it works."

They had reached the lobby.

"Is it possible you don't know that the United States was attacked yesterday?"

Shannon froze. "What?" It was close to a scream.

"I thought it might interest you."

Before she could answer, he led her out of the door.

"I had no idea that CNN had a bureau in Düsseldorf," he said as they parted.

"We don't," she said absently, before regaining her composure. "I made the trip over especially. I still had a little gas left in the tank."

"I wish you a good trip back then."

———

Hartlandt stood in front of the entrance and watched the woman leave. As she drove off in her bright Porsche, he gave a single nod. As soon as she had left the parking lot, the gray Audi A6 with Pohlen at the wheel started up and followed her at a distance. Hartlandt pulled the printout out of his pocket that showed Lauren Shannon reporting the attack on the power grid on television and, in a photo taken by surveillance camera, in a hotel room in The Hague with Piero Manzano.

"Do you think we're stupid, girl?"

———

Shannon checked her rearview mirror again. The gray Audi had reappeared. The streets were so deserted that every car drew her attention. She spent a few minutes trying to find a radio station, but only static came through the speakers. She could barely concentrate on driving as her thoughts jumped from her parents to her grandparents and her half siblings, scattered across the United States. She thought of friends, people she knew from school, people she hadn't seen in years. The gray Audi was still there. For a few minutes she was distracted by a military convoy that stretched for a kilometer in the oncoming lane. By the time she reached the outskirts of Düsseldorf, the Audi was still there.

She had saved the location of the hospital in her navigation system. She could take a few detours and it would still lead her back there. Acting on impulse, she turned from the route indicated, her eyes darting back and forth between the road and the rearview mirror.

The Audi was still visible.

One more test.

Yep. It was definitely tailing her.

It could only be one of Hartlandt's men. She had become familiar with their methods. They had shot Manzano cold-bloodedly when he tried to flee. Shannon accelerated. Felt herself being pushed back into the seat. A test with the pedal, a quick look in the mirror. The Audi was falling behind. The motor roared, the speedometer climbed up to 130 kilometers per hour. At the next intersection, Shannon braked hard, swerved right, and accelerated again. When she came to another intersection, she repeated the maneuver. Now she hadn't the faintest idea where she was. Somewhere in the industrial district. After the seventh or eighth turnoff, she risked a look behind her. The Audi was gone. She slowed and took a deep breath.

The female voice of the GPS gave her a new route. Shannon followed it.

Her stomach dropped. There was the Audi in her mirror again. Resigned, she let the GPS lead her back to the access road. Shannon slid the laptops out of the bag on the passenger seat, then the cameras and everything else. From the glove compartment, she took the user manual, chunky as a phone directory, and stuck it in the bag. With the press of a button she slid open her window and tossed the pack out. In the side mirror she watched the bag roll over and over. The Audi slowed. A man leaped from the car and picked up the bag. Shannon floored it. Quickly the car in the rearview mirror grew smaller. At the next intersection, she turned off onto a side street and reemerged in a web of small avenues that made up a residential area. The Audi did not reappear.

Shannon smiled with thin lips; she wasn't celebrating. After ten more minutes she risked following the GPS's instructions again. The race had used up a quarter tank of gas. She would have to "fuel up" again at the hospital.

NANTEUIL, FRANCE

Annette was scared out of her wits. There were two men in hazmat suits standing at the door. Luckily, they had come to their aid.

"One piece of luggage per person," said the crackling voice behind one of the masks.

Behind them, frightened people were crowded into the back of an open truck.

"We'll get to come back here afterward, right?" asked Celeste.

"We don't have no information," answered the man in the hazmat suit. "Our job is to evacuate."

Annette had read about Chernobyl and Fukushima. She'd wondered then what it must have been like for people, having to leave their homes in a hurry, afraid they may never return. Panicked that they might already have been severely, even mortally affected by the radiation. With the prospect of starting again in a strange place instead of living out their twilight years in their own home. This was the fear she now heard in Celeste's voice. For eleven generations, over three hundred years, the family had lived on this property, despite the upheavals of the French Revolution and two world wars.

Never had Annette imagined that one day she herself would have to join a refugee convoy. When she and

Bertrand had left Paris, she'd told herself it was nothing more than a brief vacation. Only after they had killed all the Bollards' chickens and used up all their supplies, having been barred from leaving the house, did she admit to herself that she was now a displaced person.

Her attention shifted to her body. Did anything feel strange? Unusual? Some sensation that would indicate that the radiation was already gnawing away at her cells?

While the two men in suits stowed their luggage in a compartment under the cargo bay, Bertrand gave her a hand up. The people on the wooden benches slid closer together to make room for them. Celeste sat down next to her, her eyes never leaving her farm.

As the doors closed and they set off, all Annette could see of the Bollards was the backs of their heads. They were both watching their beloved home grow smaller, not knowing if they would ever see it again.

DÜSSELDORF, GERMANY

Shannon parked the Porsche in the underground parking lot, right in front of the door to the staircase. She grabbed the laptop and the flashlight, jumped out of the car, and hurried up the stairs to Manzano on the third floor. She stumbled, out of breath, into the ward where she had left him. He was lying on one of the beds, covered in blankets, his head turned to the side.

"Piero?" she said, breathless.

When he didn't move, she called to him more loudly and hurried to his bedside.

"Piero!"

His eyelids fluttered, and he raised his head sluggishly.

"We have to get out of here!" she said, holding up the laptop and waving it around. "Come on!"

"Where...where did you get that?"

"Later!"

She tore the blankets off his legs. A glistening dark spot the size of a plate stood out on his right trouser leg. When she froze, he said, "It's fine. Give me the crutches."

As fast as his injury allowed, Manzano limped after her. In the stairwell Shannon lit the way. When they reached the door to the garage she put a finger to her lips and signaled for him to wait. She turned off the flashlight, opened the door a crack, and peered out. In the darkness she could barely see a thing, no Audi either.

"The Porsche is right by this door," she whispered. "I'm going to unlock it now with the remote. Then you come through and climb in."

Shannon edged the door open. The lights of the Porsche flashed as she unlocked the doors.

Manzano hobbled forward, catching the shadow that fell over Shannon's face. Someone was standing in the doorway, blocking his way. Manzano recognized Pohlen's powerful figure. With all his strength, Manzano rammed his crutches into the policeman's stomach. Pohlen doubled over, and Manzano brought the crutch down hard on his head. Once, twice, a third time. Pohlen fell and held his arm up in defense. Manzano kicked him in the chest with his good leg, the injured one almost giving out. He heard a whistling sound and landed one more kick. Pohlen cringed, but he didn't fight back. Behind the Porsche a second man was kneeling over Shannon. Manzano could only make out the back of her head. Before the man could defend himself, Manzano had already knocked him in the skull twice with the crutches. He fell to one side, unconscious.

Shannon pulled herself up to sitting, looked around in a panic, and screamed, "The keys! The laptop!"

Manzano saw that Pohlen was getting to his feet. He limped over to him and struck him in the face once more with the crutches.

"Got it!" cried Shannon.

As Manzano turned back toward the car, Pohlen reached out to grab him. The passenger door was already open, and Shannon had started the engine. Manzano threw himself into the seat and the Porsche tore off, motor revving and tires squealing, Manzano panting in the passenger seat as the door snapped shut on its own.

Shannon skidded around a curve, braking so suddenly that Manzano almost hit the dashboard, and came to a stop next to a gray car. She ripped open the door, a hand in the side compartment.

"Ouch! Damn it!" She kneeled next to the car, jabbing at the front tire with something. When she ran around the back he spotted a small blade in her hand. She punctured the rear tire too, let go of the scalpel, and was back in the driver's seat before the clatter of the blade against the asphalt had died away.

She steered carefully onto the street. Manzano saw that her right hand was bleeding.

"Where are we going?" he asked.

"The hell out of here," Shannon answered.

BERLIN, GERMANY

"Conference room," the chancellor's secretary whispered to Michelsen. He hastened his step, Michelsen following in his wake. The cabinet members and crisis team were already tapping fingers impatiently in front of the screens as they awaited the start of the teleconference. Only the chancellor was missing. European heads of state, ministers, and top officials peered down from the monitors.

"Urgent crisis meeting," explained the defense minister.

Whispers, murmurs.

"What's this all about?" the chancellor called out as he stormed into the room.

The defense minister shrugged.

The chancellor lowered himself into his seat, where the

camera would capture him, pressed the button to activate the mic, and shouted his question into the virtual round.

Michelsen had become familiar with these faces over the past few days. It wasn't always possible for the same individual to represent his or her country at every meeting, but it had been agreed that each member state would confine its choice of representatives to a maximum of three. So Michelsen was surprised when she saw a new face on the Spanish screen. At second glance, she realized that the man wore a uniform. An uncomfortable feeling crept over her.

The Spaniard, a bullish man with a mustache and heavy bags under his eyes, answered: "We wanted to inform our coalition partners as soon as possible that the prime minister and the entire government of our country consider themselves no longer capable of fulfilling the duties of office... In order to maintain public order, the army chiefs of staff under my leadership have declared themselves prepared to command the affairs of state until further notice."

Michelsen felt as though she had been trampled by the stampeding bulls at the annual fiesta in Pamplona. The military in Spain had seized power in a coup.

THE HAGUE, NETHERLANDS

"There was something important I had to do," said Bollard sourly. He had no interest in defending himself for having to find food for his family. "When the people in charge don't provide enough food, then we have to find it ourselves."

Wrapped in a thick jacket, Bollard sat with the Europol director and the rest of the leadership team. Since the previous night the building management had reduced the supply of electricity to cover essentials only. The heating had been dialed down to eighteen degrees. Most of the elevators had been shut down. Those who still made it in to work were all wrapped in thick layers.

"We should arrange for a special provision for Europol employees and their families." Bollard grew heated. "Or soon we won't be able to function. Half of the staff has already stopped reporting for duty."

"I'll see what I can do," Director Ruiz said guardedly.

———

"Message just in from Interpol," one of the team called out as Bollard walked into the incident room. "I can't work out if it's good news or bad."

"Don't talk in riddles," snapped Bollard, striding across the room to look at the monitor for himself.

A photograph of a corpse filled the screen. He scrolled down and more images appeared: a close-up of the dead man's face. Several bullet wounds to the chest…

The images were accompanied by a police report from Bali, describing how the victim had been found that morning, local time, by farmers in a patch of forest near the village of Gegelang. The dead man had been provisionally identified as the missing German national, Hermann Dragenau.

Bollard repeated the name while he sifted through his memory. "That's the Talaefer employee they're looking for—the chief architect of their SCADA systems!"

They compared images of Dragenau with the photos of the dead man.

"They do look similar," Bollard's colleague said.

"Is there anything there about who killed him?" asked Bollard.

"No. They found neither money nor valuables nor identification on him. Could be a straightforward case of robbery-homicide."

"You think this is a coincidence?" asked Bollard. "A man on our short list of suspects for tampering with the SCADA systems of Europe's power plants flies to Bali a couple of days before the devastating blackout that he might just be complicit in, and as soon as we start looking for him he turns up dead. Whatever he knew, he can't talk now!"

Bollard stood up.

"I don't believe in coincidence. Hartlandt's going to have to go through every aspect of this Dragenau's life and shine a light in its darkest corner!"

BETWEEN DÜSSELDORF AND COLOGNE, GERMANY

The Porsche's headlights cut through the twilight.

"Shit," cursed Manzano.

"What's up?"

She heard him typing frantically. For the past half hour, Manzano had been bent over his laptop, totally absorbed. He had murmured unintelligible things to himself, interspersed with outbursts of surprise.

"Well, what is it?"

"There's an IP address here," said Manzano, excited. "We need power. And an internet connection. Urgently."

"No problem," Shannon replied. "Plenty of those to go around."

"I'm serious," Manzano insisted. "Every night at 1:55 a.m. my computer sent data to a certain IP address. You know what I'm talking about when I say IP address?"

"IP as in internet protocol. It's a computer's address within a network and on the internet as well."

"Exactly. Theoretically, you can use it to locate any computer. And my laptop sent data to an address I don't recognize. My guess is that he broke in through the Europol network."

"So it was the Euro-cops then?"

"I don't know. I need an internet connection to find out more." He clapped his hand against his forehead. "I'm such a jerk! I know where we have to go!" He leaned forward, inspected the GPS. "Do you know how to use this thing?"

"Where do we have to go?"

"Brussels."

Shannon pressed a few buttons to bring up the route. "A good two hundred kilometers," she said. She cast a look at the dashboard. "There's enough in the tank. So, why Brussels?"

"I know someone there."

"And they've got power and internet access?"

"If the Monitoring and Information Center of the European Commission has no power and no internet connection, then we really are fucked. Pardon my language."

"Fine. The GPS says it'll take two hours."

"But first, I need something to eat," Manzano said.

"Where do we get that?"

BRUSSELS, BELGIUM

Sophia hurriedly stuffed a piece of bread into her mouth while the others trickled into the conference room. Last to come in was the head of the MIC, Zoltán Nagy. He got straight to the point.

"We can forget about help from the United States," Nagy said. "What's more, any help we can expect from the Russians and Chinese, from Turkey, Brazil, and others, must now be shared between Europe and the United States."

For a few seconds there was a stunned silence. Then they started to run through the latest updates.

"NATO high command has invoked Article 5," Nagy said in a morbid voice. "According to the principle of collective defense, members of the alliance will proceed with full resolve against the aggressors. There remains, however, no indication as to who those aggressors are."

Sophia was thinking of Piero Manzano. She hadn't

heard a word from him. Had he been able to help Europol in tracking down the culprits?

The International Atomic Energy Agency had raised the accident in Saint-Laurent to level 6, one step below the catastrophes in Chernobyl and Fukushima. "The evacuation zone has been expanded to thirty kilometers," reported the team member tasked with following the matter. "Cities such as Blois and certain neighborhoods in Orléans are among those affected by this. It's possible that the area surrounding the power plant, including parts of the Loire Valley, a UNESCO World Heritage site, will be uninhabitable for decades, possibly centuries. France has officially asked us for help. Japan has offered to send experts."

"I guess they should know what they're doing," someone commented sarcastically.

"A similar scenario threatens the area around Temelín in the Czech Republic, which now stands at INES 4," the man continued. "The IAEA reports level 1 and 2 incidents at seven other nuclear power plants across Europe."

"It doesn't directly affect us," said a colleague, "but a serious breakdown is also being reported at the Arkansas Nuclear One facility in America. The same failure of the backup power supply we've seen reported here."

They understood little about conditions for the civilian population across Europe. They could only extrapolate; all they knew were their own personal experiences here in Brussels. The early sense of solidarity had started to diminish. It was as if good deeds were now rationed too, with most people reserving their help for friends or family only.

"Reports of unrest and looting are coming in from several cities," said a female colleague.

Not even a hint of good news, Sophia sighed. The situation was as bleak as the night outside.

BETWEEN DÜSSELDORF AND COLOGNE, GERMANY

Out of the darkness ahead of them a house appeared.

"There's a light up ahead," said Manzano.

Shannon steered the car toward it. A narrow, paved road led off the street. Shannon followed it until a large farmhouse appeared before them. Three windows were lit on the ground floor. The residents must have heard the engine, because within minutes someone had opened the door. At first they could see only a silhouette against the light.

"What do you want?" asked a man; he was pointing a rifle in their direction.

"Please, we're looking for something to eat," said Manzano in broken German.

The man eyed them warily.

"Where are you from?"

"I'm an Italian, and she's an American journalist."

"Nice car you've got there." The man gestured toward the Porsche with his gun. "Still runs too. Mind if I take a look?" He took a step toward them, letting the gun drop.

Shannon hesitated, then she walked over to the car with him.

"Never sat in one of these," he said. "Can I give it a try?"

Shannon opened the door, and he sat down in the driver's seat. Manzano had walked over to join them.

"The keys," the man said and held out his hand. When Shannon didn't react, he pointed the barrel of the rifle at her.

"I said, the keys," he repeated.

Shannon handed them over.

The man turned the ignition. The car door was still wide open. The gun, held above his thigh, was pointing at Shannon.

"Sounds good. And there's fuel in the tank too."

He slammed the door and, before Shannon or Manzano could react, drove at high speed through an open barn door.

Shannon and Manzano gave chase. When they got to

the barn he had already climbed out and was pointing the gun at them.

"Get out of here!"

"You can't—" cried Shannon in English, but Manzano held her back.

"As you've just seen, I can."

"Our things," said Manzano. "At least give us the things we have in the car."

The man thought for a moment, then he pulled Shannon's rucksack out of the backseat and threw it at their feet.

"The laptop too," pleaded Manzano, adding, "But don't throw it. Please!"

He took a few steps toward the car, and the man raised the gun barrel. Manzano froze.

"What do you need a computer for?"

"It's no use to you," Manzano responded. And repeated, "Please."

"Get it yourself," the man said. "But no false moves."

Manzano pulled the laptop out from under the passenger seat.

"Now get out of here!"

He closed the door from inside.

Manzano and Shannon looked at each other and took a few cautious steps over to the front door of the house, which was swinging open, weak light coming out of it.

"That asshole," hissed Shannon, then a shadow appeared in the door.

"I said get out of here!" the man shouted. A shot shattered the silence. Dirt and gravel sprayed from the ground.

"Shit!" swore Shannon, and she jumped back. When the next shot landed close to her, she grabbed Manzano by the elbow and pulled him away.

"And don't come back neither!" the man yelled after them. "Next time I won't miss!"

THE HAGUE, NETHERLANDS

"It tastes disgusting!"

Bernadette threw her spoon into the vegetable stew that Bollard had brought back from the Hotel Gloria.

"You won't be getting anything else," answered Bollard.

"I want spaghetti!"

Marie rolled her eyes. The flu medicine had helped; her fever had dropped.

"You can see for yourself that the stove doesn't work. Where are you going to boil the water for the pasta? In the living room fireplace?"

Really, the kids didn't have it that bad, Bollard thought. They had no school and got to play all day long. The situation meant he and his wife were more lenient with them than usual.

"I don't care! And I wanna watch TV!"

"Bernadette, that is enough!"

"No! No, no, no!"

She jumped up from her chair and stomped out of the kitchen.

Marie gave him a desperate look. Bollard pushed back his chair and followed his daughter. He found her sitting on the living room floor in front of the fire, combing the hair of one of her dolls.

Bollard sat down on the floor opposite.

"Listen, sweetie…"

Bernadette lowered her head, fiercely knit her eyebrows, pushed out her bottom lip, and combed the doll's hair more urgently.

"I know things are difficult at the moment, but all of us…"

He heard his daughter's quiet sobs and saw her little shoulders shaking. He hadn't seen her cry like this before. This wasn't just her being moody or stubborn. The kids might not know what's going on, he thought, but they sense it. Our helplessness, our tension, our fear. Bollard stroked her hair and took her in his arms. Her delicate body was racked with sobs now, and her tears spilled onto his shirt as he held her in his arms and gently rocked her.

That's how we all feel, honey, he thought. That's how we all feel.

BETWEEN COLOGNE AND DÜREN, GERMANY

Shannon and Manzano struggled to gain a footing over the loose earth. Ahead of them was a wooden shack of about five square meters; it had no windows, and the door was unlocked.

She rummaged in her rucksack and found the matches that she had packed in Paris. She struck one and lit up the interior. As far as she could tell in the faint circle of light, the hut was empty save for a few old fence posts and some hay.

"It's no warmer in here," Manzano pointed out.

"We'll fix that," said Shannon.

The moonlight glimmered through a large hole in the ceiling. After a few minutes she had kindled a small fire with straw and bits of wood. The flames threw dancing shadows on the wall. Manzano huddled up in front of the fire and held his hands out to warm them.

"This is brilliant," he sighed. "Where'd you learn this?"

"Girl Scouts," she answered. "Who would have thought it would come in handy one day?"

She knew it wasn't exactly safe to fall asleep next to this fire. Stray sparks could set the shack alight and they would suffocate from the smoke in their sleep.

They stared into the flames for a while.

"What insanity," Manzano finally remarked.

Shannon said nothing.

"There's one thing I can't stop thinking about," Manzano went on. "What are the attackers hoping to accomplish by cutting off the lifeblood of our civilization?

Do they want us to start robbing each other and bashing each other's skulls in—like cavemen in the Stone Age?"

"If they do, then they've succeeded," Shannon said bitterly. She stood up, emptied out her rucksack, and handed him a few pieces of clothing. It wasn't much.

"Something to lie on and something to use as a blanket."

"They haven't succeeded with everyone yet."

"What?"

"The acting like it's the Stone Age thing. Thank you."

Manzano bunched together two T-shirts and a sweater for a pillow. Shannon crumpled up a pair of pants. They lay across from one another, each facing the fire. Shannon felt the cold at her back, less intense than outside. Manzano had already closed his eyes.

Shannon cast another look at the tiny embers that popped out of the glowing wood, one by one. She closed her eyes too and hoped she would wake up again the next morning.

DAY 8—SATURDAY

RATINGEN, GERMANY

"Dragenau wasn't Dragenau," Hartlandt began. Dienhof was there, the rest of Talaefer AG management, even Wickley. "At least not at the hotel. There he checked in as Charles Caldwell. Does the name mean anything to any of you?"

The group shook their heads.

"My theory is that Dragenau is our man. He didn't travel to Bali for a vacation; he went there to disappear. To his—and our—misfortune, his accomplices or employers didn't trust him. And for that reason, he had to be silenced."

"This is all speculation," Wickley said indignantly. "For all we know the dead man is Charles Caldwell. Why would Dragenau be involved in something like this?"

"Money?" Hartlandt suggested.

"Wounded pride," Dienhof offered. "Delayed revenge."

Wickley threw him a nasty look.

"Revenge for what?" asked Hartlandt.

"Many years ago," sighed Wickley, "while still a student in computer science, Dragenau started a company that made automation software. The guy's a genius, but a lousy salesman. Despite his excellent products, the business never really took off. For a while he was a competitor, but he didn't stand a chance against Talaefer. By the end of the nineties his firm was deeply in debt, not least because of various copyright disputes with us. We bought him out—primarily it was a strategic move to get Dragenau on the team. He became our chief architect."

"A frustrated, failed competitor who was driven into bankruptcy—in your industry, you don't consider such an employee an extreme security risk?" asked Hartlandt in disbelief.

"At first, sure," answered Wickley. "But over the years he made such a positive impression that at some point all doubts were forgotten."

BETWEEN COLOGNE AND DÜREN, GERMANY

Shannon opened her eyes. A few orange embers were still burning amid the ashes. Manzano was breathing heavily in his sleep; sweat glistened on his pale face. Through the holes in the roof she could see patches of blue sky.

She lay uncomfortably on her makeshift pillow and pondered their predicament. Panic was beginning to rise within her; she recognized the feeling from school, before an exam; from her travels, when she had nowhere to go or had run out of money. And she knew what she had to do. Freezing like a deer in the headlights would get her nowhere—she needed to take action.

Slowly she picked herself up, laid a piece of wood on the fire, and blew on it carefully until the first flames started to lick. Then she slipped outside and took a shit in the undergrowth. The night's frost had covered the surrounding fields and forest in a white layer that sparkled in the sun. For one moment she felt free of the worries that had been weighing her down.

She leaned against the wooden wall, which had been warmed by the morning sun. Up until the day before, her goals had been clear: to secure the story of a lifetime. But what kind of news did she want to hear now? The answer was simple: that it was all over.

She wanted to be the one to deliver the good news. But first she had to be sure of the facts. Maybe it was time to stop reporting what others were doing. Maybe it was time to do something herself, just as Manzano had done when he discovered the code in the Italian meters.

Her raw mouth and the rumbling in her stomach were a reminder of their basic needs. She had eaten nothing since Hartlandt had fed her yesterday morning. She had drunk only once, when they passed a stream earlier. Things looked worse for Manzano. He hadn't even benefited from the policeman's snacks.

She went back inside the hut.

Manzano opened his eyes. They were glassy.

"Good morning," she said softly. "How are you doing today?"

He closed his eyes and coughed.

She laid her hand on his forehead. He was burning up. He mumbled something, delirious.

"We have to find you a doctor," she said.

Step one.

THE HAGUE, NETHERLANDS

Marie pushed her way through to one of the vendors in the square. He was selling kohlrabi, turnips, and spotty apples. She pulled out the watch that her parents had given her for her high school graduation. She clasped two gold rings and a chain in her hand, her last reserve. She held one of the rings out to the vendor.

"Real gold!" she cried. "This is worth four hundred euros. What can I get for it?"

The man's attention was caught by someone farther along who was offering cash. She called out several more times before he looked over.

"And how am I supposed to know it's real?" he asked.

Before Marie could answer, he took money from someone else and handed over two full bags of vegetables.

Deflated, Marie withdrew from the crowd in front of his stall. She wasn't going to give up so easily though. At least thirty vendors had spread out over the square. Crowds of hungry people jostled one another, trying to get closer to the vendors. In the middle stood a man with a long beard who wore only a white sheet wrapped around his body. Arms raised, he chanted, "The end is nigh! Repent!"

Everywhere she looked, there were people squabbling, yelling angrily, brawling. At one edge of the market people had gathered to listen to a speaker who was spewing rage and hatred.

As she fought her way past the stalls, she came upon one that didn't seem to be selling anything. Though it was smaller than the others, it was guarded by six burly men with unsmiling faces. Marie drew closer. Through a glass clamped to his right eye, the stallholder appraised a piece of jewelry.

"Two hundred," he called out to the woman before him.

"But it's worth at least eight hundred!" she wailed.

"Then sell it to someone who will give you eight hundred for it," he sneered, handing her back the brooch.

The woman hesitated to take it. Then she reached out, and her hand closed around it. The man was already accepting the next piece offered to him. The woman was still hesitating when she was pushed.

Marie felt for the pieces of jewelry in her coat pocket. She bit her lip, then turned away.

She stood helplessly in the crush and roar of the crowd. She wasn't prepared for such extortionate dealing. The masses around the chanting speaker had grown and by now occupied half the square. They were shouting something in unison. It took a while for Marie to make out what they were saying:

"Give us food! Give us water! Give us back our lives!"

BETWEEN COLOGNE AND DÜREN, GERMANY

Shannon heard the sound of the engine before she saw the car. Then from the left a truck appeared.

"Hopefully it's not the military or the police," mumbled Manzano.

"Doesn't look like it from the color," said Shannon. It was too late to hide anyway, so she stuck her arm out, thumb in the air.

She made out two people in the truck's cab. The vehicle pulled up alongside them. Through the open window a young man with short hair and a stubbly beard peered down at them. Shannon wasn't sure he understood her request; there was a pause and then, apparently coming to a decision, he opened the door and held his hand out to them. Shannon helped Manzano up first, then climbed in after him.

An older man—also bearded and with a substantial paunch—sat at the wheel. In a thick accent, the young man said, "He's Carsten. And I'm Eberhart."

It was gloriously warm inside the cab. Behind Carsten and Eberhart's seats a bench offered enough space for her, Manzano, and their few possessions.

As soon as she and Manzano were buckled in, Carsten shifted into gear; slowly the truck started moving again. Manzano sank back against the wall and closed his eyes.

"We're reporters," explained Shannon. "While we were out doing research our car ran out of fuel…"

"Pretty hard reporting, from the looks of your colleague," said Eberhart, gesturing toward Manzano's head injury.

"Car accident after the traffic lights went out," Manzano informed him.

"…after a few days our hotel closed too," Shannon continued. "Now we're trying to get to Brussels."

She realized how stupid that sounded.

"You think the EU is going to help you?" laughed Eberhart.

BERLIN, GERMANY

"We have to agree now what our response to the Russians will be," the chancellor demanded. "The first planes take off in two hours."

"We need all the help we can get," Michelsen spoke up. "What's the case for stopping Russian aid? We've no more evidence against them than we have against the Turks or the Egyptians, but we're not turning down their aid."

"Until we can be certain that the Russians are not behind this, we should regard their 'help' with suspicion," replied the defense minister. As the leader of the smaller party in the coalition government, his role would become crucial in the event of a military conflict. By this point, Michelsen felt the man might provoke a war for that very reason.

"The first wave Russia is sending consists almost exclusively of civilian forces," said the interior minister. "The military units are only there to coordinate things at the command level."

There was a knock on the conference room door. One of the chancellor's aides answered, stuck his head around the door, then walked purposefully over to the head of state, and whispered something in his ear.

The chancellor pushed back his chair and stood up. "You should all see this." Then he left the room.

The others followed him, puzzled. The chancellor left the secured area and continued into the corridor from where they could see out on to the street.

Michelsen felt goose bumps running up her back to the nape of her neck. "I can understand where they're coming from," she said to her neighbor, as they watched the massive crowd making their way toward the Interior Ministry. There were thousands of them. They chanted slogans that Michelsen couldn't catch through the windows. She saw open mouths, raised fists, banners.

We're hungry!
We're cold!

We need water!
We need heat!
We want power too!

Modest demands, thought Michelsen. And yet harder and harder to meet. She was painfully aware of the image they must present to those below, standing in a centrally heated, well-lit building, gazing out as if from a fortress.

The crowd moved this way and that, surging toward the building, retreating, coming back, unable to gain entry because the gates below were locked and guarded by police.

"I have to get to work," Michelsen said and turned away. A muffled noise made her look back. Her colleagues had stepped away from the windows in horror. A shadowy object struck against one of the glass panels, and a snarl of cracks spread out like a spider's web. More stones flew. More windows cracked. In the corridor, even though the security glass was impenetrable, staff stepped farther back. They followed each other into the secured central rooms of the crisis center. A couple of brave souls remained.

This is exactly what I'm here for, thought Michelsen, to prevent something like this. She leaned back against the wall, overwhelmed by a sense of failure, as piles of stones smacked against the glass.

Then the hail stopped. Five of the sixteen windows in the hallway were shattered.

"We let the Russians in," she heard the chancellor tell the foreign minister.

Cautiously, Michelsen risked stepping closer to the windows. A thin spiral of smoke rose in front of the building. Fire or tear gas? she asked herself.

NEAR DÜREN, GERMANY

"What about you?" Shannon asked the man in the passenger seat. "Why are you out here on the roads?"

"Carsten works for a large food company," answered

Eberhart. "Normally he supplies the local branches with food from the central warehouse."

At the thought of food Shannon's stomach tightened.

"You speak English well."

"I'm a student," Eberhart explained. "They needed extra manpower, so I'm doing this."

"And what do you have with you?"

"Nonperishable stuff: canned goods, flour, noodles. In the towns along our route a couple of branches were converted into food distribution sites. We're supposed to hand out rations directly from the truck. Not for much longer, though." He looked thoughtfully out of the window.

"How come?"

"Our warehouse is almost empty. This is one of our last trips. Even now, we're really tight on what we give out."

Shannon hesitated before asking her next question. "So you're carrying food. We've eaten nothing since yesterday morning." When neither of the two reacted, she added, "I might have some money left."

Eberhart looked at her, eyes narrowed.

An uncomfortable feeling rose in Shannon, but it couldn't calm her aching stomach.

"Only a little," she added, downplaying it. "I thought I might be able to buy something off you."

Eberhart scratched his beard. "We're not allowed. Emergency laws. We have to distribute the stuff for free. It's strictly rationed." But as he spoke he fixed her with an intense stare, as if he were waiting for her to make an offer.

"Just a small amount," Shannon tried. "For my colleague and me. You can see for yourself he's in a bad way."

Eberhart glanced over at Manzano, who sat in unusual silence.

Shannon rummaged in her pocket.

"I have fifty euros here. That's got to be enough."

"A hundred," said Eberhart and reached for the bills. Shannon pulled them back.

Eberhart turned back to the road as if nothing had happened. They drove like this for a full minute, enough time for the acid in Shannon's stomach to spread right across her insides.

Finally, Shannon gave in. "Sixty."

"We're at one-twenty now."

Shannon cursed silently. Next thing, he would throw them out of the truck.

"Eighty."

"I had a decent breakfast this morning." Eberhart kept his gaze fixed squarely on the road. "And soon I'm going to have a proper lunch. If you'd like one, it'll cost you one fifty."

"I don't have that much!"

"Those who don't have the means, shouldn't offer." Eberhart gave Carsten a sign. The truck came to a halt.

Eberhart turned to Shannon and held a palm out toward her.

"First the food," demanded Shannon.

Eberhart got out and returned with a package.

Gritting her teeth, Shannon swapped it for her hundred euros.

She tore off the packaging and found a loaf of bread wrapped in plastic, two cans—one of beans and one of corn—a bottle of mineral water, a tube of condensed milk, a bag of flour, and another of noodles. Fuck! She had just handed over one hundred euros for a goddamn bag of flour and noodles. Useless without a stove or at least a fire. Hurriedly she fumbled the bread out of the packaging, tore off a piece, handed it to Manzano, ripped off another and stuffed it down greedily. Manzano ate beside her in the same starved manner. With his fingers he spread some of the condensed milk onto the bread.

Eberhart and Carsten were having a good laugh about something.

Shannon couldn't care less.

RATINGEN, GERMANY

Hartlandt's colleague had the radiophone glued to her ear. When she saw him she ended the conversation and hung up. "That was Berlin. I just sent them something—here, take a look."

She opened up an image file on her computer.

"These are files recovered from old hard drives found at Dragenau's place. Either the guy wasn't especially careful, or it didn't matter to him if something was traced."

The group photo brought together at least sixty people of all nationalities, with a city in the background that Hartlandt didn't recognize. The faces were hard to make out.

Shanghai 2005, read the photo caption.

"In 2005 Dragenau took part in a conference on IT security in Shanghai. The photo must have been taken sometime during this conference. Here's Dragenau. And over here is somebody else we might know."

She enlarged the photo until the face was visible. A good-looking young man with a tanned complexion and black hair smiled into the camera.

"He's the spitting image of…" She brought up a second image and lined it up next to the face in Dragenau's Shanghai photo.

Hartlandt recognized one of the facial composites that had been made of the suspected smart meter saboteurs in Italy. "Five years between then and today," he said. "His hair is shorter now. But other than that…"

"Berlin, Europol, Interpol, and a bunch of others are being informed as we speak. Let's see who this is and if anyone has information for us."

"A bunch of others" meant every secret service and intelligence agency across affected territories—in the present situation, they could count on that.

COMMAND HEADQUARTERS

So they'd found the German's body in Bali. Now they'd be looking that much closer at Talaefer AG. Well, they'd be looking for a long time. Nobody sifts through several decades' worth of code—millions of lines of it—in just a few days, even if they put the entire BKA on it. And those guys were so incompetent, they couldn't even hold on to a single hacker.

Their internal arguments about Saint-Laurent and the other nuclear power plants, plus various chemical factories on both sides of the Atlantic, had calmed down. They had deliberately not infiltrated these facilities' IT systems; the responsibility for any accidents or failures therefore lay solely with the operators and their insufficient backup systems. Anyone with a conscience had to accept this.

When it was all over, the people who had suffered most wouldn't let the corporations and politicians get away with any more lies or excuses. Under the new order, they would be called to account. Only then would things really begin to change.

ORLÉANS, FRANCE

Annette stood in front of the cloudy mirror. Holding her breath as the stench from the toilets assailed her, she ran her fingers through her hair, then stopped dead when she saw the strands of hair in her hand. She ran her fingers through her hair again, pulling gently. More gray strands came away. You always lose a few hairs, she thought. I've been losing them all my life. She began to recall images from an antinuclear war film from the eighties. In it the main characters began to lose their hair a few days after they had been irradiated by the bombs. Within weeks they had suffered an agonizing death. She felt her face growing hot.

To her left, a woman her own age was scrubbing her

arms with a washcloth; to her right, a young woman bathed a baby in the sink.

Trembling, Annette ran her hand through her hair once more. This time nothing came out. But she hadn't dared to pull on it. She hurried to leave the communal bathroom. Its tile floor was so filthy that even with shoes on she could barely stand to tread on it.

The air was clammy and cold in the broad corridor that circled the arena, and the light of a few forlorn neon lights flickered from the ceiling. Throughout the day a shroud of whispers, talk, snoring, crying, and screams filled the shelter, which had been built to serve athletes and crowds. Annette walked up to the entrance gate, where volunteers assigned space to new arrivals, distributed food and blankets, and answered queries. A man in uniform, who might have been the same age as her daughter, sorted cans of food.

"Excuse me," said Annette.

He stopped for a moment, then turned to her with an open expression.

"We came here yesterday from near Saint-Laurent," she went on, noticing how hoarse her voice had become. "When are we going to be checked for radiation?"

The man put his hands on his hips. "Don't worry about it, madam," he replied.

"But don't we need to be checked?"

"No, madam. This evacuation is only a precautionary measure."

"After the Fukushima accident in Japan in 2011, they showed people on television in the emergency shelters with these devices—"

"This isn't Japan."

"I want to be checked!" demanded Annette. Her voice sounded strange and shrill.

"Well, we're short of the equipment right now. But, like I said, there's no need for you to be afraid. Nothing in Saint-Laurent is—"

"But I am afraid!" she cried. "Why else would we have been evacuated?"

"I've already told you," the man replied, brusque now. "As a precaution." He turned back to his work.

Annette felt her body shaking, her face burning. Tears came to her eyes. She shut her eyes to hold them back.

NEAR AACHEN, GERMANY

Eberhart and Carsten distributed food in two other towns. Manzano and Shannon stayed in the cab. Shannon thought his forehead felt less hot. Maybe the medicine from the hospital was beginning to work.

Twilight stars appeared in the sky. They were close to Aachen, rambling through a low-built area broken up by fields and woods, when Carsten braked so suddenly that Shannon was thrown forward. When she straightened up she spotted a tree lying across the middle of the road.

The doors on either side of Eberhart and Carsten were ripped open. There was shouting. Shannon saw gun barrels, then the tops of heads. Bandannas wrapped over faces, caps and hats pulled low over foreheads.

"Out!" the masked men screamed, and they pulled themselves up onto the truck. Carsten slammed the truck into reverse, but one of the armed men struck his hand with the butt of his gun. Another shoved the top of his gun to his head. With a howl of pain, Carsten let go of the gearshift and raised his hands. The men grabbed him. He came close to falling out of the cab and was just able to catch himself. He tumbled out, as Eberhart had done on the other side. Shannon flattened herself against the back of the seat; automatically, she put her hands up. The men waved guns in their faces, screaming. Shannon undid Manzano's seat belt and hauled him up so he would be able to try to climb out of the cab on his own. She threw her rucksack, still with Manzano's laptop inside, over her shoulder. A man pulled Manzano out and was about to fling him down onto the street. Shannon held Manzano back, pushed herself past him, and cried out, "Easy! Easy!" Leaning against her shoulder, Manzano climbed out without falling onto the asphalt. On the roadside, Eberhart and Carsten were writhing on the ground. One was holding his head; the other, his groin.

A masked man had already taken over the driver's seat. Two crowded into the back of the cab. There were three more in the passenger seat. They slammed the doors.

The driver reversed, steered the truck onto a dirt road, turned the vehicle around, and drove off in the direction they had come from.

"Assholes!" Eberhart shouted after the truck as it grew smaller and vanished in a cloud of dust.

Look who's talking, thought Shannon.

Eberhart had sat up by then but was still groaning.

Shannon felt no pity. He had earned himself a beating for extorting them. All the same, she asked, "Everything OK?"

"The cargo bay was empty anyway," groaned Eberhart.

Carsten was sitting up.

"How much farther is it to Aachen?" asked Shannon.

Eberhart pointed down the street.

"Maybe four kilometers."

BERLIN, GERMANY

Michelsen was checking statistics on the country's remaining food reserves when someone whispered in her ear: "Into the conference room. Now."

Michelsen watched as, one after another, her colleagues received the same whispered summons. It made no sense: why whisper if you're going to invite every person in the room?

In the conference room the chancellor was already

seated, along with half the cabinet. They had long since discarded their ties.

"Ladies and gentlemen," the interior minister began once everyone was assembled. "The attack has escalated to a new level. Our IT forensics team has just informed us that our communications system has been infiltrated by the attackers. We still don't know how they did it, but one thing is clear: your computers are compromised. We have further confirmation from Europol and the French, British, Polish, and three other crisis teams on the continent." He raised his hands in a placating gesture. "To avoid any misunderstanding: we don't believe anyone present has anything to do with this. The intrusion into the systems must have been organized at the same time as the attacks on our energy infrastructure."

He lowered his hands and cleared his throat. "Most important, the attackers are not content merely to eavesdrop on our communications. No, they are manipulating them quite deliberately in order to sabotage our activities. Unfortunately, it was only after several such instances that we became aware of what was going on. You must assume that all of your messages are being read, every telephone call and every conversation tapped."

Michelsen, listening in disbelief, heard a whisper from the other corner of the room.

"Yes, conversations too," repeated the interior minister, who apparently had heard what was said. "Your computers are equipped with cameras and microphones that someone with the right software can activate remotely. In this way they hear and see everything that the cameras and microphones pick up." He spoke more forcefully now. "The attackers have their eyes and ears here, in the middle of our operations center! It's the same in France, Poland, Europol HQ, and at the Monitoring and Information Center of the EU. We haven't heard anything yet from NATO, but it wouldn't surprise me…"

He had to take a breath to calm himself. "Every exchange of information with external authorities, whether domestic or foreign, must be confirmed through a separate communications procedure, effective immediately. When you receive information or a directive via the internet, you must call the other party over the radio to verify its authenticity; likewise, if you send information, you must call to make sure not only that it has been received but that the contents are consistent with the message you sent. For the moment we can assume that the official radio channels have not been infiltrated and are secure."

He looked around to assure himself that everyone in the room had understood him.

AACHEN, GERMANY

"Damn, it's cold!" exclaimed Shannon. Manzano watched her as she looked for a sweater in her rucksack.

"I am so done with all of this," she groaned. "What I wouldn't give for a warm bed in my own apartment and a hot shower or, even better, a hot bath!"

Manzano hadn't the energy to reply. He couldn't stop shivering—whether from fever, the cold, exhaustion, or all three. They'd spent the whole evening searching in vain for somewhere to stay. By the time they'd reached the train station, it was snowing steadily. Shannon had led the way to a rear entrance; inside, dozens of people were encamped under the roof that covered the platforms, lying side by side, wrapped in sleeping bags and blankets. The underground passageways that connected the platforms to the main hall were blocked off by rolling shutters, with sleepers leaning against them.

It was far from ideal, but at least they'd be somewhat protected from the wind and snow here. Most of the unoccupied spots stank of piss, but eventually they found a free corner. Manzano sat down and leaned his back against the wall.

"Lean against me," he told Shannon. "That way we can keep each other warm."

Shannon sat down between his legs, pressed her back against his torso, stuck her hands under her arms, and pulled in her legs. Manzano put his arms around her. She felt his warm breath in her ear and then, slowly, the warmth of his body, radiating through the layers of clothing.

"Helps a little, at least," he whispered.

She turned around and tried to see how he was.

Manzano had let his head fall back against the wall; his eyes were closed. His chest rose and fell evenly; his arms went slack. Gently Shannon tucked them under her own, let her head sink back against his chest, and stared at the hall's dark ceiling, stray snowflakes drifting through it. Then she fell into a dreamless sleep.

DAY 9—SUNDAY

THE HAGUE, NETHERLANDS

Bollard had cut the last heel of bread into eight slices: four thick ones, four onion-skin thin. They were in desperate need of supplies. In the house, there was barely anything left to eat. Bollard caught himself staring out the kitchen window, lost in thought. He, who was usually so in control. The lawn of the little yard was green even in winter. The bushes around it were leafless, like the neighbors' hedges. Behind one of them he saw a man crouching on the deck of the house next door. Probably Luc. Motionless, his arm held out toward the lawn. Now Bollard spotted a cat a few meters away who sloped cautiously toward the neighbor. He seemed to be luring it with something. It raised its tail and approached with a bound, reached Luc, and licked at his fingers. With a lightning-quick motion the neighbor grabbed its neck with one hand and struck its head with the other. In his hand was a T-shaped object that Bollard in that moment recognized as a hammer. His neighbor rose, the bloody hammer in the one hand, the lifeless legs of the slaughtered animal dangling from the other.

Gingerly, Bollard set down the knife with which he had sliced the bread.

The children stormed into the kitchen. Marie followed them wearily, though with more strength than the previous day. Bollard, glad for the distraction, set each of the four thick slices on a plate and placed them in the center of the table. Then he took the thin ones and held them up in front of the children's faces.

"Let's pretend that these are tasty salami slices that we're putting on the bread."

He placed the thin slices on top of the thick ones and watched the children expectantly. He still couldn't get what he had just seen out of his head.

"That's bread, not salami," argued Bernadette and looked dismissively at her plate.

"It's salami for me," insisted Bollard. He bit off a piece of his bread.

"Mmm! That's goood!"

Bernadette copied him skeptically. Marie tasted her piece and likewise made a show of how good it tasted. Bollard chewed with relish and nodded at his bread with approval.

"De-li-cious. You two don't want to miss out on this."

Georges, who like his sister had sat there, skeptical, let himself go along with it and placed his "piece of salami" on the bread and took a big bite like his parents, accompanied with "mmms" and "aahs."

Bernadette stared down at her bread, unsure; her parents and her brother stepped up their show. Shaking her head, she reached for her slices, said, "You're all totally nuts," and took a bite.

AACHEN, GERMANY

"Good morning," whispered Manzano into Shannon's ear. Despite the freezing cold and the uncomfortable position, he must have slept for a few hours. He felt better than the day before; the fever seemed to have gone back down.

Shannon started, restlessly moved her head this way and that, then buried her face in his neck and went back to sleep. He could barely feel his hands and feet, buttocks, or back thanks to the cold. A little way ahead of them, a sleeping bag appeared to be moving. The train station was slowly waking up. Tired faces, rumpled hair. Most of them seemed to Manzano to be long-term street dwellers, with weathered faces and matted hair.

Not even an hour and a half from here to Brussels with the regular connection, he thought. Over two days on foot. He rocked Shannon gently, then whispered in her ear again until she opened her eyes.

She looked at him, blinking.

"Nightmare," she groaned.

"You had one?"

"No, I woke up and landed back in one."

She sat there a moment longer, then rose, sluggish, and stretched dramatically. Manzano did the same. He could feel his injured leg.

"What do we do now?" said Manzano.

"I've got to… You know."

"Oh." An awkward pause. "Me too."

After they had done their business in separate corners, they wandered across the platform looking for a map or some other clue as to how they could get to Brussels.

They asked some of the people who were also starting their day.

"Do trains come through here?"

"Very rarely. Freight trains," answered one.

"Where are they heading?"

"No idea."

"Is there anywhere nearby where you can get something to eat?"

"In the street in front of the train station there's a soup kitchen. It's not always open, though."

An hour later Shannon and Manzano were sitting in a room heated by a coal oven. No one had questioned them in the food line. Each of them had received two large ladlefuls of vegetable soup, which they sipped gratefully directly from the bowl, seated at long crowded tables. Those who had empty bowls were requested to give up their seat for the next consumer. Which meant most of them lingered a long time before finishing. Shannon and Manzano were in no hurry either, but after repeated demands they were finally forced back outside to the cold. "We've got more important things to do," Manzano said. "Come on, back to the train station."

Manzano paced up and down the track, before finally deciding on a direction, and pulled Shannon with him. After about two hundred meters they went under a bridge. Beyond them, the tracks branched out in several directions. Two of them disappeared into buildings; others merged again after another few hundred meters. In between, dozens of railway vehicles were parked, from simple locomotives, regional train cars, and freight cars to strange machines that were probably used to lay rails or make repairs. One of them looked like a short, yellow truck that could drive on rails.

Manzano climbed up next to the driver's door and tried to open it. A second later he was sitting at the wheel inspecting the controls.

Shannon watched him doubtfully from the ladder beside the door.

"Doesn't this thing need electricity?"

"Nope. Runs on diesel."

"If the tank's not empty."

Manzano removed a panel under the dashboard, behind which a tangle of wires appeared. He looked over the cables, pulled out a few, reconnected others. Suddenly, with a loud rattle, the engine sprang to life.

"What are you waiting for?" he asked. "See if there's anything like a route map in here."

"Hasn't it got a navigation system?" she asked. She climbed in, sat down on the passenger seat, and looked through the giant glove compartment until she found a thick book filled with diagrams and maps.

"Got it!"

Manzano tested whether he could put the vehicle in motion. It gave a lurch and started.

Shannon studied the thick tome and found Aachen and Brussels on a full-page spread.

"Now all we have to do is figure out what this means."

"You're the navigator. I'm the driver!" cried Manzano, and he sped up to walking speed.

"Since when does a man trust his female passenger to map read?"

"Since the thing he's driving isn't a car but a... Oh, just bloody well tell me where to go!"

BERLIN, GERMANY

"*Rosinenbomber*"—raisin bombers. That was what her mother and all the other Berliners had called the American aircraft that had supplied the west sector of Berlin with food after the Second World War. Michelsen wondered if any of today's youth knew the word. And now, sixty years on, military planes were once again landing at Tegel Airport—only this time, they were Russian.

The passenger planes grounded since the beginning of the power outage had been cleared away. In their place a staggering number of dark green, large-bellied colossuses were lined up beside each other, the symbols of the Russian Federation emblazoned on their tail fins. In the night sky, Michelsen saw the chain of lights from incoming planes and the formations of those flying out again.

Berlin wasn't their only destination. At that very moment, similar scenarios were playing out in Stockholm, Copenhagen, Frankfurt, Paris, London, and other large airports across north and central Europe, while in the south hundreds of planes, chiefly from Turkey and Egypt, delivered their loads. At the same time, truck convoys and mile-long trains brought more life-saving provisions from Russia, the nations of the Caucasus, Turkey, and North Africa.

"Looks like an invasion," muttered the foreign minister.

NATO had still not made a decision about Chinese offers of aid. The view that China was responsible for the catastrophe was gaining increasing acceptance among hardliners. So long as this suspicion could not be refuted, they would not, under any circumstances, tolerate Chinese soldiers or even civilian aid personnel setting foot on Western soil.

"Let's go welcome the general," said Michelsen.

BETWEEN LIÈGE AND BRUSSELS, NETHERLANDS

Up until then, they had traveled no faster than seventy kilometers per hour so as not to miss any switches or obstacles.

"What's that light back there?"

Behind them, Shannon and Manzano saw a tiny, flickering light.

"No idea. Getting bigger and brighter, though," said Shannon. "A lot bigger and brighter—and fast," she realized. "It's on the tracks. That's a train."

"On our track?"

"I can't tell, but it's a train all right," Shannon repeated, getting anxious. She could already make out the locomotive. "If it is driving on our track, it's going to ram us. Go, now—we need to go!"

Their car-on-rails shuddered forward. The train behind them was only a hundred meters away now.

"Faster!" screamed Shannon. She felt the car accelerating, but nowhere near fast enough. Then to her relief it became apparent that the train was traveling on the other track. As it drew closer, she saw dozens of freight wagons behind the locomotive, hundreds of people sitting on top of them.

"Like in India," remarked Manzano. "Only those people must be frozen stiff!"

Slowly the train caught up to them, until they were

driving right alongside the locomotive. Shannon saw the engineer and waved at him until he snapped opened his window. Shannon did the same. Over the noise of the two engines she shouted in French, "Where are you going?"

"Brussels!" he replied.

BERLIN, GERMANY

"Oh my God," Michelsen stammered.

"How could this happen?" asked the chancellor. His face was as white as chalk.

"From the way things look, there's been an accident," said the secretary of state for environment, nature conservation, and nuclear safety. On the screen appeared photos of burned-out truck skeletons that lay scattered over the highway and neighboring fields. Faces grimaced in horror.

"We don't know how it happened," said the secretary of state. "The investigations are still ongoing. The fuel trucks were pulling trailers and were accompanied by two troop vehicles, front and behind, each with a ten-man crew."

He pointed at two of the blackened wrecks in the fields.

"There are no survivors."

"Was it an accident or an attack?" asked the chancellor.

"We can't say at present. All we know is that from the time of the inquiry made by the Philippsburg nuclear power plant until the discovery of the accident site, ten hours had elapsed."

"Lord, why so long?"

"Because everyone out there is at their limit!" growled the secretary of state. "Because fewer and fewer are even available. Because the BOS radio doesn't work in many regions. Because…" Words failed him, his lips began to tremble, he fought back tears.

Please don't have a nervous breakdown, Michelsen prayed. They had already lost two people.

"The next diesel transport could not be sent out till this morning and will reach Philippsburg in six hours at the earliest."

On the screen there appeared a large basin like a swimming pool.

"This is the pool for spent fuel rods in the Philippsburg 1 nuclear power plant. In some power plants there are more used fuel rods sitting in the spent fuel pool than are active in the reactor itself. Since they are still very hot, they have to be cooled year-round. The pool in Philippsburg 1 was always a safety risk, as it lies outside the containment structure for the reactor. The spent fuel pool didn't even have a backup system prior to the plant's early decommissioning in 2011, at which time it was provisionally equipped. According to the operators, diesel for cooling the spent fuel pool ran out sometime last night. The power plant management chose not to risk diverting diesel from the emergency cooling systems for the reactors.

"The water in the pool is evaporating due to the heat of the fuel rods. By the time the replacement diesel reaches the plant, the pool will be dry. It's likely that the fuel elements have already begun to melt. I don't need to explain to anyone here what that means. Or maybe I do. Since the spent fuel pool is not located within the containment structure, this meltdown would take place in the middle of the building. As a result, the inside of the building will be so severely irradiated that it truly can no longer be entered. In the event of an explosion, even the cities of Mannheim and Karlsruhe could be endangered.

"For God's sake!" shouted the chancellor, and he pounded his fist on the heavy table so hard that it shook. "You close the damn reactors down and still things go wrong!"

"The residual risk people always like to cite," murmured Michelsen.

"Do we need to evacuate the area?" asked the chancellor.

"Even if we want to, there's no way we can do it quickly," answered the secretary of state. "Contact with local emergency crews has long been patchy. Even if we're only talking about a radius of a few kilometers, we'll need hundreds of vehicles, drivers, fuel. In the present situation"—he looked down at the table in front of him, shaking his head—"all we can do is pray."

BRUSSELS, BELGIUM

There had been enough fuel in the tank to make it to the next switch. Shannon and Manzano had then simply hooked the railway vehicle to the train. The engineer way up front hadn't noticed a thing.

Forty-five minutes later, they stopped in what seemed to be a major train station.

Soldiers with rifles across their chests stood on both sides of the train.

"Hopefully, they're not waiting for us," said Manzano.

"Don't be so full of yourself," Shannon replied. "I'm sure they're here because of looters."

A soldier without a gun but with a megaphone walked up and down the train and ordered the people in French to get off and calmly disperse. They climbed down from the containers and freight cars and carried their possessions past the line of soldiers. Manzano and Shannon blended in with the crowd. The station signage confirmed they had reached Brussels. Here too hundreds of people had set up makeshift sleeping rigs in the main hall of the train station. The booths were closed, but Manzano spotted a man in a yellow security jacket who was watching from the sidelines.

"Where do you want to go?" he asked, after Shannon and Manzano had tried out their English on him.

"To the Monitoring and Information Center of the EU," repeated Manzano.

The man shrugged. "No idea where that is. I only know the seat of the European Commission."

"How do we get there?"

COMMAND HEADQUARTERS

At first they were worried. Since the previous day, more computers used to communicate with crisis centers and important organizations like Europol had been shut down. Email traffic had markedly decreased. Had their surveillance been discovered? They waited, conducting no active manipulations. Really, it had almost been too easy. They had procured thousands of email addresses belonging to employees at various power companies and government institutions via social media. Then, using personalized emails, they had lured them to a website with "special discount travel deals for select employees."

One visit and the deal seeker's computer was infected with a malicious code.

Within a few months they had infiltrated practically every target—several corporations and the systems of the largest European nations as well as the United States. In the same way they identified laptops that had Skype or other internet telephone programs installed. They had activated their built-in cameras and microphones, without the users being notified.

But now more staff were turning off their computers. And in doing so they took away their eyes and ears inside the enemies' operations centers.

In an email from the French crisis center, their automated keyword search had finally seized upon a message. It came directly from the office of the president. In it he ordered all staffers at government authorities to turn computers and other technological devices on only when absolutely necessary, in order to conserve backup power. Within a few hours they dug up similar emails in several other government networks.

That was a welcome surprise. If after just a week even the most important institutions were having to conserve backup power, it couldn't be long till the final collapse. The day when the people would finally take back their lives was growing ever closer.

BRUSSELS, BELGIUM

It was getting dark by the time they stood in front of the massive building. Big letters beside the entrance proclaimed: *Europese Commissie—Commission européenne.*

Lights were on inside. A few men dressed in navy blue stood in the window and looked out on to the street.

Shannon took a close look at Manzano, from his stitched-up forehead to his filthy shoes. His fever had abated, but he still looked like a vagrant. A glance at herself reminded her that she didn't look much better.

"Yeah," said Manzano, "we look like welcome visitors. I'm sure we smell like it too."

They hadn't even pushed the door open before a security guard came to greet them.

"Entry is for staff only," he said in French.

"I am staff," Manzano answered confidently in English. He tried to push past him but ran into an outstretched arm.

"Your ID," the man demanded, also in English now.

"Escort me to reception," Manzano told him. "I'm an independent contractor with the Monitoring and Information Center," he lied. "Ask Sophia Angström— she's an employee here. If you don't let me through there's going to be trouble, I can promise you that."

The security man hesitated but quickly came to a decision. "Come with me."

———

Sophia stepped out of the elevator and scanned the lobby. Only at second glance did she recognize Piero Manzano. Sitting next to him was a young woman with matted hair. Coming closer, Sophia recognized her face.

"Piero! My God, just look at you!" She took a step back. "And the smell…"

"I know. A long story. By the way, this is Lauren Shannon, American journalist."

"Oh, I know her," said Sophia. "She was the first to report on the attack on the power grid. And now I know where you got the story," she said to Shannon. "Piero here…"

"We met in The Hague," Manzano explained, "through François Bollard. Do you remember him? Another long story."

Sophia couldn't help but wonder if Manzano and the young American had been through more than just "long stories" together.

"What are you doing in Brussels? Another scoop? Or are you here for Europol?"

"I might have a clue that could lead to the attackers," answered Manzano.

"The whole world is in the dark about who's responsible for this disaster, and you're telling me you know who it is?"

"I didn't say that. But I might have a clue. My hunch turned out right once before."

Sophia nodded.

"What I need right now, though, is power and an internet connection. I thought I could maybe get them from you here."

Sophia laughed wearily. "Oh sure, it's not like it matters. Everything's gone nuts here anyway." With a motion of her head, she signaled for them to follow her. "This could cost me my job. But first you two have to check in and shower."

"We'd like nothing better."

"We have sanitary facilities, so we'll go there first. Do you have something to change into?"

"I do," said Shannon.

"I don't," Manzano admitted.

"Maybe I can rustle something up," said Sophia.

She stood at the desk.

"Two visitor passes, please," she asked the receptionist, whose nose was upturned in a sneer.

RATINGEN, GERMANY

"We've got them," announced the caller from Berlin on the radiophone. "A team carrying out surveillance on a transmission substation spotted them after they started a fire."

"Where?"

"Near Schweinfurt."

Schweinfurt. Hartlandt didn't bother to guess how far that was. On his computer he brought up a map of Germany. Around three hundred kilometers southeast of Ratingen.

"Did they catch them?"

"They called in a helicopter. It's under way and will continue surveillance from a safe altitude. The GSG 9 has already been notified."

"I have to get there."

"Chopper should be landing in the Talaefer parking lot in twenty minutes."

BRUSSELS, BELGIUM

Two minutes, no longer. That was all that was allowed; Sophia had made that clear to him. He had never enjoyed a shower so much. When he stepped out of the stall, towel around his waist, the Swede was waiting with a stack of clothes.

"Shirt and pants. From a colleague who had them stowed away on a shelf but hasn't shown up for days. They'll be a bit too small, but better than nothing."

"What happened there?" she asked and pointed at the stitches on his thigh.

"Took a dumb fall," he lied.

"Looks nasty."

"Feels like it too. And how are you managing otherwise?" He changed the subject while he got dressed.

"I more or less live here," she answered with a shrug. "I only go home to sleep. And sometimes not even that. The special buses for employees aren't running anymore. And it's an hour and a half by bicycle—quite a haul. But it keeps me warm, and I'm getting a workout to make up for the one I would have had on the ski trip."

"Have you heard anything from your friends and Old Man Bondoni?"

"Not since we left," she admitted gloomily.

In front of the bathrooms they ran into Shannon.

"I'm never leaving this place," the journalist sighed. She wore a fresh pair of jeans and a sweater.

"Oh yes you are," said Sophia. "You're coming with us—to the MIC."

She led them into a small office on the seventh floor.

Manzano had pictured the central reporting and control center for Civil Protection and Disaster Management as being more impressive.

"This is a conference room," she explained. "We have a guest network; you can access it via WLAN."

"I can't access a thing." He showed her his laptop. "The battery is dead. I'll need a charger. Do you have one?"

Sophia opened a side cabinet. "Here are two laptops; maybe you can find something that'll work?"

Manzano tried them out. One of the cables fit.

"If anybody asks you anything," said Sophia, "send them to me."

"Say that we're from IT. There are thousands of you here; not everybody knows each other anyway."

"That's true. I'm two rooms down, on the left. I'll stop by now and then."

She left the room and closed the door.

Manzano plopped down into one of the chairs and started up the computer.

Shannon took a seat at the desk opposite.

"When I imagine that for over a week millions of people have been going through what we went through last night," she said and looked thoughtfully out the window, "I'm amazed that all hell hasn't broken loose out there a long time ago."

"It probably has, to an extent," replied Manzano. "But most people are too busy surviving. They don't have the time or the energy for rioting."

He jumped as the door was opened.

Sophia walked in and set a tray down on the table.

"Hot coffee and something to eat. You two look like you could use it," she said. "If you need anything, like I said, two rooms down. My extension is 27. See you in a bit." With that, she went out and closed the door behind her.

"She might as well be telling you what size bra she wears." Shannon grinned with her mouth full. "She likes you."

Manzano felt himself turning red.

Shannon had to laugh. "And you like her too!"

"Cut it out. We have things to do."

"You have things to do." Shannon chuckled contentedly and gulped down her mouthful. "All I have to do is eat, drink coffee"—she pushed her chair around the table and next to his—"and watch you."

Someone knocked on the door, and before they could respond it was already being opened.

A man with fashionable designer glasses stuck his head in and looked at them in surprise.

"Oh, I thought... Who are you?"

"IT department," answered Manzano. "We're supposed to fix something here."

"Ah. OK then, please excuse the interruption."

He closed the door. Manzano and Shannon were not bothered again.

THE HAGUE, NETHERLANDS

They had chosen a special conference room in which there were no computers except for Bollard's. And it wasn't connected to the internal network. After the presentation, Bollard would have it wiped before he hooked the computer back up to the internet.

"The man's name is Jorge Pucao," Bollard declared. "Born in 1981 in Buenos Aires. Grew up there as well. Even as a high school student he was politically active—he took part in a number of demonstrations against the economic crisis."

Visible on the projection screen was the angry face of a young man raising his fist against unseen enemies.

"During the peak of the crisis around the turn of the millennium, he studied political science and computer science in Buenos Aires. He continued to be involved politically, at demonstrations and in the organization of an exchange ring. These were popular in Argentina at the time, as the value of the state currency, the peso, had plummeted in the economic and financial crisis. The country was going bankrupt, and large parts of the middle class were impoverished. In 2001, Jorge Pucao was arrested at the protests against the G8 summit in Genoa."

Even the unflattering mug shots of Pucao with sweat-soaked hair couldn't mask his good looks.

"Around this time his father took his own life. Pucao returned to his home country and ramped up his activism. By 2003 Argentina was over the worst of it, and Pucao began a master's degree at Georgetown University's School of Foreign Service in Washington, DC. He was able to fund his education by working as a freelance IT specialist in online security. Concurrent to this he was involved in the antiglobalization movement. Articles and a so-called manifesto that he published on his website indicate that he had started to become more radical.

"You will find all documents, later ones as well, under 'Pucao_lit' on the server," Bollard added, in the expectation that all present would take a close look at the documents. He had skimmed through a few of them himself but hadn't delved deep. What stood out at first glance was the discipline of the argument, which was missing in most pamphlets by radicals of all stripes, whose tirades got lost in a mess of slogans and accusations.

"In the United States, he also came into contact with primitivist factions. For any of you who don't know what that means, essentially, the proponents of primitivism call for a return to preindustrial ways of life; many also reject our form of civilization. These contacts don't seem to have been particularly strong—hardly surprising, given that Pucao earned a living with the most modern of technology. But we already know that our man here is thoroughly ambivalent.

"In 2005, he successfully completed his studies in Washington. He protested at the G8 summit in Gleneagles in Scotland. Back in the United States, he continued to work as an IT specialist. There is speculation, but no proof, that he was also active as a hacker all those years."

Now Bollard came to the group photo at the conference in Shanghai that the Germans had sent him.

"In 2006, he took part in a conference for internet security in Shanghai. At the same conference, Hermann Dragenau was also present, as this photo indicates. Dragenau was head of products at Talaefer, the technology firm whose control software for power plants is believed to have been manipulated."

"Aside from this similarity between our facial composite and the photo of a man who attended the same conference as Dragenau, do we have anything else that suggests he's our man?" asked Christopoulos.

Bollard brought up a list of letters and numbers.

"As you know, the United States began collecting data on passengers traveling by plane after the terror attacks of 9/11. In 2007 the EU announced that it was also prepared to give the United States information on passengers in and outside of the United States. Therefore, we know that Pucao frequently shuttled back and forth between the United States and Europe between 2007 and 2010. Düsseldorf was often his preferred destination in Europe—a stone's throw from Dragenau's place of residence. But it gets even better. In 2011 Dragenau went on vacation to Brazil. We've got photos and even travel documents. Pucao flew down there at the same time and stayed two days. Too short for a vacation."

"But there's no evidence that the two of them met?" asked Christopoulos. "Even if there were, that in itself wouldn't mean anything."

"That's true, of course, but—"

"Excuse me for interrupting you, but something else occurs to me: if the two of them are such computer geniuses and they're planning the apocalypse, then they have to know that everything they do leaves behind a digital trail. Why don't they proceed with more caution or cover their tracks?"

"Because they feel safe?" countered Bollard. "Because they don't care? For now, all we can do is speculate."

"Nor have you mentioned anything about his political activities in the last few years."

"I'm getting to that. After 2005, Pucao changed his behavior quite strikingly. He ceased to show up among protestors at meetings of the G8 or similar occasions—though here one has to add that protests by opponents of globalization declined in these years. But he also completely put a stop to his publications. The last political post on his blog appeared November 18, 2005. And he's not been active on social media, at least not under his real name."

"I can see two reasons for that," reasoned Christopoulos. "He's either given up his involvement, or he continues to push forward with it but no longer wants to draw attention to himself…"

"…because he's planning something in secret. Exactly. Think of the 9/11 attackers, who appeared to be well-behaved students or something along those lines. Inconspicuous, assimilated. Meanwhile they were quietly planning the worst terror attack since the end of the Second World War."

"But he's got to expect that he's still on our radar."

"Of course. We have him in our data bank. Unfortunately, the images we have of him are poor quality, so the facial recognition software couldn't establish a sufficient degree of similarity between them and the facial composite."

"How many millions did that cost? It didn't recognize any of these faces?"

"We'll find out if that's the case."

"But even if Pucao is one of the attackers, we still don't have the others," Christopoulos pointed out, still playing the skeptic. Bollard had nothing against that—to the contrary.

"Right this minute, every intelligence agency in Europe, the United States, and all allied nations are checking out every contact of Dragenau's and Pucao's that they can find."

"Insofar as they're able to." Christopoulos sighed. "If things are playing out the same way in the United States as they are here, they'll have trouble finding a lot of them. And not because they're terrorists, but because they're sleeping on a mattress among hundreds of other people in some sports arena or civic center—or standing in line for food."

BRUSSELS, BELGIUM

"Remember the suspicious IP address I discovered before the battery went dead and we lost the Porsche?"

Hy typed it into the browser's address line. In the browser window the word RESET appeared, followed by the fields user and password.

"Amateurs," Manzano blurted. "I'll try an SQL-Injection. I'll spare you the details but someone here felt hugely overconfident."

A few minutes later, he whispered, "I don't believe it..."

"What?" Shannon whispered back.

"The username field," said Manzano. "It's vulnerable. I can get through and access information on the website practically without putting in a username."

"How'd that happen?"

"Bad security measures by the people behind it."

"And what kind of information are we talking about?"

"Let's take a look right now."

A long list appeared on the screen.

blond
tancr
sanskrit
cuhao
proud
baku
tzsche
b.tuck
sarowi
simon
...

"What is that?"

"If we're lucky, what we've got here is a list of this website's users," said Manzano. "Now let's go look for the passwords."

He downloaded the file to the computer. A few seconds later, he opened it.

A massive jumble of letters and numerals popped up.

```
Downloaded table: USERS
sanskrit:36df662327a5eb9772c968749ce
9be7b
tzsche:823a765a12dd063b67412240d5015
acc
tancr:6dedaebd83531823a03173097386801
b.tuck:9e57554d65f36327cadac052a323f
4af
blond:e0329eab084173a9188c6a1e9111a7
f89f
...
```

"Look, look" was all Manzano said.

Someone knocked. The door was opened, and Manzano reached for the laptop so that he could close it if necessary.

Sophia.

"You scared us," said Manzano.

"What are you up to?"

"We've found something interesting."

"Come on over," said Shannon. "It's fascinating what he's up to over here—if also completely incomprehensible…"

Sophia gazed at the screen.

"Might as well be Chinese to me," she said.

"Same with me," Manzano agreed. "How can anyone be so careless? Look here," he pointed at the beginning of the lines. "These are usernames for this website. Plain and clear, stored without encryption. That means we can go ahead and fill in the upper field. The keystroke combinations that follow are the passwords, or, to be more precise—and this is the problem—so-called hashes of the passwords: encrypted versions of the same."

"Does that mean we won't get any further with them?" said Shannon.

"Depends," replied Manzano. His fingers flew over the keys again.

"If the people behind this did clean enough work, then this is the end of the road for us. But one continues to be surprised at how sloppy even the pros can be in this area."

There was another knock at the door. Sophia, nervous, turned, crossed the room, and opened the door but didn't give whoever it was the option of coming inside. Behind her, in the hallway, Manzano recognized the man with the designer glasses again.

"Ah, they're still there..." he said.

"I called them," explained Sophia.

Manzano could see the man trying to catch a glimpse of him and Shannon over Sophia's shoulder.

"IT," the man repeated. "When I need them it takes two weeks for them to show up. I guess I'd have to look as good as you..."

"Thanks," Sophia responded.

"Well, I guess I'll be..."

He cast another look inside the room and disappeared. Sophia closed the door and came back to the table.

"Did he want something?"

"Seemed to me he was curious."

"So am I," said Shannon. "How are you proposing to get the passwords?"

"I'm betting on more human fallibility. First, I'm hoping that the programmers haven't built in additional security mechanisms. I'm also hoping that a few of the users were too lazy to enter long or complicated passwords. Because the shorter and simpler a password is, the fewer combinations there are that the computer has to cycle through and try out in order to crack the password."

"But there have got to be more than enough."

"And for that reason there are so-called rainbow tables."

"You sound like you're doing brain surgery here," said Sophia.

"Well, I am operating on the nervous system of our society."

"More jumbled numbers."

Manzano's use of the rainbow tables for unencrypting the passwords had produced a long list:

```
36df662327a5eb9772c968749ce9be7b:Nu
nO2000
1cfdbe52d6e51a01f939cc7afd79c7ac:kie
mens154
11b006e634105339d5a53a93ca85b11b:
99a5aa34432d59a38459ee6e71d46bbe:
9e57554d65f36327cadac052a323f4af:gat
inhas_3
59efbbecd85ee7cb1e52788c54d70058:fus
aomg
823a765a12dd063b67412240d5015acc:439
42ac9
6dedaebd83531823a03173097386801:
8dcaab52526fa7d7b3a90ec3096fe655:080
4e19c
32f1236aa37a89185003ad972264985e:pl
us1779
794c2fe4661290b34a5a246582c1e1f6:xin
avane
e0329eab084173a9188c6a1e9111a7f89f:r
ibrucos
```

"Look closer," Manzano directed them.

"Behind some of the alphanumeric sequences, there are shorter ones," said Sophia. "Some of them look like—"

"Passwords. They don't just look like them. They are passwords: NunO2000, kiemens154, gatinhas_3, fusaomg… And, as you can see, they're mostly either shorter, or use

only lower or uppercase letters, or are more simple for some
other reason. And of course we were lucky that no other
security mechanisms were used."

"So this means that now you can log on to the site that
your computer was being made to transfer data to every
night?"

"And that's exactly what I'm going to do."

Manzano brought up the site and filled in the username
and password fields with a valid combination.

```
Username: blond
Password: ribrucos
```

"Enter."

"And now even more lists, tables…" Shannon remarked.
"What do they tell us? Like that one there."

She pointed to a line.

```
tancr topic 93rm4n h4rd $4b07493
```

"Looks to me like 'Leet.' It's a hacker language. I think
what it says is 'topic german hard sabotage.' Let's see what's
behind it. 'Tancr' is confirming some kind of action. At
the end, he says he's satisfied that everything is going
according to plan."

"And now can you translate it so that we also know
what's going according to plan?"

"To do that, we'd have to read more of the thread.
Maybe then we'll find out more."

He scrolled down; hundreds of lines appeared.

"Wow, they've been talking for a long time. Ah, it looks
like they start here."

Manzano scrolled up again.

"That's interesting. There's a date at the beginning of
every new discussion. For the first one it was Monday the
third…"

"But the third wasn't a Monday."

"Right. For the last conversation, it's Sunday the tenth."

"Today is Sunday," said Shannon.

"But again, not the tenth," Sophia added.

"Wait, wait!" cried Manzano. "Let me do the math here!" He counted silently.

"The power went out on Friday of last week. From then up to today that's..."

"Ten days," Shannon finished his thought.

"The calendar for this chat begins on day zero of the blackout."

"Then this thread would be from this morning."

"If our guess is right."

"We still don't know what it is they're talking about."

Manzano closed the thread and returned to the original list.

"All manner of discussions are being carried out here."

"Apropos discussions," said a deep voice from the door. "The police would very much like to speak with you."

Sophia jumped. In the door stood Nagy, leader of the MIC; behind him were three meatheads in dark security guard uniforms and the curious colleague from earlier. Before Sophia could say a word, they had barged into the room. Out of the corner of her eye she saw Manzano frantically type something on the keyboard and then close the laptop. The next moment one of the uniformed men grabbed him, and another reached for the American journalist. They pulled their arms behind their backs with such force that Shannon let out a yell.

"What are these two doing here?" Nagy asked in an icy voice. "They are not employees in our IT department."

"No!" cried Manzano. "But I've just—"

The security man behind Manzano's back pulled upward on the Italian's arm and he went quiet, his face twisted in pain.

Sophia was speechless. When Manzano had turned up

in front of her that afternoon she had been happy to see him again, despite his ragged appearance—happier than she had admitted to herself in the moment. "This man was the first to lead Europol and every one of us to the true cause of the blackout," she said, noticing that as she spoke her voice was shaky. This uncertainty—it wasn't like her. Sophia tried to make her voice firmer. "A few minutes ago he discovered a communications portal used by the attackers."

Even as she was saying the words, the blood flooded back into her face at the thought that Manzano might have known about this website the whole time. Had he put on a show for her?

Nagy gave the two security guards a sign. The two of them led Manzano and Shannon out.

"Listen, Mr. Nagy," said Sophia. "This is, I believe it's really, very…"

Nagy nodded at the remaining security man.

"…important." Sophia went quiet as the man grabbed her roughly by the arm.

"Tell it to the police," said Nagy.

EC 155, BAVARIA, GERMANY

The ground troops had radioed with info on the route. By the time the EC 155 had reached the stretch of road, it was getting dark. They were flying high enough that the targets wouldn't be able to hear the helicopter. Through the night vision goggles mounted on his helmet, Hartlandt searched the country road for the vehicle, the road winding its way below them like a narrow footpath. He was now wearing his bulletproof vest.

"I have them," announced the copilot. "One o'clock, approximately two hundred meters."

"Drop altitude," ordered the commander.

Now everything had to play out with the greatest

precision. The pilots had to bring their aircraft to street level within a matter of seconds, so that the sound of their motors wouldn't give their quarry too much advanced warning.

Hartlandt saw the road growing quickly larger and sighted the other helicopter as well, as it executed the same maneuver. He flipped up the night vision.

When they were still about sixty meters above the van, the pilots turned on the spotlights. The vehicle was immediately bathed in a dazzling circle of light.

Hartlandt watched it slow down abruptly while the helicopters continued to dive. His stomach dropped for a second when the pilot finally leveled out a few meters above the ground and behind the vehicle. The other helicopter had blocked the road in front, its light shining directly into the van. The brake lights flashed red, then the vehicle started to reverse, making such an expert turn that it swung a full 180 degrees and was now speeding right toward them.

Their pilot stood his ground and almost set the runners down on the road. The van braked so sharply that the front end pitched downward, then the doors were flung open. In the glaring light of the van's headlights the GSG 9 men jumped out of the helicopter.

Hartlandt felt the hard asphalt under his boots.

Muzzle flashes flared up next to the van. He dived off the road and crawled out of the range of the headlights.

"Don't shoot!" he shouted. "Cease fire."

Through the speaker in his helmet he heard the short, sharp orders of the commander.

The lights of the van had been shot up by then, and the helicopters' spotlights bathed the bullet-riddled vehicle in glaring light. A body lay motionless next to the passenger door. Members of the team from the other helicopter were kneeling at the rear of the van, taking cover. One of them crawled over to the man lying flat out on the ground, kicked his gun to one side, and quickly felt his body for more weapons; others secured the vehicle from the side.

Then came the signal from the other side of the van. "Secure."

Hartlandt jumped up and ran to the van.

"One target dead," announced a voice in Hartlandt's helmet.

The man on the road looked dead all right. His torso and his head had been hit by several bullets, and only about half of his face was still recognizable. Furious, Hartlandt went around the front of the van to the other side. The officers did not have a choice; the men in the van had begun exchanging fire. To neutralize the targets without killing them was impossible. Next to the front left tire lay a second man with a dark complexion; he too was dead. The third had been fired on in a field a few meters away. Next to him kneeled two police officers, and a third rushed over with first aid. Like his comrades, the man had been hit several times. Hartlandt would have described his facial features as typically Mediterranean, but at that moment he could barely tell the color of his close-cropped hair.

Part of the attack squad had carefully opened the back doors. Inside they found dozens of canisters and boxes. Hartlandt spotted lighter fluid and explosives. Inside a bulky box were stored food and sleeping bags. To judge from the amount of food they were carrying, they must have been close to the end of their trip or near a base with supplies.

A second team was going through the drivers' cabin. Two laptops—they would have to take a close look at them. A well-worn road map of central Europe was the first interesting find. The saboteurs' route was indicated on it in purple marker. The route had two more legs through Germany, then led across Austria toward Hungary and farther on to Croatia, where the map ended. There were three kinds of symbols to be found along the line. Hartlandt had quickly deciphered them.

"These are substations," he explained, pointing at small squares, the northernmost of which was in Denmark, the next at the first German target, Lübeck. "They set these on fire. The triangles indicate the transmission towers. These ones between Bremen and Cloppenburg, for example, have been blown up already. As for the places that are marked with a circle, we don't have any reports of sabotage for them. I'm guessing that's where they stashed their food and munitions."

"So far we haven't found any phones or other communication devices," said one of the men.

"They don't need any," said Hartlandt. "As soon as they set their route, they could act independently. Shield the rest of the troops."

"Here's a second map," said one of the men, his face covered up. He unfolded a less ragged road map—the purple line led all the way to Greece.

Out of the corner of his eye Hartlandt watched the officers struggling to save the life of one of the terrorists. He hoped to God they didn't lose him.

BRUSSELS, BELGIUM

The women were packed into a small bus in front of the police station, the men into a larger one with bars on the windows. Four armed police officers escorted them. They had to stick their legs into leg irons attached to bars under the seats. The police checked them over and clamped them shut.

Like a hardened criminal, thought Manzano. He stared through the window bars at the dark facades of buildings passing in the darkness. The only vehicles he could see were the military's armed cars; and only a couple of soldiers were standing around in the street. They carried flashlights or lanterns or had lights on their helmets. Like in a disaster movie, he thought.

NEAR NUREMBERG, GERMANY

Standing in the middle of a field illuminated by the helicopter's spotlight was a shack. It measured maybe seven meters square, guessed Hartlandt. The pilot set the machine down a few meters away. The runners had barely touched the ground when Hartlandt and the GSG 9 special unit men jumped out into the cold. They sprinted toward the shack, ducking under the beating of the rotors.

The helicopter's engine grew quieter. When the men got closer to the shack, they began to tread cautiously. They pushed a cable with a tiny camera and a light mounted on it through the gap under the door. On the monitor that displayed images from the camera, Hartlandt saw an empty interior, a floor strewn with straw. The officer with the remote turned the camera toward the inside of the door and inspected it.

"Secure," he confirmed.

Two men broke the door down with a battering ram. Their bright flashlights lit up only an empty interior. They pushed the layer of straw aside with their feet. One of the police officers stamped down harder.

"There's something under here."

It was a door, built into the floor.

———

The officer let down the small mobile eye. Hartlandt spotted white plastic packets to the left, canisters on the right. In between sat three packs of canned goods wrapped in clear tape.

The cameraman gave the OK to break the door open. Crouching low, two of the men carefully sliced through the white plastic, then inspected the contents.

"Plastic explosive," said one. "Unmarked. An analysis will show what it is exactly."

In the canisters they found diesel.

"Explosives, fuel, food," the commander summed up. "Nothing else here."

"No phone or radio?" said Hartlandt.

"No. Looks like this would have been their next stop. The trail ends here for now."

BRUSSELS, BELGIUM

The bus stopped in front of a barely lit building. Still has power, thought Manzano. An imposing iron gate opened, and the bus drove into a large courtyard. The smaller van with the women followed. The courtyard was bordered by four four-story outbuildings, the facades bathed in a gloomy yellow light from lamps set at regular intervals. The women's bus turned off to the left; the men's bus drove straight on, through a large gate. Behind it a cordon of armed police officers awaited them. The escort officers opened their leg irons, then shouted at the prisoners; the men stood up, and Manzano followed. They left the bus and were led down a long passageway. At the end of it more officers were waiting in front of a tall double door. It opened onto a giant, gloomy hall, a beastly stench pressing out from it. They were driven forward, and the doors slammed shut behind them with a resounding clang.

Four fluorescent lights shone from the ceiling, flickering. Manzano could dimly make out crowded rows of metal bunk beds. The room was teeming with people. Hundreds of us, thought Manzano grimly.

The prison guards had not issued instructions or assigned any spots. Some of the men sitting on the floor closest to the beds were murmuring to the newcomers in threatening tones.

Manzano couldn't understand. But from their body language, he concluded it would be best not to approach.

"No beds left," whispered a young man, in English.

Someone in their group seemed to know what was going on; the young man translated the essentials for Manzano.

"Several Brussels jails were evacuated into this one, which is to say they were all thrown together in here. The cells are full to bursting. This is actually the gymnasium," he said. "There are all kinds of prisoners in here. Pickpockets, white-collar criminals, serial killers... We should act calm and do as we're told."

Manzano looked around for a space for himself.

DAY 10—MONDAY

BRUSSELS, BELGIUM

Noise and shouting. Manzano opened his eyes. There was an overwhelming smell that was not the stench he recognized.

Fire.

Panicked, he struggled to stand up between the bunk beds and immediately saw the flames, blazing two meters high in the middle of the floor. Black smoke rose to the ceiling and collected there.

Prisoners were retreating to the edges of the hall or toward the door. A few were leaping hysterically around the fire, screaming, tossing mattresses into the flames— whether to extinguish or to feed the blaze, Manzano couldn't tell.

The smoke grew thicker and slowly sank down from the ceiling.

The only windows were about six meters high and too narrow to squeeze through.

More prisoners rushed toward the large doors and toward smaller exits that Manzano saw only now. They cried for help, pounded against the doors with their fists, and tried to ram them or force them open with the metal bed frames.

The smoke began to scratch his throat. The prisoners coughed and held towels to their mouth and nose.

Shots rang out.

Suddenly one of the big doors was flung open. Men shoved their way through. There were more shots, barely audible over the deafening yells.

Another door sprang open, and the men dashed toward it, despite steady shooting. The smoke grew thicker inside the hall. The flames, stoked by the airflow between the doors, leaped from bed to bed, blazing ever higher.

Some options, thought Manzano: suffocate, get burned alive, or get shot. Outside, however, the shots seemed to be more scattered and to come from a greater distance. He crawled on all fours beneath the black cloud to the exit, leaving the last of the madmen behind him, dancing around the flames.

Dozens of wounded or dead lay in the doorway. Manzano passed two lifeless bodies in uniform. Had the inmates killed the officers and grabbed their weapons? In the midst of the crowd he made it to the entrance of the large courtyard. Smoke from the burning gym had seeped outside. Manzano felt it scratch the back of his throat and sting his eyes. He buried his face in his elbow. He kept on going. There was no place to hide out here in the courtyard. Bullets were still raining in from all sides. He staggered forward, convinced that at any moment he'd be hit by a bullet and it would all be over.

BERLIN, GERMANY

"I need an update on Philippsburg," ordered the chancellor.

"We're working on it," a woman from the Ministry for the Environment, Nature Conservation, and Nuclear Safety assured him. "The latest report, an hour ago, indicated that minute amounts of radioactive steam had escaped. Yesterday we began advising the population within a five-kilometer radius not to leave their homes or emergency shelters."

"Do the rest of the nuclear plants at least have the supplies they need?" barked the chancellor. The woman didn't answer. Her hands began to shake.

"What?" the chancellor asked in an empty voice.

"It would seem there's been a severe incident at the

Brokdorf power plant on the Elbe. More precise information is not yet known."

"More precise information is not yet known?" the chancellor exploded. "Just what *do* these worthless plant operators know? They have no idea who breached their IT network, why their power plants don't work, when they can get the power running again—nothing! I want to see the CEOs of the plant operators for Philippsburg and Brokdorf here in person or on the screen, immediately!"

"I…I'll take care of it," stammered the woman.

The chancellor closed his eyes for a moment, then opened them again.

"Forgive me," he said. "I know there is nothing you can do about it. I hope that was everything?"

The woman bit her lip.

Again the chancellor closed his eyes.

"Go ahead, out with it."

"The French plant at Fessenheim on the Rhine is also reporting a serious incident resulting from undefined difficulties with the backup cooling systems."

On the map of Europe, she pointed at a spot on the German border, near Stuttgart. "According to the IAEA, mildly radioactive steam was let off. There is no reason to evacuate, the plant operators say. Yet. The map would envision a zone of up to twenty-five kilometers. Under normal circumstances that would affect almost half a million people, including Freiburg."

"Half a million…" groaned the chancellor.

"And Temelín," the staffer went on. "It may have come to a core meltdown there, like in Saint-Laurent. The Czech authorities have started their evacuation. But the power plant lies about eighty kilometers away from the nearest German border. Plus, at present, the prevailing winds are moving northwestward. Therefore, radiation will likely be carried more toward Austria."

"Until the wind turns," said the chancellor.

BRUSSELS, BELGIUM

The cell door sprang open with a loud clank. Sophia was the first to notice, as she was the only one not trying to get a glimpse out the window of the courtyard.

She grabbed Shannon.

"They're opening up!" she cried and pulled the American out into the hallway. They were almost trampled by the others. They ran with the crowd to the stairwell, stopping only at the entrance to the courtyard. The shooting had stopped. Hundreds of men were flooding toward the exit from the men's cell blocks. Smoke was rising, and flames leaped out of the windows.

"Shall we wait till they're gone?" asked Shannon. "Hundreds of men on a rampage, hardened criminals among them…"

"No," replied Sophia. "In the chaos no one will notice us. Come on!"

They started running, and Sophia prayed there would be no more shooting.

They reached the large gate without incident. It was open. The escapees were spreading out onto the street in all directions.

"Where are we?" panted Shannon, jogging alongside Sophia.

"On the outskirts of town," answered Sophia.

"And now?"

"Let's make sure we get home safely. The police won't be so quick to look for us there. They've got bigger game to catch."

THE HAGUE, NETHERLANDS

Hartlandt had a hard time hearing Bollard over the satellite phone. He had returned to Ratingen while the GSG 9 set about digging through more of the saboteurs' storehouses.

"We've identified the men," he said. "Mercenaries. A

South African, a Russian, and a Ukrainian. Turned up in the data banks of several intelligence agencies. One of them was recently in Iraq working for Blackwater; the other two had been there earlier."

"Have you questioned the survivor yet?" asked Bollard.

"No. He was hit by twelve bullets. Three of them in the brain. We won't get a thing out of him."

"Did you come up with anything else?"

"We found a map in the car showing the route they'd planned, the attack targets, and the way stations. But there were no communication devices. Intelligence agencies are analyzing the men's histories, including their financial records. Personally, I would pay guys like that in cash, but you know what they say: 'Follow the money.' With luck, it will lead us somewhere."

BRUSSELS, BELGIUM

Manzano limped through the streets as quickly as his leg allowed. In the distance he heard the sirens of police cars. During the first minutes of his escape, pure instinct had guided his actions. Now his senses were slowly returning. The first thing he needed was a place to hide, then he had to try to find an internet connection where he could look more closely at the RESET site. He weighed up his options. He didn't know a soul in the city, except for Sophia Angström. Had the women been able to break out? He hadn't even thought about it till then.

He had to try. He'd memorized Sophia's address from the business card she'd given him. All he had to do now was find someone who could tell him how to get there—and some form of transportation, in case Sophia's apartment was too far away. He rattled every bicycle that he could find chained to railings or street signs. After a few tries he found one whose owner had been careless enough to leave it unlocked.

THE HAGUE, NETHERLANDS

As she had the day before, Marie waited in vain at the food distribution site for the truck carrying supplies. In the end, even the price gougers and black-market traders had been forced to flee from the angry crowd. The speakers on the square had succeeded in inciting the mob to vent their anger on those responsible, namely the politicians. The masses had been set in motion as slowly and inexorably as a mudslide after a dam break. Feeling a confused mixture of fascination, anger, and curiosity, Marie let herself be swept along all the way to the Binnenhof, the seat of the Dutch parliament.

On the way through the city, more people joined the procession. She estimated that thousands filled the square, chanting as they arrived. A few police officers tried to stop them but were simply shoved aside. The crowd was so large that the complex's giant inner courtyard couldn't contain them. They spilled out into surrounding streets, all the way to the seat of the second chamber on the opposite side.

Marie had been a student when she attended her last demonstration, and that was only to provoke her parents. She felt uneasy among these loud, disgruntled people, and yet strangely secure within this large, warm, moving organism. Both worried and fearless, she could feel its energy pass into her. She didn't go so far as to join in the screaming. Though she remained intent on keeping her distance, as the fury of the mob around her grew, she began to feel something primitive within her responding to their cries...

BERLIN, GERMANY

"We have further indications that China is behind the attack," announced the NATO general from the screen. Behind him, Michelsen sensed the buzz of activity in the NATO crisis team's command center.

"Well, sure," grumbled Michelsen. "People are quick

to find proof when they need it—like weapons of mass destruction…"

The general hadn't heard her, but the defense minister threw her a withering look.

"Wars have certainly been started for lesser reasons," remarked the NATO general. "China has been working intensely for at least a decade to infiltrate the IT systems of Western states and corporations."

"The motive continues to be a mystery to me," the interior minister spoke up. "The world economy has long been so closely interconnected that bringing Europe and the United States to the brink of ruin would only have devastating consequences for the rest of the world."

For the first time since the beginning of the discussion, the general moved more than his face. He leaned toward the camera.

"Look, Mr. Chancellor, I'm a soldier of the old school, but even I have come to realize that the wars of the future aren't necessarily going to be fought with rifles, tanks, or fighter jets. They'll be fought the way we're seeing now. We cannot—no, we must not—wait for someone to take the first shot at us or drop the first bombs on our cities. The enemy isn't going to do it. That's because he no longer needs to. He can destroy us while sitting behind his desk ten thousand kilometers away.

"Do you understand? The first blow has been dealt! The enemy doesn't need nuclear weapons—they've turned our nuclear power facilities on us. The first meltdown has already laid waste to parts of France. It's only a matter of time before we see more. At least we can still prevent these if we take immediate action. And I'm not talking about launching nuclear missiles at Peking," he explained. "We too command the means of modern warfare. As the first step, it would be conceivable to respond in kind: by cutting off power to certain key cities."

"Who has that capability?" asked the interior minister.

"Do you think the militaries of the West have been asleep these past years?" asked the NATO general. "Look, Mr. Chancellor, the one thing you're not going to see in this conflict is a smoking gun. But if you step outside the door you'll see that the shot has been fired. And it has seriously wounded us. Let's start shooting back before we bleed to death."

BRUSSELS, BELGIUM

Sophia parked the stolen bike against the five-story apartment building; Shannon leaned hers next to it.

Sophia lived on the top floor. As soon as they were in the apartment, she turned all four locks twice.

They both looked a sight: sweaty, covered in soot, their hair frazzled.

"Come with me," Sophia said. In the bathroom she handed Shannon a few individually wrapped wet wipes. "This'll have to do, sorry."

Shannon cleaned herself as best she could. At least she could get the dirt off her face and hands. She even had a wet wipe left over for her underarms and neck.

In the kitchen, Sophia opened some bread and set honey and a bottle of water on the table.

"I've got corned beef too, if you'd like some meat with your breakfast," she offered.

"Thanks, but this is plenty."

"You met Piero in The Hague?"

Shannon told the story: how she had sought out Bollard and in doing so had come across Manzano. She still had a feeling that Sophia was interested in the Italian, so she kept quiet about the fact that she had shared a room with him.

"How did things play out over the past few days?" Shannon asked finally. "I'm sure you must have a good overall sense of it."

"Is this the journalist coming out again?"

Shannon shrugged. "It's not like I can get anything on the air at the moment."

"We have no overview of the situation," said Sophia. "Most means of communication have failed, leaving the authorities with no telephone, no official radio, a little military and amateur radio, and a few satellite connections. The only links still functioning are those between the national crisis centers, but each country has a fragmented sense of what's going on out there.

"Black markets are flourishing, public structures and institutions are being dissolved by private initiatives or parallel structures, the police and military can no longer maintain public safety. People are starting to take the law into their own hands. Since Spain fell, there have been military coups in Portugal and Greece. In France they're contending with a meltdown at a nuclear plant; the same in the Czech Republic, and conditions are critical at a dozen more facilities across Europe.

"There have been accidents at industrial facilities, particularly chemical factories, some of which have claimed dozens, if not hundreds of victims and caused severe damage to the environment. But here too we lack precise information. It's impossible to be sure of the scale of the devastation. Those few areas that still have a power supply have been overrun with refugees."

"And in the United States?"

"You have family over there?"

Shannon nodded.

"It doesn't look much better. The same drama, but a few days behind us, since the blackout started later."

There was a knock at the door.

Shannon's heart shot up into her throat. "Who's that?" she whispered.

"No idea," Sophia whispered back. "Maybe my neighbor."

"What about the police?"

"Would they knock?"

PARIS, FRANCE

"We've reset almost all the computers in the grid control room," Blanchard explained to Tollé, the aide to the French president—the one person in the place who wasn't sleep deprived and malodorous.

"Does that mean," asked Tollé, "that you can monitor the flow of electricity in the grids again?"

"In theory, yes," answered Proctet. "We were also able to get the majority of the servers that control grid operation functional again. Starting tomorrow morning, we'll begin rebuilding the first small grids. If we're successful, we'll keep expanding over the course of the day."

"And why wouldn't you be successful?"

"The systems, the processes. They're complex. And they're dependent on various factors."

"Where do the problems lie? Is there anything we can do? You only have to say the word."

"I'm afraid," said Blanchard, "you cannot make the necessary amount of reactive power available, nor can you accelerate the grid-building process without causing more problems. At this stage, the power plants must run in unfavorable operating conditions that they can only maintain for a few hours. On top of that, it's hard to determine how many users one can connect in order to keep the grid stable.

"There's also the possibility that automatic protective mechanisms will be triggered, which will entail load-shedding, shutting generators off, and so on. For example, switching on transformers that have lain idle can result in bottlenecking; on top of that, the Ferranti effect can activate excess voltage triggers—need I go on? In short: none of it is simple, and unfortunately you can't help us."

Tollé nodded, as if he had understood everything but didn't know what to say.

Blanchard relished the moment, but then Tollé spoiled it by saying, "So I can tell the president that the power supply is going to return?"

THE HAGUE, NETHERLANDS

When the first plumes of smoke rose up from a corner of the Binnenhof, the crowd fell into a frenzy. Flames billowed from windows on the second floor and soon enveloped the building in smoke. Marie stood trapped at the back of the square, the statue of William I rising before her. The noise had taken on a new timbre. In place of the rhythmic, pounding slogans, there was fevered, confused shouting interspersed with fearful screams. Marie now felt an ever stronger pressure from behind, but the streets around the square were too narrow and too packed for anyone to get away. Ghastly images of people getting trampled, crushed, suffocated raced through her head, and she could not suppress the rising panic in her chest. As the adrenaline coursed through her veins, all she could do was allow herself to be swept along with the flow. How could she have let herself get carried away like this? The children needed her.

BRUSSELS, BELGIUM

"I have to get on this site!" cried Manzano.

He was, at least, in better shape than before. Half an hour ago, when Sophia had opened the door, he had simply stood there staring at them: bloodshot eyes in a blackened face.

"Every time I see you, you look worse than the last time!" Sophia had found herself saying. She had spent the worst night of her life because of him, but the joy of seeing him alive outweighed any anger.

He had arrived at her apartment by bicycle. With the help of a few wet wipes, some soap, and a precious half bottle of water, they had cleaned him up as best they could.

The three of them could only guess why the guards had opened the cells. Probably fear. The fear of having to answer for the deaths of hundreds of prisoners by fire.

"I don't have any internet here, obviously," said Sophia.

"Then I've got to get into your office."

Sophia thought she had misheard him.

When she didn't answer, he continued, "That's the only way we can investigate this site properly. Don't you get it? We might have discovered the attackers' communication platform! I have to gain access!"

COMMAND HEADQUARTERS

The images first appeared on the Japanese network's website. Its correspondent in The Hague had sent them via satellite. The Dutch parliament building was in flames.

"It's starting," one of his coconspirators, Lekue Birabi, remarked with satisfaction. He'd first met the Nigerian during his time as a student in London. The son of a tribal chief from the Niger Delta, Birabi had been in the final year of his doctoral thesis at the renowned London School of Economics and Political Science. The two had bonded from the start. Since his youth, Birabi had opposed the exploitation of the Niger Delta by the central government and multinational oil corporations.

It was back then that he, together with Birabi and a few others, had begun to develop the idea that had been sparked during their all-night discussions. Others had signed up in the years that followed. People of different backgrounds, nationalities, social classes, and education; men and women, united in the same vision, the same goal. Now they had achieved their first step. The citizens of Europe and the United States had moved beyond the stage where they'd be satisfied with discussions, petitions, or demonstrations. After a few days of shocked inaction and the illusion of a peaceful maintenance of the old order, events were stacking up. From Rome, Sofia, London, Berlin, and many other European cities, journalists were reporting on increasingly violent attacks against public institutions. And now the same thing was happening in America.

He nodded to Birabi, who made no effort to hide his gratification. A broad smile had broken out on his face. Their fantasy construct had become reality. The uprising had commenced.

THE HAGUE, NETHERLANDS

"Our cooperation with international authorities has provided us with the names of several possible accomplices of Jorge Pucao," Bollard informed the group. "There is solid evidence that he has been in contact with six of them. Moreover, flight data analysis has revealed overlapping stopovers in the same locations over the past few years."

He pulled up a photo of a black African.

"Dr. Lekue Birabi from Nigeria. You'll find the details of his biography in the data bank. There are many parallels to Jorge Pucao: member of the middle to upper class of a developing country, politically engaged, antagonized by the ruling system, family drama, high intelligence, educated at one of the best universities in the world. On one of his several blogs, back in 2005, he wrote: 'Today's economic-political system in its current form reinforces existing power relations. History tells us that peaceful attempts at reform have fallen apart from within. Therefore, one must consider a violent destruction of the system as the road to renewal.' His radicalization mirrors Pucao's. As does his participation in various anti-G8 protests, beginning with Genoa in 2001."

Bollard showed a world map on which locations were

connected with red lines. Number combinations labeled every line, every location.

"These are the documented trips made by Jorge Pucao, starting in 2007."

With a click of the remote he added blue lines to the red. In some places the blue ends met up with the red.

"These are Lekue Birabi's trips during the same time frame. As we can see, they are frequently at the same destination at the same time. When we last checked, Birabi was living in the United States. In the fall of 2011 he disappeared. There's been no trace of him since then. The American authorities are currently checking over his computer, which he left behind in a storeroom.

"It had been carefully wiped, of course, but it was possible to recover a few files. Among other things, his email correspondence. From this it emerges that from 2007 he was in frequent contact with a certain 'Donkun'—who, according to IP addresses, was located wherever Pucao happened to be staying at the time. The investigators found further contacts all over the world.

"A number of these individuals have also disappeared and are now being investigated. Siti Yusuf, for example. From Indonesia, same age and similar CV to Pucao and Birabi; his family lost its fortune during the Asian financial crisis of the late nineties and suffered during the subsequent unrest.

"Then there are two countrymen of Pucao: Elvira Gomez and Pedro Munoz, both political activists. Two Spaniards: Hernandes Sidon and Maria de Carvalles-Tendido. And the list goes on: two Italians; two Russians; a man from Uruguay; a man from the Czech Republic; three Greeks, a woman and two men; a Frenchman; an Irishman; two Americans; a Japanese man; a Finnish woman; and two Germans. Some of them are proven IT experts, like Pucao. In total, there are at the moment about fifty persons under suspicion."

"Do we really believe," someone spoke up, "that a handful of overprivileged, overgrown adolescents could bring Western civilization to its knees?"

"Why not?" asked Bollard. "In Germany in the seventies all it took was a handful of terrorists in the Red Army Faction to change the lives of sixty million citizens of the republic. The societal consequences could be felt for decades afterward. The founding group of the Red Brigade in Italy consisted of fifteen members, and fewer than two dozen men carried out the 9/11 attacks. I'd say we can absolutely assume that a few dozen people with sufficient know-how and financial means are capable of causing the devastation we're now looking at."

"That's the crux of it," Christopoulos spoke up. "Finance. Even if these guys have the relevant know-how, for such an undertaking you need serious money."

"Which brings us to Balduin von Ansen, Jeanette Bordieux, and George Vanminster. What makes them distinct from the other persons of interest on our list is that they are heirs to substantial fortunes: von Ansen, son of a British aristocrat and a German banker; Vanminster, U.S. citizen, heir to the multinational conglomerate Vanminster Industries; and Bordieux, daughter of a French media baron. Together, they are worth over a billion euros. All three generously fund social and political projects. All three have been in close contact with Pucao and the other suspects for years."

"Why should such people—"

"Why not? There are enough examples. We owe the publication of global literary successes like *Doctor Zhivago* and *Il Gattopardo* to the Italian publisher Giangiacomo Feltrinelli, son of one of the richest families in Italy. But that same Feltrinelli was also responsible for the famous image of Che Guevara that still today adorns millions of T-shirts and teenagers' bedroom walls. Not only did he have connections to Italian extremist groups, he founded his own, joined the underground, provided weapons to German terrorists—and died in an attempt to blow up a transmission tower. And then there's that other millionaire and godfather of terrorism, Osama bin Laden. Trust me, there are extremists among the rich too."

ORLÉANS, FRANCE

Annette had grown used to the smell and the constant noise in the shelter, but the faces depressed her. The woman from the Red Cross had assigned the Doreuils and the Bollards four beds in a row, near the back of the hall. True, it meant a long hike to the showers and toilets, but any disadvantage was outweighed by the benefits of escaping the noxious stench that surrounded her now, as she stood in line to use the bathroom.

Annette had demanded to be checked for radiation several times but had always received the same answer: insufficient personnel and no equipment.

She heard raised voices from the entrance. A few people hurried into the sleeping area and spread out. Across the vast room, she could see her husband and the Bollards asking their neighbors what all the commotion was about. More and more people began flooding toward the exit loaded with packs, bags, and suitcases. They were fleeing the shelter! There were so many trying to get out that bottlenecks were forming at the exits.

"There was another explosion at the power plant!" Vincent said urgently as Annette reached them. "The wind is blowing a radioactive cloud straight toward Orléans!"

He began to stuff the few possessions that lay on their beds into his suitcase.

"We have to get out of here!" her husband shouted.

Annette hesitated. "Come on," Bertrand urged her. He pressed the lighter of the two bags into her hand while he took the suitcase. He grabbed his chest for an instant, his face twisted. Then he marched off, ensuring that Annette was following.

The grimace on his pale features unnerved her more than the latest evacuation, but she took the bag and hurried after the others in silence as they weaved their way between the beds. By now there were huge crowds trying to force their way out of the exits, which were completely jammed with the crush of bodies. Ahead of Annette, her husband turned to look over his shoulder. He called out to her, but she couldn't hear him above the terrible din of panic and disorder. And then he staggered, dropped the suitcase, and collapsed to his knees. She threw down her own bag and raced to his side, screaming his name.

He looked up at her, and in his eyes she saw the pain and the fear.

"Bertrand!" she sobbed, clutching her husband's shoulders, trying to support his weight. The Bollards, unaware of what was going on behind them, were continuing toward the exit. She screamed their names as loud as she could. Celeste turned, saw her, tugged Vincent's arm to get his attention, and the two of them abandoned their suitcases and pushed their way back through the exodus.

By the time they got there, Bertrand's face was chalk-white and covered in sweat; his lips had turned blue and his whole body was trembling. His fingers clutched weakly at his chest. Annette laid one hand over his, all the while stroking his face and murmuring words of comfort. His eyes stared at her, but he didn't seem to see her.

"His heart!" Annette screamed at the Bollards. "A doctor! He needs a doctor!"

His eyelids fluttered. His lips opened and closed like a fish's. He tried to speak.

As Vincent and Celeste looked helplessly around them, calling for a medic, while Celeste cradled him in her arms, Bertrand stopped gasping for breath.

BRUSSELS, BELGIUM

"I can't believe I'm doing this," Sophia whispered as they parked the bikes in front of the European Commission building.

"Me neither," Shannon replied.

As casually as they could, the trio ambled up to the building's entrance. They made it to the lobby without being stopped, but when Sophia held her ID up to the electronic lock on the door, it remained locked.

"Damn!" she hissed. "Already deactivated."

They had caught the attention of a security guard. He came across to where they stood, one hand hovering near his holstered weapon. "Show me your ID," he said.

Sophia handed the plastic card to the guard. He studied it, then raised his eyes to Sophia and back to the card. He handed it back, then eyed Manzano and Shannon.

"They're with me," said Sophia.

"The electronic entry has been deactivated," the guard said. He opened the door with a key and looked at the clock over the reception desk: quarter past eight. "Don't work too late."

Sophia managed a laugh. "We won't, thanks."

When they were out of the guard's sight, Sophia ordered the other two to wait while she crept ahead, casting a glance into every office left and right. At last she signaled for them to follow. Manzano and Shannon hurried along the corridor and darted into the open doorway next to her. As soon as they were inside, Sophia closed the door behind them. It was the room they had been led out of the night before.

"Hey, my rucksack's still here!" Shannon was amazed.

"But my laptop is gone," said Manzano.

THE HAGUE, NETHERLANDS

"I ask myself whether we're safe here," Marie said to her

husband. They were sitting by the fireplace, wrapped in blankets. The kids were already asleep.

"It's no better anywhere else," he said. She'd never seen him so exhausted. "I'll be right back."

She heard him go down to the basement. Two minutes later he came back, a small bundle in his hand. He unwrapped it. In the flickering light of the flames she saw a pistol.

"Where did you get that?" she asked, shocked. "You know we're not allow—"

"You never know, my love," he cut in, looking into her eyes. "I brought it for safety's sake. It's been locked away in the basement."

When they went upstairs to the bedroom, he set the gun on his bedside table.

BRUSSELS, BELGIUM

"Here, I've got another laptop," whispered Sophia. She closed the door quietly behind her and set the computer down on the table.

Manzano flipped it open.

Sophia went back to the door to listen for anyone approaching.

Thankfully, Manzano had memorized the IP address. He logged into the guest Wi-Fi, typed it in, arrived at the RESET site, and entered the username and password that had got him in last time.

The list of conversation threads appeared before him. He scrolled down until he found a subregister.

"There sure are a lot of them," Shannon observed.

Manzano clicked on one at random.

Proud: Did you get the codes from deelta23?
Baku: Yep. He set up a nice little back door.
See attachment.
Proud: Ok. Put them in.

"Back door?"

Manzano didn't respond. He clicked on an attachment. A document popped up on the screen, full of lines of letters and numerals.

"What the hell is that?"

Manzano was silent, reading intently. "It's a code fragment," he said. "In a nutshell: the back door to a computer system. Programmers write something like this into a program so that if anything happens they'll still have access to it later, even if it's not designed to allow them access. And of course such a thing can be built in after the fact as well, if you're clever enough."

"Does that mean they're talking here about how they tampered with the networks?"

"They're not just talking," confirmed Manzano. "They're putting it together... Give me a minute while I..."

He scrolled down and opened another thread.

    Date: thur, -1,203, 14:35 GMT

"Kensaro: B.tuck signed Stanbul," Manzano read out. "The transaction should be completed by the end of the month."

    Simon: ok. Send it by Costa Ltd. and
    Esmeralda, fifty/fifty.

"What's that supposed to mean?"

"No idea. Transaction could mean a money transfer."

"What's Stanbul?"

"Haven't the foggiest... Istanbul?"

"What are you two whispering over there?" Sophia hissed from her position at the door. She came over and crouched by the table. "What have you got?"

"The holy grail," Manzano replied quietly. "Maybe."

"What is all this gibberish?"

"It's possible our friends made a capital error when they planted emails on my computer. They did it directly from their central communications platform, without rerouting it. Or at least, that's what it looks like. And if that's the case, then…"

"Then?"

"We've got a problem," said Manzano. "This site could give us all the information we need to put a stop to the catastrophe out there—and maybe even to catch these bastards."

"Hell, if you're right—that's a goddamn monster of a puzzle!" said Shannon. "A little info here, a little there. To read through it by ourselves would take years!"

"I said we had a problem." He turned to face the two women. "We can't do this by ourselves. We need to get the pros involved so they can analyze everything, put the puzzle together. Fast. It's going to take hundreds, thousands of them."

"And who are these pros?"

"No idea! The NSA, CIA—every intelligence agency in the world and every institution that investigates terrorism."

"The police always did think highly of you, right from the beginning," Shannon teased.

"I know," sighed Manzano. He closed his eyes and pinched the sides of his nose with his fingers. "But what choice do we have?"

DAY 11—TUESDAY

THE HAGUE, NETHERLANDS

"Wow." It was all Bollard could manage.

He bent over the computer, spellbound, and clicked through the RESET site that Manzano had led him to a few minutes earlier. Christopoulos and two more of his colleagues stood staring over his shoulder.

"You have to secure this information as quickly as possible," Manzano's voice commanded over the telephone. "Before our break-in is discovered."

Bollard nodded, thoughts spinning inside his head. He whispered to Christopoulos. "Tell IT—they must start immediately."

The Greek ran to the telephone at the next desk.

"How am I supposed to know this is real?" said Bollard, wondering if the Italian could have fabricated this site to put them on the wrong track. He clicked through a few threads at random. Fortunately, he knew this hacker language well enough to follow the discussions.

"Are you kidding! You can see for yourself how much there is. It would be impossible to fake something like this."

"How did you find it?" asked Bollard.

"I tracked down the IP address they were using to access my laptop. Turns out these jerks have been seriously careless in the security department. I'll give you the whole story when I have the chance."

Bollard stopped randomly clicking through the data bank. He had seen enough. If this was genuine, the Italian had hit the jackpot. He had to admit he was impressed by the man's fervor—and his stubbornness.

"If this platform holds what you say it does…"

"I'm pretty certain it does. But you'll need a hell of a lot of resources to analyze it fast enough. Who can you tap?"

"Everybody."

"Who's everybody?"

"From the NSA to the Police Nationale to the BKA. Everybody…" There was a pause, and then Bollard said, "I heard you got shot. How are you doing?"

A snort of derision from the other end of the line, then, "I've been better, thanks."

BRUSSELS, BELGIUM

He's never hugged me like that, thought Shannon as she watched Manzano say good-bye to the tall and lovely Sophia. She felt a tiny stab of jealousy, although she wasn't sure what she'd been expecting from the Italian. They had gone through so much together. Probably some of the most emotional moments of her life.

Manzano pulled himself away from Sophia's embrace. An officer was waiting by the SUV parked in front of the Commission building.

Shannon climbed into the backseat; Manzano sat next to her. In the front passenger seat, their escort pulled four sandwiches and two large bottles of water out of a bag and handed them back.

"With warm regards from Monsieur Bollard," he said, then ordered, "Buckle up, please. Even if there's almost nobody on the road."

THE HAGUE, NETHERLANDS

The Hague offered a grim picture: burned-out cars and smoldering ruins lined the streets.

"Where are we headed?" Manzano asked their driver.

"The hotel is full. You'll be put up in provisional quarters at Europol."

Tanks were patrolling the streets surrounding the compound.

"Did I just hear gunshots?" asked Shannon.

"Could very well be," said the driver.

To reach the building they had to pass a checkpoint that was guarded by heavily armed soldiers.

"This place looks like a war zone," Shannon remarked.

"It's pretty close to one," said the driver.

———

"What is she doing here?" asked Bollard, pointing at Shannon.

Manzano went to the window and looked out over the city. Columns of smoke rose above the buildings from east to west. In the distance, he heard the sirens of emergency vehicles, the rattling of helicopters crisscrossing the murky skies.

"Without her, we wouldn't have gotten my laptop back and would never have found RESET," he said.

Bollard clamped his eyes shut and worked his jaw.

"OK. But no reporting," he ordered.

"You have my word," Shannon promised. "Not until you give the OK."

She whispered to Manzano, "But I really do need some equipment: cameras, a laptop."

"We need laptops," Manzano told Bollard. "And she gets a camera."

He could see that Bollard was close to exploding, but he figured they were entitled to make a few demands.

"Fine, I'll get you the gear." Bollard shot them an angry glare. "But remember: no reporting."

Shannon nodded fervently. "Only when you're ready

to see the monumental work you're doing documented for the public."

"Find somebody else to bullshit," Bollard snapped.

"How far are you with RESET?" said Manzano.

"The information is now with Interpol, NATO, the Secret Service, the NCTC, and a number of others," said Bollard. "We're dividing responsibility for the analysis between us."

In the conference room, two dozen people were seated in front of computers. Bollard, Manzano, and Shannon placed themselves behind one of them.

"Using what parameters?" asked Manzano.

"Whatever we can come up with. Search terms, for example. We found a number of chats in which the topic was 'zero days.'"

"What are those?" asked Shannon.

"Vulnerabilities in systems and programs that the manufacturers themselves are unaware of and there's no protection against," Manzano explained.

"We're also looking into the various users," Bollard continued, "scanning their discussions for certain terms…"

"Terms," echoed Manzano. "Am I one of those 'terms'?"

Bollard nodded. "That was one of the first things we looked for. Do you want to see?"

The man at the keyboard tapped away, and some text popped up on the screen.

6, 11:24 GMT
tancr: Looks like the Italian escaped from the Germans.
b.tuck: But he's still under suspicion?
tancr: Don't know, think so.
b.tuck: Caused us enough trouble.
tancr: Yeah, well. Somebody had to catch on sometime. In I, in G.

"The Italian," said Manzano, "that's me. And the Germans, that's that guy Hartlandt."

"There's more," said Bollard.

```
5, 13:32
tancr: The Italian's getting annoying. Tipping
them off about Talaefer. Would really like to
give him something else he can deal with
b.tuck: What's that?
tancr: Fake mail
b.tuck: Ok
```

"Thank you!" Manzano cried out in relief and gave Bollard a triumphant look. "I hope that finally convinces you that I'm innocent."

"If you're with them," Bollard replied without batting an eye, "you could have gotten your buddies to set this up."

Manzano groaned. "Do you believe anybody?"

"No."

———

"What I'd be interested to know," said Manzano, "is how these guys got the idea to plant the emails on my laptop, and how they knew I was on my way to Talaefer."

Bollard gave him a long look. "After you insisted to Hartlandt that the information had to come from us, our IT people checked over our system."

"And they found something in Europol's systems?"

It was clearly painful for Bollard to admit it. "They found programs that could read the email correspondence on most of our computers and could also activate cameras and microphones."

"Well, I wouldn't want to be the guy in charge of security here…"

"Nor me. And the same goes for the German, French,

British, and other government crisis teams. It seems these guys got in everywhere. They read, saw, and heard everything."

———

Manzano saw no sense joining in on the analysis of RESET. Thousands of highly qualified specialists across half the world were taking care of it. That fake email—*Headed to Talaefer. Looking for a bug. Won't find a thing*—was still bothering him. And so he had withdrawn to one of the quieter rooms and was studying the error reports from power plants that had come in to Talaefer.

"Do you ever get tired?" asked Shannon.

All day long he had watched her as she looked over the men's shoulders, studied the diagram on the wall, filmed, and photographed. Bollard had given his blessing after Manzano had made clear yet again the role Shannon had played in the discovery of RESET. "Might actually be a good idea," the Frenchman had said, "if someone documents us working."

Manzano stretched, feeling his limbs popping. She was right; he needed a break.

"Coffee?" she suggested.

Together they found the small kitchen a few doors down. At the tables sat two Europol men with bags under their eyes and steaming cups in front of them.

Manzano stuck a coffee capsule in the machine. As he watched the cup fill, he marveled at the backup power system that even now allowed Europol this luxury. "Small but strong for me," Shannon said.

He pressed the button again, waited, and handed her the cup. A red light indicated that the container for used capsules was full and had to be emptied. Manzano pulled out the compartment and saw that there were only two capsules inside. He took them out, pushed the container back in, and made his coffee.

He had no sooner sat down than he got up again and walked over to the coffee machine. The little red light was still lit up, even though he had emptied the container. Manzano pulled it back out and pushed it back in again. The red light was still on. "The instruments," he whispered. "It's probably the instruments."

"What are you muttering about over there?" Shannon asked.

Manzano knocked back his coffee in one gulp. "The error reports might just be the instruments' fault!"

"What instruments?"

"In the SCADA software."

"And the coffee machine told you this?"

"Exactly."

MADRID, SPAIN

blond
tancr
sanskrit
zap
rtwo
cuhao
proud
baku
tzsche
b.tuck
sarowi
simon

"These twelve are the ones leading the majority of the discussions," Hernandez Durán, interim leader of the department for cybercrime and terrorism in the Brigada de Investigación Tecnológica in Madrid, announced to those present. "Some are obvious, like *blond* and *rtwo*. Presumably the latter is a *Star Wars* fan. We're not so sure about Proud, *zap*, *baku*, *tzsche*, *b.tuck*, and *sarowi*." He paused for effect, then continued. "Our colleague Professor Belguer has an interesting theory, which could provide us with information about the motive. Proud, Zap, Baku, Tzsche, and B.tuck *could*—emphasis on the conditional—be abbreviations. More specifically, Proudhon, Zapata, Bakunin, Nietzsche, and Benjamin Tucker."

"Zapata and Nietzsche I get," one of the listeners spoke up. "As for the others, I know I've heard of them, but…"

Initially, only IT forensics specialists had analyzed the information. They'd soon realized that they needed to bring in experts from other fields, among them the sociologist, Belguer.

"Pierre-Joseph Proudhon," explained Durán, "was a Frenchman who lived in the nineteenth century. He's considered to be the first anarchist. He was the one who came up with the line '*La propriété, c'est le vol*'—'Property is theft'—which became a standard quotation. Mikhail Bakunin, a Russian nobleman, was another influential anarchist in the nineteenth century. Benjamin Tucker was an American who translated and published the writings of Proudhon and Bakunin."

"Revolutionaries, anarchists," noted another. "Sounds as though we're on the right track with this theory, given what these bastards have done."

BERLIN, GERMANY

"What do we know about the incidents in the correctional facilities?" asked the chancellor.

"Wherever possible, inmates were transferred from facilities lacking provisions and consolidated into centralized facilities," said the minister of justice. "We couldn't very well let them starve to death or die of thirst."

"How many criminals are we talking about?"

"I can't say exactly," the minister admitted. "In addition, news has come in from Dresden that angry citizens have stormed the Saxony state parliament building in an attempt to remove the crisis team from power."

His gaze froze. With his eyes locked on a single point, he stood up and went to the window, which overlooked the Spree. The others followed, curious.

Michelsen could not believe her eyes. Across the river, on Holsteiner Ufer, behind the leafless willow trees, wandered a giraffe and two of her young. The sight of the animals striding past with such dignity threw them all into a stunned silence.

"What the hell?" said the interior minister.

"The animals from the zoo," answered Secretary of State Rhess. "It's only two and a half kilometers away, and nobody's left to run the place."

"What about the—" someone asked.

"Rest of the animals." Michelsen paused. "Jesus Christ. Lions? Tigers?"

Rhess nodded. "I'm afraid so," he said.

RATINGEN, GERMANY

"There," said Dienhof. "No idea how the guys at Europol figured this out, but they're right. We cracked the code half an hour ago. For simplicity's sake, we've translated it into pseudocode, so everybody can understand what it says." He handed the printout to Wickley:

```
If time = 19:23 + (random number
between 1 and 40)
for 2% of all objects,
change object status to different value
display the corresponding different color
communicate the change in status back
to the calling program
```

"This means," explained Dienhof, "that…"

"By adding an element of randomness, you cause more and more instruments in the control booth to start reporting errors that aren't there," Wickley completed the explanation. "That," he added in a whisper, "is insidious."

Wickley's mind raced ahead. If this was true, Talaefer was indeed among the main parties responsible for the disaster.

"It truly is," Dienhof agreed. "The false displays don't themselves disrupt the machines, which continue to function properly throughout. There was nothing preventing power plants from starting up again and continuing to operate. Whoever implemented this was betting on the most critical weak point of the system…"

"People." Wickley nodded. He couldn't deny a grudging respect for whoever had designed this code. Here was somebody who knew what it all came down to. A brutally intelligent mind. Diabolically clever. "So even though the power plant is running smoothly…"

"The staff in the control room are bombarded with error reports and system alarms," said Dienhof. "They respond by taking action that results in damage to the facility. Because of the erroneous instrument readings, they do the exact opposite of what is required."

"How do we address this?"

"We write a new version of the library, without the malicious code, and install it at the power plants. With a working internet connection on both ends it could be done in a matter of hours. But I'm guessing that, given the circumstances, the BKA will ensure we have sufficient technicians and transportation to—"

"Can we not keep the BKA out of it?"

LONDON, ENGLAND

"We struck the mother lode," sang Phil McCaff, deep in the bowels of MI6 headquarters. He hadn't left the building in Vauxhall Cross in a week. His neighbors at the computers looked up.

"Look here," he called out, hitting a key to project the contents of his screen onto the wall where everyone could see. He had highlighted two lines of a conversation thread.

rtwo: Ok, got it
tzsche: Almost midnight. time to go to bed.
Enjoy your breakfast

"These lines come from a thread that's a few weeks old," he explained. "Tzsche and Rtwo belong to the inner circle. It's almost midnight where Tzsche is, and meanwhile Rtwo is supposed to enjoy his breakfast. What does that tell us?"

"That they're on opposite sides of the world," reasoned Emily Aldridge.

"Exactly. Here I've got another one…"

Fry, -97, 6:36 GMT
baku: Raining cats and dogs. Thought this was
a sunny country.
zap: Full moon here. No clouds

He brought up a world map.

"On this map I can load the position of the sun, the phases of the moon, weather reports, and more from various data banks. Together with the date and time when the conversation took place, I can be relatively precise in establishing Zap's location to be in a time zone between five and seven hours behind Greenwich Mean Time."

"Somewhere in America," Aldridge concluded.

"After evaluating other remarks like these, I've come to the conclusion that there are at least two groups."

He looked around and let the news sink in.

"You should all double-check this one more time, but

I'm pretty certain that one group is in Central America, the other on the eastern Mediterranean."

THE HAGUE, NETHERLANDS

"This is brilliant!" cried Bollard. He tore the paper from the printer. His eyes flew over it. "*Bien*," he murmured. "*Très bien*."

Printouts, images, and notes detailing the most essential findings now covered three walls of the incident room. One wall was reserved for the suspects. They still didn't know for certain if Jorge Pucao and his contacts were involved with the power outages, but the evidence was mounting.

More than three dozen portraits were scattered on the wall. In the last twenty-four hours the notes had piled up around one photo in particular, that of Balduin von Ansen. The subject was a skinny man in his midthirties. He wore a three-day beard and fashionable, rectangular glasses, his mid-length hair carefully parted on the left. Below the photo were six sheets of A4 paper arranged in two rows. On them was an elaborate graphic: dozens of lines connected boxes in which names and combinations of letters and numbers were noted.

"We've had confirmation," Bollard announced, "that the two million from the account on Guernsey belonging to Karyon Ltd. flowed in seven installments over a six-month period to an account in the Caymans belonging to Utopia Enterprises, as well as to the Hundsrock Company in Switzerland. From there it went to an account registered to Bugfix in Liechtenstein and a numbered account in Switzerland. One of the owners of Bugfix—which is listed as a software consulting firm based in Tallahassee, Florida—is Siti Yusuf. His partner in the business, John Bannock, is one of Jorge Pucao's two U.S. contacts. Bannock hasn't been heard from since 2011."

He added the corresponding entries to the graphic.

"From these accounts, the money immediately went on to others. We're looking into this. And I've just received word from the analysts in London that the attackers are working from two bases: one in Mexico, the other on the eastern Mediterranean or in the Middle East. That means we're going to prioritize our analysis of money transfers headed to these regions."

Follow the money. "That was the…" he heard Manzano mumbling. The Italian was rubbing his stubble as he leaned over one of the analysts, peering at the screen.

"Look for…Stanbul! Type Stanbul in there."

DAY 12—WEDNESDAY

THE HAGUE, NETHERLANDS

Bollard stuck the photo of a building alongside the other notes on Balduin von Ansen. The architecture didn't immediately register with Manzano.

"This complex on the Asian side of Istanbul was purchased by a firm named Süper Kompüter, which, according to information we've received from Turkey, rents the building out to six companies, all operating in different industries. The building lies in a part of town popular with international companies. Foreigners don't draw attention here. The Turkish investigators have dug deeper into the companies' ownership structure and business dealings, going over bank accounts and data from the Ministry of Finance over the past few years. The first match to come up was one of the owners: John Bannock. Then Dr. Lekue Birabi, Pucao's contact from Nigeria, showed up as a partner in a second company."

He pinned up another printout. "They've also identified a transfer of two million euros from Costa Ltd, Esmeralda, and two other companies to Süper Kompüter." He tapped the image of the nondescript building with his finger. "One of the terrorist cells is probably here. Our Turkish colleagues have begun surveillance."

RATINGEN, GERMANY

"Did you follow up on the lead?" asked Hartlandt.

"The instrument displays, yes," answered Wickley. "We didn't find anything."

"Show those parts of the program to my people," Hartlandt ordered. "They will double-check your findings."

Wickley and Dienhof exchanged nervous glances, which didn't escape Hartlandt.

"What?" he asked sharply.

"No problem," the executive replied suavely. "You'll get them. Dienhof, take care of it."

It seemed to Hartlandt that the two of them were hiding something. Wickley was never going to crack, but Dienhof was sweating heavily and looking distinctly uncomfortable.

"Functioning power plants are essential for rebuilding the grid," Hartlandt reminded them, determined to make clear to Dienhof what was at stake. "The grid cannot function until there are enough power plants to supply it—and they cannot get their generators up and running so long as these problems with the SCADA system persist. Extremely critical situations are playing out in two nuclear power plants. I realize you don't develop software for nuclear facilities, but the backup systems at those two plants rely on the regular grid for their power. Already, thousands of people have been exposed to radiation, forced to evacuate their homes…"

He paused, observing the reaction to his lecture.

"Ghastly," said Wickley.

Dienhof grimaced, swallowed, and managed to nod.

"If the grid is not restored, the same thing could happen in Germany…"

"I'd like to, um"—Dienhof cleared his throat—"show you something."

Wickley closed his eyes for a couple of seconds. When he opened them again, Hartlandt could see that he had won.

MCLEAN, UNITED STATES

Richard Price, interim director of the National Counterterrorism Center, studied the printouts his deputy had spread out on the table. Europol's investigation into the suspects' revenue streams had led them to an address in Mexico City. The building in question had been purchased two years previously by a U.S. citizen.

"What do we have on this Norbert Butler?" asked Price.

"The guy's a fanatical opponent of the state. He was active in the Tea Party for a while, then disappeared four months ago."

Price looked up from the photograph of Butler. "A Tea Party member and he's working with Pucao and Birabi—a Latino and an African, both of them left-wing anarchists?"

"Left, right, doesn't seem to matter to Butler as long as they're against the state. Natural enemies united by their hatred of the ruling system and their determination to dismantle it."

"But why would Butler actively enable these bastards to kill American citizens?"

"Why not? It didn't bother Timothy McVeigh when he planted his truck bomb in Oklahoma City. One hundred and sixty-eight American citizens killed, nineteen of them kindergarteners."

"Plenty of U.S. citizens buy real estate in Mexico."

"But only Butler has connections to Pucao and his cronies going back decades. The Mexican authorities have turned up a picture similar to the group's Istanbul HQ: the building's occupied by firms with convoluted structures and powerful internet connections. They've put the place under surveillance."

"I'll inform the president."

THE HAGUE, NETHERLANDS

"You want to leave? Now?"

Bollard heard the panic in his wife's voice. He knew how close she was to breaking point, but he had no alternative but to leave her.

"Marie, we are so close to ending this disaster and catching the people who caused it—I have to go."

They stood in front of the fire, the only warm place in the house. The kids pressed up close against their mother and looked up at him with frightened eyes. He gestured toward the boxes that he had placed next to the door.

"That's food and water for three days. You might already have power again by tomorrow morning. And the day after that, I'll be back, I promise."

"Is it dangerous, what you're doing?" Bernadette asked, worried.

"No, my darling."

She looked doubtful.

"Truly," he assured her. "The special forces people will take care of me."

His wife nudged the children off to the side. "Go play."

The two obeyed reluctantly, but they didn't stray far.

"It's anarchy out there," she hissed.

"You have the pistol." The terrified look on her face revealed that she saw the gun more as a threat than as protection. "The day after tomorrow, when the power is back…"

"Can you guarantee that?"

"Yes," he lied.

His wife looked at him for a long while before she asked, "Have you heard anything from our parents?"

"Not yet. But I'm sure they're fine."

ORLÉANS, FRANCE

"You shouldn't be watching this," said Celeste, resting her hand on Annette's shoulder.

Annette didn't try to shake off Celeste's hand, but she resisted her attempt to turn her away from the scene in front of them.

At a distance of about fifty meters, men with gloves and face masks were unloading lifeless bodies from the back of a flatbed truck. They grabbed them by their hands and feet and threw them into a ditch about twenty meters long and five meters wide. She could only guess at how deep it was.

A priest stood at the edge of the grave, sprinkling holy water. Stone-faced, hands clasped together, she watched the scene unfold. A few steps away, an older woman was standing by herself; a little farther on, a young couple hugged each other, sobbing. Altogether, more than two dozen people were in attendance for the makeshift burial.

Then Annette recognized the slender figure of her husband in the hands of the undertakers. They swung his body, picking up momentum, then he vanished into the hole. Annette thought of their daughter and of the grandchildren whose visit he had so looked forward to. She crossed herself, whispering a final "*adieu*."

COMMAND HEADQUARTERS

Siti Yusuf had been analyzing the authorities' communications since the beginning of the blackout. As the communications decreased in volume, something occurred to him. He went back and checked the frequency of certain key words and encountered an interesting fact. In the first week after the attack, the crisis centers and authorities had exchanged information not only about coordinating aid, but also about the search for the perpetrators. Words like "investigation" and "terrorist" featured again and again. But as communications had decreased, the incidence of these words had decreased too. Drastically. In fact, they had all but disappeared.

On Sunday they had become aware of the emails in which government institutions advised staff to turn on their computers only when strictly necessary. That had explained the decreased communications. Now Yusuf speculated that these emails had actually been directed at them, intended to lull them into a false sense of security after their surveillance had been discovered.

When he voiced his suspicions, some began to panic, while others dismissed the possibility. Arguments had raged, but in the end they had agreed to exercise greater vigilance, just in case the police and intelligence agencies were on their heels.

Not that it would make any difference to their mission, either way. They had made contingency plans to ensure that, even if they were discovered, the final blow would be delivered.

TRANSALL AIRCRAFT, SOMEWHERE ABOVE EUROPE

"Yes!" said Bollard, punching the air in celebration. No one heard him over the noise of the propellers.

Soon after the terrorist's possible headquarters had been identified, Bollard had been flown by helicopter to the Wahn military airfield. There he had stepped onto a German army Transall aircraft, while GSG 9 teams began arriving from nearby Sankt Augustin.

Taking advantage of the working satellite connection in the plane, Bollard had been keeping himself updated on the latest developments. It made up for his frustration at not being allowed to participate directly in any operation against the terrorists. Director Ruiz had reminded him that he was neither authorized nor trained to do so, but he had conceded to the request that Bollard be allowed to tag along as Europol's representative. Which was how he came to be sitting in a noisy aircraft with sixty men in peak physical condition who appeared to be passing the time by telling jokes, judging by the laughter that rippled through their ranks.

Bollard was sharing a table with the two team commanders. He turned the computer so that they could see the screen and pointed to the latest photos of the building in Istanbul. Unfocused, grainy images showed two men leaving and entering, plus a third man and a woman standing at the window.

"Pedro Munoz," Bollard announced triumphantly and pointed at the first surveillance photo. Next to it he brought up a photograph of Munoz. He pointed at the other individuals. "John Bannock. Maria Carvalles-Tendido. Hernandes Sidon."

One by one he loaded photographs from the database, so that those seated around him could compare the faces with those on the surveillance shots.

"Gentlemen, the target is confirmed. Your men can start preparing themselves for an operation."

BRAUWEILER, GERMANY

Pewalski sat nervously in front of the screens, watching as Amprion's operators attempted to rebuild the grid for southeastern Germany.

So far, he and his family had been well looked after. The backup power system in the basement had provided them with electricity, the cistern, installed for just such an event, with water. The hardest part for them had been dealing with neighbors and relatives in need. Pewalski had turned them away without exception; his wife, on the other hand, had let those who were freezing come inside, at least for an hour at a time. She had welcomed the hungry and the thirsty too, which dug into their own supplies. But Pewalski had stocked up for three weeks. He didn't have to worry yet. In any case, the crowds had started to peter out the day before yesterday, when word spread that they'd used up the last drop of their diesel reserves.

Pewalski felt he'd more than earned the preferential treatment his family had received. The facility had been operating with a skeleton crew for days now, and he'd had to spend every waking hour at the operations center, filling in for absent coworkers. Which was how he came to be sitting at a desk, keeping an eye on his own screen while trying to follow developments on his neighbor's monitor, which showed work in progress on the eastern sector of the grid.

"Markersbach and Goldisthal look to be back online," Pewalski confirmed. The two pumped storage facilities near the Czech border had black start capabilities. All they had to do was allow water to flow down from the elevated storage reservoirs so it could pass through the turbines and generate electricity. Should this small grid-building succeed, it would create an island from which the country's eastern grid would then be built up, bit by bit. In the process, the complex in which he now sat would also be supplied with voltage.

"Come on!" whispered Pewalski. "Come on!"

BERLIN, GERMANY

They were all gathered together on the screens again, including the new heads from Portugal, Spain, and Greece. For the top brass at NATO, one screen had to suffice this time; the White House was also patched in.

On the six screens in the bottom row, Michelsen saw the buildings in Istanbul and Mexico City, captured from a variety of surveillance and helmet-mounted cameras. The images from Istanbul, where it was already nighttime, were green and full of shadows; in Mexico City the sun was shining.

The moment the location of the terrorists' headquarters was identified, elite units scrambled to take them out of commission. All communications had been conducted over absolutely tap-proof systems; they risked the attackers finding out that they had been discovered. Units of Bordo Bereliler, the Turkish special forces division, would make the assault in Istanbul, backed up by teams from GSG 9 and the Secret Service. Two hundred Navy SEALs had touched down a short time ago in Mexico City to carry out the raid there, in cooperation with Mexican troops.

The two attack teams on opposite ends of the world stood poised to launch a synchronized assault the moment the command was given. But first, all internet and power connections for each building would be cut off. Then it would be the special units' turn.

"The indicators are overwhelming," announced the chancellor. "We say go. Any objections?"

No one said a word, not even the NATO generals whose China theory had been blown to shreds.

"Then let's give our people the order to engage," concluded the U.S. president.

ISTANBUL, TURKEY

He needed fresh air. They'd been sitting in front of the screens for eighteen hours a day or more. His head would explode if he didn't get out once in a while.

He took the exit through the basement. They'd had this passageway specially built. Even though he knew some of the others weren't observing the security measures, he stuck to them. So when he first stepped out into the night air, through the exit of the neighboring building, he was two hundred meters away from their base. Outside it was five degrees above zero. The pavements were bustling with activity; traffic was backed up in the street. Hard to believe that just a few hundred kilometers across the Bosporus, life had come to a standstill. In the coming weeks, the consequences would be noticeable here too, and then the people would follow the citizens of Europe and the United States in rising up against the old order.

He zipped up his jacket and took a deep breath. Relaxed, he strolled past shop windows without a sideward glance. Nothing but junk on sale. Soon people would have more important things on their minds. When he heard the muted bang behind him, he wheeled around in surprise. There were flashes in the windows of one of the buildings a block away. Their building. A helicopter descended to hover over it, bathing it in blinding light.

Passersby turned toward the scene, transfixed. Bright spotlights were shining on the facade from all sides now. Announcements rang out that he didn't understand. But their message was immediately clear. He felt his hands clench into fists in his pockets. Cautiously he looked around, observing the people, the cars. He had to make himself as inconspicuous as possible. Most of the pedestrians were still gawking; others hurried on their way. As he followed their progress down the street, he spotted a delivery van with dark windows. The back doors were open, and he saw several police officers inside. One of them he recognized immediately. It was the Frenchman from Europol.

THE HAGUE, NETHERLANDS

Christ, it's not a soccer game, thought Manzano when they'd invited him to join everyone in front of the big screens to watch the raid. He'd resolved not to watch, but the blurred images on the monitors—from Istanbul and Mexico City, four cameras in each location—had him transfixed. Manzano wondered who was selecting the angles. Was there a director somewhere in Langley or Berlin—or maybe in Hollywood?—giving orders to his crew: "Screen One, cut to Helmet-Cam 3!"

At that moment the special units in Istanbul were running through a dark hallway and crashing into a room full of desks and computers. Several people jumped to their feet. Some put their hands up; others threw themselves under desks, behind chairs. The helmet cameras showed images of panicked, enraged faces. The microphones picked up screaming, shouting of orders, heavy footsteps, gunshots.

It didn't take long for the special troops to secure the premises. The cameras showed several prisoners lying on their stomachs, hands tied behind their backs. At deserted desks, screens were lit up; Manzano couldn't make out anything on them. Two police officers stealthily worked their way into a neighboring room. There was no one inside, but racks of servers were stacked up to the ceiling.

In Mexico City, two SEALs were kneeling next to a wounded man, applying bandages. The man cursed at them but then grinned and hissed something that made them flinch. Ten minutes later, the report came in from Istanbul. "Mission accomplished. Target location captured. Eleven target persons found—three nonfatally wounded, three dead."

Two minutes later, Mexico City reported. "Thirteen target persons, one badly wounded, two dead."

"Good work!" They heard the voice of the American president in the speakers. Other patched-in politicians joined him in their own languages, filling the airwaves with a veritable babel of hearty congratulations.

ISTANBUL, TURKEY

He took public transportation to Atatürk Airport. He always kept the key to the locker with him when he left the building. Forged papers and money were waiting for him inside.

If the police had found their headquarters, it was likely they now knew the cause of the outages and could reverse them. It would be only a matter of time until the first flights took off toward the major European cities. One question remained: How had the police discovered their group?

He had to assume, since they knew of the group, that they suspected him of being involved. Now that they had control of the building, they would start to pore over the evidence, trying to track down the ones who'd escaped the raid. Little did they know half of them were in Mexico. They'd no doubt be watching the airports, but he trusted his new papers, his changed haircut, and his handsome new mustache.

He found a comfortable seat in the terminal, overlooking a large-screen TV tuned to a news broadcast. Had they uncovered Mexico City too? Even if he couldn't hear the anchorwoman delivering the news, the images would tell him enough. Well, he could wait. The precautions they had taken would carry forward their mission. Let them think that they'd won, that it was all over. He knew better.

YBBS-PERSENBEUG, AUSTRIA

Oberstätter looked over the three red giants in the generator room of the southern power plant. The radio speaker crackled in his right hand.

The update from Talaefer had arrived three hours ago with a special messenger from the military.

"That's it?" The IT technicians were amazed. Someone had manipulated a part of the program so that the displays would go crazy with false readings.

The company responsible is ruined, thought Oberstätter. They'll never get a contract again; claims for damages would finish them off.

After the technicians had modified the system, Oberstätter and his colleagues in the control booth started the tests and preparations for resuming operations. No problem.

At first he heard nothing. Then the air began to vibrate, telling him that the control booth had diverted the Danube's current over the turbines and on to the generators, inducing voltage in the coils for the first time in days. The quiver in the air grew into a faint, deep hum, rose, sounding richer, then stabilized into a mild drone, which Oberstätter greeted inwardly like the first cry of a newborn child.

DAY 13—THURSDAY

ROME, ITALY

Once again, Valentina hadn't slept a wink. Now she sat in the operations center, where the IT forensics specialists had just declared the workspaces ready for use. It was still dark outside, but the news that the bug had been fixed was coming in from most of the deactivated power plants. They were ready to start. Neighboring transmission grid operators in Austria and Switzerland were already making voltage available at the key international connection nodes.

On the large board the first lines on the northern borders were turning green. The lines were connected from node to node, and one after another green lines began replacing the red ones. At the same time, the green glow from individual power plants was spreading, blanketing the entire country like rapidly growing roots.

THE HAGUE, NETHERLANDS

"They've got a good setup here," Bollard's voice announced as his helmet camera conveyed the images from the Istanbul command headquarters. "Every one of the captured and the dead features on our list of suspects. Some of the individuals on the list are missing—which doesn't necessarily mean anything. It's possible they weren't involved after all."

"And are they saying anything?" asked Christopoulos.

"Some of them are only too happy to talk," answered Bollard. "Though a lot of it's nonsense. They wanted to set up a new world order, more humane, more just. They believe the only way this can be achieved is through a massive rupture in society."

"Sounds like neoliberal shock doctrine," said Christopoulos.

"Look outside!" someone cried.

———

Marie was staring out at the wintry yard, lost in thought, when suddenly the refrigerator began to emit a tired buzzing. She turned in amazement, cautiously approached the appliance, and opened the door. The light came on inside. Flickering and dim, but light all the same. In a rush she flipped the switch on the neighboring wall. The ceiling lights came on.

"*Maman!*" she heard her children calling from the living room. "*Maman!*"

She hurried through. The floor lamps next to the sofa were glowing. Georges hit a button on the TV remote. Flickering grays appeared on the screen, and a hiss came out of the speakers. Bernadette played around with the light switch for the chandelier, switching it on and off, on and off.

"Papa was right!" cried Georges. "The power's back!"

In the house across the street she saw lights going on and off. She skipped over to the window; the kids followed her and pressed their faces against the glass. The houses were lit up as far as they could see.

She wrapped an arm around each of her children, pressed them tightly to her, and felt their arms hugging her waist.

"Is Papa coming home now?" asked Bernadette, looking up at her. Marie hugged her even tighter.

"Yes, he is. I'm sure he'll call soon."

"Then we can finally go and see Grandma and Grandpa in Paris," said Georges.

"Yes, we'll do that too," said Marie, stifling a sob.

BRUSSELS, BELGIUM

Sophia stood with the others at the window and looked out over the city. Individual lights flickered on in the office towers: neon advertisements, decorative lights on the facades of office buildings, shimmering against the dark sky. Her colleagues laughed, clapped, hugged one another. Telephones were ringing, but for a few minutes, no one picked up.

Then everyone began trying to reach the loved ones they hadn't heard from. She too wanted to hear from a few people, find out where they were, how they were. Sophia thought of Piero Manzano. She hadn't heard from him or Shannon since they had left for The Hague. As she walked back into her own office, the telephone rang and she picked up.

"Hey," she heard Piero Manzano's voice. "How's it going?"

BERLIN, GERMANY

"And now the big cleanup begins," announced Secretary of State Rhess. He had the attention of everyone present. "Our first priority is to establish the supply of water, food, and medicine. Ms. Michelsen will take you through what happens next."

So I get to be the bearer of bad news all over again, she thought.

"With a relatively stable power supply, we've taken care of the basic prerequisites," she began.

"'Relatively'?" queried the defense minister.

"Certain facilities were severely damaged due to the power outage. As a result, capacities are diminished."

She brought up the image of a simple tap, the kind found in millions of households, on the monitor.

"With no water being pumped through the pipes, air pockets developed, some were left completely dry, and others froze in unheated buildings or were damaged by fires and explosions. Those pipes will need to be repaired and decontaminated. This process will take several weeks."

There had been enough pictures taken of overflowing toilets in the first days of the blackout that she could now bring up one of them. "Eeeuuugh!" called out someone in the audience.

"The outlook isn't much better for waste disposal," Michelsen continued, unfazed. Only by using images like this could she make clear the extent to which ordinary citizens had suffered in the past twelve days.

"Most toilets stopped flushing on the very first night. After that, the volume of water left in the sewers wasn't enough to carry the waste away. As a result, blockages formed in individual homes and buildings as well as in the sewers, which have now dried up. The department in charge of reestablishing wastewater treatment is prepared for short-term power cuts, but the duration of this outage has significantly reduced stocks of the bacteria cultures they rely on to purify water. New cultures will have to be introduced to the tanks, and this will take many weeks."

Photos of deserted supermarkets with empty shelves.

"Stores of frozen goods have spoiled, and practically all fresh produce was sold or looted during the blackout. We have limited quantities of canned goods and dried foods. Many supermarket chains will reopen in the coming days, but after the necessary cleanup and repair work has been completed, the selection will be very limited."

Images of a poultry farm.

"Many companies involved in food production have lost everything. Disregarding the issues of hygiene that continue to assail us with the disposal of millions of carcasses, when it comes to meat, we will be reliant on imports for several years to come. It is vital that we start thinking about the mid- and long-term consequences and find solutions fast.

"Domestic companies *must* be supported so that we can

reestablish our own production. The same applies for the majority of greenhouse cultivation of fruit and vegetables. Germany is not as severely affected in this area as other countries, like the Netherlands and Spain; nevertheless, significant losses have been sustained.

"In many instances it would, therefore, be best if people remained in the shelters until the regular supply in their regions is up and running. This news is liable to dampen the euphoria that has greeted restoration of the power supply; if we are to avoid further unrest, it is vital that we consider carefully how to communicate the setbacks to the population at large."

THE HAGUE, NETHERLANDS

"The terrorists have been caught," Shannon announced on the screen. "No one can yet estimate the extent of the damage done, but one thing is certain: this is the worst terrorist attack in history. The number of casualties in Europe and the United States runs into the millions. Economic damages amount to trillions; the national economies that have been affected will have to bear them for a long time yet."

Shannon had put them up in one of the best hotels in The Hague, at the network's expense. They each had their own room. Manzano enjoyed the clean sheets, the bathroom, the moments of calm. Now he lay on the bed, freshly showered, wrapped in a soft bathrobe. He was happy for Shannon. This was her moment. The first journalist in the world who could report on the capture, she had also been able to deliver exclusive background material. Although she had barely slept in days and had worked through the past night, she looked like she'd just returned from a health spa. How did she do that?

"I'm now on the line with the lead investigator from Europol, who was involved in the capture of the perpetrators."

In a window on screen, Bollard was patched in from Istanbul.

"Monsieur Bollard, what kind of people are they? The people who would do something like this?"

"That's something that will come out over the course of our investigations in the coming days. Among those in custody are members of both the radical left and the far right. The majority come from middle-class families. All of them appear to be well educated."

"Do these profiles show that such a stereotype-focused approach is obsolete and no longer represents social realities?"

"Perhaps. Among terrorists, there's one type that is prevalent, independent of the worldview: we call this the 'righteous' type. They firmly believe that they are in possession of the one legitimate truth and that they have the right to implement that truth through every conceivable means. For the achievement of their supposedly higher goal, they have no qualms whatsoever about sacrificing innocent people."

"Were all the perpetrators captured? How many are there? Where and when will they stand trial?"

"I am not in a position to answer those questions as yet."

ISTANBUL, TURKEY

The televisions at the airport told him everything. Only a few hours after the raid on the building, the first networks were showing images. To his disappointment, there was footage from Mexico City. And as if that weren't enough, the power was back in large parts of Europe and the United States.

A few hours after the end of the blackout, he was on a plane headed from Istanbul to The Hague. The airlines had resumed most of their regular flights to Europe as quickly as possible.

This was not the way they had planned it. Europe

should have been without power for at least a month after the first outage. And it would have been, had it not been for that fucking Italian. His face had flashed briefly on the television screen—one of the heroes of the hour. They should have taken care of him as soon as he'd gone running to Europol about the smart meters. The bastard had denied them the fruits of their years of work, and the world had been robbed of its chance at a new beginning. For this the Italian must pay.

It pained him to admit that he was taking this matter more personally than he should, more than was professional. The anger had been burning corrosively inside him ever since he'd learned that their planned second wave had been blocked. He still didn't know who was responsible. He might never know.

But in the meantime he could at least wreak vengeance against the Italian.

RATINGEN, GERMANY

"We've traced the origin of the malicious codes in the SCADA system," said Dienhof. "Dragenau had built it in as early as the last millennium."

"He'd been planning his move for that long?" asked Hartlandt.

"That we'll never know. Maybe it was just an exercise. Or he wanted, even at the time, to have something in his back pocket to one day have his revenge for the takeover of his company."

"Why wasn't the manipulation noticed?"

"Dragenau picked a good time. Do you remember the Y2K hysteria shortly before the turn of the millennium? Every computer was going to crash on account of the date change. We had our hands full, modifying programs that had been designed with a two-digit year by the original developers. The proofers and the testers were all tied up with work related to the millennium switch. In the end, the predicted disaster didn't occur. But the IT consultants made a killing. And in the confusion, the few lines were overlooked. And they were never found afterward either."

"He did nothing with them for fifteen years."

"And look where his betrayal got him," said Dienhof. "I can't help wondering how the terrorists came upon Dragenau. I daresay that's something you will find out in the course of your investigations. Presumably they would have approached insiders at several companies—a risky undertaking, if you ask me, but clearly it worked."

Hartlandt wasn't about to be drawn out on what they had learned about Dragenau. He decided it was time to conclude the meeting. "We appreciate the help you have given us, Mr. Dienhof," he said, extending his hand to Dienhof. "Particularly in providing the scrubbed versions so quickly."

He turned to Wickley, who had followed Dienhof's presentation with a blank expression.

"And as for you: if I'd had enough to issue an arrest warrant, believe me, I would. But your attempt to hide the discovery of the malicious code will not go unpunished, you can be certain of that. I'll see you in court."

And then he turned on his heel. There was one more phone call to make, something Hartlandt wasn't too excited about but felt he needed to do.

THE HAGUE, NETHERLANDS

"Manzano speaking."

The concierge spoke. "A Mr. Hartlandt for you."

Manzano hesitated for a moment before responding, "Put him through."

The German greeted him in English, asking how he was doing.

"Better now," Manzano answered skeptically.

"You've done damn good work," said Hartlandt. "Without you, we wouldn't have managed. Or at least, it would have taken us much longer."

Manzano, surprised, was silent.

"I'd like to thank you for your help. And to apologize for the way we treated you. Only, at the time…"

"Apology accepted," replied Manzano. He hadn't expected to hear from Hartlandt ever again. "It was an extreme situation. We all behaved irrationally at times, but at least we got there in the end."

BERLIN, GERMANY

"We still don't have an accurate death toll," began Torhüsen from the Ministry of Health. "However, provisional estimates for Germany assume a high five-figure to low six-figure number for fatalities resulting directly from the blackout."

Michelsen could sense everyone in the room holding their breath for an instant.

"Like I said, these are provisional numbers. We can't rule out the possibility that they might rise substantially. Across Europe, we're looking at several million. And that's without taking into account victims of radioactive contamination or sufferers from chronic conditions—heart disease, diabetes, dialysis patients—that went untreated. For the ten-kilometer radius around the Philippsburg nuclear power plant, with its compromised spent fuel pool, a mortally high level of radiation was measured."

Torhüsen changed from pictures of power plants to graveyards with large patches of freshly dug earth.

"One aspect we cannot neglect is the disposal of human remains. In the past few days, out of necessity, the dead have been buried in mass, unmarked graves. Worse still, the identities of some individuals weren't even known. This is going to be controversial, to say the least—particularly among relatives of the deceased. Many bodies will likely have to be exhumed and identified, at great cost."

The photographs of deserted hospitals came from Berlin.

"Hospitals will be able to resume operations more quickly, though not overnight. The supply of water, food, and medicine will play an important role here. In the midterm, we have to prepare for shortages of medications. We're assuming for the moment that in about a week a majority of the population will have adequate access to medical supplies again."

THE HAGUE, NETHERLANDS

Laughing, Shannon pointed the camera at Manzano. She was only stopping by his room for a moment. She didn't have that much time.

"You're a hero!" she cried. "Now you'll be famous!"

Manzano held a hand in front of his face. "I'd rather not be."

"But I do get an interview, right?"

"Why don't we turn the tables? I'll ask you the questions. After all, you're the one who saved the computer we found RESET with."

Shannon's cell phone rang. She exchanged a few words with the caller and put the phone away.

"I get bothered enough as it is," she groused coquettishly.

"You're a celebrity," he said.

"I'm just the messenger."

She dialed back her playfulness a little, sat down on the sofa, and gave him a thoughtful look. "What's up?" she asked.

"Why should anything be up?"

All at once her voice grew gentle but firm.

"Look, we've gone through so much together—I can't ignore the fact that something's obviously bothering you."

"Maybe it's what we went through?"

If my face is as red as it feels, then it doesn't look good, she thought, embarrassed. She still wasn't sure what to think about her feelings for Manzano. They had become very close over the course of their odyssey together, in more ways than one. But she had to admit that it wasn't so much attraction, more that he was the older brother she never had.

He must have noticed her embarrassment.

"I meant, what we saw and experienced. The consequences of this insane attack, what people suffered."

A little offended, and yet relieved, she replied, "It's not something any of us will forget in a hurry."

He nodded, looking out the window. "One thing I don't understand," he said. "These people, the ones who did this. They devoted so much time and effort to carrying out the attacks... You remember, I discussed it with Bollard after he flew to Istanbul."

I remember, thought Shannon. Can't he ever turn off?

"I ask myself: Did they achieve their goal? Was this a victory for them? Their pamphlets and manifestos talk about a more just, more harmonious order, one that could only be achieved by enforcing a completely new start. RESET: bringing the system back to zero. By taking away the foundation of our civilization, they'd see to it that every structure had to be built anew—that was the idea.

"It's true we don't know the long-term consequences yet, but the conditions didn't last long enough to achieve their goal. In most of the targeted countries, the elected governments are still in power, and they're reestablishing the traditional structures. Twelve days wasn't enough. Could they have known that? Did they plan to keep the power off for longer? All this time I've been thinking about how I'd have acted in their place... If I'd gone as far as these guys, I'd have put a contingency plan in place, in case I got caught early. I'd have made sure that my goals would be achieved no matter what. Look at the photos from the arrests and from afterward. They don't look defeated. If you ask me, they look satisfied. Triumphant even."

"They probably just wanted to be famous, like every other mass murderer. They accomplished that much, and they know it too."

He shook his head, looked at the floor, as if the answers to his questions were there.

"I have a bad feeling," he said. "Like there's something else coming, something bad."

"You know what?" said Shannon. "I'm supposed to go to Brussels; I've got a few meetings there with top politicians…"

"You're a sought-after woman now."

"What I was going to say was, do you feel like coming along for the ride?"

ISTANBUL, TURKEY

"What would you have done in the attackers' place?" asked Bollard. His room even had a window. Outside, the sun, glowing red, descended over the roofs of the city.

"I don't know the latest results from the RESET analysis," Manzano answered on Bollard's computer screen. "Have the elements of the malicious programs been reconstructed yet?"

"The first parts."

"Do they correspond to the attacks of the past weeks?"

"We don't know yet. We're dealing with thousands of coordinating discussions between software developers and millions of lines of code. What are you getting at?"

"All the attacks so far seem to have been triggered on the first day. Or are there signs now that the terrorists were continually tampering with the systems?"

"No."

"OK, you want to know what I would have done in the attackers' place. Well, I'd have made sure that the attacks could continue even if I was no longer free to carry them out myself. I'd have hidden time bombs in the power system, set to go off as soon as the grid was up and running again."

Bollard stared at the monitor. The terrorists hadn't been wrong in their online conversations: Manzano thought like them. That, or after everything he had gone through, he was completely paranoid.

"The first time I went on RESET, I ran across a thread in which there was talk of a back door," Manzano continued. "Why bother with a back door when you're already inside?"

"So you can get in when everyone thinks that the systems are secure again…" Bollard finished Manzano's thought.

"There's no way I'm the first to think of something like this," said Manzano. "Has there been any sign of Pucao, Yusuf, and von Ansen?"

Bollard shook his head, then answered with a question of his own. "You think there's more to come?"

"I don't know," answered the Italian. "Right now, I'm headed to Brussels. I'll check in again from there."

The screen went blank.

Bollard gave a sigh and tried calling his contact at the French Red Cross again.

"François," the wrinkled face greeted him. "I'm sorry, we haven't found your parents and in-laws yet."

ORLÉANS, FRANCE

"No!" a soldier called out to a few people farther ahead, loud enough that Annette and Vincent could also hear. "No one is allowed back into the restricted zone!"

"But where are we supposed to go?" someone called out.

"You need to stay here!" declared the soldier.

"Christ, I'm not staying here for another second," Annette shouted to her companions above the noise.

Vincent didn't answer. In his eyes she could see the terrible fear of never again being allowed to return home.

"It's only 130 kilometers to Paris! There has to be some way for us to get there. If the power is back on, they can pump fuel again—maybe we can take a taxi or rent a car. I'll pay any price. Or maybe the trains are running."

Bollard shook his head doubtfully.

"It's got to be a damn sight more pleasant in our apartment than it is here!" she screamed. She had automatically said "our," she noticed. She still couldn't get used to the fact that Bertrand was no longer alive. Perhaps it was because she had yet to grieve properly; she'd been afraid to give in to the urge to cry uncontrollably, fearing that once she started she would never be able to stop.

"Celeste and you, you'll both come with me, of course," she shouted, trying to stay strong though she wanted to crack into a thousand pieces. "You'll stay with us—with me—until you can go back to your home."

BRUSSELS, BELGIUM

Laughing, Manzano hugged the older man.

"I've never been to Brussels," Bondoni announced with a grin. "So I thought, now's the time." He clapped Manzano on the shoulder. "You look bad, my boy! Is it true what I'm hearing? That you beat the terrorists pretty much single-handedly?"

"I never even came close to them," Manzano replied. He hugged Bondoni's daughter too. Lara was sharing the luxury suite in the hotel until the water in her apartment was running again.

"Your friends all got back safely?"

"Not a scratch on them."

"May I introduce you to Antonio Salvi?" said Bondoni, pushing a thin man with even thinner hair forward. He had been standing back. "His network is paying for all of this"—he gestured around the room—"the flight from Innsbruck too. He'd like to do a story on me. Somehow he found out that it was my old Fiat that got you to Ischgl."

BERLIN, GERMANY

Michelsen and a few colleagues had nabbed a car with a willing driver to take them home for the first time in over a week. The city seemed alien to her somehow. Advertising billboards, shop names, and company logos were lit up on most of the buildings' facades, but on the streets below, bags of rubbish were stacked high on the pavement. Many had been torn open, leaving packaging and rotting food pouring out onto the street. There were bags spilling into the roadway that would suddenly pop up in the light of the car's headlights. Dogs and rats darted between them.

Ahead of them, on the side of the road, were strangely curved poles jutting up several meters high between two wrecked cars. Ribs, Michelsen realized as they drove past, the gigantic ribs of an animal carcass.

"What was that?" she cried out to the driver. It was too big to have been a cow.

"The remains of one of the elephants from the zoo," he answered, unfazed. "A lot of animals have escaped in the last few days."

She thought of the giraffe with its young.

"Most of them were slaughtered by people who were starving," the driver went on. Could you eat elephant meat? Michelsen asked herself, disturbed.

The driver stopped, and they agreed on a pickup time for the next morning. As she stepped out of the car she felt a few cold drops of rain land on her cheeks. She found her way between the stinking piles of trash and climbed the steps to her building.

Her apartment was cold and clammy, and there was a stale smell in the air. The lights were working. It was almost as if she were merely coming home from an extended vacation. She could already tell that she wouldn't be able to sleep tonight. She opened a bottle of red wine, poured herself a glass, and went to the window in the dark kitchen. She took a long sip and looked out into the night, out at the lights of the city, which began to swim before her eyes. A shiver ran through her and then the tears came.

BRUSSELS, BELGIUM

Sophia knew she was laughing too much and too loudly, but after the fifth glass of wine she really didn't care. Fleur, Chloé, Lara, and Shannon wouldn't notice. They'd knocked back quite a few themselves.

The hotel had been able to reopen quickly. Most important, the alcohol reserves hadn't been depleted during the blackout. So here they were, Fleur and the Italian reporter propping up the bar next to her while the others danced. Sophia wasn't surprised that people were so cheerful, downing the contents of their glasses as if nothing had happened. Today they wanted to party away the fear, the suffering, the death and despair of the preceding days.

Manzano observed them. "I'd like to dance now myself," he said, emptying his glass. "But I feel so tired. Like Lara's dad. I'm becoming an old man."

"I'm going to head out too," Sophia replied and noticed how dizzy she was as she slipped off the barstool. She gave Fleur a light tap on the shoulder and waved to the Italian journalist.

On the way through the hotel lobby, Manzano said, "I have to apologize again for what I pulled you into. I... didn't know where else I could have gone."

"I didn't have to bring you into the office with me," she replied. "But I'm glad that I did."

"Can you get a taxi?" he asked.

"Sure. The gas stations are pumping again, even if the

water pipes in my building aren't yet." She giggled. "But I'm used to it by now."

"You can shower at my place," Manzano offered with a grin. "Wouldn't be the first time."

"You're just trying to lure me to your room."

"Of course."

They had reached the hotel exit. There were, in fact, a few taxis waiting out front. They held each other tightly and then kissed. Sophia felt his hands rubbing her back, her shoulders. Then her hands were on his hips and on the skin of his neck. Holding each other close, they walked quickly to the elevator, ignoring the other guests' amused looks. They spilled out into the hallway on the third floor, where Manzano fumbled the key card out of his pants and opened the door to his room.

He gave her a gentle push. Sophia turned to pull him after her, and her hands caressed him under his sweater; he slipped his hands under her blouse and onto her breasts. His hands moved softly around them. They stumbled around in the darkness, coming close to falling over. Sophia caught herself, found the card still in his hand, and pushed it into the slot next to the door, which completed the electric circuit in the room.

A warm light came on with a soft click.

"So long as we've got it," she whispered, lifting her head as he kissed the sides of her neck. "I'd like to see you."

His hand felt for the switch, and he dimmed the light till it was almost off. "But we should be sensible with it. I'm not such a pretty sight right now anyway."

She kissed his forehead gently around the scar.

"That'll get better."

THE HAGUE, NETHERLANDS

"I'm afraid he checked out, sir," said the receptionist apologetically.

"Did he say where he was going?"

The receptionist looked at him, sizing him up. "What is it you want with him?"

He pulled out his wallet, removed a two-hundred-euro bill, and pushed it across the desk. "If you could tell me where he moved on to, I'd really appreciate it."

"You want to interview the guy—that's it, isn't it?" said the receptionist. "You're probably wasting your time. We were overrun with journalists once it got out he was staying here. After a while, he made me stop putting the calls through. And then he left."

The receptionist's tongue flickered from his mouth as another two-hundred-euro bill appeared on the desk. "C'mon, man, help me out here. I could really use an exclusive…"

DAY 14—FRIDAY

BRUSSELS, BELGIUM

"Good morning," said Manzano, as Sophia opened her eyes. Half-asleep, she blinked and squinted at him, then looked around.

"My hotel room," he explained. "You stayed on account of that shower."

"So I remember." She stretched, pulled a sheet around her, and went off to the bathroom.

Manzano walked barefoot to the windows, pushed the curtains aside, and stared out into the day. From the bathroom he heard the water running. The receptionist had explained to him that the hotel had priority when it came to the supply of, among other things, water, because it was frequented by diplomats and politicians. That was why the pipes were flowing here, while most of the homes in Brussels still had to do without.

They dressed and went downstairs to the breakfast lounge. At the long buffet they found bread, slices of cheese, and cold cuts, just one variety of each, as well as open wrappers of chocolate, pitchers of water, tea, and coffee. A handwritten sign apologized for the modest selection. They were making efforts to resume their usual high standards as soon as possible.

"Good morning!" Shannon greeted them with a big grin.

She was sitting by herself at one of the tables; in front of her were a laptop and a cup of coffee. She gave Manzano and Sophia a long look.

"Good time last night?"

"How about you?"

"So good, I've no idea how long we danced."

"Where's Bondoni?"

"Probably still asleep."

With fast fingers, she typed something on the computer.

"Sorry, an email. I've got to get going in a second. Have either of you heard from Bollard?" She gave them both another look. "That'll be a no then. I guess you had more exciting things to do, right?"

Manzano was irritated by her insinuations. "I need my breakfast."

Shannon closed her computer and jumped up. "You'll keep me in the loop if there's any news from Bollard, OK?"

And she was gone.

Manzano took a deep breath. "Hard to believe the energy," he remarked.

Sophia put her long arm around Manzano's thickening waist.

"Let's get ourselves some fuel too," she suggested and pulled him over to the coffeepots.

ISTANBUL, TURKEY

Bollard watched through the two-way mirror as the Japanese suspect was questioned. The man seemed calm, composed, despite having been allowed to sleep for only two hours since his capture. Like the others, he had demonstrated from the start that he spoke English perfectly.

When he had shown up in the list of suspects, it had caused some surprise among the civilians assisting the investigation. Japanese terrorists? Bollard had reminded them of a couple of historical incidents, for example the poison gas attack by the AUM Shinrikyo sect in the Tokyo subway in 1995 and the massacre at Tel Aviv airport in 1972.

Across six rooms, they were interrogating seven men and one woman. Three of them had come away with gunshot wounds; they were placed under medical supervision, and the interrogations were kept brief.

On the morning after the operation, representatives from several European intelligence agencies and the CIA had arrived. Alternating with the Turkish officers, they quizzed the attackers. None of them denied taking part in the attack—quite the opposite—but they refused to reveal anything about their methods.

"How much do you get paid to lock us up and torture us here?" the Japanese man asked his interrogator.

"You aren't being tortured."

"Sleep deprivation is torture."

"We have a lot of pressing questions. As soon as you've answered them, you get to sleep."

"Can you afford a Rolls-Royce on your salary?"

The man led the conversation like a corporate recruiter, thought Bollard.

The Turkish officer was unmoved. "We're not here to discuss my salary."

"On the contrary, that is exactly why we are here," the Japanese man replied coolly. "Because your bosses can afford fancy cars, and their paymasters can afford a whole fleet of cars that cost more than your apartment. While you're down here, doing the dirty work, they sit in their mansions. They don't wait for paradise; they treat themselves to their two and seventy virgins in the here and now."

"I have to disappoint you: I don't believe in such things."

"Do you think that's fair? That you've got to spend the night with someone like me while they're out with pretty women, driving around in Ferraris?"

"This is not about justice."

"Then tell me, what is it about?"

Bollard's laptop came out of sleep mode. Christopoulos's face shone in the video chat window.

"Look here," said the Greek, and he entered lines of code in another window. "We've already got it in pseudocode."

> *If no block code in the past 48 hours*
> *activate phase 2*

"Activate what?" asked Bollard.

"We don't know yet," said Christopoulos. "All we know is that it's not there to activate Dragenau's SCADA code and it's not for the Italian or Swedish smart meters. And the really worrying thing is, unlike phase 1, the attack strategy requires no command in the software."

BRUSSELS, BELGIUM

"That's exactly the command I was talking about!" cried Manzano.

Bollard's face had a greenish tinge to it, but maybe that was the light. "There are still time bombs hidden in the systems, sleeping," said Manzano. "Instead of needing to be activated, until now they've been actively blocked. At least every forty-eight hours. If they're not blocked— boom! Everything starts all over again."

Shannon and Sophia were peering over Manzano's shoulder, but, like Bondoni, they kept themselves out of view of the laptop's camera.

"How long ago was the raid?" whispered Sophia.

Manzano counted. "About thirty hours," he whispered back.

"But the block command didn't have to be given right before the attack," whispered Shannon. "Maybe it was already sent the day before."

"If that were the case, you'd already be reporting on the consequences," Manzano whispered back.

"What's that you're saying?" asked Bollard.

"Get me access to the RESET data bank!" Manzano told him. "And we need the logs from all the devices in Istanbul and Mexico City. ASAP!"

BERLIN, GERMANY

"It's difficult at present to estimate the consequences for large sectors of the economy," began the minister for economic affairs.

It struck Michelsen that most people in the room were looking better today. The bags under their eyes weren't as heavy; they sat up straighter—yes, a better mood all around.

"Most companies in the manufacturing industry had to suspend operations," said the minister. "Many firms will be inactive for weeks because of a lack of raw materials and supplies. There are shortfalls in the power supply. About ten percent of power plants in operation have sustained damage; repairs may take several months. Energy-intensive branches of industry like paper, cement, and aluminum manufacturing will suffer as a result. We should consider bringing recently decommissioned nuclear power plants back into operation."

"Absolutely out of the question!" roared the head of the Ministry for the Environment, Nature Conservation, and Nuclear Safety. "No one will tolerate that, not after the accidents in Philippsburg and Brokdorf."

"If we don't, German industry will suffer. And then there are the small and midsize businesses, the backbone of the German economy. They're facing even greater problems, because less attention is paid to them individually than to the large corporations, and they have a harder time getting finance from the banks. In order to prevent the collapse of the German economy, we must implement a rigorous development program. Even then," he said darkly, "the question remains whether the German economy will ever again achieve its former status in the world. We can't hope for a Marshall Plan from the United States this time. They're almost as hard hit as we are.

"And we're not the only ones who need support—our fellow EU members are in the same boat. That means many of our most important trade partners are out of the picture and will only recover slowly—if at all. And this is only the beginning. Emerging markets depend on European and American consumers; that means China, India, Brazil, and others will soon be struggling with higher unemployment and social conflict, as well as political instability. And with that we lose the biggest growth markets in the world. It's a vicious spiral. Here at home, unemployment will rise drastically without support programs. Economists are foreseeing conditions for us that resemble those in Latin America, with a small, wealthy upper class, a disappearing middle class, and the majority of the population in impoverished circumstances."

"You could, of course, counteract this with the appropriate political measures," the chancellor interjected.

"If the majorities are there to support such initiatives... I fear that many people, including some in this room, are not yet aware of what far-reaching consequences this event might have."

"And where is the money for economic programs supposed to come from?" asked the foreign minister. "Most of the affected nations were already deep in debt or bankrupt."

Domscheidt returned the foreign minister's look with a blank expression. "Hopefully, the finance minister can tell you that."

ISTANBUL, TURKEY

"What kind of block code is it? What happens if it doesn't get entered?" asked Bollard. Leaning across the table, he propped himself up with one arm and tapped the index finger of his free hand on the printout.

"I already said that I don't know," answered the suspect, one of the captured Frenchmen. Bollard was glad of the opportunity to converse in his mother tongue, but it infuriated him that one of his countrymen should have played a part in the attack.

"Listen," Bollard hissed, so quietly that the cameras recording them wouldn't pick up what he said, grabbing the guy by the collar. "If the power goes out somewhere in Europe or the United States and more people die because you won't tell me what this block code is for, then I can do things differently. Very differently. And it won't just be sleep you'll be losing."

Bollard knew he could be taken to court for making threats like that, but his anger had gotten the better of him. He pushed himself away from the man and tried to compose himself.

"You can't do that," the young man protested. "You can't threaten me with torture."

"Threaten you? Who's threatening you?"

"You are! That's a human rights violation!"

Bollard leaned toward him again, their foreheads almost touching now.

"You want to tell me about human rights? Millions of people have died. Died of thirst, of exposure, of radiation sickness, untreated diseases. Did these people have no rights? What is the block code for?"

"I really don't know," the man insisted. His face was pale, sweat beading on his upper lip. This Frenchman hadn't been trained for rough interrogations. He would surely break down eventually. Bollard wondered how long it would take, how far he would have to go.

And what if, at the end of it all, the guy really didn't know anything?

BERLIN, GERMANY

"The good news is," the secretary of state for finance commenced his presentation, "most banks are open again. The supply of cash for the population is, for the time being, secure. The less good news is that, to prevent bank runs, withdrawals will be limited to one hundred and fifty euros per person per day until further notice. The European markets will remain closed until the middle of next week, as will markets in the United States.

"The technology is ready for use, but traders need time to digest the new developments. European and American indices have lost around seventy percent of total value since the crisis began. Despite the European Central Bank flooding the market, the euro tanked. As a result, oil and gas imports became prohibitively expensive—although things eased a little when the United States was attacked. That made imports somewhat cheaper again, since oil and gas are accounted for in dollars. Thankfully, our strategic oil and other fuel reserves are sufficient to last for several more months, and price increases will only take effect several months from now, since the prices in most cases are based on long-term contracts."

He paused to draw breath. "In a few months, Germany will no longer be able to service its loans or to pay state employees and pensions. Many European nations will be confronted with this problem significantly sooner. As a result, the international financial markets are facing collapse. It is incumbent on those in the political arena to prevent the worst. Possible scenarios are to be presented and discussed in"—he looked at his wristwatch—"four hours, at a video conference between the heads of state of the G20 nations, representatives of the European Central Bank, the Federal Reserve, the International Monetary Fund, and the World Bank."

PARIS, FRANCE

The train ride from Orléans to Paris took forever, and it was well after midday by the time they arrived. Annette and the Bollards waited at the taxi stand, together with a few dozen other travelers. When a cab finally appeared, pushing and shoving broke out among those waiting in line. Two more cars arrived. They bore no taxi sign, but stopped nevertheless, one of them right in front of Vincent. The driver rolled down the window. "Where to?"

Annette told him the address.

"A hundred and fifty euros," the man demanded.

"That's…" Annette began, but then restrained herself. It was five times the normal fare.

"Fine," she said with a hardened expression.

"Half in advance," demanded the man and stuck his hand out.

Annette placed the cash in the man's grimy hand.

"Where are you coming from?" the driver asked, curious, as he sped off.

"Orléans," Annette answered curtly. She had no interest in conversing with the price gouger.

"I thought that was a restricted area," he said. "That's what they said on the news."

The streets were even dirtier than in Orléans, with bloated animal carcasses in the gutters. Here too it was mostly troop transports and armored vehicles driving past, though the speedometer showed eighty kilometers per hour. The driver laughed. "Well, things aren't much better for us here in Paris!"

Annette hated him for his presumptuousness, but now she had to ask, "Why's that?"

"A cloud from the power plant that blew up down there is supposed to have carried over to us. It's not so bad though, the authorities are saying." He shrugged. "The next rain washed it away again, so there's no more danger. Or at least, that's what they claim." He made a gesture as if he was tossing it aside. "Personally, I'd rather just go ahead and believe it. If I don't, I'll worry myself to death."

Annette said nothing. She ran a hand through her hair, almost casually, then secretly inspected her hand, front and back.

"Is there anything else you need?" the man continued

cheerily. "Food? Drinks? I can get things for you. It's not easy these days, finding stuff."

"Thanks, but no," Annette answered stiffly.

In front of her building she paid him the balance of his overpriced fare and took note of the license plate. As soon as she opened the door to her family apartment, her heart swelled with fear and joy. "Finally!"

The air here was stale, though the foulest smells had stayed outside for now. She put down her suitcase and went to the telephone, looking so familiar on the hall table. The line was dead. She went to the computer in Bertrand's study—her heart constricted as she perused his shelves, the unfinished novel he had left face down in their hurry to depart. The Bollards followed her. Since her daughter had moved to The Hague with their grandchildren, even Annette had mastered the latest means of communication. She turned on the computer, started Skype, and clicked on her daughter's name. After a few seconds the slightly pixelated face of Marie appeared on the screen. Tears welled in Annette's eyes. Through the microphone she heard Marie calling out, "Kids! Come here! Grandma and Grandpa are calling!" Her daughter turned back to the screen. "My God, *Maman*, am I happy to see you! Where's Papa?"

ISTANBUL, TURKEY

"François? François! Are you still there?"

As if through gauze, Bollard heard Marie's voice coming from the computer. He stared into the monitor. The thin, pale face of his wife was swimming. Bollard fought back the tears.

"He…" Her voice broke. "He's got to be…dug up again. So he can be buried in Paris."

She repeated it for the second time. The fact had her almost as shaken as the news of her father's death itself.

"I…I'm so sorry," answered Bollard in a thick voice. "I

have to go now. Take care of yourselves. We'll see each other soon. I love you all."

For a few seconds Bollard sat there without moving. He pictured his children, Marie. He had to get home. He was the one who had sent her parents there, imagining they would be safe in the idyllic hills along the Loire. For an instant he saw himself as a young boy, chasing a butterfly over a field in front of Chambord castle. Never again could he return to his childhood home. Nor would Bernadette and Georges play there ever again.

He jumped up, walked to the interrogation rooms, and stormed into the first one he saw. Two American officers were putting one of the Greeks through the mill. Dark sweat stains showed on his shirt under his armpits and collar, and his lips were quivering.

Ignoring the Americans, Bollard grabbed the Greek by the collar and yanked him off the chair.

Hoarsely he whispered, "A few days ago my father-in-law died near Saint-Laurent. Heart attack. Nobody could get help. Saint-Laurent—you know what happened there?"

The Greek stared at him, eyes wide. He didn't dare move. Of course he knew.

"My parents," Bollard continued, breathing heavily, "were forced to leave the house my family has lived in for generations. It was my childhood home. My children loved the place. Now none of us will ever be able to go there again."

He pressed the knuckles of his fist against the man's throat, smelling his fear. "Do you know what it feels like?" Bollard went on. "Do you know what it's like when you realize that you're going to die, in agony, and no one is going to help you?"

He could sense that the Greek was about to pass out on him, but he tightened his grip. The man's eyes began to swim, filling with tears. "The block code," Bollard asked, his voice low, "the one that has to be sent every forty-eight hours. What's it there for? What does it prevent? How much time do we have left? Speak up, you smug piece of shit!"

The man's entire body was shaking; the tears flowed down his round cheeks.

"I...don't know," he whimpered. "I really don't know!"

BRUSSELS, BELGIUM

He hurried over to the young receptionist. "Which room is Piero Manzano in?" he demanded, laying his hands on the desk.

The receptionist immediately set about looking it up on the computer. "Room 512," he said, smiling.

It was so easy when you acted with confidence.

———

"So there are still a few of them," determined Manzano.

"What?" asked Shannon, who never stopped filming.

"Somewhat regular logs on static IPs."

Manzano pointed to some of the network addresses. Shannon and Sophia leaned over his shoulders, and Bondoni moved his chair closer to see better.

"This one, this one, and this one we know. They belong to the headquarters in Mexico City."

He called Christopoulos in The Hague over the video chat program. After a few seconds, Bollard's colleague answered.

"I've got a list of IP addresses here," explained Manzano. "I need a comparison as soon as possible, of these ones and the ones where we already know what's behind them."

"I'll see what I can do."

It was a blessing, thought Manzano, that the internet connection was working without a hitch again. So long as the electricity was flowing.

"I wouldn't always send the block command right at the last minute," he said, thinking out loud. "There'd be a risk I might forget to do it."

"Plus," Shannon added, "several people have to be able to send it. In case they lose one of them."

"If we'd been sitting in their headquarters, in charge of blocking the trigger," Sophia joined in with the thinking aloud, "what would we have done?"

"I would have sent the command at a particular time each day," Shannon offered her opinion. "To be on the safe side."

"Why have the blocker at all?" asked Bondoni. "If without it all that happens is you trigger another power outage, which is what the jerks wanted anyway."

"It's so that they wouldn't waste ammo when they didn't need to," said Manzano. "The block code stops the time bombs in the electric system from going off and leading to a blackout. But so long as the power is out anyway, you don't need the time bombs. They're intended for the very situation in which we now find ourselves: the grids are up and running again, and the attackers have had the plug pulled on them. If the time bombs activate new malicious programs now, the whole thing starts over again from the beginning."

His video chat window announced a caller. Christopoulos. Manzano picked up.

"Yeah?"

"I sent you the list of IPs. Addresses with known background are marked."

"Thanks."

Manzano opened the table. More than half the lines were highlighted in yellow.

"Good. That narrows down our selection. Let's compare these with the results of our latest search..."

He refreshed the lists in his data bank.

"Still too many."

He called Christopoulos again.

"I'm sending you a list of logs," he told him. "Examine what kind of data went to each of the IPs as quickly as possible. We're looking for a block command."

"We're working at full capacity right now," said Christopoulos. "I'm sending you access to the data. So you can look for yourself."

"But that might take too long!"

"Sorry! We're really busy over here!"

"OK, go ahead," grumbled Manzano. A second later, an email landed on his computer. He logged into the data bank on which the investigators had secured all the data from the servers and computers from the two terrorist headquarters for analysis.

He checked the files that had been sent to the first addresses at the times of day on the list of IPs. He would first look at just one file per IP. It was likely that the IP had been set up exclusively for the time bomb activation mechanism. At least, that's how he would have done it.

Someone knocked on the door.

"I'll get it," Sophia offered.

Arduous, thought Manzano. This way, every time, he had to look first at the IP list for a time and a computer, in order to then search through its security files for the corresponding data. And dangerous. If he was right, every minute counted. From outside Manzano heard somebody call, "Room service."

On the seventh attempt, he found something.

"This could be it," said Manzano. He looked at the time when the last command had been sent.

Forty-seven hours and twenty-five minutes ago.

"Numbers and letters," groused Bondoni. "Who can read anything in that…"

"He can," said a voice behind them in English.

Manzano jumped. Sophia was standing in the doorway, a knife glinting at her throat. A man's unruly dark hair appeared from behind her. Manzano recognized the face immediately. He had seen it often enough over the past days in Bollard's base of operations.

Jorge Pucao shoved Sophia brutally forward, toward Manzano. He could see the panic in her eyes. He felt his whole body tense up.

"Ms. Shannon, go get the cords from the blinds; use them to tie your friends up."

Shannon followed the order with trembling fingers. She ripped out the cords and started tying Bondoni's thin old hands behind his back.

"You could always work with us," said Pucao to Manzano.

"There is no 'us' anymore," replied Manzano. "Your comrades have been arrested."

Pucao laughed pityingly. "You're wrong—there are billions of us. People who have had enough of Western civilization with its predatory capitalism that enslaves and exploits them. We're through with being ruled over, lied to, and robbed by a small group of criminals who call themselves politicians, bankers, and managers. And you, Piero—I know deep down you count yourself among the people who have had it up to here."

He held the knife under Manzano's nose. His voice lost its preacherly quality and took on an almost friendly tone. "You're one of us. Or have you forgotten how you took to the streets against the corrupt political caste in Italy? How you fought against the injustices of globalization in Genoa? Maybe you've gotten older. Maybe you're disillusioned. But don't tell me that you've given up on your dreams."

"In my dreams, hundreds of thousands of people didn't die from hunger, thirst, lack of medical care…"

"In your dreams they didn't, but they do in real life! Every day, all over the world. That's what you were rebelling against in Genoa! That's what you still get worked up about, even today! But only with old war buddies over a nice glass of wine."

He looked at Manzano, adding, "Isn't that so?"

Manzano had to admit that Pucao had hit a sore spot. But he couldn't worry about that now. They had to send the block command.

"Even if my dreams were the same as yours," he said. "My methods of realizing them are most definitely not."

"And that's why nothing has ever changed," Pucao answered indulgently. "It was the same thing, even with the sixty-eighters. Protested, moved into a commune, threw stones—and today? They're bank directors, doctors, lawyers, lobbyists for industry—anything to pay for their mansions. What did they achieve? The rich got richer, the poor poorer. Young people today are as conservative, apolitical, and spineless as their great-grandparents. We're destroying our environment more than ever. Do I have to keep going down the list?"

He checked the cords that Shannon had tied around Manzano's wrists. Then he continued, "When and by what means did the real changes take place? When were societies actually revolutionized, new systems brought in? When did democracies oust aristocratic power and later fascism in Europe, colonial power in the United States? Only after big catastrophes. The masses at large need to experience an existential threat. Only when they have nothing left to lose but life itself are they ready to fight for a new life."

"That's all nonsense! You're just babbling!" Shannon yelled, interrupting him. "What about the fall of communism in Eastern Europe? The change from military regimes to democracies in lots of countries in Latin America? Or the Arab Spring? They didn't need world wars!"

"Shut your mouth and keep working," Pucao ordered and waved the knife in her direction. "The fall of communism was preceded by a decades-long war throughout the world. The Cold War, remember? Oh, you were still a little girl then."

"But you were already a wise old man, is that it?" Shannon retorted. Manzano fired a look at her, trying to get her to stop.

But Pucao seemed to enjoy the discussion. Perhaps he liked having an audience. "You have no idea what a war is," Pucao lectured Shannon. "In Latin America, the United States and Europe used their puppet terror regimes to lead brutal campaigns with hundreds of thousands of victims. Later it was the International Monetary Fund and the World Bank, instruments of established nations, formed to keep the competition small in so-called developing countries. A similar thing happened in the Arab countries. That's why the people eventually rose up. Only in Europe and North America was the suffering not great enough for the uprising, for the change toward something better. Now it is. That's why we can't stop too early. We've got to push through. Then everything will change."

Pucao checked how Sophia's bindings were holding.

"Do you actually hear what you're saying?" asked the Swede. She was obviously feeling braver now. "You sound exactly like the people you claim to be attacking. Feebleminded slogans about the sacrifice that's necessary to make it to paradise, about purification through fire, painful measures before everything gets better…"

They had to sit on the couch.

"Bring me a cord for yourself too," Pucao ordered Shannon.

"People are dying out there!"

"And that's terrible, horrible, but it can't be avoided. It's like a hijacked plane that you have to shoot down so that something worse doesn't happen. A few have to die so that many can be saved."

"You piece of shit!" yelled Shannon. "You're not the one who has to make the decision to shoot it down; you're the hijacker!"

"He's crazy," Sophia whispered to Manzano.

Pucao pulled the cords tight around Shannon's wrists and pushed her toward the others. "I'm hoping I don't have to gag you. More screaming like that and you all die immediately."

Be reasonable now, Manzano wanted to say, but he knew it would be useless to appeal to the reason of such people.

"Don't worry," Shannon spat back. "I've talked to you enough."

Pucao ignored the remark, sat down at the computer, and studied the data. Manzano thought feverishly about what he could do.

"Bastard," whispered Pucao, abruptly turning back to them. "You never learned, did you? Not a thing. Not even after you got shot by the police."

Manzano felt the anger rising within him and knew that it was the wrong moment to lose his composure.

"You're well informed," he said instead, deliberately calm.

"We were watching the whole time. Long enough, anyway…" he corrected himself. For a moment he stared off into nothingness. "How did you find us?" he said finally.

Manzano considered for a moment whether he should tell him the truth. The man before him was, like all megalomaniacs, a hopeless narcissist. The slightest criticism could set him off.

"Did you plant the emails on my computer?"

"I wrote them," said Pucao. "Somebody else loaded them on there."

"Well written," replied Manzano. "The police fell for them. But the guy who put them on my computer directly from your central communications server? Him you should fire."

Pucao hissed something in Spanish that Manzano didn't understand. It sounded like a curse.

"And while you're at it, everyone else who was in charge of server security," Manzano went on. "Hard to find good people, eh?"

"Enough!" Pucao made a dismissive gesture. "Do you think I don't know what you're trying to do? You think you can butter me up?"

"We'd be happy to call you names too," Shannon offered coldly. "Really, I'd much prefer it. You goddamn madman!"

Pucao smiled.

"This conversation bores me. Say good-bye to one another. I'm sorry that you were all here; really, I only came for Piero. You were a real pain in the ass, you know that?"

"I've been getting that a lot lately."

Pucao stepped toward the couch from behind, the knife in his hand. He reached for Sophia's hair.

Manzano jumped up. After a moment of shock in which no one had moved, including the surprised Pucao, the others followed. "Together!" shouted Manzano. He hurtled forward and rammed his head with all his might into the man's side. Pucao stumbled, fell to the floor behind the couch, caught himself. Instead of running away, Bondoni kicked him in the knee with all his strength. Pucao buckled. Manzano had gotten up off the couch—not so easy with his hands tied—climbed over the back and knocked Pucao in the shoulder with his hip. Together they fell backward against the wall, and Manzano felt a burning pain in his chest.

Pucao was hit from behind with a nasty kick between the legs from Shannon. He doubled over. Manzano saw the knife in his hand, the blade bloodied to the hilt. Shannon kicked him again. Manzano couldn't breathe, but kept going all the same and threw himself with all his weight at Pucao, so that they fell to the ground together. Manzano saw Sophia's foot land on Pucao's face, right next to his own; blood spurted out of his busted lip. Manzano struggled to stand up and got to his knees. Pucao's shirt was soaked in blood. While Sophia kept on kicking Pucao, Manzano dropped on him with both knees.

"The knife!" Manzano panted. "Where's the knife?" He was dizzy. He couldn't spot it in Pucao's hands, which he held around his head in defense.

"Here," said Bondoni, who was holding it in his bound hands and using it to cut Shannon's bindings.

Manzano kneeled hard on Pucao. He wasn't moving anymore. The newly freed Shannon had placed a foot on his head and was putting her entire body weight behind it. She cut off Bondoni and Sophia's cords, then Manzano's. With the rest of the cord, she tied Pucao's wrists and ankles together. He was bleeding from a wound on his lips and a cut over his eyes. His eyelids fluttered, he was breathing heavily, then his eyes opened and closed.

"Too many mistakes," groaned Manzano, pressing his hand against the left side of his chest, where he had crashed against Pucao. He must have broken a rib. "Especially for someone as infallible as you."

He went to the computer. His vision went dark. He stumbled but caught himself. Ten more minutes. Where was the command? Here. Send it. Hopefully that was the right code. Where was all this blood on the keyboard coming from? Hopefully he had done everything right. The screen swam before his eyes. Video chat window. Christopoulos.

"Yeah?"

Breathlessly he said, "I sent you an IP address and a block code. I think that's what I was looking for." Why couldn't he breathe?

"What the hell happened to you?" cried Christopoulos.

Instead of an answer, Manzano said, "Check it anyway. Please. Fast. Right now." His head almost fell on the table. He shot up and muttered hoarsely, "We've only got nine minutes left."

"What?"

"Just do it!"

"Piero!" Sophia screamed. She rushed over to him. Shannon came right after. Sophia felt his chest, where blood was gushing from a cut under his ripped shirt. She pressed her hand on it.

Pain overtook Manzano. He felt himself sliding feebly out of the chair into Shannon's hands. He grew cold. Sophia bent over him and Manzano looked up at her. Why this panic in her eyes? As if from far away, he heard her calling his name, over and over again, quieter and quieter. All he wanted was to sleep, just to sleep. He closed his eyes.

Would Christopoulos get it done in time?

Cold. Sleep.

DAY 19—WEDNESDAY

PARIS, FRANCE

A sea of flashbulbs greeted Bollard when he entered the arrivals hall. He stopped, had to shield his eyes with his hand, and wondered what celebrity they were expecting.

"Monsieur Bollard! Monsieur! Monsieur Bollard!" The journalists thrust microphones in front of his face, bombarding him with questions, not one of which could he make out amid all the noise. Bollard spread his arms out protectively in front of the children. Bernadette skipped past him, laughing into the cameras and finally—to Bollard's horror—sticking her tongue out at them. The journalists flashed away all the more eagerly, but many were laughing too, and that eased Bollard's tension. How did the reporters know about his arrival, and why were they even interested?

He spotted his parents and Marie's mother among those who were waiting. Bernadette and Georges rushed over to the three of them and were taken in their arms. The perfect tableau. For a few seconds all the cameras turned to the reunited group. Bollard and his wife made use of the opportunity to push past the reporters.

"Is it true that you're being awarded the Grand Cross of the Legion of Honor?" he heard from the pack.

"Have all the attackers been caught?"

"How did your family endure the weeks in The Hague?"

"James Turner, CNN! Is it true that you'll be leaving Europol?"

"When will the president be meeting with you?"

"What do you say to rumors that you're being considered as the next interior minister?"

Bollard answered no one. With Marie by his side, he reached his arm to touch the rest of his family. The children were talking excitedly to their grandparents. For them the death of their grandfather was far away in this moment. Bollard squeezed Marie's arm before she hugged her mother.

Finally, security personnel arrived to help shield his family from the media scrum and escorted them out to a taxi. Only after his family had climbed into a minivan did Bollard finally turn and face the horde.

"Thank you for the thrilling reception. But I was only one of many who ended the attackers' mission. Direct your thanks to them. I have nothing more to say."

He climbed in, the car drove off, and the clamor of the crowd receded behind them.

DAY 23—SUNDAY

MILAN, ITALY

A cool wind whipped around the cathedral roof. The lights of the city glittered below them. On the square in front of the church, thousands of people had been protesting for days against the government, demanding better provisions. Sometimes they drowned out even the noise of traffic, which reached them only as a muffled rush.

"Can you imagine I've never been here before?" asked Manzano.

"Isn't it always like that?" said Sophia. "If you live somewhere, you think you can do it anytime. But you don't do it. Only when someone comes to visit."

The knife had opened a flesh wound in Manzano's chest and nicked his lungs, but the injury wasn't life threatening. He had had to spend a few days in the hospital, which had provisionally resumed operations. After that, they had stayed in Brussels. Sophia had taken time off. They had recuperated in the hotel, spoken on the phone with friends and relatives, exchanged emails, trying to find out how they had endured the two weeks of terror.

The internet and television were working without a hitch; the media knew only one story. Jorge Pucao was still being questioned, along with his accomplices in Mexico City and Istanbul. The airport police in Ankara had arrested the fleeing Balduin von Ansen. Siti Yusuf would also be caught one day. It would take years to process their cases. Even longer to deal with the consequences.

Despite a basic supply of electricity, the general state of provisions in many regions was still poor. The accidents in the nuclear plants and chemical factories had made whole stretches of land uninhabitable and driven millions from their homes. The economy would be ruined for years; a massive depression was expected.

There were still no authoritative death counts; it was said there were millions, if Europe and the United States were counted together. But that didn't include long-term victims. And still it could all have been even worse. In the days after Jorge Pucao's arrest, the IT forensics experts had found the malicious program with which many grids in Europe and the United States would have been shut down once more.

When people learned of the perpetrators' motives, they were outraged; thoughts of lynching were given voice. But after a few days, their anger turned on the official institutions that had failed to prevent the catastrophe and were now dragging their feet instead of reestablishing normal conditions. The unrest increased; none of the new military regimes in Portugal, Spain, or Greece gave power back to the elected institutions.

Manzano wondered if in the end Pucao and his comrades had been successful after all, at least with their destructive work. He didn't want to think of it just then. He put his arm around Sophia's waist and enjoyed the view over the roofs, the sparkling lights under the night sky drawing down. The chanting of the crowd rose softly from below. They stood side by side touching like that in silence.

In his trouser pocket, Manzano heard a loud *bing*.

He took out his new cell phone and read the text.

"Lauren arrived safely in the United States," he said.

"I don't think Pucao was right," Sophia said, gazing down at the demonstrators in the cathedral square, small as ants.

"Me neither. We can do it a different way, a better way."

He let his gaze sweep over the panorama, putting his arm more tightly around her waist.

"So let's go back down to the street and join the others."

AFTERWORD AND THANKS

As a thriller writer, naturally, one is happy about placement on bestseller lists, translations, and selling film rights.

But since the book's publication in spring 2012, to my surprise, I have also been invited by numerous national and international political institutions, public and private organizations, as well as corporations, to give lectures on *Blackout* and to hold discussions. Also, the book has become standard literature in many companies and administrations.

Blackout wasn't only highlighted in the culture pages and on television segments focused on books; it was also discussed in the economic, scientific, and information technology media.

In December 2012, a highly respected jury of economic journalists recognized *Blackout* as Germany's "most thrilling topical book of the year." *Blackout* was already being assigned in schools as well.

Blackout is fiction. But while I was working on the manuscript, reality caught up to my imagination more than once. Accordingly, my first draft in 2009 predicted a manipulation of power plant SCADA systems. At that time, even experts considered this possibility as either barely feasible or completely far-fetched—until Stuxnet was uncovered in 2010. It was the same story with the danger presented by the backup cooling systems at nuclear power plants—until the disaster in Fukushima.

Just before Christmas 2015, three years after the first edition of *Blackout*, the first cyberattack causing a large power-outage was reported from Ukraine.

In the years following 2012, other international media have also shown acute interest in the scenario, such as extensive documentaries running on Channel 4 in Britain and on the National Geographic Channel in the United States in 2013. Also, more scientific, security, military, and other studies dealing with the subject have been conducted worldwide.

In doing research for this book, I availed myself of a variety of sources. I spoke with experts—for example, those in the energy and IT sectors, as well as those in disaster management. They were all quite willing to provide information, but no one wanted to be credited by name. The internet, of course, offers inexhaustible sources of information. Some of them I'd especially like to highlight.

Without the online encyclopedia Wikipedia and its ten thousand authors, an author like myself would have to spend a significantly longer amount of time researching for a book like this one. (And before anyone asks: yes, I support Wikipedia financially.)

My research was corroborated shortly before completion of the manuscript in May 2011 by the report presented by the Committee on Education, Research, and Technology Assessment (eighteenth committee) as directed by Article 56a of the rules of procedure for the technology assessment project: "Endangerment and Vulnerability of Modern Societies—as Seen in the Example of a Wide-Reaching and Long-Lasting Failure of the Power Supply." I have included some of the results of this study in this book. The report can be found on the home page of the German Federal Ministry of the Interior under its German title: *Bericht des Ausschusses für Bildung, Forschung und Technikfolgenabschätzung (18. Ausschuss) gemäß § 56a der Geschäftsordnung zum Technikfolgenabschätzung-Projekt: "Gefährdung und Verletzbarkeit moderner Gesellschaften—am Beispiel eines großräumigen und langandauernden Ausfalls der Stromversorgung."*

Sheri Fink's Pulitzer Prize–winning article from August 25, 2009, in the *New York Times* on the dramatic days in the Memorial Medical Center in New Orleans after Hurricane Katrina in 2005 provided inspiration for the hospital scenes.

The scenario I've described is one of many that are possible. The fact is, no one can predict what would happen in such an event. Since I wouldn't like to provide instructions for a terror attack, I have left out or changed sensitive technical details. I've simplified the presentation of some facts for the sake of narrative and readability; for example, I have placed grid control rooms within corporate headquarters, kept telephone and internet connections intact longer than would be probable—and various other technical details. Possible inconsistencies or inaccuracies can be traced back either to this—or to mistakes that slipped past me, for which I ask forgiveness.

I would like to give my heartfelt thanks to all sources, named and unnamed. Without them, I wouldn't have been able to write this book.

Additionally, special thanks goes to my agent, Michael Gaeb, and his team, who believed in the manuscript, and to my editors Eléonore Delair and Kerstin von Dobschütz, as well as to my publisher, Nicola Bartels, who have helped me to make this into the book it is. I must give particular thanks to one of my anonymous helpers, who unflaggingly provided me with information dealing with the IT aspects above all and even proofread the manuscript on top of that. It goes without saying that I might thank my parents, for everything one can thank parents for. Finally, and ahead of all others, I thank my wife for her endless patience, her tough criticism, her countless suggestions, and her continuing encouragement.

And then, of course, I say thanks to you, dear reader, for your interest and your valuable time.

If *Blackout*, on top of a few thrilling hours, should also

have imparted a bit of knowledge or even given you some small cause to stop and think, that would make me especially happy.

Marc Elsberg, Fall 2016

ABOUT THE AUTHOR

Marc Elsberg is a former creative director in advertising. His gripping and meticulously researched thriller *Blackout* is a frighteningly plausible drama of an international blackout caused by a hacker attack. An instant bestseller in Germany, it has sold more than a million copies and has been translated worldwide. The book established Elsberg as a sought-after dialogue partner for industry and politics. Marc Elsberg lives in Vienna, Austria.